1

Born and brought up in Wales of English and Russian parents, Kate Sharam studied at London University before pursuing a career in advertising. This gave her the opportunity to travel all over the world while filming commercials. She now lives in Devon with her husband, two sons and three cats. *Power Cut* is her first novel.

SCEPTRE

Power Cut

KATE SHARAM

SCEPTRE

First published in 1995 as a Sceptre Book by Hodder and Stoughton
First published in paperback in 1996 by Hodder and Stoughton
A division of Hodder Headline PLC
A Sceptre Paperback

10 9 8 7 6 5 4 3 2 1

British Library Cataloguing in Publication Data

Sharam, Kate
  Power Cut
  I. Title
  823 [F]

ISBN 0 340 63977 6

Typeset by Palimpsest Book Production Limited,
Polmont, Stirlingshire
Printed and bound in Great Britain by
Cox and Wyman Ltd, Reading, Berkshire

Hodder and Stoughton
A division of Hodder Headline PLC
338 Euston Road
London NW1 3BH

For Norman
with all my love and thanks

1

The knife cut deep into the flesh.

She eased it very carefully through the soft tissue, watching for the spurts of clear liquid that, to her eyes, ran red.

She increased the pressure with infinite care and the blade slid through the dark skin. A thin slice, an almost perfect circle, fell on to the chopping board. She drew in her breath sharply, as exquisite pleasure flowed through her. She lifted the knife again, and again the sharp steel sliced into the firm skin. It was so effortless and the effect was so irreversible. She felt the warm familiar glow and—

'Jenny, what the hell are you doing?' His voice, full of impatience, shattered her fantasy. 'You're grinning like a demented clown. For God's sake, hurry up with that salad or we'll never finish eating in time.'

Jenny Cranshaw obediently speeded up cutting the cucumber, then quickly chopped up the tomatoes. But with a sense of loss. They were her favourites and she had been saving them till last.

Punctuated by warnings of being late and urgings to hurry, she finished preparing the meal and placed it on the table in front of her husband. She slid into the seat opposite. At last David relaxed and savoured the flavour of the chicken chasseur.

'You know I hate eating in a rush,' was his only comment.

Jenny picked at her food, unable to work up any enthusiasm for the meat. She ate the salad with concentrated care, placing each piece of cucumber and tomato separately in her mouth and sucking all the juice out before letting it slide smoothly, unchewed, down her throat. Her sense of loss and frustration began to ease. She was able to make token replies to her husband's carping comments about the couple they were to join for drinks at the local pub at eight o'clock.

'. . . and Susannah doesn't know what the hell she wants, does she? It's all cordon bleu one minute, language courses the next, and then redoing the whole house. And now it's golf. If she treats us to another stroke-by-stroke account of her latest triumph on the course, I'll walk out. Or get drunk.'

He laughed. And Jenny didn't know if it was at the idea of getting drunk, or at Susannah.

The breeze from the river was warm and the garden was full of eager young couples determined to take advantage of the fine weather and the long June evening. It was an old, whitewashed pub that had managed to retain its character and warmth, despite attempts to popularise it with added timbers, soft lighting and hanging baskets. Its name, The Riverside Inn, gave an accurate picture of its situation and appeal. Encircled by the meandering river, the well-tended lawn at the rear of the inn sloped gently down to an elegant stone parapet, designed to deter any over-enthusiastic drinkers from demonstrating their prowess in the cool waters.

From the dozen or so tables spread out over the lawn, there was a happy murmur of voices. The comfortable sound of social satisfaction, splintered every now and then by a high female laugh or a deeper male roar of approval.

At a table near the parapet, the voices were soft and the two couples seated there appeared confident and successful. The tall slim woman with short dark hair, and dressed in a light summer frock, was the only one of the four who gave a hint of disharmony. She sat silent, gazing out across the gleaming water with a slight smile on her quiet face.

'Wake up, Jenny,' the stocky man sitting opposite her urged laughingly. 'You're in a mist out on that river, instead of listening to Susannah. She just asked you if you wanted to go with us next time. David's keen, aren't you, David?'

Jenny winced, as she felt the painful pressure under the table of David's heavy foot on her open-toed sandal.

'I'm sorry, Robert. I was miles away,' she apologised.

She looked quickly into Robert Benson's grey eyes, but saw no genuine reproach there. They were warm and laughing in his round face, openly reflecting his cheerful outlook on life and trusting nature. Sometimes too trusting. Especially where his wife, Susannah, was concerned. Despite the warmth of the summer evening, he had arrived wearing a dark suit and tie in an attempt to disguise the outline of his short, portly figure, the result of too many good business lunches.

'I'm sorry,' Jenny repeated. 'It's the heat and the wine getting to me.' She turned to her husband and asked cautiously, 'What is it you're so keen on, David?'

David Cranshaw repeated the pressure on his wife's foot, as he replied, 'Susannah and Robert have invited us to join them when they go golfing again in Scotland at the end of September.' He looked meaningfully at her and again pressed her foot. More gently this time.

She knew he wanted to use her to say 'No'. He was always complaining that that was the trouble when you got too friendly with others. They wanted to take you over, start living your life for you.

But Jenny would have liked a trip to Scotland. And the company of Susannah and Robert would make the journey and hotel less claustrophobic than their own brief silent holidays. She didn't play golf and David did so only for business reasons, but perhaps he was working towards a business deal with Robert and in fact wanted her to say 'Yes'. He may have told her something about it already, perhaps even over the meal that evening. She knew she didn't listen to much of what he said to her. As long as she mouthed an occasional 'Oh yes?' and 'Oh no', he seemed not to notice her inattention.

She looked at her husband more closely, searching for a clue in his expression, but he was wearing his polite, social face that told her nothing. Gave nothing away. It was certainly a good-looking face – tanned, blue-eyed, with fair hair swept back and only just beginning to recede. She was used to seeing other females casting openly covetous glances in his direction. The arrogant set of his mouth and jaw only increased his attraction.

At nearly forty years old, he sat there sipping his wine, cool and assured. In his casual clothes, effortlessly elegant, he appeared relaxed and amused. Yet Jenny could sense the tension in his every move. He wanted her to say something. But what? For a split second, she felt the old misery of failure flood over her. Then with an effort of will, she turned to Susannah. Simple, sunny Susannah. Golden-tanned, golden-haired.

'What a lovely idea.'

It came out before she knew what her answer would be.

'That sounds like great fun. Up in the wilds of the Highlands. I'd love to go, but you'll have to let me off the golf or I'll ruin it for you all.' She certainly did not want to be roped into that humiliation.

Susannah Benson laughed indulgently, shaking her head to set her silky blonde hair dancing round her shoulders. 'Of course we will. You can go for one of your lonely treks while we bash the ball around.'

She leaned forwards towards Jenny, ostensibly to emphasise her point. But Jenny knew, as she saw Susannah's peach silk dress fall loosely to reveal even more of her generous, golden brown breasts, that Susannah liked to see the desire spring into David's eyes. Despite her friend's tendency to lust after any attractive male body within reach, available or not, Jenny was fond of Susannah. Her laughter and determined enjoyment of life were contagious and always lightened any sombre mood.

Susannah shook one carefully manicured finger at Jenny in mock disapproval. 'But you're silly not to at least have a go at golf. It's a fabulous game. You're so keen on exercise that I'm sure you'd love it if you gave it a try.'

'Stop bullying Jenny,' Robert grinned, as he made his usual ineffectual effort to curb his wife's enthusiasms. He always felt the urge to protect Jenny, with her soft brown eyes and elfin face. 'Let her go for walks, if she wants and we can all get together on the nineteenth green.'

His delight at the whole idea overflowed into a deep, warm laugh that startled a bold sparrow pecking for crumbs in the grass at their feet. It flew urgently across the garden and perched safely on the sundial.

David said nothing.

Jenny knew she had got it wrong. She wanted to take the words back, turn the clock back, start the conversation again. She'd do it right next time.

There was a sudden interruption from a nearby table. A young couple had started an argument and in a flurry of anger, the girl stood up, incensed. The paleness of her skin was emphasised by the blackness of her tee shirt and leggings. Tossing back her long straight hair, she snatched up her shoulder-bag and strode furiously from the garden. There was a momentary hush, as everybody turned to watch the embarrassment of the abandoned youth. Blushing desperately, he paused to down the last of his pint and then hurried after his girlfriend.

As people's interest returned to their own drinks and half-finished sentences, Jenny looked round at David. He was sitting calmly on her left, a slight smile of wry amusement on his lips. But as she looked at him, his gaze turned to her. The blue eyes were ice-cold.

She instantly dropped her eyes to her drink. Her grip on the glass was too tight. If she wanted to go to Scotland with the Bensons, why shouldn't she say so? If David did not want to go, he should come out and state it clearly.

But perhaps he had.

Now came the guilt, familiar and all-invasive. Why did she always let him make her feel this way? She quickly, eagerly, offered him an escape route.

'But don't you have to go to Germany on business some time around then, David?'

She wanted him to see she was sorry. To see she was trying to help.

His intense blue eyes held hers for a moment. Then he reached forward for his glass of wine and smiled reassuringly at Susannah.

'Don't worry, Susannah, I won't let it interfere with your plans. I do have to go to France, not Germany,' he added pointedly, 'for Filmer Industries, but the date hasn't been fixed. I can be fairly flexible about it. So keep practising that elegant swing of yours and we'll give you ample opportunity to show it off in Scotland. Won't we, Robert?'

'We certainly will,' Robert agreed, 'but we won't let her get the better of us up there.' He laughed and looked admiringly at his young wife, clearly willing to let her get the better of him any time.

Out on the river a group of ducks paddled past, their beaks dabbling in the water, searching for the odd titbit of crisp or bread roll.

David turned to Jenny and she knew her mistake would not be allowed to pass. He smiled patiently at her. 'You know I told you the Filmer trip wasn't settled yet.' He winked at Susannah. 'It's always the same with Jenny. She refuses to remember anything I tell her.' He turned again to his wife. 'Don't you, my dreamer?'

His laughing expression said he was amused, but his voice betrayed his annoyance as he warmed to his subject.

'The other Saturday, we were supposed to meet for lunch at the Terrazza. I sat there like a bloody fool for over an hour. She didn't turn up. Forgot all about it.'

Susannah and Robert exchanged glances and Robert hastened to defend Jenny.

'We all forget things sometimes,' he said quickly. 'I know I do. I don't know where I'd be without my secretary.' Oblivious to the unintended meaning of his words and Susannah's sharp snort of irritation, Robert continued, 'I have to be reminded of my appointments all the time.'

But David would not let the subject drop. 'I'll have to start writing down notes about everything for you, Jenny.' He leaned forward. 'You're in a world of your own, aren't you?'

They all smiled at her indulgently. Jenny tried to smile back, but it came out awkwardly.

Seeing her embarrassment, Susannah hastened to reassure her. 'Don't you worry, Jenny. We love you just the way you are. I'd give anything to be as mysterious as you are.'

Robert and David both chuckled at the idea of the vivacious and voluptuous Susannah ever achieving mystery.

'But perhaps we underestimate Jenny,' David suggested as

he finished his wine. 'Perhaps she doesn't really want to go to Scotland. Maybe she's looking for an excuse, like my trip to France, to avoid the holiday. Is that it, Jenny? Tell us if you don't really want to go.' He looked hard at her and then turned to Robert for support. 'We won't force her to go, will we?'

'Of course we won't,' Robert Benson chipped in. 'It's completely up to you, Jenny. We wouldn't dream of pressuring you.' His warm generous eyes smiled encouragement.

Jenny felt the colour creeping up her face, her cheeks starting to burn. She wanted to stand up and run away like that girl had. To leap into the dark depths of the river and drift into oblivion. Her eyes sought the relief of the cool water, but the calmness she saw there only served to emphasise the turmoil within herself.

He had trapped her. Whatever game he was playing, he had won. Again.

They did not talk on the journey home, but drove in moody silence. Only when a boy-racer in a Golf GTI pulled blindly out of a side-road in front of them, did David's excessive cursing betray the tension.

They parked in silence at their comfortable suburban home with its mock-Tudor beams and cosy gables. But its warmth did nothing to thaw the ice. Jenny walked straight into the kitchen and poured herself a glass of clear water from the water-filter jug. She stood looking out the window at the darkness beyond. She felt weary. As she sipped her water, staring blankly into the black night, she heard David come into the kitchen behind her.

'What the bloody hell do you think you're playing at?' His loud voice filled the quiet kitchen.

She didn't turn round. She didn't answer.

'For God's sake, I told you last weekend and I reminded you again tonight that I thought Robert was going to invite us to Scotland. I explained to you why I couldn't go. So why the hell did you say "yes" tonight?'

Jenny continued sipping and staring. 'I forgot,' she said quietly.

'Don't be so bloody stupid,' he exploded. 'How could you possibly forget? I had only just reminded you. I told you I'm trying to put together a deal with Manfields and they're Robert's main competition. They'll put up with my having a social drink with him, but going away on holiday with him is quite a different matter. I've already told you all this.' He paused. 'You know I want that deal. But I don't want Robert to get wind of it.' He came and stood directly behind her. 'So just what the bloody hell *are* you playing at?'

She wished he'd go away. She looked at his reflection in the window and she felt squeezed between his face in front of her and his presence behind her.

'I'm sorry,' she murmured.

'For God's sake, what sort of answer is that? You're getting worse and worse. I can't rely on you for anything. You're a bloody shambles.'

His voice was growing louder and louder at her ear. Battering her. Numbing her.

'You've got to pull yourself together. Stop that stupid dreaming. This is the real world we're in.'

The words roared in her head.

'Haven't you got anything to say? Why the hell did you do it?'

She stared at the angry face in front of her. The glaring eyes and clenched jaw floated, disembodied, in the window, with a halo of darkness.

She shook her head.

She watched as his face seemed to grow, as if made larger by the intensity of his anger. For a moment she thought he was going to strike her, but instead he turned and strode furiously from the room, slamming the kitchen door behind him.

She waited while the vibrations that shook the window subsided. She saw her reflection shudder and then settle into a welcome stillness. She felt numb and lifeless.

She might have stood like that for a long time, glass in hand, staring out into the night, had she not felt a gentle, insistent pressure round her ankle. Immediately she looked down at the cat and smiled, then scooped the purring animal up into her arms. She hugged him tightly to her, as he pushed his face into hers with feline eagerness. She pressed her cheek against the soft, black fur and felt his warmth melt her indifference to life.

'Shadow,' she murmured. Cradling the animal in her arms, she walked out of the kitchen and went reluctantly upstairs.

As Jenny slid between the cool sheets in the dark, she tried not to disturb the unforgiving back that was determinedly turned towards her. Night after night, month after month, it was the same: silently back to back. Only a sense of desperation kept them coming together every few weeks in the act that was supposed to be love. A monthly affirmation that their marriage still existed. A brief and wordless coupling.

Gentle padding of paws interrupted her thoughts. A small round head popped up beside her, warily peering over the edge of the bed.

'It's all right. It's safe,' Jenny whispered to the black shape.

She lifted her corner of the duvet and the cat leaped easily into its warmth. Jenny instantly dropped the cover back down, quick to muffle the motor sound of the contented purr. David hated the cat in bed. If ever he caught him curled up under the duvet, he lost his temper and kicked the animal to the floor. David had all the right arguments, of course: it was unhygienic; it made the sheet dirty; it disturbed their rest.

No mention of the pleasure of touching silky fur, as the cat nestled in the curve of her body.

Shadow had learned to be cautious. Only when he was sure David was asleep did he come into the room. At one time, David had tried shutting their bedroom door to keep the animal out, but the scratchings and miaowings each night had proved too disturbing. So he had been allowed back into the room, but supposedly, only to spend the night on the carpet.

Now, as she felt the gentle vibration flow from his warm body to hers and the sensation of soft fur pressed against her bare skin, Jenny slowly relaxed and drifted off to sleep.

2

The music blared out, filling the large hall with an insistent, driving beat.

'Up, two, three, four . . . Stretch, two, three, four . . .' The voice never stopped. On and on it pounded, pushing them, driving them, exacting every ounce of effort. The young blonde woman in her purple leotard and tights called out each action, always demanding more and more. '. . . Knees up, to the chest, five, six, seven, eight . . .'

Lifting her own slim legs up with ease and twirling her outstretched arms in large circles, Amy Stafford was the epitome of all that the women in front of her yearned to be. Only twenty-four, with flat stomach, tight buttocks and high breasts. A body that was firm and fit. Arrayed before her in all shapes and sizes, they watched with longing as she bent and stretched with straight limbs and boundless energy. Her fair hair was swept up into a ponytail, bouncing and flicking with every beat.

'Keep it going, keep it going . . .' she chanted to the rhythm.

She glanced round at some of the bulging thighs and flabby stomachs, then, with determination, stretched her tendons further, worked her muscles harder. She enjoyed watching the class struggle to keep up with her.

At last, as the music slowed and died, there was a collective sigh of exhaustion. Hearts were pounding and lungs heaving. It was hot in the hall as the sun streamed through the high windows, making broken patterns of light on the woodblock floor. Wall bars ran down one side of the room and a basket-ball net perched high on each end wall. The air-conditioning hummed away, but as always, was erratic at keeping an even temperature.

Jenny wiped a trickle of sweat from her cheek and breathed deeply, as she waited for her heartbeat to slow down. She had enjoyed the exercise, even if Amy had worked them extra hard. She glanced to her right to see how her friend Caroline Palmer had fared and could not help laughing when she saw her vermilion face and desperate expression.

'What the hell's got into Amy?' Caroline panted, flicking her damp, dark curls off her neck. 'She's like a demon driving us today. I'll never last the distance,' she groaned.

Already the music was building up again and the demanding voice was starting to call the next routine.

'You'll make it,' Jenny encouraged her. 'This bit is not so bad.'

Caroline grimaced doubtfully. She obediently took up the required stance and stretched her arms above her head. Her pale blue leotard was drenched and stuck to her like an ill-fitting second skin. She knew only too well that the trouble was that she was overweight. Each pound of extra flesh made every movement more of an effort and she determined, yet again, to go on a diet.

'. . . to the right, two, three, pull down and hold it there, one, two . . .' The music gave no respite.

With her head hanging in front of her knees and her bottom stuck self-consciously up in the air, Caroline felt ridiculous. The blood rushing to her head made her ears pound. She gritted her teeth and as she walked her hands around to the left, fingertips only just touching the floor, she caught sight of Jenny in a similar pose. But Jenny's tiny waist bent so completely that she was folded tight against her legs, palms flat on the floor and head dangling loosely between her ankles. How on earth did she do that? Make it look so easy? Their eyes met and they exchanged upside-down smiles of sympathy.

By the end of the hour, with everyone's muscles stretched and aching, the lesson came to a stop. With a last toss of her ponytail, Amy turned off the cassette player and the sudden silence shattered the sense of group effort. There was a feeling of relaxation and release of tension. They sprawled on the floor or leaned against the wall bars, chattering and towelling themselves dry before pulling on tracksuits.

Jenny Cranshaw was talking to a thin, ginger-haired woman who was trying to persuade her to join a new circuit training course.

'No, Sally, I don't think I'll be able to come,' Jenny said, shaking her head regretfully. 'It sounds great, but I can't come on a Thursday. Sorry.'

Standing in her red and black leotard, Jenny looked fit and relaxed, her skin and dark eyes glowing. As Caroline Palmer walked over to her, she was amazed to see Jenny had, yet again, been transformed by the pumping adrenaline. Caroline herself arrived at the class, groomed, calm and confident, but after an hour of hell, was reduced to a sodden jelly of self-doubt, which only a long, hot shower and a bar of chocolate could banish.

But Jenny was different. Each week Caroline watched her arrive in the hall looking tense and miserable, her delicate features pulled tight with strain. Caroline had tactfully tried to probe, but her casual questions were always gently brushed aside with, 'I'm fine. Really.' But after an hour of total dedication to the exercises, she was a changed woman. Confidence shone in her eyes. Caroline knew exercises caused all sorts of chemicals to race through your blood, which were supposed to give you a high, but how come it never seemed to happen to herself?

Caroline listened to Sally Wright becoming more insistent. 'Oh, come on, Jenny. Surely you can spare an hour on a Thursday? You'd love it.'

Jenny again shook her head. 'Sorry, Sally, I can't. The morning would be all right for me. But not the evening.'

Sally pulled off the ribbon that held back her frizzed mane of ginger hair and her thin, freckled face took on an expression of impatience.

'What's the matter? Does David need you sitting there, darning his socks and warming his slippers of an evening?' she laughed. 'Doesn't he let you out?'

Caroline saw Jenny's flush of colour. Watched the light of confidence die in her eyes. She wanted to kick Sally.

'We're not all fanatics like you,' Caroline snapped. 'Some of us actually enjoy putting our feet up in the evening instead of weights, tracks and gyms every second of the day. Haven't you got anything else to think about?'

Sally stared in surprise at the unexpected attack, then turned again to Jenny. 'Well, if you change your mind, let me know. I promise you, you'd enjoy it. Circuit training gives you a great buzz..'

'Perhaps I'll come and have a look at it sometime,' Jenny offered without any conviction.

'Come on, Jenny,' Caroline interrupted. 'I want you to give me a lift into town. My car's in dock, so I'm desperate.'

Sally gave Caroline a quick glance of annoyance and walked away.

'Never mind her,' Caroline commented. 'Is it all right about a lift to town? I've just got to get to a shop or Andrew and I will be eating dry bread and no cheese tonight.'

'Of course. You know I always do my shopping before I go home.'

She picked up her jeans and slid them over her long legs. 'It's certainly too hot in here for leotards, isn't it?' She pulled her tee shirt over her head and ran her fingers through her close-cut hair. 'I think I'll change to shorts next week.'

'What I need is a change of body, not clothes,' Caroline joked ruefully.

Jenny laughed and together they left the hall.

The sports centre was on the edge of town. Jenny turned into the flow of traffic and drove along the dual carriageway into Hambury. It had once been a thriving market town, but in recent years its character had changed completely with the advent of the shopping malls, industrial estates and the commuter train to London. The High Street had managed to salvage some of its original charm. Tall, black and white timbered buildings leaned precariously over the shops below and strange carvings leered at passers-by from unexpected corners. But they were being steadily elbowed aside by the acres of glass of new shops.

Jenny carefully manoeuvred round a Metro that suddenly decided to pull in on the double yellow lines.

'Bloody moron,' Caroline yelled at it automatically.

'Don't be so hard on him,' Jenny said, as she changed down into a lower gear. 'That's exactly the sort of thing you would do yourself if you wanted to go to one of the shops along here. You know you would.'

'You're right, I admit it,' Caroline laughed. 'But I'm a great believer in one law for me and another one for everyone else,' she added unabashed.

'That's no way for a solicitor to talk.'

'Don't tell my clients that.'

Jenny envied Caroline her total self-confidence. Though they were both about the same age, close to thirty-six, Jenny looked a good five years younger and Caroline tended to treat her like a sister who still needed a guiding hand. Jenny dimly remembered a time when she also had been so sure of herself and full of bright plans for the future. Had believed in herself.

'By the way,' Caroline continued, 'have you heard Susannah Benson's latest?'

'No, she didn't mention anything last night. What's she up to now?'

'She's talking of adopting a child.'

Jenny froze and the car almost stalled but she quickly over-revved the engine, grateful for the diversion.

Caroline did not seem to notice anything amiss and expanded on her theme. 'We all know Robert is down on the old fertility count. I'm sure that's why Susannah leers at any prospective studs within reach, but it's all show really. She would never hurt Robert.'

'Robert adores her.'

'But I ask you, can you imagine her up to her manicured nails in nappies and teething gel?' Caroline chuckled at the memory of her own twins' antics at an early age. 'And sticky fingermarks all over those silk blouses? Heaven forbid.'

Jenny kept her gaze rigidly on the windscreen, forcing only casual interest into her voice. 'Is anything settled?'

'No, not yet. Anyway you know what Susannah's like,'

Caroline added cheerfully. 'She will be off on some other whim before long.'

Jenny jerked her thoughts away from the dark shadows and pressed hard on the accelerator pedal, as her foot clamped down on the memories.

The car shot forward and Caroline called out, 'Whoa there. This is Hambury High Street, not Silverstone, you know.'

Luckily the traffic had momentarily cleared, so no harm was done. Jenny quickly eased back on the pedal and reverted to the usual stop-go crawl up the hill.

'Sorry. I got carried away for a moment.'

'Don't worry, I do the same myself. That's why my Escort is in the blasted garage today. I only took my eyes off the road for a second. Well, maybe two. But the idiot in front chose that moment to brake and that was the end of my bumper and his rear light.'

Jenny knew how proud Caroline was of her flashy white convertible and sympathised with her temporary loss.

'As long as I get it back for next week's great escape, I won't grumble. I'm in the office for the next two days, so Andrew can ferry me to and from work. That's why I've got to get the dreaded shopping done today.'

'I'd forgotten you're off on holiday so soon. Won't the business collapse without you two beavers?'

Caroline laughed, shaking her dark curls. 'No, Andrew may think he's indispensable, but I've screwed his courage to the sticking place and nothing, but nothing, is going to come in the way of this holiday.' She sighed with exaggerated pleasure. 'A whole month in the sun. Sheer heaven. No more contracts, no more clients and best of all, no more telephone.'

Caroline's husband, Andrew Palmer, was a partner in a law firm in nearby Tonbridge and Caroline, also a qualified solicitor, worked in the office two or three days a week.

'It sounds wonderful,' Jenny enthused, as she pulled up at the traffic lights. 'A month in the South of France.' She turned and looked across at Caroline's contented face and felt a stab of envy. 'I wish David and I were going somewhere. Anywhere would do.'

'Don't tell me you haven't booked anything again this year? You're mad not to yank David out of that office of his and whisk him away to somewhere exotic for a few weeks.'

Jenny pushed the gear stick forward, a little harder than was necessary and followed the flow of traffic round to the right.

'You know what David's like. He never wants to take a holiday.' She could not quite keep the bitterness from her voice. 'Even when we have a rare long weekend away, he's always up to his eyes in paperwork or sitting with a telephone clamped to his ear.' She pulled a face as she flicked on the indicator. 'Last night we had the chance to go to Scotland in September with Robert and Susannah Benson, but in the end I had to say "no" because David didn't want to.'

'For heaven's sake, Jenny,' Caroline snorted in exasperation, 'if you want to go, then just do so without David. He'll soon learn to take more notice.' She stopped as she sensed Jenny's unhappiness. More gently she added, 'You need a holiday. And so does David. It would do you both good. Perhaps he would come to his senses if you took off without him for a few days.'

Jenny drove into the huge, flat car park at the side of the supermarket and pulled into an empty space. She turned off the engine and looked across at Caroline.

'Thanks for the thought, but no thanks.'

Caroline's heart sank, as she saw her friend withdraw into herself and bring down the protective shutters. 'Okay,' she smiled affectionately. 'It's your life. I'll keep my nose out.' She opened the car door and looked across at the ugly squat building. 'Come on, let's go join the trolley-truckers.'

She waited.

The evening was warm, as the last of the June sun streamed in through the French windows. They stood open, so that as Jenny sat quietly in her armchair, she could look out and see the bees crawling in and out of the lupins and smell the fragrance of freshly mown hay that hung in the air.

She was used to waiting. She never knew what time David would arrive home. Usually she heard his Mercedes' tyres crunching over the gravel before seven o'clock. But frequently, like tonight, it was gone eight and he was still not home. Once it had worried her. She had fretted over what could be keeping him. Meals had spoiled and tempers had flared.

Eventually she had stopped fretting. She had learned to adjust the meals to flexible times. David liked to unwind with a glass of wine before his dinner and moan about the unpredictable habits of British Rail. But not even she believed that every late arrival home was due to the inefficiency of the commuter service. It was then, over his drink, that he relaxed back in his chair, stretched out his long legs and told her about his day.

She used to be genuinely interested at one time. She had enjoyed hearing of his triumphs and had been proud of his achievements. But gradually things had changed and she was no longer willing to sit there, applauding his actions and listening to his self-congratulation. She realised that over the years, she had changed from being a partner to being no more than an audience.

So she had started to withdraw her unquestioning support. She queried his decisions and argued with his opinions. But by then it was too late. David was used to her ready agreement and refused to accept the change. He ridiculed her ideas and condemned her faults. Before long, the fragile roots of her belief in herself were destroyed.

Instead, she had turned inward, into a world of her own, where his infidelities and disdain could not touch her. So she still sat each evening, apparently listening to David's one-sided conversations, but his empty words flowed past her deaf ears and her mind was preoccupied with her inner thoughts. Yet despite everything, she was meticulous in fulfilling her side of the marriage bargain. She kept the home running smoothly. She provided the meals, kept herself fit and well-dressed and played her required role in social situations. And never said 'no' in bed.

Jenny's mind was jerked abruptly to the present by the sound of a car pulling into the drive. A few moments later, she heard David's footsteps in the hall and then the door opened and he strode into the room. For her, the peace was shattered. She tried to cling on to a few remnants of her earlier tranquillity, but it was in vain.

'God, it was a bloody awful journey,' were David's first words.

It was like playing the same tape over and over again.

He shook off the jacket of his grey suit, yanked the tie from his neck and threw them roughly on to a chair.

'It's too bloody hot for commuting,' he complained, as he released his collar button. 'That's better.' He sank into his customary armchair, kicked off his shoes and breathed deeply, drawing in the fragrance of the summer evening. 'Half an hour we were stuck on the track. Would you believe it?'

No, she would not.

'And no attempt for an explanation for the delay. The stupid idiots have no idea how to run a railway. The sooner the whole damn system is privatised, the better.'

Jenny stood up and murmured sounds of sympathy. She automatically bent and picked up his shoes, then his jacket and tie. As she walked to the door, David asked his usual, 'Get me a drink while you're up, will you?'

She crossed to the kitchen, where she hung his jacket over the back of a chair. The cat appeared from nowhere and wound itself around her ankles, hoping for food. She ran her hand along its arched back, then turned to the fridge and took out a bottle of white wine. It used to be a scotch each evening, but like most of his colleagues, David had given up drinking spirits and taken to the more socially acceptable glass of wine instead. Jenny poured out two glasses, though she knew her own would sit virtually untouched beside her. He would complain if she made him drink alone, so each evening she went through this charade of joining him.

She carried them on a tray back to the sitting-room. As she opened the door, she was struck by the harmonious picture the room made. The handsome man, with his blond head tilted back against the cushioned headrest, was perfectly framed by the elegance of his surroundings. The rich, russet colours of the Chinese carpet, echoed in the soft folds of the curtains, gave the room a glow that was warm and welcoming. Shafts of sunlight highlighted the figured grain of the walnut cabinet and the watercolours that hung above it. A crystal vase with long stemmed roses stood proudly on a side-table. She had bought the flowers that morning and had chosen the red roses because she knew David approved of them. She preferred the sweetpeas from the garden herself.

Jenny placed David's glass on the table beside him and returned to her own chair. The sound of a blackbird's noisy alarm call drifted through the open window and she assumed the cat was on the prowl again.

'You'll be pleased to hear, it looks as if I'm going to get the Manfields account,' David announced. He smiled smugly. 'I've spoken to Philip Wareham. You know, I told you, he's their managing director. He was very impressed with that report I did and looks ready to sign a deal. So it was worth all those late nights at the office, thank God.'

Jenny looked at her husband speculatively. Did he really believe she fell for all those late night excuses?

David worked for the firm Dern & Fairchild, a marketing consultancy in the City. Jenny knew they handled some large accounts, but she only had a vague idea as to exactly what David did all day. He seemed to divide his time fairly equally between poring over a computer keyboard and taking clients to expensive lunches. He had recently been made a member of the board and had his sights firmly set on deputy chairman. One of the original partners of the firm had died years before, but old Richard Fairchild, the present chairman, was still going strong and ruled over the company with hawkish control.

As David drank his cool wine and told her more of the details of the Manfields account and the idiosyncrasies of the company's managing director, she watched him relax. His long, angular body softened and his voice mellowed to a slower, more intimate tone. He gradually shed the bombastic and strident intonation that served him well at the office. Eventually he turned to her and asked, 'And what have you been doing today?'

She saw his lips form the words, but she had already stopped listening to what they were saying. A frown of annoyance flitted across his face and his sense of wellbeing evaporated. It was enough to warn her of her error. She became aware of the silence in the room.

'I'm sorry,' she said quickly. 'What was it you asked?'

His mouth tightened, then he repeated, 'What have you been doing today?'

'Oh, nothing much.' Seeing he expected more, she added, 'Just the usual.'

'Well, that tells me a lot, doesn't it?' he snapped. His contented mood of a few minutes before was gone. 'What's the matter? Can't you say anything about what you do? Is it top secret or something?'

She watched his irritation build.

'Jenny Cranshaw, the top MI5 agent. It's certainly a damn good disguise you've got. I'm sure nobody suspects.'

She looked away.

'Or perhaps you've taken a lover. And drive around the local motels for secret assignations.' He leaned forward in his chair and gripped the glass hard in his hand. 'Is that it?'

'No. That's not it.'

'Then for God's sake, what did you do today?'

She looked at his set face. He didn't really want to know. He was only proving a point. And she knew he would not let it drop until he had an answer. She let the silence sit there between them for a moment and then dropped her eyes to the patterns on the carpet.

'I went to my aerobics class this morning and then shopped in Hambury with Caroline Palmer. This afternoon I went for a walk along the river. On my own.' She stopped speaking, but did not raise her eyes from the carpet.

'Off on one of your communing with nature sessions, were you? You won't talk to people, but you've got all the time in the world for the fauna and flora.'

She did not reply. Anything she said would be distorted.

David finished off his drink and stood up. He walked across the room to the open French windows and looked out across the lawn at the peaceful garden. He breathed deeply, as if trying to inhale some of its tranquillity and for a few minutes, neither of them spoke. They were accustomed to the impasse.

Then Jenny rose from her chair. 'I'll get the meal if you're ready for it.'

He remained with his back turned towards her and nodded briefly. 'Fine.'

She left the room quickly, relieved to be out of his presence.

Jenny placed the two thick slices of fillet steak on the chopping board. She lifted the knife and cut a thin section off the end of one piece. She smiled as she heard the clatter of the cat-door and the urgent purrs that greeted the smell of fresh meat. Shadow leaped on to the work surface beside her and Jenny held out a blood-smeared finger. Ravenously he licked the red drops with his rough pink tongue and looked round eagerly for more.

Jenny rinsed her finger under the tap and resumed slicing pieces off the meat until about a quarter of one steak was chopped up. The cat thrust his face determinedly towards the tempting pile on the board, perilously close to the sharp blade, but Jenny pushed him away.

'Don't worry,' she laughed, as she looked into the amber eyes. 'This little lot is all for you, you greedy monster.' She held out a scrap of meat between her fingers and Shadow snatched it quickly from her grasp. Piece by piece she fed the chopped pile to the hungry mouth.

'What the hell are you doing, giving that animal steak?'

David's voice startled them both. She had become so absorbed in the ritual that she had not noticed his entry into the kitchen. The cat shot off the counter in a flurry of fur and fear, and skulked nervously under a stool.

Jenny turned to face David, angered by the disruption. 'You frightened the life out of him.'

David paid no heed to her annoyance and repeated his complaint more vehemently. 'Nobody feeds a cat steak. It's ridiculous. You were giving it our dinner.' He shook his head in exasperation. 'A pet should eat bloody petfood, not our meat. I don't give you good money to feed it steak.'

His reminder of her financial dependence on him stung Jenny into retaliation.

'I will give Shadow whatever I choose,' she said emphatically. 'If I wish to feed him steak, then that is what I will feed him. But don't you worry, it wasn't yours. It was only slices from mine.'

Seeing Jenny's and David's attention locked on each other, Shadow slid out from under the stool and leaped again on to the counter.

'And if I decide to give him some of my food,' Jenny continued, her voice becoming more strident, 'whether it be steak, chicken or even smoked salmon, I do not need your permission to do so.'

The animal crept silently nearer the chopping board.

Jenny's control was slipping. She could not stop. 'So don't think you can walk in here and—'

At that moment, David spotted the dark shape over Jenny's shoulder.

'That bloody animal,' he shouted and lunged for the cat.

With lightning speed, Shadow seized the larger of the two steaks in his jaws and turned to flee.

David grabbed at the dangling end of the steak with his left hand and with his right, knocked the cat away. He had intended only to push him off the counter, minus the meat, but the movement exploded in a release of pent-up anger and the blow he gave the small animal sent him flying across the room.

Jenny looked on in frozen horror as the black body slammed into the wall with a sickening crunch and slid silently to the floor. Before she could react, he dragged himself to his feet, then scurried stumbling from the room, his movements odd and erratic.

Jenny screamed.

Where the cat had crashed into the wall, a long smear of blood stood out starkly against the white paint.

'You bastard!' Jenny shrieked, and flung herself at David, hands flailing and nails raking his face.

David stepped back defensively, but she kept coming at him. He caught her wrists and held her firmly at arm's length.

'For God's sake, I didn't mean to hurt the bloody animal. It was stealing my meat.'

He pushed her away from him and for a moment they stared accusingly at each other. For a second he thought she was about to hurl herself at him again, but instead she whirled round and rushed from the room. He could hear her calling the cat.

*   *   *

'Shadow, Shadow.'

She knew he would not come. All his instincts would be to hide. She hunted through the rooms downstairs, her heart racing and her blood pounding in her ears. At last, when she bent to the floor to look in the low gap under the oak dresser in the dining-room, she spotted a dark shape cowering at the back against the wall. In the gloom, she could only just make it out, but she knew it was him. With her cheek pressed to the floor, she whispered, 'Shadow, it's all right now.'

She was about to slip her arm into the gap, when she heard David's voice behind her.

'I wouldn't do that, if I were you,' he said. 'An animal that's hurt will attack you. It wouldn't mean it personally, but your hand would be torn to shreds. Just wait until the cat is ready to come out.'

She did not turn her head. 'I have no intention of letting him bleed to death.'

Pushing her arm as far as it would go under the dresser, she touched the soft fur and ran her fingers over the trembling body until she was holding his back. She could feel something wet and sticky in the fur. Murmuring low sounds of reassurance, she gently pulled the tense but unresisting body towards her.

As the dark form emerged from under the dresser, Jenny's throat tightened.

The cat lay still on the floor, his head stretched out, his eyes closed. The black fur was matted into sticky clumps and from one ear, a gaping wound extended right across his head. The point of impact had obviously been the fragile skull.

Jenny's hand rested gently on the moving animal's back and it was with relief that she could feel the shallow breathing beneath.

David leaned over her shoulder. 'How is . . .?' He did not finish and Jenny heard his sharp intake of breath.

A low moan issued from Jenny's throat. 'Go away,' she growled. 'You've done enough.' She had to get to the vet right now. 'Get me the carrier. Quickly.'

'Where the hell is it?'

'Under the stairs.'

'It's only a cat, for God's sake. We can always buy another.'

'Just get it,' she hissed.

With a curse, he left the room.

She kneeled by the still, black form on the floor. She wanted to stroke it, but was frightened that the slightest touch might increase the pain. When David returned with the carrying box and car keys in his hand, she stood up slowly.

'Go away. Don't come near him.'

'Don't be so damned stupid, Jenny, it's not a child. It was a simple accident.'

She had heard those last words before.

'I said go away.' It came out as a snarl. 'I don't need you.'

'For heaven's sake, Jenny, I—'

'Go away.'

He stared at her, her eyes huge in a white face, then turned and walked out. As Jenny took the towel from inside the carrier, she saw her hands were shaking and hoped she was fit to drive. She kneeled down again beside the cat and very gently wrapped the towel around him. Then with great care, she lifted him into the carrying box. Shadow made no sound and she wondered if he was conscious. His breathing was very light, but as long as she could feel the slight rise and fall of his body, she clung to hope.

She raised the box in her arms, but when she tried to walk, found her legs weak. It was as if they had been disconnected from her brain. She stood still for a moment and breathed deeply. Thinking of Shadow. Thinking of David. Then she strode more firmly to the door.

3

David Cranshaw sat in the kitchen drinking a cup of black coffee. He could not face any breakfast. It had been three days now. Three days that she had been up in that room, never coming out while he was in the house. It was ludicrous. She was over-reacting.

He regretted now indulging in a few too many scotches last night. His work demanded a clear head and it was unlike him to let anything jeopardise that. He ran a hand over his stubble. Blast the woman. What had got into her? Why did she have to make this cat business into such a drama? He hadn't intended to hurt the animal. It was just an accident.

She had returned from the vet with the cat still in the carrying box. David had been surprised to see it still alive. Ignoring him, she had walked straight upstairs with the box clutched tight and had disappeared into the guest room. The door was shut firmly behind her. David's repeated questions through it had been met with silence. When he had tried to open the door, she had started screaming incoherently at him and he had quickly retreated.

Instead, he had telephoned the vet's surgery and eventually managed to speak to the man who had treated the injured animal. He told David that Mrs Cranshaw had been advised that the cat should be put to sleep because he was beyond help. But she had refused. She remained adamant and nothing the vet could say would dissuade her. In the end, he had given the cat a pain-killing injection and after dressing the wound, had been forced to allow her to take the animal away. The vet assured David that the cat must be in a coma by now and would probably not last more than a matter of hours.

That was three days ago and David had not seen Jenny since. Each morning, before leaving for the office, he had taken up a coffee and told her he was leaving it outside the door. But not once did she touch it. The cup was still standing there, a congealed skin over the cold liquid, when he returned in the evening. Presumably she used the bathroom and kitchen while he was out, so why not remove the cup? What was she trying to prove?

It was a relief to get out of the house each morning, to walk into his office and take control. He was equipped to deal with the problems and demands of business. He knew he could handle those. It was in the churning waters of his home-life that he was out of his depth.

He had talked to Jenny through the door, quietly at first, explaining that he had not meant to hurt the cat. But finally, when he received no response, he had tried to force the door open. A chair under the doorknob effectively barred his way. Exasperation had shortened his temper and he had given her the ultimatum that if she did not give some sign that she was at least still alive in there, he would take an axe to the door.

Only then did he hear a low 'Go away'. He had repeated the ritual each morning, so that he was certain that she was still there, even if she was refusing to see him.

He would just have to wait until she decided enough was enough. After all, she would have to come out sooner or later and pick up the threads of her life. She couldn't stay in limbo forever. In all honesty, he did not care for cats himself, but he would never have inflicted suffering on the creature deliberately. Nevertheless, he was annoyed that Jenny was getting the whole thing out of proportion. It was only a cat, for heaven's sake. Not a child.

He downed the last of his coffee and let his mind turn with relief to the day ahead. He would have to give Philip Wareham of Manfields Importers a call and arrange lunch. He had to keep him sweet. Then the research sheets should be in with the data from the Nottingham test. He would have to give it the once-over and get his assistant, Simon Grey, to compare them with the Manchester results. He felt the surge of adrenaline at the prospect before him.

He got up quickly and hurried upstairs to shower and dress. When he was ready to leave, he stood quietly outside the guest room door for a minute, but could hear nothing inside.

'I'm off to the office now,' he informed the closed door. Impatiently he waited for a response, but after a few moments' silence, he turned and left.

Dern & Fairchild, marketing consultants, was on the fifth and sixth floors of a modern office block in the City. They had moved there five years before and as a result of expansion at the right moment, the company had prospered. Richard Fairchild, its chairman, demanded dedication and hard work from his staff and when his expectations were fulfilled, the reward was high.

David Cranshaw had impressed him from the start. His hours of number crunching produced insights into marketing and demographics that others seemed to miss. And clients loved him. The rapid appointment to the board had been inevitable, but Fairchild knew he would have to keep an eye on his newest and ablest director. David's ambitions were high.

He stood now in David's office and looked around him. There was the usual array of electronic hardware, monitors and keyboards, but nonetheless, David had managed to make the room welcoming. It was no wonder his clients chose to come and lounge in the comfortable chairs over a drink or two, relaxing and dropping the occasional indiscreet remark. Remarks that were often useful.

As Fairchild was flicking through the papers on the desk, the door opened and David walked in.

'Ah, David, glad you're in early,' Fairchild greeted him.

'Spot of bother?'

'Not exactly. But I'm uneasy about this latest report for Harrisons Hardware. They might get cold feet when they get wind of these results.'

David hastened to reassure his boss. 'I'm certain it's nothing I can't sort out.'

'Good. Let's get some coffee in and get down to this damned Nottingham report then. The figures don't look too good. I think we'll have to advise Harrisons to try another test market.'

He looked keenly at David. They were testing a new product for Harrisons Hardware and initial results were not promising. The High Street was very sluggish at the moment.

This was where David excelled. He slipped off his jacket and swung it loosely over the back of his desk chair.

'Okay, Richard. Let's have a look at them.'

Fairchild sat down purposefully in the chair opposite, as David leaned over and pressed his intercom button.

'Bring in some coffee, will you, Sarah? For two.'

Almost immediately, the door was pushed open and his secretary walked in with a coffee tray. They both watched her place it on the low table in the centre of the room.

'White for me, please, Sarah,' Fairchild requested, his eyes travelling up her shapely legs.

Sarah Archer picked up the coffee pot and as she leaned over, her short navy skirt rode higher up her thighs. She was small and slim and was always immaculately dressed in figure-hugging suits and soft clinging blouses. David liked to watch the way she flicked her long dark hair over her shoulder as she poured the coffee, causing her small breasts to push firmly against the restraining fine material. He smiled at her as she handed them their coffee and she raised a questioning eyebrow in Fairchild's direction.

'Mr Fairchild and I will be busy for some time,' David told her. 'So hold my calls until later, will you?' Just in time he remembered the guest room at home. 'Unless there's a call from my wife.'

He saw Fairchild look at him sharply and cursed the need to bring his marriage to the office. As Sarah left the room, David picked up the documents on his desk and turned with relief to the problems of Dern & Fairchild.

David sat back in his chair as the door closed behind Fairchild. He stretched his legs out and smiled. It had been a tough couple of hours, but it had gone well. They'd made real progress.

He buzzed down to his assistant, Simon Grey, and arranged a meeting for that afternoon to discuss further tests. He was just crossing his office to pour himself another coffee, when the door opened again and Sarah Archer came in.

She replaced the cups on the tray that lay on the table and then turned and stood in front of David. His tall figure towered above her.

'I missed you last night,' she said simply.

Before he could respond, she slid her arms around his neck and pulled his face down to hers. Her mouth sought his hungrily and her body moulded itself against his. Though David was used to Sarah's sudden displays of sexual need, he was taken by surprise this time. His mind was full of the problems of his clients, but as always, he could not deny his instant response to Sarah's physical nearness.

His arms curved round her slender waist and held her tighter to him. He ran one hand up into her dense dark hair and twisted the long strands into a knot in his fist. He pulled it down so that her head tipped back and he buried his lips in her throat, tasting the faint scent of sandalwood on her skin. For a moment, his urgent need of her overwhelmed him, but with an effort, he dragged his senses back to reality and forced himself to release her and step away. He looked at her flushed cheeks and her open mouth and he wanted her so much that he did not trust himself. He stepped quickly behind the desk and sat down.

'Not now,' he reminded her. 'Fairchild could walk in again any moment.'

Sarah's brown eyes stared solemnly at him for a second and then she resumed her role as efficient secretary. 'Fairchild looked pleased when he left.'

'So he should. I'm the one doing all the work.'

'Were you working last night? Is that why you didn't come round to the flat?'

'Partly, but also I've got a bit of trouble on the domestic front at the moment.'

She stepped nearer the desk. 'Your wife?'

''Fraid so,' he nodded, then smiled at her invitingly. 'But I feel all the better for seeing you.'

She responded by perching her small bottom on a corner of his desk and mischievously crossing one leg over the other with exaggerated care. She grinned down at him, then reached out and lifted one of David's hands. She placed it inside her jacket on one of her breasts.

'Can you feel that my poor heart is broken? When you didn't come to see me, I thought you didn't love me any more.' She pouted playfully and David found her irresistible.

He gently squeezed a handful of her soft breast, then bent over and kissed the tip of her knee. 'I'll always come for you, my precious one,' he murmured to her kneecap, 'but right now, I've got to put a call through to Philip Wareham.' He rested his cheek against the soft, cool flesh of her leg and ran his fingers up and down from her knee to her ankle, over the silky smoothness of her skin. He felt Sarah's hands entwine possessively in his hair.

'I've had a call from him this morning for you, while you were closeted with Fairchild. He wants you to ring him back.' She tightened the grip of her fingers.

David slipped his hand under her heel and lifted her leg higher. He slid his lips down its gentle curve and kissed her calf, her shin and eventually her ankle.

'Then you had better get him on the line for me,' he mouthed against her skin and gently placed his teeth around her delicate ankle bone.

Sarah released his hair. 'I'll go and do that now, before he gets caught in meetings.'

David deliberately closed his teeth on the bone and felt her wince. It made him laugh, but he quickly kissed it better. Releasing her leg, he stood up and pulled her into his arms for a lingering kiss on the mouth.

'You're good for me,' he smiled down at her.

Sarah clung close to him for a moment longer, then reluctantly turned towards the door. 'I'll go and make that call to Manfields now.'

He watched the round, red mark on her ankle walk out of his office.

The morning sunshine splintered into dazzling motion on the

surface of the river and was reflected in fluid patterns of light up in the branches of the overhanging trees. A song thrush on the bough of an old oak peered down curiously at the figure below. Its practised eye searched for the worms exposed as each clod of earth fell to the ground.

The spade sank easily into the sandy soil under the oak tree and it was not long before a hole, two foot square, was cut into the grassy slope to the river. Jenny kept digging. She wanted to make it deep. When she was satisfied with her labours, she went over to the cardboard box lying at the base of the tree and kneeled down beside it.

As she reached out to lift the flaps, she could not stop the trembling in her hands. She paused to make herself calm down. Inside the box the body lay wrapped in a white, lacy shawl, pulled high to cover its head. She ran a finger along its cheek, but the fur was cold and lifeless. Quickly she closed the box and carried it to the hole, where she lowered it gently into the bare earth. She picked up the spade again.

There were no tears. As each clump of soil fell into the small grave, Jenny whispered softly under her breath. When the work was finished, she sat down nearby on the riverbank and stared across the gleaming water. The thrush abandoned hope of finding a meal and flew off downstream. Jenny picked a smooth stone and threw it out over the river. She watched it arc high up in the air, then curve and fall inexorably downward to be swallowed by the waiting water below. Where it broke the surface, a circle formed and spread towards her in ever-increasing ripples.

The first step was taken. The cat was buried. Buried far away from David. Here he was safe.

For a long time she sat there, remembering the hours spent in that hot room, clutching the sick body to her and willing it to live. Replaying the dark scene that stalked her nightmares. And just before dawn, she had made the decision. She would not leave. That would be too easy.

She continued to gaze at the hypnotic flow of the water. The sun warmed her hair and skin, and as she ran her fingers over the tufts of grass, she saw her hand was steady now. There would be no more trembling.

She stood up and her eyes rested for a moment on the unmarked grave, then she turned and walked briskly along the winding path. She had a letter to write now. She had to word it carefully. A satisfied smile spread over her face, when she thought how Fairchild would react to the information she would give. David would not know what hit him.

David Cranshaw turned into the drive. It was already gone eight o'clock, but he had been reluctant to return home and had lingered in the warmth of Sarah's bed. He parked the car in the garage and let himself into the house. All was silent. He walked across the hall and opened the door into the sitting-room.

She was there, sitting in her chair as usual. The French windows stood open and the evening birdsong drifted into the room. Everything was the same. Except Jenny. Despite her summer tan, her skin was grey and her dark eyes were sunk in purple shadows. She looked ill.

Her mouth formed itself into a copy of a smile of greeting. 'Hello,' she said.

He sat down in his chair and kicked off his shoes. 'How are you feeling?'

Again the awkward smile. 'I'm all right.'

She didn't look all right.

He had to ask. 'And the cat?'

'He's dead.'

'I'm sorry. You know I didn't mean to hurt it. I just tried to—'

'Don't, David. It's over. I buried him.'

'You can get another cat. A kitten that—'

'I don't want another cat,' she interrupted. 'I told you. It's over.'

Thank God for that. She wasn't going to make any more fuss.

There was an uncomfortable silence.

'I feel like a drink,' he said to break it. 'You look as if you could do with one too.'

'Thank you, yes.'

He stood up and the darkness in her eyes lifted slightly as she recognised his relief to get out of the room.

When he returned with the wine, she smiled at him as he placed her glass beside her. More successfully this time. He carried his own glass to his chair and to forestall another of those silences, he gave an exaggerated sigh, as he drank the cool wine. 'That feels good. I needed it.'

And then, from long years of habit and because they had nothing else to talk about, he started to tell her about his day.

The weather was warm but a fine drizzle had fallen for most of the morning, making the roads wet and slippery. Jenny turned carefully into the sports centre car park. She was about to pull into one of the allotted rectangles near the main building, when she suddenly spotted a car parked alone at the far end of the tarmac. She quickly reversed and drove along the aisles. When she reached the empty space next to it, she parked neatly within the white markings and pulled on the handbrake. She looked across at the little car beside her and smiled. It was a bright red Mini.

It was not hers. The numberplate had told her that. It was a couple of years younger and had special wheels and fat tyres. Otherwise it was the same. Her eyes ran over its familiar shape, its stubby bonnet and flat square roof, and she felt a tug of affection. And loss.

Eight years old, that's all hers had been. Not a wreck by any means. She was willing to admit it had been suffering a bit towards the end and had needed a new drive shaft and then a replacement subframe, but it had never actually let her down. She studied the condition of this younger Mini and could tell by the gleaming chrome bumpers and door handles that it was well cared for, well loved. Its paintwork was somewhat soiled, but then it had been raining all morning and the roads were dirty. She could tell the car had been recently waxed by the way the raindrops beaded on the bonnet.

Jenny had not been quite so meticulous with her own Mini. Its death knell had tolled last year. On her thirty-fifth birthday. She had been woken by David with a cup of tea and then led downstairs and out to the garage.

With a flourish, he had swung open the up-and-over door and burst into song. 'Happy birthday to you, happy birthday to you . . .'

Standing on the concrete floor next to David's Mercedes was a brand new Honda Prelude. There was no other car.

David turned to her, beaming proudly and seeking her reaction. He had taken the shock on her face to be an expression of surprised delight and had drawn her to the car to admire its many features. Its shining maroon paintwork, its reclining seats, electric windows and generous boot. No more cramming boxes of shopping on to the back seat of the Mini.

The tour of the car had given Jenny sufficient time to recover, so that when David suggested that they should go out in it, she had managed to appear enthusiastic. He had held out the keys to her and asked, 'Isn't it just great? Don't you love it?'

She had ducked down to slide into the driver's seat, so he could not see her face, as she answered, 'Yes, it's lovely. Thank you.'

'I knew you'd be thrilled. The Mini was completely finished. And anyway, I didn't like you driving around in crap like that.'

She clutched the padded steering wheel so tightly that her fingernails sank painfully into her palms. David had climbed in beside her and she was able to use her preoccupation with the new controls to avoid the necessity of replying.

She had never asked what had happened to her Mini. Where it went. But every time she caught sight of one of the small red boxes on wheels, she went to check if it was hers. Just to say goodbye.

Now she opened the car door and stepped out into the light rain. She locked the Honda and as she passed the Mini, she ran her finger along the curve of the chubby wing. She was starting to hurry over to the sports hall, when she hesitated, then stopped. She turned and looked back at the two cars side by side. She walked slowly back to them and opened her handbag. From her purse she took out a fifty-pence coin. Its corners would suit her purpose.

She stood by the front wing of the Honda on the driver's side, where the bodywork flared gracefully. She placed one edge of the coin on the flawless paintwork above the wheel and pressed firmly. Then, very deliberately and carefully, she drew a line about six inches long. Parallel to the arc of the wing. The two metals grated together, uttering a slight screech.

Jenny straightened up and inspected the damage. It was exactly where she could see it each time she got in and out of the car. As she turned for a second time to hurry out of the rain, she noticed two young boys standing watching her. They had swimming towels clutched under their arms and were staring at her, whispering to each other.

'It's all right,' she called. 'It's my husband's car.'

She smiled broadly and set off for her class.

Amy Stafford was disappointed. There were only seven today. Attendance numbers always dropped during the summer, as people were away on holiday or otherwise occupied with children home from school. But today there were hardly enough to make it worth her while and it was hard to inspire enthusiasm in such a small group. They were lost in this big hall. She turned the music up louder to fill the empty spaces, but it was clear that everyone was finding it hard grind.

'. . . Keep those legs straight and scissor, two, three, four . . .' she shouted over the beat of Queen.

Amy's eyes flicked critically over the display of limbs in the air and her glance settled on Jenny. She was definitely having to work harder at it today. The effort was showing. Well, what do you expect if you miss two weeks? She said she had been ill, and Amy had to admit she did not look at all well. Her arms and legs were like sticks and she obviously didn't have her usual enthusiasm or energy.

As Freddie Mercury's tones faded away and the class reluctantly started on the next routine, Jenny caught Amy's eyes casually inspecting the straightness of Jenny's leg, as she swung it over her head. Today she was wearing black cycling shorts and the silky material clung to her slender thighs.

She watched Amy intently, never breaking the rhythm of her movement and was rewarded by a look of sudden surprise on the instructor's face. Her eyes were focused on Jenny's thigh and then she quickly looked up at her face. Their eyes met and Jenny managed to keep the smile from her lips.

Sally Wright was sitting on a bench, pulling on her trainers as she talked to Amy. They were discussing the low attendance numbers, as Jenny came up to them. She noticed Amy's eyes travel quickly to her leg, as Sally commented sympathetically, 'I saw you puffing a bit, Jenny. It takes it out of you if you haven't been well.'

'I know. It was tough today. But I wanted to speak to you about that circuit training course on a Thursday evening, Sally.'

'Oh yes?'

'I've decided I would like to have a go at it after all. I can't start just yet, but in a while I'll give it a try.'

'Oh good. Are you sure you're up to it?'

'Don't worry,' Jenny laughed. 'I'll soon be fit again.'

Amy's expression was concerned. 'I'm sure it won't take you long to get back into shape, Jenny, but what's that mark on your leg?'

All three pairs of eyes turned sharply to Jenny's left thigh. The black shorts covered most of it, but where the shorts ended, a purple smear could be seen. Before Jenny could reply, Amy leaned forward, flicked a finger under the hem of Jenny's shorts and raised it a few more inches.

It was a huge bruise. An ugly black and purple discolouration swollen into a hard lump. Amy drew in her breath and Jenny heard Sally gasp beside her.

'How the hell did you get that?' Sally demanded.

Jenny quickly jerked her leg away and pulled the shorts down further. 'I tripped in the garden and knocked it on a stone wall.' The excuse sounded unconvincing.

Amy was surprised by Jenny's embarrassed reaction. It made it quite obvious the culprit had not been a wall. She looked at Jenny speculatively and wondered if she had got it during love-making. Was that why she was embarrassed about it? But it was a heck of a knock to have got in bed. What antics did they indulge in, for heaven's sake?

'It's nothing,' Jenny assured them, as she moved away to pick up her clothes. She hoped she had not overdone the bruise. The hammer had produced a more dramatic effect than she had intended. She would have to go a bit easier next time. She wondered how many more she needed to inflict before people began to suspect David.

Amy and Sally watched, as Jenny dressed and, with a 'See you next week', walked out of the hall.

The report on his desk just wasn't good enough. If Simon Grey thought he could get away with this, he was mistaken. David glanced up at the young man sitting opposite him, assessing his reaction.

David sat back. 'Some of the sections are very thorough, Simon.' Always praise them first. 'But I think you've missed some important points.'

'The new figures we're getting in from York and Cambridge are not complete yet,' Simon responded instantly. 'But I did draw a few preliminary conclusions.' He had worked damned hard on that report.

'Yes, I can see that, but we're trying to make Harrisons Hardware a household name. They're going into the High Street in a major way and we've got to get their marketing strategy right.' Did he have to spell it out again? 'This isn't your corner CTN we're talking about here.'

'I'm aware of that, David.'

David stood up and walked over to the table to pour himself another coffee. If he couldn't rely on his assistant for better work than this, he'd have to go. Perhaps he'd promoted him too soon.

'More coffee?'

Simon drained his cup and passed it across. 'Thanks.' He saw David's face and knew he had to make up ground fast. 'What direction do you suggest we go in, then? Obviously you don't agree with my ideas. So where do you think I've gone wrong?'

David handed Simon his coffee and sat down again. 'Study

the figures, Simon. We know Harrisons want a good practical image, but they've got to attract the "I-don't-want-to-get-my-hands-dirty" customer, who is looking for her new range of kitchenware as well as the paint and screws enthusiast. The ad agency is coming up with some good ideas for making the shops more user friendly. The whole operation is going up market.'

Simon nodded in agreement and for the next hour, listened to David's examination of and solutions to the problems. He had to admit, he was good. A bloody slave-driver and arrogant with it. But good. Simon smiled to himself. He had made the right choice. It had taken him only a couple of months after joining Dern & Fairchild to recognise that David Cranshaw was the one to watch. He had latched himself firmly to Cranshaw's elbow and as his star had risen, it had carried Simon with it.

He noticed David glance at his watch and realised drinks weren't on offer today. He started to gather his papers together.

'Well,' said David, 'that's a good morning's work. You get it sorted out this afternoon and bring me the amended report tomorrow. We'll go through it then, and afterwards I'll take you out to lunch. How's that?'

'Great. I'll get on to it right away.'

At the door, he turned and asked, 'Is Fairchild going to look in on this? Or are we on our own?'

'No.' David hid his irritation. 'Don't worry, he'll be in on it. As always.'

He closed the door behind Simon and returned to his desk. He buzzed the intercom. 'Get me Fairchild on the line, will you, Sarah?'

He waited impatiently. Fairchild was supposed to have turned up this morning at his meeting with Simon, but hadn't shown – which was just as well, now he had seen Simon's work. But it wasn't like the chairman. You usually had to fight to keep his fingers out of your pies.

'What is it, David?' Fairchild's voice was curt.

'Just to let you know we're making good progress on the Harrisons presentation. We should have it finalised by tomorrow.'

'I'll look at it then.'

'I'll set up a lunch with Hargreaves, their marketing man, for next week. I thought it would look good if you could join us.'

Silence for a moment. 'I'll see.'

Another surprise. 'All right, then. I'll let you know when we've got everything together tomorrow.'

'Fine.'

As David replaced the receiver, he decided to forget Fairchild and take Sarah to lunch. The very thought stirred his loins.

The small directors' washroom was one of the perks of being on the board. You didn't have to pee in front of junior employees. David stood before the washbasin and let the hot water flow over his hands and trickle through his fingers. It was the end of the day and he closed his eyes thankfully.

When he opened them, he saw dark spectacles watching him in the mirror above the basin. He had not heard Don Lerner come in.

He glanced over his shoulder in casual greeting. 'Hi, Don, how's your day been?'

The deputy chairman was tall and thin and there was some-thing faintly menacing about him. Perhaps it was the tinted lenses. He crossed over to the urinal and turned his back on the younger director.

'Not too bad.' His voice was cold. After a studied pause, he enquired, 'How's the Manfields account going?'

David turned off the tap and picked up one of the soft white towels that were neatly folded in a pile. 'Very well. Philip Wareham has gone along with our suggestions. He's a bright guy.' He'd have to give Philip a call again. He had tried to reach him all afternoon, but hadn't managed to get hold of him.

Lerner zipped his fly, and walked over to the other washbasin. He concentrated on soaping his hands and did not look at David. 'I hear Harrisons is giving you a spot of bother.'

David tossed the towel on to the washbasin in annoyance. 'That's rubbish. We're making great progress.'

'Good,' Lerner commented drily. 'It's amazing how rumours start.'

Their eyes met in the mirror and David tried to assess the

threat he heard in the words. Then he abruptly turned away. 'Goodnight,' he said and walked to the door. In the full-length mirror on the wall, he saw the tall reflection of Lerner. Using his own towel like a glove he was leaning over to pick up the soap and towel that David had used. He dropped them both into the rubbish bin.

For a second, David resented the action, but then dismissed it as another of Lerner's eccentricities.

The lift came to a stop on the ground floor and David hurried out across the reception hall. He waved a hand in acknowledgement of the concierge's 'Goodnight, sir', and pushed open the glass doors to the small car park at the front of the building. There were only half a dozen cars still there and he easily spotted Sarah's gold Fiesta.

'What kept you?' she asked, as he got into the driver's seat.

'Sorry, I got caught up and then met old Lerner in the washroom. He's even worse than usual.' He slipped into first gear and joined the traffic heading west.

'Don't take any notice,' Sarah told him and ran her fingers softly along his thigh.

David forced himself to keep his eyes on the traffic, but he could feel her warm breath on his cheek as she leaned over and kissed him on the ear. As he changed gear, she quickly thrust out a moist tongue, probing into his ear and he almost stalled the engine.

'You'll have me arrested for dangerous driving.'

Sarah sat back in her seat again. 'We certainly couldn't allow that, could we? I'd miss you too much.' Again her fingers started to run up and down his thigh.

'Do you know what was up with Fairchild today? He was distinctly preoccupied. Not himself at all.'

Her long nails started to scratch against the linen of his trousers, as she pressed more firmly on his leg. 'I wouldn't have thought he could get anything up any more,' Sarah replied with a grin. Her eyes were on the lights ahead.

The first traffic lights they had passed had been green, but these were just changing to amber. As David pulled on the handbrake and they waited in the queue of cars, Sarah's hand slipped over the top of his thigh, down to his groin. She rubbed gently against the soft material and felt the responding hardness inside. They continued to look ahead through the windscreen, both silent, in a secret world. As the lights changed to green again, Sarah withdrew her hand and they resumed conversation.

It was a game they played. David knew exactly how many traffic lights there were between the office and Sarah's flat in Kensington: thirty-two. Sometimes, when the traffic was particularly bad, they could be caught at every single one. This time, to David's chagrin, they sailed through at least half of them on green.

David parked the car and with his jacket slung over his arm, walked impatiently up to Sarah's second-floor flat. It never failed to amaze him, when he stepped through her front door, that someone as immaculate in her clothes and her person as Sarah could live in such a mess. He knew she shared the flat with two other girls, but he could not blame it all on them, because Sarah's own room was just as bad. Blouses and tee shirts lay abandoned on floor and furniture. Yesterday's mugs of coffee stood half-finished on the bedside table. The bed was an untidy jumble of underwear and bedding, which Sarah instantly swept on the floor in an impatient gesture.

But nothing could dampen his desire for her. If anything, the chaos around him heightened the abandoned passion of their love-making. He dragged her down on to the mattress and his hands pulled urgently at her clothes. A button tore from her blouse, but neither noticed. When she was wearing only transparent bra and panties, he eased back to gaze at her as she lay on the bed. Breathing heavily, he ran his fingers through her long silky hair, then over her nose and full, sensual lips. Her pink tongue snaked out and licked each fingertip. His hand slid down to her narrow throat and he could feel the strong pulse surging beneath the soft skin.

Her eyes were fixed on his face, watching him staring at the fast rise and fall of her breasts as she lay there. He slipped his hands under her to undo the catch at her back, and then slowly pulled the filmy material away. He murmured longingly as her small firm breasts were exposed and sank his face into the softness of her body. She moaned eagerly at his touch and clutched at his broad back.

His hand slid down over the concave smoothness of her belly and his fingers crept into the dark mound of hair below. She wriggled free of her pants and once naked, Sarah could hold back no longer. She swept her bare legs up and entwined them round his body, clinging to him and sliding her naked body over the roughness of his zip and buttons.

Her mouth pressed to his and his lips parted to receive her probing tongue, as she pulled him to lie down beside her. Slowly and sensuously, she removed each piece of his clothing, stroking and caressing his body, her lips enticing each part to desire. When they were both completely naked, David lay back on the pillows and she rolled on top of him, her hair tumbling over his face.

His hands ran down her arched spine and on to the round curves of her bottom. She moaned softly in his ear and he felt the urgency within her. He pulled her tight against him and as he buried his face in her hair and his flesh in her body, she was the only world that existed.

4

The train pulled noisily into Charing Cross Station and immediately the dash took place to get out of the door. Jenny Cranshaw waited until the barging and trampling had eased and then stepped down on to the platform. People swirled around in heedless, headlong rush.

It was some time since she had been up to London and the dirt and smells struck her anew. She thought of David commuting to the City each day, crammed between outspread newspapers on the train and then forced to strap-hang on the underground, jostled against strangers' bodies at every jerk of the carriage.

But now she smiled happily to herself, as she emerged from the station into the bright sunlight. Dressed in a well-cut, cream linen frock, fashionably short, with a matching short-sleeved jacket, she knew she looked good. She had worked hard to gain a little weight, so that the lines of her body had softened and the hollows of her cheeks filled. Her skin glowed with its summer tan and there was a new eagerness in her step.

She crossed to Trafalgar Square and mingled with the crowd of tourists, watching a party of French children shrieking in delight as the pigeons descended on to their outstretched hands. Cameras clicked and whirred, and Jenny carefully walked round each posing group. She trailed her fingers in the cool waters of the fountains, but did not delay long.

She turned up St Martin's Lane and found herself enjoying the atmosphere of life and energy that surrounded her. There was a sense of purpose and determination in the figures that strode past her and in the continuous torrent of cars and buses that poured down to the square. Only the tourists were happy to drift along at a slower pace, gazing in shop windows or standing awkwardly in the middle of the pavement to study a map, while the flow of people broke and reformed around them.

At the top of the road, Jenny turned left and crossed to Old Compton Street, narrowly avoiding the aggressive wheels of a double-decker bus. Her pace slowed and she felt more uncertain of herself. She had to admit that she was a little uneasy about her destination now that she was almost there. Firmly pushing aside such thoughts, she started to look about her for the shop she wanted.

She was not familiar with Soho and was surprised to find its narrow streets less busy than the main thoroughfares. Her image of the area was still one of numerous strip-clubs, sex shops and sleazy bars, but to her surprise many of them seemed to have gone, replaced by Greek restaurants and Italian bistros.

As she turned a corner, her eyes at last found what they had been searching for. It didn't look much from the outside. So much the better. She stood on the pavement on the opposite side of the road and was trying to study the shop unobtrusively when its door suddenly opened and a blond young man, clutching a brown paper bag, strode off down the street.

Perhaps it would be empty now. It was impossible to see inside because the shop's narrow frontage was discreetly masked and only entry through the door would reveal the details of its contents.

The door opened quietly and the bored young man behind the counter glanced up casually from the magazine. His interest was immediately caught. It wasn't often a woman came into the shop, certainly not a looker like this one.

She stepped inside and gazed around. Her eyes met his and flicked away quickly. It was obvious she was embarrassed and unused to magazines like these. He leaned his elbows on the counter and settled down with amusement to watch her progress. There was only one other person in the shop at the moment, browsing over the displays, and the newcomer kept well clear of him.

She moved rapidly past most of the shelves, hardly glancing at the abundance of naked breasts and thrusting bottoms. Clearly she knew what she wanted. His eyes rested on her own bottom, as she stood with her back to him. Very nice little arse, good and firm. Great legs too. He guessed she must work out. But he liked long hair on a woman himself. Something to grab hold of. To pass the time, he conjured up a vision of himself and this willowy brunette entwined in his bed together and he wondered what her breasts were like. Too often tall slim women had no tits worth a damn. And he didn't mind bedmates older than himself. Often they appreciated him more. But what was she doing in here? Didn't her man provide her with enough of it?

He watched her quickly find what she wanted and could see she was eager to get out of the shop. Her choice amused him, but he had learned in this business that there was no accounting for taste. As she offered the money, he smiled invitingly at her, but she would not look at him. He pulled out a bag and slipped the three magazines inside.

'A bit cooler out today, isn't it?' he commented.

She nodded silently, staring down at the counter.

'Still,' he laughed, 'warm enough to make you want to sink your teeth into a nice, moist, juicy peach.'

He was rewarded by seeing her glance quickly up at him and then turn a burning red.

'Have a nice day,' he called after her, as she hurried from the shop. The magazines were tucked safely inside her handbag.

David smiled at Jenny. She was certainly looking better these days.

'So what sort of exciting day did you have?'

They were sitting out on the terrace, watching the last rays of sun streak the clouds blood red. She picked up her glass of Pimms and sucked a cold slice of peach from the rim.

'I had a lazy day at home,' she answered casually. Just the memory of the shop brought the colour to her cheeks again. 'I did some gardening though. I've improved that rambler.'

David glanced over at the deep pink rose that climbed in glorious abundance up the side of the house and arched over the French windows. Instead of the usual riot of unruly shoots hanging loosely down to snare the unwary passer-by, it was now restrained by strands of wire and neatly trimmed to frame the window.

'You've not made a bad job of it. Well overdue.'

She lifted her hands, palms towards him and smiled ruefully. 'I paid a price though.'

A multitude of tiny scratches and snags covered her hands and forearms. The soft evening light gave her face a glow and David suddenly found her unexpectedly desirable. His eyes dropped to her white tee-shirt that clung to her breasts and he could see clearly the outline of her nipples. He liked her with no bra.

He reached out and took one of her torn hands in his own. He gently drew it to him and pressed his lips to the red cuts on the palm.

'I'll kiss it better for you.'

For a moment, she let it lie unresisting in his hands, but when his lips sought the scratches on her wrist and the inside of her arm, she carefully withdrew it.

'You should have worn gloves.' He was disappointed.

'Don't worry, the scratches will soon go.' She smiled at him. 'Especially now you've kissed them better.'

David glanced up at her face and was caught unawares by the amusement he saw in her eyes. There was a definite change in her.

He picked up the tall jug of Pimms mixture that stood on the table and the ice cubes clinked softly against the glass. He had been surprised after their meal when she had suggested a drink on the terrace, and though he had some paperwork to go through, he had agreed. It would be good to relax for a while, before starting on those figures. And he had to reread Simon's new report.

As he poured out the cool brown liquid, David thought again about the chairman. 'I don't know what's got into Fairchild. He's obviously got something on his mind. He's acting very strangely. Very distant.'

A sprig of mint and an apple chunk slid into Jenny's glass. She promptly picked out the floating piece of fruit and sucking it between her teeth, asked, 'Distant? What do you think the trouble is?'

David replenished his own glass and shook his head. 'God knows. I just hope he's not in any financial trouble.'

'What do you mean? I thought the new accounts with Harrisons and Manfields meant the company would be doing well.'

Another surprise. Since when did she actually remember any of his clients' names?

'I'm just guessing. Fairchild usually handles everything so smoothly, but he's not himself at all. Whatever is worrying him must be serious.'

'You're probably right.' Jenny was studying him closely.

'I couldn't get him to come and give our report the once-over today. Normally nothing gets passed without his approval. But he seems to be always "in conference" these days. In the end, he told me to give it to his secretary and he'd look at it tomorrow.' Again David shook his head. 'It's not like him.'

'Perhaps there's a problem with his family or health.'

'No, he would never let his home life interfere. And he's as fit as a fiddle. Always bragging about his "robust constitution".'

He leaned back in his chair, stretching out his legs, and looked at his wife as he sipped his drink. There was no doubt about it. Something was different. Her mouth was softened in a smile and her eyes held his, instead of instantly flitting away. Ever since the death of that damned cat.

He smiled as he remembered her when they had first met. Only eighteen, an elf of a creature with huge brown eyes that brimmed with enthusiasm and vitality. She had been ready to fly high on the wings of youth and spread gossamer on the world's wounds. He had met her at university. She had just come up to read History and he had gone there to a party thrown by a colleague of his, who was doing a post-grad degree in Economics. The older students had roped in the prettiest of the new crop of girls to come to the party and David had ended up sitting on the floor with her, knocking back the cider and planning to change the world. He had been entranced. The inevitable had happened. Within two months she was pregnant and he had married her.

The first couple of years had been tough. He had only just been appointed to a position in a marketing consultancy and was still on the first rung. But between them, they had managed to get Jenny through the BA degree course, even with a baby in tow. Then things had started to change. Jenny had stayed at home to care for the child, and David worked doubly hard to earn the income for them all. He had wanted to get to the top fast – be the best – and he had certainly succeeded, but something had come adrift along the way. It had started with having to work late, putting in the extra hours, but then he had discovered that with each step up the ladder, the girls had made themselves ever more available. The late-night meetings had become late-night dinners. And then hotel rooms. And now there was Sarah. As always, the thought of Sarah roused him.

He tipped his head back and stared up at the rosy fingers of cloud tracing the last vestiges of the day across the sky. He did not like to look back. There were too many black holes. Like the day his first company had folded. He had been too green to see it coming and had gone down with the rest of them. But he had fought his way back. He sighed with satisfaction. Then, catching him unawares, came the unbidden image of his son, blond and laughing. He closed his eyes, shutting down on the memories. All that was finished with. That was before the accident. Before Jenny had come to tell him their son was dead. They had moved house, moved town.

Don't look back. It's the future that counts now. So what lay ahead for him at Dern & Fairchild? Deputy chairman? Chairman? Without thinking, David found himself telling Jenny his fears about the internal politics on the board. No one was safe. Not even directors. He even related the incident in the washroom with Lerner, the man he had every intention of replacing.

He opened his eyes to find Jenny staring at him intently. He could not fathom her expression, but somehow it made him faintly uneasy.

A light breeze had sprung up and rustled softly in the trees. It was just enough to chill the evening air and break the mellow mood. David finished his drink and stood up.

'Well, I've got to get down to some work. It's no good putting it off any longer.' He started towards the house, then turned and added, 'It's getting cool now. Are you coming in?'

Jenny continued to gaze out across the lawn at the gently waving heads of the delphiniums. 'No,' she answered quietly. 'I like it like this.'

David nodded, his thoughts already with Dern & Fairchild.

As Jenny looked over the edge at the turquoise water below, her face wobbled slightly and then splintered into a thousand shimmering facets.

'Come on in,' Susannah Benson shouted, as she slipped smoothly into the pool. She scooped up handfuls of water to splash at Jenny. 'It's absolutely wonderful.'

Laughing, Jenny retreated a few steps to avoid the spray and shook her head. 'No, I'm fine here on dry land. I'll just dip my feet in.'

The sun reflected fiercely from the mirrored surface and as Jenny walked around the warm stone paving that edged the pool, she watched enviously as Susannah sank completely under the cool waters, where her slim figure was suddenly distorted into a squat dwarf. Then the underwater image transformed into a sleek line, as Susannah swam effortlessly along the bottom of the pool to the deep end. When she reached the wall, she burst up out of the water and ran her hands over her face to clear her eyes and smooth her hair. She laughed and squinted up at Jenny, silhouetted against the sky.

'It's heaven. Why don't you join me? There's a spare bikini on the lounger over there.'

Jenny grinned down at the seal-smooth head. 'It looks very tempting, but I don't want to risk any more sunburn. I overdid it yesterday while I was gardening, so I'm keeping covered up today.' She grimaced. 'I don't want to peel.'

'God forbid.' Susannah pushed off from the wall and floated on her back. Eyes closed, she stretched out and abandoned herself to the sun. The full curves of her breasts and hips were highlighted by her skimpy white bikini and by the myriad water droplets that dappled her golden tan.

Jenny sat down on the paved edge and swung her feet into the water. Behind her the elegant Georgian house stood surrounded by an abundance of immaculate flowerbeds, its tall windows seeming to stare blankly at her. The summer had been so free from rain that the lawn was just beginning to turn a dust brown, another victim of the hose-pipe ban. Jenny knew Susannah would not risk soiling a manicured fingernail and that the garden was maintained in its perfection by a dedicated menial.

Jenny gently kicked her feet, circulating the water. 'How's the golf going? Any more trophies?'

Susannah flipped on to her front and swam leisurely to the Roman steps at the shallow end of the pool.

'Not yet,' she answered, 'but I'm down for the Trentworth competition in two weeks' time. I intend to make mincemeat of them.' She stood up on the marble steps and shook herself vigorously, then walked over and picked up a towel from one of the sunbeds. 'God, it's hot. Are you ready for another drink?' She lifted the iced jug on the table beside the pool and poured the cool liquid into tall glasses.

Jenny joined her at the table and accepted the proffered drink. 'That's marvellous,' she murmured appreciatively, as she tasted the concoction of fruit juices and wine.

Glass in hand, Susannah stretched out on the sunbed. 'It's nice to see you over here, Jenny, on a day like this. You're not like some of Robert's freeloaders. As soon as they know you've got a pool and a well-stocked drinks cabinet, you can't keep them away.'

Jenny sat down on a chair beside the table. The wood was warm on her skin. 'I was shopping in Tonbridge and thought I'd pop in on my way home. It's such a glorious day, I knew you'd be in the pool.'

Susannah laughed. 'I can't resist it on a day like this. It's a shame you won't come in as well. In this country you've got to grab every bit of sun that comes along.' She reached down beside her and picked up a pair of sunglasses. 'Not off on holiday yourself?'

'Nothing's arranged. It just depends on what David's got on.'

'God, these men and their work. They're gluttons for punishment. Poor old David. Working too hard, is he?'

'As frenetic as ever, especially now he's snowed under with all the work on the new accounts.'

'What new accounts are those?'

Jenny sat back in her chair and watched Susannah closely, as she said, 'He has just won a big hardware account and an import business.'

Susannah's interest quickened. 'An import business?'

'Yes. It's a bit like Robert's, I suppose.'

Susannah slipped the sunglasses over her eyes and two black circles stared back at Jenny. 'Like Robert's? Why, what sort of imports do they deal in? What's its name?'

Jenny caught the sudden sharpness in the tone.

Robert Benson had based his company's success on importing goods cheaply from East European countries and selling them at highly inflated prices to shops throughout Britain. His major achievement had been the introduction of an inexpensive range of watches, which was now in every High Street and on almost every wrist. The watches were manufactured in Poland, where low wages and government subsidy meant that Robert could purchase large quantities of them for comparatively little outlay. At a time when the watch market was dominated by the Japanese and the Swiss, Robert's competitors had laughed at the idea of anyone wanting a Polish watch. But their derision had changed to amazement and then dismay as they saw his watches seizing an ever larger slice of the market.

Jenny looked around her. The status house, the pool, the gold Cartier watch and emerald ring lying discarded on the table before her, all derived from cheap watches mass-produced by Polish peasants.

She turned back to the black lenses and smiled helpfully. 'Manfields I think it's called. It imports watches. Isn't that what Robert does?'

'You know damned well he does.'

'But, Susannah, David's new client is into Japanese watches. Not European, like Robert.'

'That's not the bloody point, is it?'

Jenny was aware that Robert Benson had for years used Dern & Fairchild for the odd marketing job – a product test here, an analysis there. Never anything big, but enough for David to know all the details of their pricing policy and marketing strategies. Useful information to a competitor.

'Robert won't like this. Not one little bit.'

Of course he wouldn't. That's why David hadn't told him. 'I'm sorry, Susannah. I thought David might have already mentioned it to Robert.'

'No, I'm sure he hasn't.'

'Perhaps he's been too busy.'

'Too cowardly is more like it,' accused Susannah. 'He could have let him know the other evening at the pub, if he had wanted to.' She stood up and placed her sunglasses on the table beside the watch for safety. Her wet hair clung in long strands to her shoulders, as she looked down at her guest.

'But hell, Jenny, I don't want them to fall out over this. You know what men are like – so bloody touchy. Hackles raised at the slightest threat to their territory.'

Jenny smiled up at her. 'They'll get over it.'

'I hope so, but I wouldn't count on it.'

'Don't let it spoil today. Forget about them and enjoy your swim.'

'You're right. This sun is too good to waste.' She laughed and launched herself into the inviting waters. As she disappeared from view, Jenny continued to sit thoughtfully for a moment, staring at the sunglasses, watch and ring on the table, glinting in the sunlight. Then she placed her drink on the floor and slowly stood up. Keeping one eye on Susannah's subaqua form, she very deliberately tipped the round table precariously on to one leg. The highly polished surface sloped at a sharp angle towards the pool and Jenny watched as the little pile of possessions slid inexorably down towards the edge. She tilted the table just a little more and caught the gold watch and ring in her hand as they slid over the rim, but let the sunglasses tumble into the blue water. Instantly they spiralled down into the depths. Jenny released the table with a loud cry and it fell on its side on the ground. Quickly she placed the watch beside it.

Susannah's head popped up abruptly out of the water. 'What's the trouble?'

'Oh Susannah, I'm sorry. I stood up suddenly to watch you underwater and I accidentally knocked over the table. The watch is safe, but your ring and sunglasses have fallen into the water. I'm terribly sorry.'

Susannah's face took on a look of horror. 'Not my emerald.'

'Don't worry, I'll find it,' Jenny promised.

Instantly she tore off her dress, and wearing just bra and panties, she slid over the edge into the pool. The ring was still clasped tightly in her fist. The cool water took her breath away for a moment, but without delay she sank to the bottom. Susannah joined her and together they scanned the marble floor of the pool, their eyes fighting to make sense of the swirling, distorted images. Susannah quickly found and rescued the sunglasses but could see no sign of the ring.

Jenny did not want to distress her friend any longer than necessary, so she made a brief pretence of searching every inch of the area and then, with lungs bursting, rose to the surface. She held the ring aloft.

'Eureka.'

'Thank God for that,' Susannah gasped, as Jenny dropped it into her outstretched hand. The emerald and diamonds gleamed in the sunlight, none the worse for their ducking.

'Bloody hell, Jenny, that was a close thing.'

'I know. I'm awfully sorry. I don't know how I could have been so careless.'

Susannah slipped the ring safely on to her finger. 'It's okay. It was an accid—'

She broke off and stared aghast at Jenny's right shoulder. A livid bruise the size of a grapefruit disfigured the skin where her bra strap lay. And on her thigh was the fading mark of another.

'Good Lord, what on earth happened to you?'

Jenny stood up. 'Oh, nothing much. I was trying to get something off the shelf in the garage and a paint tin fell on top of me.'

'God, it looks awful. No wonder you were keeping them covered up.' Susannah studied the rest of Jenny's shoulder. 'There's no trace of sunburn though.'

Jenny smiled self-consciously, wrapped herself in a towel and after removing her sodden underwear, slipped her dress back on. She ran her fingers through her short wet hair and turned to face Susannah's concerned gaze.

'Jenny, are you sure you're all right?'

'Of course I am. What do you mean?'

'The bruises.'

Jenny shrugged. 'It's nothing. Really. I was just clumsy.'

It was again her self-conscious, embarrassed smile that made Susannah uneasy. 'You should look after yourself better. Make David do it in future.'

The sudden look of distress on Jenny's face made Susannah aware of the unintended meaning of her words and she quickly added, 'Get things off high shelves, I mean. Not make the bruises.' She stared, appalled, at Jenny. 'Don't tell me David is involved in causing the bruises?'

'Of course not. I told you—'

'Yes, I know, it was the paint pot.'

'That's right.'

Susannah refilled their glasses and sat down, spreading her wet hair in a fan around her to dry in the sun. 'Then why are you hiding your shoulder behind a story of sunburn?'

'Because it's so darn ugly. That's the worst of it. Not being able to strip off when it's hot.'

'Are you sure that's the worst of it?'

'Yes.' Jenny did not lift her eyes from the glass in her hand. She hated lying to Susannah.

Susannah eyed her sceptically, then stretched luxuriously on the sunbed. 'Okay, I'll take your word for it. But now that I've seen your guilty secret, you might as well make use of that spare bikini and have a swim.'

Jenny grinned. 'Sounds good to me.'

She stood up, changed into the skimpy black two-piece and with relief, slipped into the pool. A few brisk lengths would rid her of the tension and now that she had accomplished both aims of the visit, she could relax and enjoy herself.

What the hell was going on?

David Cranshaw marched again into Sarah Archer's office and demanded, 'Are you sure you got the message right?'

Sarah looked up from her monitor, but he did not wait for her answer.

'Did you speak to Philip Wareham himself?'

'Of course not.' She patiently repeated, 'His secretary rang to say he was cancelling his lunch date with you today.'

'Did she give a reason?'

'No. She just said he was caught up and couldn't make it today.'

'For God's sake, that's the second time he's cancelled. You shouldn't have let her get off the phone without making another appointment.'

'I tried to,' Sarah explained, 'but she wouldn't commit him to a definite day. She just agreed to a vague arrangement for lunch some time soon.'

David paced the tiny office. 'What's he playing at? How can we do business if he keeps backing out of meetings?'

Sarah tried to pacify him. 'I think Simon has seen a lot of Lesley Carter. She's Philip Wareham's chief assistant, so—'

'I'm not interested in Simon's bloody sex life,' David snapped. 'What has she told him about the account?'

'That's what I meant,' Sarah answered calmly. 'He's been having business meetings with her and she says that Manfields are extremely pleased with our work.'

David glared at her for a moment. 'Get hold of Simon and tell him to get himself into my office right now.' Then he turned on his heel and walked out.

By the time Simon Grey hurried into the office, David had calmed down. Everybody was forced to cancel appointments at times. He'd just had a run of bad luck with Philip Wareham. It did not mean anything.

Simon stood uncomfortably in the middle of the room and enquired what the problem was.

'I want to know what Lesley Carter has been telling you about our handling of their account.'

'She says Wareham likes what we've produced so far,' Simon

responded quickly. 'He's impressed. Great background knowledge. She tells me he intends to follow our guidelines for market penetration.'

That sounded reassuring. David relaxed a little.

'I want you to contact Miss Carter this afternoon, find out if anything is amiss with Wareham. See if there are any problems that are making him keep his distance.'

David sat down in his chair and waved his assistant into the seat opposite, but to his surprise, Simon chose to remain standing. 'And for God's sake, use a little subtlety, while you're at it. We don't want them to think we're worried.'

Simon backed slightly towards the door. 'I'll give her a ring now.'

'There's no point. She'll be out to lunch.'

'I may just catch her before she goes.' He took another step backwards.

'This afternoon will do. And make damned certain you don't alarm her,' David reiterated. He stood up and walked over to his drinks cabinet, then turned to Simon who still hovered near the door. 'I certainly need a drink. How about you?'

Simon's eyes darted uneasily away from David's face. 'Not for me, thanks. I'm in the middle of some numbers for . . .' He hesitated.

'For whom?'

Simon again looked away. 'For Mr Lerner.'

'Why the hell are you doing work for him?' David demanded. 'He may be deputy chairman, but you damned well work for me, not him.'

'It's nothing much. Just some figures on Manfields.'

David stood with his hand on the cabinet door and looked hard at his assistant. He took in the embarrassment in his manner and his eagerness to leave the office. Slowly he took a few steps towards Simon, then smiled reassuringly. 'As long as it doesn't take up too much of your time, that's all right.'

'No, no. Don't worry. It won't.' Simon turned, as if to go, but David put a hand on his shoulder to restrain him. Simon instantly ducked out from under it and said, 'I'll go and give Lesley Carter a ring. I might be lucky.'

'She will be at lunch.' David's voice was now relaxed and inviting. 'I tell you what, Simon. I've got a table for two booked at Schofields. Now that Philip Wareham has cried off, why don't you join me?'

'Sorry, I can't. I've arranged lunch with . . . Bill Stanton.'

Bill Stanton was the assistant advertising manager of Harrisons Hardware.

David stared at his assistant for a moment, then nodded. 'Some other time, then.'

'Right.' Simon quickly opened the door.

David watched him leave, then went and poured himself a large scotch.

David had looked for Sarah. He had decided to invite her to accompany him to Schofields restaurant instead, but she had already left the office for her lunch hour. He determined to enjoy the meal anyway. Probably he would meet someone he knew there.

As he walked into the street, his eyes searched the stream of traffic for an available taxi, but his mind was preoccupied with his meeting with Simon Grey. He ran over the exchange in his head and sought for an interpretation of Simon's behaviour. And what the hell was Don Lerner up to?

David waved his arm in vain at a disappearing cab and then turned down a side-street to take him in the general direction of the restaurant. On the corner, he passed a sandwich bar, one of those tiny establishments that churn out Cellophane-wrapped rolls by the thousand to fill the empty stomachs of the local offices. David glanced briefly at the queue inside and suddenly checked his stride. Halfway along the row of hungry secretaries and young executives inside the shop stood Simon.

After a brief pause, David continued along the street.

Pierre greeted David Cranshaw warmly. A valued customer.

'And how are you today, sir?' he enquired with professional ease.

'Just fine. Overworked as usual.'

Pierre smiled and wondered as always how two-and three-hour lunch breaks fitted into overworked schedules.

David glanced around the tables. 'My companion can't join me after all, so it's just a table for one.'

'Certainly, sir. This way please.' He led David across the restaurant to a small table against the wall, but with a good view of the room, pulled back the chair and shook out the fan-shaped napkin.

'Thanks, Pierre. This is fine.'

The maître d' raised an eyebrow at a young waiter, who instantly approached with the large menu sheet.

David noticed a familiar face at a nearby table and nodded a greeting. 'Just bring me my usual first, Pierre, while I decide what to order.'

'Right away, sir.' Pierre turned to the wine waiter and within a couple of minutes, a bottle of Chablis '89 arrived at the table in an ice bucket and was opened with a flourish.

'Thank you, Emile,' David murmured, as he savoured the wine. His eyes flitted round the various groups of diners clustered around the immaculate white tablecloths. Several business suits he recognised, but none that he cared to join. He acknowledged their waves but remained seated. He assessed the significance of who was lunching whom and was amused to see one of his fellow directors closeted in a corner with Richard Fairchild's secretary. It certainly couldn't be her mousy looks that were the attraction.

He picked up the menu and studied the sepia italics, but Simon Grey's furtive face kept getting in the way and David tried again to make sense of his behaviour. He looked round for a waiter, but seeing they were all occupied, decided to take the opportunity to go to the men's cloakroom.

He stood up and moved towards the far end of the room. The restaurant was L-shaped, with the cloakrooms situated round the corner. There were a few tables occupying that section, but most customers preferred to be in the main part of the restaurant where they could see and be seen. David turned into the more secluded area and headed for the door in the corner. As he did so, his glance fell on two men deep in conversation at one of the tables. He stopped dead in his tracks.

Neither man looked up nor broke off from their discussion. Both were leaning forward, elbows on the table and voices lowered. The shorter man on the right was overweight and held a large Havana cigar in his stubby fingers. He was listening intently to the words of his companion. The other was lean, with grey hair and tinted glasses. He was wearing an immaculate grey suit with razor-sharp creases. It was Don Lerner.

David stared for a second, then pulled himself together and hurried into the cloakroom. He had to think. What the hell was going on? His heart was racing and his palms were moist. He walked over to the basin and splashed cold water on his face.

Don Lerner and Philip Wareham. That's why Wareham had cancelled lunch. What the hell were they up to together? David knew Lerner of old, before he became deputy chairman of Dern & Fairchild – knew of his love of intrigue and the silent stiletto in the back. Somehow he had spread his web and ensnared Wareham, but what would he achieve by taking Manfields Importers away from David? That was only too damned obvious. It was a big account. If he could erode David's power base, then that made David more vulnerable.

He flicked water on his face once more, straightened up and looked again at his reflection. The blue eyes were cold and the jaw clenched. Well, he wouldn't let it go without a fight. He had to speak with Wareham. And he had to get to Fairchild. He forced a smile and made it look convincing, then dried his hands and walked casually out of the door.

He glanced sideways as he passed the table for two. Both men were still engrossed in their conversation. David stepped nearer their table, just as Lerner sat back and was raising a wine glass. Their eyes met and Lerner's hand froze, only halfway to his lips. David derived pleasure from the momentary alarm he saw behind the lenses, but it was only for a split second. The deputy chairman recovered himself quickly and continued the movement of the glass.

'Well, look who's here. We didn't expect to see you, David. Did we, Philip?' Lerner sipped his cold wine and smiled unpleasantly.

Philip Wareham looked up in surprise. 'David, I was going to

call you. Sorry I couldn't make lunch today, but I had a few . . .
er . . . things to discuss with Don here.' He puffed on his cigar
to fill the awkward silence.

Lerner continued to sip his wine and watch David.

'That's all right, Philip. We can make it some other time,'
David smiled reassuringly at his client. 'Are there any problems
you need to discuss with me?'

Wareham started to look more comfortable again. 'No, not
really, David. You're doing a great job.'

'So why this hush-hush meeting then? If there's a problem,
let's thrash it out together.'

Don Lerner stood up and took a step towards David. 'It's
all under control, David. There's no reason why Philip and I
shouldn't have a quiet lunch together. In peace.'

David stared into the hostile eyes and knew he could not make
waves here.

'I will speak to you back at the office, Don,' he said icily, then
turned to Philip Wareham. 'I'll give you a ring, Philip. Enjoy
your meal.'

David walked away with a confident, easy stride, but when he
reached his own table, he found his churning stomach rebelled
at all thought of food. He apologised briefly to Pierre and left the
restaurant.

5

The soft sandy soil was warm on Jenny's toes, as it trickled in through her open sandals. She loved this walk along the river. Thickly wooded on either side, it gave a sense of seclusion and privacy.

She bent down and slipped off her sandals, so that her bare feet could enjoy the dusty warmth of the soil of the path. In the heat of the day, the river itself seemed too tired to exert much effort and slid smoothly through its shallow course. The path she followed wove through the trees, keeping close to the grassy bank that sloped down to the water's edge.

Jenny quickened her step as she saw the ancient gnarled oak ahead that stretched its limbs far out over the river. She came here most days, even for just a brief moment or two. She rounded a clump of tangled briar that bordered the small clearing and stepped eagerly into the patch of warm sunlight.

All was quiet. The small grave under the protection of the oak's broad spread of branches was already covered with the first green shoots of young grass. She dropped down beside it in the dappled sunlight and stared out at the lazy motion of the river. Here was the peace she sought, the stillness she needed to forge the strength of will to carry her forward. To steel herself for what lay ahead.

The hardest part to face was misleading her friends. They did not deserve such shoddy treatment. 'Don't forget, I'm here if ever you need a shoulder to cry on,' had been Susannah's parting words that afternoon. The genuine concern on her face and the affectionate hug as Jenny was about to drive off had brought forth a surge of guilt.

But there was no other way. Her path was set and she would let nothing deter her. The result would have to justify the means.

The next step was to make use of the magazines she had suffered such embarrassment to obtain. There had been an extraordinary variety of gay magazines to choose from, going from pretty boy seductive poses to downright pornographic. She had quickly selected the three most explicit she could find and escaped from the shop as speedily as possible, cheeks burning. Now it was time to put them to work.

She rose from the grass and wandered down to the river's edge. The crystal water felt icy to her warm toes, but nevertheless, she waded out into the deeper stretches of the sluggish flow. Here lay the bigger rocks and boulders, so that she had to tread with care. She took her time peering down into the clear current, until she found what she sought. The boulder she selected was broad and heavy, but straining her muscles, she managed to raise it from the river-bed and stagger back to the bank with it clutched to her body. She struggled up the slope and finally deposited it on the spot where the box was buried. The burgeoning shoots of grass were crushed under its weight, but as Jenny stood back and inspected the result, she nodded with approval.

'That will keep you safe from scavengers.'

She took one last look round the sunlit clearing and at the tranquil river, then she picked up her shoes, brushed down her sodden dress and set off on the path back home.

That evening David arrived home tense and irritable. After throwing his jacket on the stool, he had slumped in his armchair and drunk his wine in morose silence.

Later, as he and Jenny sat down to eat, he continued to show more enthusiasm for the contents of the bottle than of his plate. When he started up a diatribe against some fellow on the tube train who had incurred his displeasure for some misdemeanour or other, Jenny gave up listening.

Instead she let her mind return to the green glade by the river where she had spent a peaceful hour after her return from Susannah's. She had even been lucky enough to catch a glimpse of a kingfisher flashing its vivid blue above the water, before it darted further upstream. Such a rare sight she took as a good omen.

'For God's sake, you might as well listen. It's your bread and butter too that I'm talking about,' David raised his voice accusingly.

She had obviously missed a cue.

'I'm sorry?' she murmured.

'We'll both be sorry if that bastard Don Lerner gets his way.'

'What is he doing now?'

'I've just been telling you,' he said exasperated. 'Don't you ever pay attention?'

'I'm sorry. Tell me again.'

She focused on his face and this time listened intently as he related the ominous twists of his day. She watched him become increasingly despondent as he revealed the extent of Lerner's manoeuvrings. Her carefully sympathetic responses seemed only to irritate him further.

'Can't turn my back on the bloody man for a second. God knows what line he has spun Fairchild. But it's obvious he's after my account.'

He picked up his glass and drank the wine down in one draught. 'Fairchild's a fool if he goes along with him. He knows I'm worth ten fucking Lerners. He damned well needs me.'

'Of course he does,' Jenny assured him. 'He wouldn't risk losing you.'

David's glance of alarm was her reward.

'Lerner's the one he'll lose. I'll make damned certain of that.'

She could feel his fear.

'Fairchild is going to have to come clean.' He poured himself another glass of wine with a hand that was not quite steady. 'It's no good his hiding away "at lunch" and "in conference" all bloody afternoon. The man's a coward.'

Jenny sat back in her chair and watched him try to wash away with a gulp of wine the stinging humiliation. Ten years of determined career building at Dern & Fairchild. It meant nothing now.

She smiled gently. 'So you didn't get to speak to Fairchild, then?'

He found it hard to admit the rebuff. Even to her. 'Only for about five minutes. Just as he was leaving.' He hesitated, but the need to vent his feelings was too strong. 'The damn fool has fallen for whatever story Lerner has pedalled him. Fairchild insisted "Everything's fine,' and "Why shouldn't Lerner have lunch with Wareham?"' David snorted scornfully. 'How many frigging times does he think I've seen an account manoeuvred out from under somebody? I've done it myself, for Christ's sake.'

He pushed his plate to one side. Jenny glanced down at the half-finished meal. There was no longer any cat to eat up the scraps. She casually picked up the wine bottle and refilled David's glass, then rested her hand lightly on his sleeve on the table.

'David, I was thinking of going up to town tomorrow. I've got a few things I want to buy at Peter Jones.'

'Oh?' He made no attempt to hide his indifference.

Her finger squeezed his arm slightly to summon greater response. 'My shopping won't take long, so I thought I'd come over and see you in your office.' That won his attention. 'It's ages since I've done that.'

Caught unawares, his reaction was slow. 'Well . . . er . . . I don't know what I've got arranged . . .'

Jenny tightened her hold. 'Oh, come on, David,' she encouraged. 'We could have lunch together. Somewhere nice. To make up for my forgetting the Terrazza.'

'I don't know what I've got on for tomorrow.'

She smiled brightly at him. 'Nothing you can't shift, I'm sure.'

'For God's sake, Jenny, I'm not in the mood for point-less lunches.' He pushed back his chair and stood up. 'Ask Susannah or Caroline Palmer to go with you. They've got nothing better to do.'

Her smile stayed in place. 'But it's you I want for company.'

The words were unexpected. David glanced down at her and the concern in her face took him by surprise.

Her eyes were soft and inviting. 'Have lunch with me, David. Please. You never know, it might even cheer you up.' She laughed softly and stood up beside him, again resting a hand lightly on his arm. Pinning him down. 'I'll come over around twelve thirty.'

David was unaccustomed to such a display of determination from his wife. Or such a desire for his company. For a moment he was distracted from his office worries and wondered if she might be right. Perhaps it would do him good to take a short break from it all.

'All right. I'll get my secretary to book somewhere.'

Sarah. He had forgotten about her. The two women had never met. The last time Jenny had come to the office was at the previous deputy chairman's retirement party and that was at least eighteen months ago. Sarah Archer had only been David's secretary for the last year. As he looked into his wife's face, he suddenly found the idea of lunching with her unexpectedly appealing.

He was gratified by her sudden interest. Especially now. God knew, he needed all the help he could get. He thought of Simon Grey. He would have to have a careful chat with that treacherous bastard. He was the weak link in Lerner's chain. David was sure he could prise some useful information out of his ambitious assistant.

He shook his mind free of that problem and turned again to the prospect of a confrontation between Sarah and Jenny. Perhaps they would not even meet. Sarah may take an early lunch. But if their paths did cross, he felt certain he could rely on Sarah to be discreet. She had never displayed any interest in his wife or demonstrated any inclination to be jealous or possessive. His pride in his sensuous young mistress reasserted itself and steadied his shaken self-image. Sexual arrogance hardened his features.

Jenny watched the confident expression return to David's face. She turned quickly back to the table to conceal her smile of anticipation and started to clear away the dishes.

Jenny stepped out of the lift at the fifth floor. The Dern & Fairchild logo was emblazoned in brass letters on the opposite wall for the benefit of visitors. To her right in the main reception area, all designer tasteful and muted lighting, the immaculately groomed receptionist raised her head enquiringly.

Jenny ignored her and turned to the long corridor on her left. Two dark-suited executives were standing deep in earnest conversation. As she passed them, despite their lowered voices, she overheard the strutting tones: '. . . like fucking melons . . . and I mean watermelons. They taste as gorgeous too . . .'

The voice ceased abruptly and she was acutely aware of the two pairs of eyes following every movement of her buttocks as she strode along the corridor. She smiled and swung her hips a fraction more.

She had dressed with care that morning. After discarding several options, she had settled for downright provocative. She selected a short jade skirt that clung tightly and emphasised her slender hips. With it she wore a cream halter-neck top and no bra. A little make-up disguised the bruises on her shoulder and leg, so that the skimpy top could show off the tan of her bare back and arms. But she was relying on it being not her tan that caught the attention, as the silky material clearly outlined her charms. She had slipped into a short navy bolero to cover some of the bare flesh until it was needed.

Now, as she turned the corner at the end of the corridor and approached David's office, she gripped more tightly the large green and white Peter Jones bag that was in her hand. First she had to steel herself to step confidently into the next doorway.

She had never met Sarah Archer. As she stared at the dark head bent over the keyboard, she was certain this was the cause of the late trains and signal failures that regularly delayed David's return home. There was something about the way he studiously avoided mentioning his secretary's name and his carefully casual dismissal of her significance at the office that instantly focused attention on her importance.

Jenny stood for a moment in the doorway. 'Hello, I'm looking for David Cranshaw.'

Sarah's head shot up and her eyes took in the attractive figure leaning elegantly against the door frame.

Jenny watched with amusement as she saw Sarah's surprise quickly smothered by professional courtesy.

'Hello, you must be Mrs Cranshaw. I'm Sarah.' She rose from behind her desk. For a second, their eyes locked. 'I'll let David know you're here.'

The deliberately proprietorial tone failed to raise Jenny's hackles.

'Thank you,' she said and stepped back to allow Sarah to pass.

David welcomed her into his office with a brush of the lips and a self-conscious glance at Sarah's retreating form. Jenny recognised at once that he was uncomfortable and preoccupied, already regretting their lunchtime arrangement.

'I've had a hell of a morning,' were his words of greeting. 'Harrisons have asked for copies of all our figures for their brown goods. And now want to try another test market.' He ran his fingers roughly through his blond hair. 'They're just making more work for nothing.'

He turned to his drinks cabinet and without asking her, poured a splash of white wine into two glasses. 'They won't listen to reason.'

Jenny placed her shopping bag on the floor beside his desk and came forward to accept the drink David proffered. 'Perhaps they're just nervous,' she suggested.

He looked at her sharply. 'Nervous of what, for God's sake? We've been over and over the market for them.' He shook his head in a gesture of despair. 'It's not that, I'm sure it's not. No, for some reason, they're trying to delay everything. The bastards are back-pedalling just as fast as they can and throwing up smoke screens.' He glared at her in frustration. 'Something smells here and you can bet your sweet life who's at the bottom of it.'

He slammed his empty glass on the top of the cabinet and took satisfaction in seeing its fragile stem snap.

'I wish that was fucking Lerner's neck,' he muttered and scooped the shards of glass into his hand to throw in the bin.

Jenny watched him stride angrily towards his desk and she began to doubt whether she could persuade him in his present mood to leave his office for a moment. Maybe a request for a glass of water would work. She glanced at the bag propped against the side of the desk and thought anxiously of the plain brown paper bag inside.

'Oh shit!'

Jenny looked up quickly to see David standing over his waste-paper basket, clutching his left hand. A thin trickle of scarlet squeezed out between the fingers that encircled the palm and dribbled down on to the clean white cuff of his shirt.

'That's all I bloody need,' David snapped. 'Even my glass is trying to get the knife in.'

Jenny hurried to his side and took the damaged hand into her own. 'Let me see,' she murmured and gently opened the fingers to reveal the extent of the cut. A miniature red geyser was filling the curve of the palm and in the centre of it stood a vicious triangle of glass, perched with one of its angles embedded in the flesh. 'Oh, David, that's horrible,' Jenny exclaimed and quickly plucked the shard out of his hand.

She reached into his pocket and pulled out his clean white handkerchief. She wrapped it tightly round his hand and pressed the centre to stem the flow of blood. He winced.

'That will be all right soon. But you'll have to go and wash it and put a plaster on for the moment.' She sensed his masculine enjoyment of her concern and her fussing. Still holding his hand in hers, she looked up into his worried face and smiled reassuringly at him. 'Don't worry. It'll soon be better.' Keeping her eyes on his, she raised the bandaged hand to her lips and gently kissed the blood-streaked handkerchief. 'It could have been worse,' she whispered.

'Like my day, you mean,' he grimaced.

Jenny stepped back and her foot touched the carrier bag on the floor.

'You go and give it a good rinse under a tap and I'll stick a plaster over it for you,' she promised and only just stopped herself offering him a lollipop for being a brave boy.

She felt her heart racing as she checked that the door was properly closed behind him. She only had a few minutes; David wouldn't be gone long. The role of wounded hero suited his present mood too well. Or someone else looking for David could walk in at any moment. She would have to rely on most people being at lunch now.

She walked quickly across the office and picked up the bag. Inside lay the flat brown package of magazines. She swiftly lifted it out and hurried round to the front of the desk.

On either side of the central kneehole was a column of three drawers. Ignoring the top two, Jenny bent down and yanked the handle of the bottom right-hand drawer. It slid forward so fast that some of its contents shot out on to the floor. She swore under her breath and swept up the few envelopes and business cards that had fallen on the carpet. The drawer was full of various kinds of stationery. She slammed it shut and glanced fearfully up at the door. It remained closed, but she was sure someone was about to burst in at any moment.

Her breathing was ragged, as she pulled more gently at the bottom drawer on the left-hand side of the desk. She cursed herself for not thinking of it before. David was right-handed and would obviously use the drawers on the right side more. This time she was in luck. The drawer contained only a few odds and ends that were clearly unwanted, but had not yet been dispensed with altogether. She quickly lifted out an old table-lighter and ashtray. Underneath, face down, lay a small photograph frame. Despite her fear of sudden intrusion, her curiosity was too great and she picked up the frame.

The smile that shone from its photograph stopped her breath. It was Mark. Her son. Laughing, with his blond head thrown back and his young hands gripping the brightly coloured ball. Her carefree, happy son.

Jenny slammed the photograph back in the drawer, as tears suddenly stung her eyes. Why did David keep this photograph in his desk, tucked away in the unwanted drawer?

The pain surged into anger and she plucked the paper bag from the top of the desk. She thrust it roughly into the drawer, but for a second, regretted that such magazines were lying on top of her young son's picture. Before she could consider altering anything, she heard the sound of the door handle.

Just in time she tossed the lighter and ashtray into the drawer and threw herself into David's desk chair. The door swung open to reveal Sarah Archer standing with some papers in her hand. She stared at Jenny in surprise.

'Oh, I'm sorry. I thought you and David had left.'

'Not yet.'

Sarah studied Jenny for a moment, seated in David's chair, and then approached the desk. Jenny instantly leaned forward, kicking the drawer shut as she did so.

'Any problems?' she enquired.

'No, everything's fine.' Sarah placed two yellow memo slips on top of the desk. 'I'll leave these here for David to see. They're rather important.' Without a smile, she left the office.

Jenny glanced down at the memos. One was a message to say that Philip Wareham's secretary had rung from Manfields to say he wanted to speak to David after lunch. The second was to inform David that Fairchild wished to see him at four o'clock sharp to discuss the Manfields account.

Jenny sat very still, a thoughtful look on her face. Then she stood up and walked over to the carrier bag on the floor. Now it contained only a set of ramekins and a new coffee grinder. She picked it up and laid it carefully on top of the desk. She stepped back and inspected the desk surface. Not a trace of the yellow messages was to be seen.

David selected sole meunière off the bone. Something he could manage to eat with one hand. He had returned to his office with a large strip of plaster from the washroom first-aid kit and had allowed Jenny to place it in position over the deep gash in his palm. His temper had not been improved by having to wait for her at the lift, because she had to retrieve her forgotten bag of shopping from his office.

The wine had mellowed his mood somewhat, but the tension still showed in his brusque manner and the constant recharging of his glass.

'Thank God Lerner is out today,' David commented, as he struggled to balance a bite of fish on his fork.

'Out where?'

'How the hell do I know? He doesn't keep me informed of his daily movements. Anal or otherwise.'

Jenny composed her features into an expression of sympathy. 'Don't let him get to you.'

She reached across the table to scoop some of his fish on to her fork and offered it temptingly to his mouth. A brief cloud of annoyance flitted across his face.

'Come on, David,' she urged. 'Let me help you.'

'I'm not a damn child to be humoured and petted, for God's sake.'

'I just want to help,' Jenny murmured and rested her other hand lightly on top of his on the table.

He looked quickly at her, then shrugged and accepted the fish into his mouth.

Jenny gently ran her fingers over his damaged hand – soft, soothing strokes. 'You'll beat the lot of them,' she assured him. 'You're much too valuable to the company. You are the one who won the new accounts for them, and Fairchild knows that. He won't risk losing them.' She observed David relax and his shoulders straighten. 'You could take those accounts with you, if you left. Fairchild is much too shrewd to risk that.'

She could see he wanted so much to believe her.

'I expect that's why Lerner is up to his tricks. He's frightened you'll oust him soon.' She sat back in her seat and raised her glass to him. 'Damnation to all deputy chairmen.'

David laughed and lifted his glass in return. 'Hell and damnation.'

They both sipped their wine and smiled at each other. It was then that Jenny took the opportunity to slip off her bolero and let it fall on to the back of her chair.

Until that instant, David had been totally unaware of what his wife was wearing. So enmeshed was he in his own cage of anxiety that he had been oblivious to her behaviour. But now he was suddenly conscious that she had slipped the latch on his cage and was inviting him out to play. As she leaned forward more intimately, her breasts in the flimsy top pressed forward temptingly. He almost laughed out loud at the blatant ploy, but at the same time, could not prise his eyes away from her cleavage.

'I think what you need is a dose of R & R,' she suggested softly.

He made himself look up into her amused eyes. 'And what the hell's that? Rhubarb and roughage?'

'No, of course not.' She shrugged her shoulders and again he found himself staring, as her breasts shifted deliciously against the silky material. 'Rest and relaxation. This business with Lerner is not doing you any good.' She reached across the table and lifted his damaged hand in hers. Slowly she turned it over, so that the palm was uppermost. Ignoring the nearby tables, she traced a finger very gently round the rectangle of pink plaster.

'Let me tell your fortune,' she mimicked in the cackle of a gypsy crone. 'I see a shining door before you. The door to your heart's desire. All you have to do is reach out and open it.'

She abandoned the accent and gazed earnestly up into David's face, whispering intimately, 'What is your heart's desire, David?'

He squeezed her hand hard in his, hurting her, and thrust his leg between her knees under the table.

'At this moment my only desire is for you.'

She gripped his leg tightly with her own and her mouth opened invitingly, allowing her pink tongue to slide wetly over her lips. 'Then why are we sitting here eating fish, when we could be eating each other?'

David was startled by this unabashed sexual provocation from his wife, but the rush of his desire for her swept him on.

She lowered her lips to his hand. 'Surely you can spare an hour or two,' she murmured and her tongue snaked out to lick the plaster.

Her hot breath on his fingers fanned the flame further. Illicit sex with his own wife. Just an hour in a hotel round the corner on a Friday afternoon. It could do no harm.

The bed sheet was tangled around David's foot and impatiently he kicked it free.

'God, I'm hot,' he complained, as he lay on his back, his naked body glistening with sweat.

The impersonal character of the room and the unfamiliar smell of the pillows had done little to curb their passion. From the moment they had sprawled entwined on the bed, Jenny had been determined to fill his mind and his senses with her body.

To block out all other thoughts. Delay any idea of returning to the office. Unfortunately, David's impatience had forestalled any attempt to prolong the encounter beyond a brief nod at foreplay, followed by a speedy conclusion.

She glanced surreptitiously at her watch on the bedside table. Only two thirty. It was too early, much too early. She thought again of the yellow memo on the desk. Four o'clock it had said.

She propped herself up on one elbow and leaned over to kiss his mouth. 'Mmmm, you taste good. All salty.' She licked his cheek and gently nibbled his ear, then snuggled close to him with her head on his shoulder. He ran his hand over her hip and up to cup her breast. Idly he tweaked her nipple to elicit a moan of protest, but she could sense his mind was already moving elsewhere. She dare not let office concerns take control once more.

She slid her leg over his and rubbed her thigh against his groin. 'A shower is what we both need,' she announced, suddenly sitting up and swinging her feet to the floor.

'Don't abandon me yet, you faithless hussy,' David responded, attempting to restrain her, but only succeeded in grabbing a handful of buttock.

Jenny laughed and slipped from his grasp. Standing naked in front of him, as he lay stretched across the bed, she performed a teasing bump-and-grind and then disappeared into the bathroom.

'Jenny, come back here,' David called after her. 'Get that gorgeous arse back in this bed.'

His only reply was the sound of running water.

Reluctantly he rolled off the bed and followed her into the bathroom. In the small shower-stall the curtain was not pulled across and Jenny was standing with her arms raised above her head, water and bubbles cascading down her body. David did not hesitate, but stepped into the cubicle beside her. With their bodies cramped together, he slid his hands sensuously over her soapy breasts and gasped as she poured bubble bath over his hair and shoulders.

'This will clean up your act,' she laughed and started rubbing the bubbles vigorously all over him. His chest, stomach and groin were each massaged in turn, but as soon as she saw the sign of his arousal, she turned him round and started pummelling his back, nervous that the make-up on her shoulder was starting to disappear, despite being waterproof. Then standing close behind him, she pressed her breasts against his back. Her body slid back and forth across his and as she slipped her hands down to his bottom, she whispered in his ear, 'Get this gorgeous arse back in that bed.'

David burst out laughing and turned to face her again, pulling her tight against his body. He kissed her hungrily on the mouth and was about to thrust himself deep within her, when she pulled away from him, ducked out of the shower and draped a tiny hotel towel over her shoulder.

'What the hell are you up to?' Frustration made the words aggressive.

With water dripping from her hair and breasts and flowing in rivulets between her legs, she held up a bath towel and smiled invitingly. 'Let me dry you first.'

David stepped out of the shower and let her envelop him in the towel. Avoiding his clutching hands, she led him back into the bedroom, where she proceeded to lay a number of towels out on the bed. Still wet and naked herself, she turned to him and grinned.

'Now it's time for the massage.'

'There's only one part of me I want massaged,' he laughed and took her in his arms. She let him kiss her and then slipped again from his grasp.

'Massage first,' she instructed. 'On the bed with you.'

Seeing no alternative, David lay down on the bed and Jenny rolled him on to his stomach. She pulled their towels away, lightly dried his hair and then kneeled on the bed beside him. She knew nothing about professional massage, but that did not deter her.

She tore open the sachet of bath oil that had been provided in the bathroom and trickled it slowly down his back and legs. David complained as the cold liquid touched his skin, but as her hands flowed smoothly over his body, softly at first, then harder and rougher, he felt his skin glow and his muscles start to relax. Her fingers dug deep into the knots of tension in his neck and shoulders. They rubbed in slowly descending circles down his spine, across his buttocks and all the way to the soles of his feet.

He was feeling warm and relaxed, so it came as a jolt when she eventually rolled him over on to his back. Her hands again resumed the massaging rhythm over his chest and arms. But this time, she sat astride him. As she bent over, he raised a hand to stroke her breast, his eyes too full of desire to notice any bruises.

'Not yet,' she breathed. 'Not yet.'

The gently circling hands moved gradually lower on to his stomach and she could feel him stirring beneath her. As her fingers touched the dense mound of hair, she raised her eyes to his face. His gaze was fixed with longing on her breasts, which rose and fell with each movement of her hands. Her fingers crept further into his groin and when she saw in his face that he could restrain himself no longer, she raised her body and sank down sharply on top of him, clutching him deep within her.

David uttered a deep moan and their bodies locked in violent spasm.

Jenny lay absolutely still. She did not want to wake him yet. She could not see her watch, but she had waited patiently as the afternoon sunlight slid inch by inch across the floor.

She glanced down at David. His head was nestled tight against her breast and his mouth had fallen open, releasing her trapped nipple. Her shoulder ached from being in one position so long, but she did not dare risk moving to ease the discomfort or to check the time. She had worked too hard to risk ruining it now. She occupied herself with composing the letter she would write tonight. Another bombshell for Fairchild.

6

Sarah Archer made herself sit at her desk and concentrate on opening the Monday morning's post. But her ears were alert to every footstep along the corridor outside. Nine thirty was his usual time. It was past that now and still he had not arrived. She tossed the last letter on to the pile in front of her and abandoned all pretence of calm.

Why the hell had he done it? David's position in the company was far too precarious at the moment for him to allow Lerner such an advantage. He could not afford any mistakes. Fairchild had come storming into her office on Friday afternoon demanding to know why David had not shown for their meeting to discuss Manfields. She had tried to cover for him, but in the end she had been forced to admit she did not know where he was. She had carefully avoided mentioning the fact that he had gone off to lunch with his wife and had not been seen since. Nor had she mentioned Philip Wareham's irate telephone calls. Eventually Fairchild had stared at her in icy silence and stalked out of the office.

Sarah rose and walked impatiently to the door. She stood for a moment in the corridor, but there was no sign of him. Back in her office, she attempted to file the letters that did not need David's attention, but when she caught herself slipping them into the wrong folders, she slammed the drawer shut and leaned her forehead against the cold metal of the cabinet.

It was not Fairchild that had got to her. It was Jenny Cranshaw. Sarah recalled for the thousandth time the carefully posed figure in the doorway, the mocking eyes and the secretive smile. She had not expected so desirable a wife. She banged her fist hard against the metal edge. No wonder he had not returned.

To distract her thoughts from the painful images that crowded her mind, she turned and picked up the bundle of letters on her desk. She walked quickly into the corridor, scanned it once more in vain for David's familiar stride and opened the door to his office. She closed it behind her and approached the desk. The yellow memos still lay where she had placed them on Friday. Why had he not seen them? She put the letters down beside them and moved round to David's chair.

This was where she had sat. His wife. Possession was nine-tenths of the law and she had certainly stamped her right to possession. Sarah remembered the gleaming eyes and the confident usurping of the seat. She recalled her leaning forward on the desk, as if to defend her territory from Sarah's approach.

Sarah very deliberately sat down in the chair. She slowly rubbed her body against the backrest and her bottom over the seat. She would wipe out any trace of Mrs David Cranshaw.

The door suddenly swung open. Sarah looked up eagerly to greet David, but the smile of welcome froze on her lips. Richard Fairchild stood in the doorway. The expression of cold anger on his face was swept aside by one of surprise at seeing her seated at David's desk.

'Thinking of dancing on the grave before the body's cold, Miss Archer?'

Sarah jumped out of the chair, as if stung.

'No, sir. I've just brought in Mr Cranshaw's post.'

Fairchild's eyes passed over the pile of letters on the desk and settled on the yellow memos beside them.

Hell, she should have removed them. Her anger and sense of betrayal evaporated. She knew she had let David down badly. She should have waited on Friday and given the messages to him herself. Made certain he was aware of their urgency. Instead, she had been only too eager to escape from the office, to flee the sight of his wife's charms.

'You may go now,' Fairchild dismissed her curtly.

Sarah quickly left the room and hurried to her own office. She had to be there to warn David as soon as he arrived.

Don Lerner dropped the three magazines on to Fairchild's desk, one by one.

'That just about confirms it then.' He pulled a handkerchief from his pocket and meticulously wiped his fingers on it.

Fairchild sat silent in his chair.

Lerner glanced at the display of seductive smiles. 'We all knew he liked the ladies, but I had no idea the bastard was into young boys as well. Literally.'

Fairchild's jaw clenched tight. He recalled the photograph of the laughing boy that had been under the magazines in Cranshaw's desk drawer and he shook his head in disgust. The second letter had been correct with its information. The sordid magazines had been exactly where it had said they'd be. Fairchild was willing to allow every man the right to his own sexual preferences, but when it came to young boys and spreading diseases, he drew the line. These perverted magazines from Cranshaw's desk certainly added conviction to the accusations of the first anonymous letter. He picked up the typed page in front of him and shook it at Lerner.

'Whoever wrote this, he or she knows Cranshaw's habits well.'

Lerner nodded. 'Probably too well for their own good.'

There was an uncomfortable silence and Lerner feared that Fairchild may be wavering. He knew the letters and even the magazines formed no real proof.

'We agreed,' he reminded the chairman.

Fairchild looked up at his deputy, hovering in front of the desk. Lerner's restrained manner did not quite conceal his eagerness for the kill.

'I know, Don. I agreed. We daren't even risk asking for a blood test.' Fairchild shook his head again. 'The danger is too great, whether it's true or not. If just a rumour got out that he was having the test, we wouldn't see our clients for dust.'

'Well, I've got Harrisons Hardware stitched up. When Cranshaw's gone, we won't lose them,' Lerner assured him.

'Friday went well, then?'

'Great success. Their guy is very sharp but I've got him totally on board with us now. He's not so wedded to Cranshaw that he'd follow him elsewhere.' Lerner sat down confidently in the chair opposite Fairchild. 'There will certainly be no problem keeping them happy without him. Manfields is the only one giving us trouble. Our older clients are secure, but Philip Wareham is very locked in on Cranshaw.' He frowned. 'I only need another couple of days and I know I can turn him round. I had a good lunch with him the other day and I can feel he's nearly there.' He indicated the palm of his hand.

'What about Cranshaw's assistant?'

'Simon Grey? Oh, he's no problem. As soon as he saw the way the wind's blowing, he was easy. We need him for continuity on the accounts, so we'd better not lose him for the moment.'

'Keep an eye on him anyway.'

'I will, as they seem to think highly of Simon as well at Manfields.' Lerner's exasperation at Manfields Importers' loyalty to Cranshaw broke through. 'God, if Wareham only knew the fatal risks he's taking. If what that first letter said is true, Cranshaw is a walking time bomb.'

Fairchild held up a hand. 'Back off, Don. We both know we have no proof. The allegations in the letters could be false. Malicious revenge.' He was well aware of some of the other directors' dislike of Cranshaw's speedy rise to power. 'I took the decision to keep this quiet for the sake of Dern & Fairchild. It may be unfair to him or it may not, we don't know, but I'm not risking my company. Not for anyone.'

His voice sank lower and his eyes grew cold. 'I don't damn well care if he's got the disease or not. Or whether it's from screwing boys or girls. Or even from drugs. It doesn't make any difference now whether it's true or not. He's become a liability. I won't have him here and I won't have him tested. It would be suicide for us.'

Lerner stood up. 'I'll contact Wareham now. A couple of days is all I need.'

'Twenty-four hours is all you've got.'

Lerner began to protest, but at the sight of his chairman's

adamant expression, he nodded and started to leave. Fairchild's voice recalled him.

'One moment, Don. There's one more thing we haven't discussed.'

Lerner resumed his seat, wondering what he had overlooked.

'And what's that?'

'Cranshaw's secretary, Sarah Archer. She'll have to go.'

'Christ, yes. I'd forgotten her. They never even attempted to be discreet about it. Off in her car together like alley cats.'

Fairchild sensed that the venom sprang from envy rather than disgust. 'God preserve her, even so, Don,' he murmured. 'But she's as big a danger as he is. If he's got the virus, he will have passed it on to her. Speak to her this afternoon. I want her gone.'

He stood up suddenly, his anger surging to the surface. 'I've worked damned hard to make this company a success and I don't intend to jeopardise that reputation now.' He seized the magazines from his desk and tossed them at Lerner. 'Get rid of that filth.'

Lerner picked them up with distaste, replaced them in their brown paper bag and walked to the door.

'Twenty-four hours,' Fairchild reminded him. 'Then he's out.'

Sarah leaned over and kissed the top of David's head. His hair felt clean and smelled of lemon. He pulled away from her, as he sat reading the memos on his desk.

'For God's sake, Sarah, why didn't you tell me?'

'I'm sorry, David. I did put the notes clearly on your desk for you to see. But you were otherwise occupied.'

He cursed himself for his weakness on Friday afternoon. If only he had come back to the office. He should have known better. At a time like this, he had to stay on his toes. But, for a second, the sight of the bubbles on Jenny's breasts and the feel of her fingers massaging his groin flooded back and he could not help smiling. It had certainly been good. But the rest of the weekend had not lived up to the promise of its beginning. After they drove home,

Jenny had become withdrawn and uncommunicative and had turned her back to him in bed.

He glanced up and saw Sarah watching him. He jerked his attention back to Dern & Fairchild. God, what a mess.

'Get Fairchild's secretary on the line, will you? See if the old man is free this morning.' He grimaced self-consciously. 'I'll have to go and do my penance. Then get through to Philip Wareham's secretary at Manfields. See if you can get her to set up a lunch. Better still, try and get hold of Philip himself for me and I'll arrange the lunch appointment myself. He's been too elusive recently.'

'I'll do what I can.'

'But make Fairchild the priority.'

Sarah nodded and leaned over to kiss him, this time on the lips. He slipped his arm round her waist and laughed. 'Is that the final kiss, before the firing squad? A dying man couldn't ask for a better wish.' He squeezed her tight. 'Don't look so worried, I'll survive.'

For a moment she held him close to her, then left to make the call.

'Hi, Jenny.'

It was Susannah Benson.

Jenny had only just managed to hear the high-pitched beep of the mobile phone above the sound of the mower's engine, and that was only because she happened to be emptying the grass box onto the compost heap at the time.

'Hello, Susannah, I'm in the middle of grass cutting. Hang on while I just turn the mower off.'

A few moments later, when she picked up the receiver from the terrace table once more, Susannah greeted her with, 'Why don't you get somebody to do your lawns for you, for heaven's sake?'

Jenny laughed. 'I know the idea may seem ludicrous to someone of your sensibilities, but I actually enjoy doing it.'

'Then you're mad. You'll end up with biceps the size of Arnie's if you're not careful.'

'No fear of that. The mower is power-driven.'

'Then get David to manhandle it around. Much more sensible than you woman-handling it.' Her grin travelled down the line. 'Not good for the nails, you know.'

'They survive.'

'Next time I see David, I'll tell him he must employ a gardener. Women's servitude has been abolished.'

'I don't think he'd appreciate that, somehow.'

'It seems to me there's a lot he doesn't appreciate.'

Fleetingly Jenny wondered whether Susannah was referring to his friendship with Robert or hinting at suspicions about the bruise. Either way, it was promising.

'So what can I do for you, Susannah?'

'It's more a question of what I can do for you.'

'In what way?'

'I've decided to take advantage of the forecast for more of this superb sun this week and hold a lunchtime binge on Friday.' Susannah Benson's occasional 'binges' were notorious. 'Bring your swimming togs and sun lotion and we'll all whoop it up round the pool.' Jenny sat down on a bench and brushed grass cuttings off her bare legs. 'Sounds like fun. Who's invited?'

'Only the cream, darling. No dregs, I promise.'

'Susannah, you're an incorrigible snob. But this time, leave the brandy out of the punch.'

Susannah's laugh was unrepentant. 'It was a bit over the top last time, I admit. The gardener was furious when he saw what had happened to the geraniums. Honestly, you'd think they were his, not ours.'

'Just think of him as their foster mother.'

'Since when do mothers have beards?'

Jenny took the bull by the horns. She had to know. 'Talking of mothers, what's this I hear about you wanting to adopt a child? That doesn't sound like the Susannah we all know and love. Might cramp your style a wee bit.'

Susannah sighed. 'I know. I can't really make up my mind whether to go ahead or not. To be honest, I'm not that crazy about the idea, but Robert's keen. He thinks I must be feeling unfulfilled without an offspring bouncing round the house. Just because he can't have kids, he wants to make it up to me.

Personally, I think I look better dripping with diamonds rather than dribbles.'

Jenny slowly released her breath. 'So it's not settled by any means yet.'

'Good Lord, no. I'm thinking of inviting a few real drones round for dinner next week. You know the type, women who are so bogged down with babies, they have let themselves run to seed and walk round with nappy pins in their hair.'

Jenny laughed with relief. 'That will certainly put Robert off the scheme.'

'That's the whole idea.'

'He doesn't stand a chance.'

'Don't underestimate him. He can be a stubborn old bastard when he wants.'

'Do I take that as a subtle hint? About David handling Manfields watches?'

'How did you guess? The old misery has really gone into a sulk about it. He thinks David is being disloyal. He goes on about what about their years of friendship, and all that kind of thing.'

'Oh Susannah, you know David. He's obsessed with work. With getting to the top. It's his life.'

A loud chattering of rival starlings drew Jenny's attention to the tree tops and she watched a miniature aeroplane trail a white thread in a high arc above them. In a thoughtful voice, she added, 'He puts himself under a lot of pressure. Sometimes he does things he doesn't mean to.'

There was a long pause.

'That sounds ominous.'

'It's not meant to. It's just that I don't want Robert to be hurt.'

She heard Susannah expel her breath impatiently. 'Or yourself?'

Jenny said nothing.

'Look, Jenny, if you've got any trouble at home with—'

Jenny cut in. 'No, of course not. Everything's fine.' Her voice was just a fraction too bright. 'I'd better get these lawns finished now. Thanks for the invitation for Friday. What time?'

'Around twelve. By the way, isn't Caroline due back from her

South of France jaunt this week? I wouldn't want her to miss out on my binge.'

'Don't worry, she's due home tomorrow. I'm certain she won't let a Susannah special go by without her being part of it. So get the sand-buckets standing by.'

Susannah giggled. 'She didn't mean to set fire to Melanie Wayne's dress last time, and anyway, the pool came in handy.'

'Just remember, no brandy this time,' Jenny laughed and hung up.

But she did not immediately return to the mowing. She sat back on the bench, staring up at the dissolving vapour trail and thought about next Friday. After some time, she smiled and went to start the engine.

Sarah Archer tore up the crust into little pieces and threw them on the ground in front of the strutting pigeons. She watched them barge each other aside in their rush to snatch the food.

She said nothing.

'Oh, come on, Sarah. It was a moment of weakness. I'm sorry. I don't know what got into my head. Or hers, for that matter.'

David Cranshaw put an arm around her shoulders and she let it lie there, but did not soften. She sat stiffly on the bench and looked straight ahead at the couple seated on the opposite side of the square. Their raised voices indicated that they too were having problems and had sought the comparative privacy of the small pocket of grass and trees that served as a brief oasis for those working in Central London. The day was unexpectedly overcast and there was a cool breeze that made most office workers opt to spend their lunch break in the warmer reaches of shops and wine bars.

She had not intended to play this role. She had always sworn privately that she would never put David or herself through this scene. Other mistresses of married men could rake their jealous nails across their lovers' hearts all they want. She had determined never to become the complaining bitch who fought for every stolen hour and ultimately destroyed what she most desired. And God only knew how she desired him. Despite all provocation, she had remained firm in her resolve.

Until she saw his wife. Until she was torn apart by the sight of the real, breathing woman who lived with him, laughed with him and probably made love with him every night. She was no longer just a name.

David pulled her closer to him on the bench. Her body felt slight under the light cotton of her blouse. 'You should be wearing a jacket,' he said and wrapped his arms around her.

The gesture broke down her fragile fences and she turned her face to his. 'David, you bastard, I know you don't need this now. I'm sorry. It's just that she got to me. And then when you didn't come to the flat as usual on Friday evening . . .' She broke off and turned aside to blink away the tears.

David took her chin in his hand and titled it up, holding her close. 'I'm sorry, Sarah,' he whispered into her hair. 'Forgive me. I didn't mean to hurt you. It happened and I can't alter that. But if I could change it all, I would.' He shook his head slightly in bewilderment. 'I should never have let her come to the office at all. It just got out of hand.'

Sarah leaned against the warmth of his body. Suddenly she decided she didn't give a damn about Jenny Cranshaw. For that moment he was hers and hers alone. When he bent to kiss her, the lonely torment of the previous weekend was swept away.

Oblivious to their surroundings, they clung to each other. Her lips pressed hungrily to his mouth and her tongue sought his. Raw longing for him overwhelmed her and she suddenly slid her hand between his thighs. David moaned aloud and was tempted for a moment to seek a hotel room, but memories of the same mistake last Friday forced him to break free from Sarah and lean back against the bench. Breathing hard, he looked across at her and shook his head.

'Not now, Sarah.'

Her dark eyes stared back at him, full of desire, but she managed to grin crookedly. 'Just you wait till I get you to my place tonight.'

'I'll be there. I promise.'

Regaining a shaky control, she picked up the abandoned packet of sandwiches and offered one to David. 'You'd better build up your strength with these then.'

'That's not what I feel like eating.'

Sarah laughed and scattered more crumbs for the pigeons that were still fighting around their feet. She turned to find David silently observing her. His expression was serious.

'You're beautiful,' he said, 'and I never want to lose you.'

Tears sprang to her eyes and to hide them she draped her arms around his neck. 'You never will.'

David held her tight, then stood up. 'Come on, back to the grindstone.' He stretched out a hand to pull her up. 'Let's see what blasted Fairchild has in store for us this afternoon.'

She rose and looked into his eyes. 'He's no match for us. No one is.'

He slipped his arm round her waist and she smiled up at him. Together they walked slowly away from the square.

The hammer swung down on to her back. A round, red mark formed on Jenny's skin where the blow had fallen. Again the metal head thudded against her ribs but she tried not to cry out.

Her arms ached from holding the heavy hammer's shaft up behind her head and she let it slide to the carpet with relief. She twisted painfully round to look in the dressing-table mirror at what effect she had achieved. It was good. Just above waist level on the left side of her back. The skin had started to turn a promising shade of purple, shot through with faint streaks of red. Just enough to keep the tongues wagging nicely on Friday.

The thought of facing Caroline Palmer and the shock that would inevitably follow when she caught sight of the bruise, made her distinctly uncomfortable. She wished in some ways that the pool binge had been last week, while Caroline was safely tucked away on her Mediterranean idyll.

But it was no good being half-hearted about it. She was just going to have to brave it out. There was no alternative. She had to force herself to be as single-minded as David himself. Emotions of guilt, disloyalty, conscience – she'd seen too often how all could be crushed if you were determined enough. And God knew, she was determined. Ruthlessly determined.

That morning, she had bought herself a new, one-piece

swimming costume, superbly designed to accentuate her slim hips and long legs. Its low-cut back came right down to her waist, so the bruise she was working on now was intended to be strategically placed, so as to provoke comment, without being too obvious.

She turned again to the long mirror and checked that the previous discolouration on her shoulder had almost completely disappeared. Only a slight yellow tinge to the skin remained and that merged easily into her smooth tan. Her reflection stared back at her. She was standing in the middle of the guest bedroom, naked except for brief panties. Draped over the brass bedstead behind her lay her clothes, discarded to enable her to observe precisely the hammer's effects.

Her eyes slid critically over the body framed in the mirror. Automatically she checked its muscle tone and searched for any drooping in the breasts. She clenched her pectoral chest muscles and saw her breasts lift up pertly. Again she twisted round painfully and peered over her shoulder to inspect the damage to her back. It was definitely swollen, but on second sight, the discolouration seemed somewhat paler than she wanted. There were still a few days until the pool party at Susannah's and though she did not want the bruise to look brand new, she did intend it to be impressive.

She glanced at the hammer lying on the floor. It was the large one. Previously she had used the small hammer from the tool-box, but today she had decided she needed a longer handle to reach so far down her back. So she had fetched the big one from the garage. The idea of using it again did not appeal to her. With a sigh, she flexed her back to test the degree of discomfort. Not too bad. She could cope with a bit more.

Jenny bent down gingerly and picked up the hammer again. God, it was heavy. With an effort, she hefted it up behind her neck again with both hands and let the head hang down behind her back. Her muscles were tense in anticipation. She had found by trial and error that a lot of small blows were often more effective and certainly less painful than one heavy one. Peering round at the mirror for guidance, she tapped the solid metal against the dark bruise on her skin. She winced and with a sudden loss of patience, she cursed aloud and hoisted the hammer for one final blow. She gritted her teeth, raised the heavy metal head as high as her shoulder and swung it down sharply.

There was a loud crack.

Her body exploded in pain. She screamed and collapsed on the floor in agony. The shaft of the hammer struck a blow to the side of her head as it fell, but she did not even notice.

She could not breathe. Her lungs were on fire. Panic swamped the pain, as she fought to drag air into her body. Each breath pierced her back with fresh torture and her head pounded with blinding bolts of light. She tried to scream but no sound came out and slowly a black fog began to blur her vision. She knew she should care. But she didn't. Her only thought was to breathe. She had to breathe.

Slowly her attempts grew weaker. Her head sank on to the carpet and a stream of blood ran down the side of her face. The black fog turned to darkness and her body at last lay still.

Simon Grey wished David good night, but did not quite manage to disguise his eagerness to leave the office. David returned to his desk and checked it for messages. He had hoped for a response to his call to Philip Wareham to repair the Friday fiasco, but he was out of luck. Nothing at all from Manfields.

He sat down in his chair. Working with Simon for the last couple of hours had left him restless and uneasy. Simon had proved a much harder nut to crack than he had anticipated. David had got next to nothing out of him about Lerner's behind-the-scenes arrangements with either Wareham or Harrisons. The bastard protested ignorance, but he protested too much.

Fighting the urge to confront Lerner head-on, David decided he had to get to Fairchild. It was the end of the day and in the hope that the chairman would be ready to unwind over his usual stiff bourbon, David headed for the upper floor. In the past he had succeeded in settling many a problem that way.

The mousy secretary was obstructive. 'Mr Fairchild is not here.'

'Has he gone home or is he still somewhere in the building?'

'I'm afraid I can't say.'

'Can't or won't?' David demanded.

A faint smile creased one corner of Jane Pearce's mouth. 'There's no need for that tone, Mr Cranshaw. I'm sure Mr Fairchild will see you when he has time.'

David hung on to his temper. 'Then let me make an appointment right now in your neat little diary for first thing tomorrow morning.'

'I'm sorry. The chairman is busy tomorr—'

'Don't give me that crap, Jane. Just write my name in for ten o'clock.'

'It's no use—'

'Just do it.' He walked out of her office, only just refraining from slamming the door behind him.

Back in his own room, he poured himself a neat scotch and struggled to regain his composure. Everything was slipping out of control. That jumped-up bitch Jane would never have spoken to him like that before, chairman's secretary or not. What the hell was going on?

Snatching up his jacket and briefcase, he walked out of his office to Sarah's. He needed her. The brief lunchtime passion in the public square had whetted his appetite. He needed to tumble her into her unmade bed and drive away all thoughts of business.

As he entered Sarah's office, he was faintly surprised to find it empty. The cover was neatly draped over the computer and her chair was pushed into the desk. Disappointed, he assumed Sarah had already gone down to wait in the car. Though she usually told him if she was going to go on ahead.

As he swung round to follow her, his eye was caught by a white envelope placed prominently on top of the desk. He hesitated, unwilling to delay his departure, but curiosity got the better of him. He walked over to the desk and looked more closely at the paper. In Sarah's rounded handwriting was written the one word, 'David'.

He picked up the envelope and quickly slit it open. Inside was one sheet of paper, dated that day, with just a few lines typed on it.

Dear David,

I regret to inform you that I find I am no longer able to work as your secretary due to personal reasons. I am tendering my resignation, effective from tomorrow. I apologise for any inconvenience this may cause you.

I have informed Personnel of this decision.

Sarah's flowing signature ended the letter.

His eyes read the words again and again, but his mind refused to accept their meaning. What on earth was she playing at? Was this one of her stupid games? Well, he wasn't in the bloody mood for it.

He crushed the letter into a tight ball and hurled it into the waste bin. Then he strode angrily into the corridor. She had better be waiting in the car park with a damned good explanation.

The taxi crawled along Kensington Road as the rush hour traffic performed its daily ritual. David glared impatiently at the offending cars as the path of his black cab was blocked by an aggressive Mondeo. Sarah's car had not been in the office car park. Neither had she. He had interrogated the concierge and been told that Sarah had left over an hour ago.

Why had she disappeared early and not told him? They were supposed to be going to her flat together.

It had taken him half an hour to find a cab and now it was hardly moving. He refused to believe the letter. It had to be her idea of a joke. She had been upset about his going off with his wife on Friday and perhaps this was her way of making him pay for it. He leaned forward on the seat, silently urging the driver to find a way through the solid wall of cars.

What the hell was she up to? Surely she hadn't found another job and was afraid to admit it? The idea of losing her appalled him. He needed her there each day.

'Damn you, Sarah,' he cursed loudly.

The taxi driver turned round in surprise and glanced at David's furious face. Another nutter. They came in all shapes and sizes.

*   *   *

David pressed a note into the driver's outstretched hand. Without waiting for change, he dashed up the four steps to the front door. The house was part of a terrace of Regency three-storey dwellings, most of which were divided into flats. David was about to ring the bell for the intercom, when a smartly dressed young man appeared at his side, smiled briefly and opened the door with a key.

David seized the opportunity. He barged past the pinstripe suit and bounded up the stairs, two at a time. Sarah's flat was on the second floor and he was breathing heavily by the time he reached it.

He hammered on the door. 'Sarah! Sarah, I want to talk to you.'

He paused a moment, listening, then heard footsteps inside. As the door opened, he stepped forward impatiently, but pulled up short when he saw the face that greeted him. It was not Sarah's.

'Hi, David.' She stepped back to allow him to enter the flat. 'What's up with you two, then?'

David had never liked Sarah's flatmate Nicola Nugent. He always thought her bouncy blonde curls matched her bouncy blank brain and he'd had no time for her in the past.

'What do you mean?' he demanded. 'Is Sarah here?'

'No, that's just the point.' Nicola walked over to the table and picked up a letter. 'I've only just got home myself and this is what I found.' She shook the letter in annoyance. 'What the hell have you done to her? What's going on?'

Ignoring her questions, David snatched the sheet of paper from her hand and quickly scanned its contents. It was addressed to Nicola and Clare, the other occupant of the flat. Sarah stated briefly that she decided to leave London for good, enclosed next month's rent and hoped they would manage to find a replacement soon. That was it. No forwarding address. No information.

He stared blindly at the words. For a moment his mind went numb. It was only when he felt fingers pulling at the letter in his hand that he became aware that Nicola was complaining to him.

'. . . bloody inconsiderate, vanishing into thin air like that without a word of explanation. Clare and I will have to start looking for—'

David lost patience. 'You've got your blasted money, haven't you? She didn't leave owing rent, so stop moaning, you stupid bitch.'

He pushed past her and walked into Sarah's room. But it wasn't Sarah's room any more. There were no clothes lying on the floor, no unwashed mugs on every surface and no crumpled duvet in a heap on the bed. There was nothing of her. The room was neat and bare. The bed looked naked, the pristine duvet and pillows laid out tidily on the bare mattress.

'She's left nothing,' Nicola said from the doorway. Stung by the earlier insult, she added, 'It's not Sarah's room any more. So you can clear out as well.'

'Sarah has paid for another month,' David snarled and slammed the door in her face.

He walked over to the bed and sat down on it. He attempted to force himself to analyse the situation calmly, to search for rational answers. But it was useless. His brain was whirling. He had been so sure he would find her here. So sure she would have a simple explanation for her antics.

He leaned over and picked up one of the pillows. He raised it to his face and inhaled deeply, trying to smell her fragrance in its soft folds. A faint trace of her tantalised his nostrils and conjured up images of their bodies locked together, her lips pressed tight against his ear, murmuring indecent urgings with every thrust of her hips. A black sense of despair and loss suddenly swept over him and he buried his face in the pillow.

Only a determined knock on the door and Clare Tilton's imperious voice roused him. He took a last look around the room before walking wordlessly past the two remaining occupants and out of the flat.

It was dark by the time David arrived home. He was surprised to see no lights on in the house and did not know whether to assume his wife was out or had gone to bed early. Either way, he was thankful for the unexpected solitude.

He parked the car next to Jenny's Honda and let himself into the house. It was dark and silent. He switched on the lights and glanced into the kitchen. No sign of recent activity or preparation of a meal. David decided he didn't feel like eating anyway. He tossed a couple of ice cubes into a glass and poured himself a stiff scotch. He carried it into the sitting-room, threw his jacket aside and dropped with relief into his usual armchair. Taking a long drink from his glass, he lay back and closed his eyes.

For the umpteenth time he went over every word, every gesture and expression of his lunchtime with Sarah in the park. He searched in vain for a clue to her actions, but could come up with no answers. What had he done to make her sneak away? It just didn't make sense. In frustration, he downed the last half of his whisky.

Then suddenly it occurred to him. What if she was pregnant? He sat up sharply and considered that possibility. It certainly fitted with her flight from London, from everyone she knew. The results could have come through by telephone from a doctor that afternoon. The more he thought about it, the more probable it seemed. She wanted to go away before it started to show. He had not noticed any thickening of her tiny waist, but perhaps it was very early days.

As each moment passed, his anger grew. No wonder she was frightened to face him. All her protestations of love and fidelity were garbage. He got up and went to pour himself another large scotch, but it did nothing to calm his mounting fury, so he carried the bottle back to his chair.

The faithless bitch. She had done a good job on him. He had actually believed her when she said she loved him. And now this. He had told her the first time he bedded her that he'd had a vasectomy years before, so there could be no doubt now of the bastard's parentage. No way was it his.

He pushed the bottle aside and decided to go up and take a shower. Anything to wash away the burning anger.

The bedroom was dark when he entered. He turned on the lamp and saw the empty pine bed and the silent room. Jenny was obviously out. She must have gone in someone else's car, as hers was still in the garage, to one of her ridiculous exercise classes, no doubt. Or maybe to Caroline Palmer's. He was vaguely surprised, as she rarely went out in the evening without him and on the odd occasion that she did, she always warned him in advance and left him something to eat.

He shrugged it off with annoyance and went into the bathroom. As he stepped into the shower, he welcomed the stinging spray of hot water and by the time he emerged, he felt more under control. He slipped into a comfortable tracksuit and started back downstairs.

As he passed along the landing corridor, he rammed his hand against the wall. 'I'll find you, Sarah,' he shouted aloud. 'I'll damned well find you.'

Somewhere there was a loud bang. Far away she could hear someone shouting. Jenny fought to make sense of the sounds and sensations. There was silence again, but she could feel something warm and prickly against her cheek. She realised her eyes were still shut and slowly she forced them open.

For a moment, she was uncertain where she was, but then realised that she was lying on the carpet in the guest bedroom. Her head lifted in surprise and instantly her lungs flared in agony, shooting pain through her back and head. She gasped and this only succeeded in intensifying the pain. Defensively, she lay very still. She mustn't move. Memory seeped back and in the darkened room, her eyes sought out the hammer that had inflicted the damage. She could just make it out on the floor near the bed, lying where it had fallen.

She kept very still, sprawled on her front and panting very lightly. She found that if she kept her breathing extremely shallow, the pain was just bearable. But the feeling that she was slowly suffocating forced her at intervals to draw a deeper breath and then her lungs and back screamed the agony.

Gradually she was able to take stock of the situation. There was something not right about her head, as well as her back. Whenever she tried to move it at all, great waves of black pain and nausea swept through her. Time passed slowly and she was growing very cold. She tried to think, but had a feeling that she kept blacking out, although she was not sure whether it was for minutes or hours at a time.

Eventually her mind came round to remembering David. Of course, David. It was dark now. He should be home. He would find her. But where was he? She tried to clear the bewildering mists that floated in and out of her mind. Was that the noise she'd heard? But how long ago was that? She had absolutely no idea. She tried to listen intently for his footsteps on the stairs, but could not focus her attention for long on anything but her breathing. And on the pain.

It came as a shock when the thought tumbled into her head that David would have no reason to look for her in here. Why on earth should he imagine she might be in the guest room? He might even have already gone to bed. Fear drove back the clouds in her mind.

She knew then she would have to move. She had to try. There was no choice. If she could get to the door, she could bang on it enough to attract David's attention, even if she could not manage to turn the handle. The prospect of David opening the door and bringing warmth and help filled her with relief. For a moment the image was so vivid that she believed it was actually happening.

She forced her eyes open again and her disappointment at finding herself still lying cold and alone in the middle of the dark room was almost more unbearable than the pain. Whatever it cost, she must get to the door.

She raised her head an inch off the carpet and for a moment, the swirling blackness threatened to engulf her. Her lungs cried out for air and she gritted her teeth against the jolting pain. She was just about to crawl the few yards to the door and safety when her eyes were caught by the black shape of the hammer beside the bed. This time she stared at it in horror. Oh God, no. How could she explain its presence to David? Or what had happened to her that left her wounded and nearly naked on the floor? She sobbed aloud. She knew what she had to do.

Hand over hand, she dragged herself away from the door. Towards the hammer. Each agonised pull with her elbows and desperate push with her feet gained precious inches of carpet. At times, her vision blanked out completely, replaced by the total darkness of an unlit tunnel. But she refused to allow herself to sink into that comforting oblivion. She did not let it interrupt her painful progress forward, for she knew that if she stopped, she might never start again.

Just when she'd reached the point where she could go on no longer, her outstretched hand touched the wooden handle of the hammer. It felt warm to her icy fingers. She allowed herself to rest a moment and dropped her head on to her arm. She was covered in sweat and her whole body was shaking, as she lay there gasping for air. She felt herself slipping away, down into the tunnel.

Quickly she jerked her head upright, so that the shrieking bolt of pain in her back would pierce the enveloping mists. Ignoring the screams of her body, she made a final desperate effort and yanked herself forward one more time until, with both hands, she thrust the heavy hammer deep under the bed.

Before she could even be aware that she had succeeded, a great wave of merciful blackness broke over her and dragged her down into its depths.

The clock struck midnight and David shook himself awake. His head throbbed and his throat felt dry. He was surprised to find himself still in his chair and glanced with distaste at the nearly empty bottle of scotch that stood beside it. God, that was a damned stupid way to go.

He stood up and looked at his watch. It was late. He had to get to bed. But where the hell was Jenny? For the first time, concern flickered through his irritation. Surely she would never stay out so late. Maybe something was wrong, but in that case, wouldn't she have telephoned him? Damn her, he didn't need this now.

He had just decided to ring Caroline Palmer, gone midnight or not, to see if she could supply the answer, when it suddenly occurred to him that maybe Jenny had in fact already returned home. Perhaps, while he had snored deep in his alcoholic doze, she had come back, decided to leave him undisturbed and gone to bed. That was sure to be the case.

Annoyed at his earlier fears, he climbed the stairs to the

bedroom. Again he turned on the light and looked around, but the room was just as he had left it. His discarded shirt lay on a chair and the bed was unoccupied. He stood in the doorway, uncertain what to do next, then walked over to the telephone and dialled Caroline's number. A sleepy voice told him Jenny was not there and had not been seen all evening. Her expression of concern increased his growing unease and he quickly rang off.

For God's sake, what had happened to her? Images of attacks in dark alleys flooded his mind, but he forced himself to stay calm. Before ringing the police, he must first search the house to be absolutely certain she was not there. He already knew she was not in the garage, because her empty car had been sitting there when he had put his own car away. A systematic check on each room would soon clear up any doubt. He walked across the silent bedroom and glanced into the en-suite bathroom. Nothing.

The unexpected thought that she may have left him fought its way disconcertingly to the surface of his mind, as he was going into Jenny's dressing-room. No, not Jenny. She would never leave. Yet only a few hours ago he had believed the same of Sarah. Instantly he flicked through her wardrobe, but could not see any difference in the number of clothes hanging there, but doubt still lingered and he left quickly to complete his search. Hurrying further down the corridor, he turned to check the guest room at the top of the stairs. Expecting to give it only a cursory glance, he opened the door.

'Oh Christ.'

Her body lay crumpled on the floor. The skin of her back was covered in blood and dried streaks of it stained the pale carpet.

David fought down nausea, his knees weak as he rushed to her side. He kneeled down, his heart racing, as he saw that her hair lay in a pool of blood that had seeped from a long gash on the side of her head. He touched her cheek and called her name, but her skin felt cold and there was no response. It must have been an intruder. A disturbed burglar. She had been lying here like this for hours, while he had sat downstairs drinking himself into a stupor.

He had to get help. If it wasn't already too late. He dragged the duvet off the bed and draped it over Jenny's still form. A slight moan escaped her lips as the cover settled on her wounded flesh.

David felt relief surge through him and adrenaline pumped strength into his limbs as he ran to the telephone. His hand was shaking so badly, he dropped the receiver, but instantly snatched it up again and dialled the life-saving nine, nine, nine.

7 *

Caroline Palmer snorted her disgust.

'Jenny, I honestly cannot believe you did all that damage to yourself just by falling on top of the foot rail of the bed.' She shook her head in disbelief. 'Brass bedsteads may be full of metal knobs and knockers, but even so! It must have been a hell of a fall.'

From the bed, Jenny smiled weakly up at Caroline's concerned expression. Guilt made her feel even worse.

'And what were you doing climbing up on top of the metal rail in the first place?' Caroline persisted.

A nurse bustled over and checked the chart at the end of Jenny's bed. 'And how are you feeling today?' she enquired cheerily.

'How do you think she's feeling?' Caroline retorted. 'Bloody awful.'

The nurse smiled tolerantly and addressed herself again to Jenny. 'How's the pain this morning? Do you need anything stronger for it?'

Jenny very carefully shook her head and whispered, 'No, thank you.'

Caroline snorted again. 'For God's sake, give the girl something that will knock it on the head.' She turned to the pale figure in the bed and wanted to hug some life back into her. The face on the pillow was grey with pain, and the bulky dressing on the side of it oddly distorted the shape of her head. She looked so fragile that Caroline was almost frightened to touch her. She leaned forward and lightly patted the hand lying still on the covers. A drip tube extended from it to an upturned bottle on a stand. 'Don't you worry, you'll be out of here in no time.'

The nurse shook her head doubtfully. 'She's lost a lot of blood and the doctor is concerned about the concussion.'

'That's right, nurse. Cheer her up.'

'She'll feel better after a few days of absolute rest. Don't tire her with too much talking. It won't help her ribs.' The nurse replaced the chart and took her smile to the patient in the next bed.

Caroline squeezed Jenny's fingers. 'She's right. I should let you rest.'

Jenny clung to her friend's hand. 'No, not yet,' she whispered. 'How was France?'

'Fabulous and fattening.' Caroline patted her waistline and pulled a face of remorse. 'Too many croissants and *pommes frites*. But I loved every mouthful,' she added with a grin. 'When you're out of here, I'll show you the photos. You won't believe it. There's one of me on waterskis that Andrew took just to prove my boasts aren't a pack of lies.'

'That's what I need to convince you my accident was real.' Each word was an effort.

Caroline smiled gently. 'You must admit, it's a bit hard to swallow. So tell me, what were you doing clambering about on top of the brass bed rail?'

Painfully Jenny tried to explain, 'I was doing my exercises on the floor. I often do them in the spare room. It's so sunny in there.' She fought to focus her throbbing mind on the story she had concocted. 'I saw a huge spider on the ceiling and I was trying to kill it.' She paused for breath.

'So you climbed up on top of the bedstead?'

'Yes.'

'And fell?'

Jenny tried to smile but it didn't work. She hated the lying. 'Yes. One of the metal balls of the bed rail got me in the back.' Her voice was barely audible.

'And you managed to crack your skull on the way down?'

'Yes.'

Caroline looked hard into Jenny's eyes and did not believe

her. She held the cold hand between her own warm ones and lightly chafed it. 'All in the nude?'

Jenny attempted a laugh but the effort was too much. She caught her breath. 'No,' she managed to whisper between gasps. 'I got hot doing the sit-ups. You know what it's like.' She made herself keep going. Keep explaining.

'So you stripped off?'

This time she did not try to reply, but nodded faintly. She was aware of Caroline's sceptical gaze and could not keep the colour from creeping into her white cheeks.

Caroline sighed impatiently. The story was plausible. Falling from that height on to the top of metal knobs and spikes could easily have caused broken ribs, cuts and concussion. Caroline should believe it, but she didn't. There was something about the way Jenny would not look her in the eye while telling the story that did not ring true. Her protests carried no conviction and her blushing cheeks betrayed only too obviously her embarrassment at the lie. Admittedly, the embarrassment could stem from having caused such a disaster so idiotically, but Caroline doubted that. She knew Jenny well and could always tell when something was wrong. She was such a hopeless liar. It went too much against the grain.

Then there was Susannah Benson. She had telephoned the previous evening with an invitation for Friday's pool party and just before ringing off, had unexpectedly asked if, since returning from France, Caroline had seen Jenny.

'No, not yet,' Caroline had replied. 'Give me a chance to unpack.'

'Oh, I just wondered.'

Instantly Caroline smelled trouble. 'Why? What's the matter with her?'

'Nothing. I'm probably imagining things.'

'What things?'

So Susannah had told her about the bruises – about the paint pot excuse and her lies about sunburn, ending with, 'It's not like her, is it?'

'No, it certainly isn't. I'll give her a call.'

Alarm bells had started to ring. She had dealt with too many

• Kate Sharam

divorce cases and listened to too many sobbing wives not to be alert to the web of lies spun by the humiliated victim of domestic violence. And David could well be the type: aggressive, dominating and always determined to be in control. Perhaps Jenny had rebelled once too often against the tight rein.

There had been no answer to her call last night. It made her feel sick now to think that while the phone had been ringing, Jenny might well have been lying there covered in blood. Then there was David's phone call. Gone midnight and he claimed to have only just noticed his wife was missing. Anger rose in Caroline, as she thought of his cowardly attempt to hide what he had inflicted on his wife. Belatedly he'd called the ambulance and produced a story of intruders, quickly swapped in favour of this ludicrous explanation about falling on the brass bedstead. Well, it wouldn't wash. As soon as Jenny was strong enough, Caroline would get the truth out of her.

In the meantime, she could only smile with concern into the troubled dark eyes of her friend and nod as if she was taken in by the lame excuse. 'You rest now, Jenny. Try to sleep and you'll feel better soon.'

Caroline's heels tapped noisily along the shiny surface as she sought to negotiate a path out of the maze of hospital corridors. When she turned a corner to bring her back to the main reception area, she glanced to her left. A row of faces, resigned to their waiting, stared at her without interest from blue plastic seats on either side of a corridor. Just past the chairs was a large drinks machine with a small cluster of people around it, hoping that coffee might break the boredom.

A tall man's blond head caught Caroline's attention and as he turned away from the machine, plastic coffee in hand, Caroline changed course and strode up to him.

'Hello, David.'

David Cranshaw looked round in surprise. 'Oh, hello.' His coffee slopped over on to his fingers and he scowled with annoyance. 'I didn't know you were here. Seen Jenny yet?'

'Yes, David, I have.' She glared at him. 'She looks terrible.'

'I know. It's a bloody stupid thing to have happened, isn't it?

But the doctors say she'll be all right eventually. What on earth she thought she was up to, I do not know.'

'I should have thought you're exactly the person who would know.'

David looked up from his coffee in surprise. 'What the hell does that mean?' His voice was raised and several faces in the nearby seats turned to stare.

'You know damned well what it means, David. Don't play the innocent with me.'

'Look, Caroline, I'm tired. I've been in this bloody morgue most of the night and my wife is flat on her back in a hospital bed. I can do without your riddles, so if you've got something to say, then just say it.'

Even those at the coffee machine had turned to listen now.

'You know perfectly well what I'm saying, David. I don't think you'd want me to spell it out here.'

'I'm not interested in playing games.' His voice was ragged with tension. 'I'm going to check on Jenny, then with luck, British Rail will still have a few of their bone-shakers in motion that will get me up to the office. Late, maybe, but at least there.'

Caroline's blue eyes narrowed and her voice was icy. 'You mean you're going to travel up to town and leave Jenny here on her own? In the state that she's in?'

David shook his head, his temper fraying. 'No, Caroline, I'm not leaving her on her own. For God's sake, talk sense. She has a whole gaggle of doctors and nurses caring for her. Anyway, she's doped up to the eyeballs, so she'll probably sleep all day and won't even notice who is or isn't sitting beside her bed.'

The hand holding the coffee was starting to shake and more of the hot liquid spilled over his fingers. He swore and quickly placed the plastic cup down on an empty chair. As he did so, he suddenly became aware of the row of eyes fixed on his every move.

'What the hell are you all staring at?' he snapped at the chairs, and an embarrassed silence filled the corridor.

Lowering his voice, he turned again to Caroline. 'If you're so keen on Jenny having company, then you stay with her.' He smiled maliciously. 'But I expect you've got an office to go to as well.'

'Not one that I put before people who matter to me.'

'Of course Jenny matters to me. What are you implying?'

'Then why did you leave her to lie for so long with her ribs smashed and her head split open? It was hours before you called an ambulance.'

The colour surged into David's face and he lost control. 'Because I didn't damned well know she was up there.'

'So what were you doing all evening then?'

'It's none of your business, but if you must know, I had a couple of drinks. It had been a bad day.' More calmly, he added, 'As soon as I found her, I called the police. I thought a burglar had attacked her.'

Caroline nodded. 'It certainly would have looked like a drunken attack – to the police as well, I would imagine. So you got cold feet at the idea of involving them, did you, and changed your story?'

Again there was silence, as David stared at her in disbelief. 'Don't you try to practise your lawyer's tricks on me. You're not in a courtroom now.' He stepped closer. 'Don't you try to imply I was involved in any way. I did not touch her. It was an accident. I wasn't even there, for Christ's sake.'

Caroline stood her ground, her voice steely. 'You may think you can hide behind Jenny's skirts, but not for long, I promise you.'

'This is ridiculous. You're out of your mind. Go back to your petty little conveyancing and leave me alone.' He turned on his heel and stormed off down the corridor.

Caroline's voice rang after him. 'You touch her once more and I'll have you in court so fast, your feet won't touch the ground.'

David did not bother to turn round but kept walking in the direction of the lift.

The telephone rang the moment David sat down at his desk.

'Mr Fairchild would like to see you right away, Mr Cranshaw.'

The chairman's secretary had obviously had second thoughts

about her obstructive attitude of the evening before. It was almost midday, so, with luck, an hour or so with Fairchild over drinks and a long lunch would set everything straight. David's magic touch had always worked before. How many times had he been called in to administer the kiss of life to an ailing account? Too numerous to mention.

He stood up and walked to the door, but the voice of unease within him would not quite be stilled. What if Lerner was there? What the hell could that bastard have up his sleeve now? David knew he wasn't in any fit state that morning to lock horns with the wily deputy chairman. His wits felt dulled and his normally sharp antennae were only functioning on half power.

A quick jolt of caffeine was what he wanted to get his energy racing, but the silent, empty office next door contained no willing hands to pander to his needs. How could she desert him now, when he needed her most? Instead, David went over to his drinks cabinet and reached for the scotch. He grabbed several swift swallows straight from the bottle and felt the smooth golden liquid kick him into a higher gear.

'Come on then, Lerner. I'm ready for you.'

He left the office and as he made his way up in the lift, he convinced himself that it was Lerner's head that would end up on the sacrificial plate, not his own. The upstairs corridor was more lavish than on the lower floor, the carpet thicker and the lighting more discreet. On the door was a polished oak plaque that said it all. 'Mr R. E. Fairchild. Chairman.' David grimaced. Until so recently, he had believed his own door was destined to bear a similar title. To hell with expectations. He just could not understand what had gone wrong.

He knocked and in response to Fairchild's brief 'Enter', he walked into the office.

The chairman was alone, seated at his desk, and did not rise. He greeted David with a curt 'Good morning' and waved him into the seat opposite.

'Hear you had a spot of bother last night,' Fairchild opened the conversation. 'Sorry to hear about your wife.'

David was surprised. He had of course rung in from the hospital earlier that morning to explain his absence till almost noon, but enquiries about a wife's ailments were not normally part of the chairman's repertoire. Family concerns were an unwelcome interruption to the smooth flowing of Dern & Fairchild.

'Yes,' David replied. 'It was a nasty accident, but she's recovering well in hospital now.'

Fairchild looked relieved to be spared further details. 'She'll be in good hands there.'

An awkward silence bridged the gap, as both men considered how best to progress to the purpose of the meeting.

'You've been with the company some years now,' Fairchild began, 'and you've done some good work for us.'

David did not like the sound of that. 'I think the extent of my client list is witness to that. I've brought in a lot of business for the company.'

The chairman shifted some papers on his desk. 'That's true, David. We have appreciated your contribution in the past.'

David sat still. He had heard the death knell in those last three words.

'But unfortunately,' Fairchild continued, 'this is a difficult time for everyone. We all have to make cutbacks—'

David was not going to take it lying down. 'Despite the tough climate,' he interrupted, 'Dern & Fairchild made a healthy profit this year. Due, in no small part, to my efforts. I'm sure I don't need to remind you, the figures so far this year are excellent.'

'Yes, thank God, but it's not as simple as that. Our prognosis for the next few months doesn't look as good as we'd expected.'

Bullshit. David had seen the reports.

Fairchild suddenly speeded up, as if eager to get it over with. 'As I was saying, we are having to make certain cutbacks to maintain our profit margin. And I'm sorry to say, we are forced to make some of those in staffing numbers. Senior management, as well as junior.'

David sat silent. He would make the chairman say it.

Fairchild cleared his throat, then looked David in the eye. 'So I'm afraid to say, David, I'm going to have to let you go. I'm sorry, but that's the way it is.'

Now he had got it out, the older man sat back in his chair, but before David could respond, he added, 'You will of course receive a full year's salary in lieu of notice. And I have decided to let you keep your company car, gratis.'

That was it. Over. And they offer him a company car as if they were doing him a favour.

'Mr Fairchild, this is grossly unfair and you know it. I have worked my damned guts out for this company. For you, in fact. And I've done a darned good job too. Two new accounts I've brought in this summer alone. So don't tell me you don't need me, because you do.'

Fairchild looked coldly at David. 'It's not a question of needing you. It's a matter of economic necessity.'

David's stomach lurched, but he held his gaze. 'If you're making cutbacks, there are half a dozen directors out there,' he gestured towards the door, 'any one of whom you wouldn't miss. You know that. I'm worth ten of them and work ten times as hard.' His voice was rising. 'So why me? What has that shitting bastard Lerner been pouring out of that sewer he calls a mouth?'

Fairchild turned away with distaste at the outburst. 'Don Lerner has nothing to do with this.'

'Like hell he doesn't. His filthy fingerprints are all over it.'

'Whatever animosity may exist between you and Don Lerner is strictly between the two of you. I repeat,' he emphasised each word separately, 'he has nothing to do with this.'

He stood up and went over to the elaborate walnut cocktail cabinet that stood in one corner of the large office and in silence, poured a scotch and a bourbon into two crystal glasses. He placed the scotch in front of David.

'It is exactly as I said. The company's welfare comes first.' He resumed his seat.

David sipped his drink and tried to keep his voice reasonable. 'If this is supposed to be for the company's good, what about the clients? They won't like this. Many of them insist on my personal attention to their accounts. You know I'm the best you've got, so what on earth is this about?' He swallowed hard, but his throat felt dry.

Fairchild stared at him and then quietly said, 'Even in that area, we've had some complaints. Some clients are definitely not satisfied with the way you are servicing their accounts recently. That, of course, influenced my decision.'

David thumped his fist on the desk. 'That's crap and you know it. That's Lerner lying through his fucking teeth. Ask any of my clients. Ask Wareham. He'll tell you the truth.'

Again Fairchild stared coolly at him. 'I know the truth.' He raised his glass to his lips.

'I don't believe—'

Fairchild cut him off sharply. 'I'm sorry, David, we have to let you go. That's final.'

There was silence in the room. David looked at the drink in his hand and placed it on the desk. 'You and I both know I don't deserve this. It's Lerner who should be sitting in this chair. He's been sneaking behind my back, somehow getting at my clients. Distorting everything. And finally he's got to you. I don't know how, but whatever he has told you, it's not the truth.'

Fairchild spoke firmly, 'David, I repeat, it's not Lerner. It's you. Believe me, I do know the truth.'

David looked at the chairman, trying to fathom his last words.

Fairchild brought the confrontation to an abrupt end. 'There's nothing more to discuss. I'm letting you go. As of today.'

David rose. 'I'll leave now,' he said tautly.

Fairchild nodded and accompanied him to the door, but did not offer to shake hands.

'Goodbye, David.'

David did not reply. He did not trust himself to speak.

The room was growing dark, but David did not stir himself to switch on the lamp in the sitting-room. The gloomy light suited him. He picked at the sandwich on a plate beside him, but he had no stomach for it, despite the fact that his last proper meal had been two days ago, for he had hardly touched the sandwiches in the park with Sarah.

Sarah. He closed his eyes. God, how he needed her.

He sat up in his chair and splashed the last of the scotch into his glass. What did it matter if he got drunk now? Who was to know? More to the point, who was to care? A hangover in the morning made no difference to anyone but himself. There was no need any more to set the blasted alarm for some god-forsaken hour in the morning. No commuters to fight for the last seat in the carriage. No need to keep the brain sharp for ever-demanding clients. Now he had only his own problems. And those he could drown.

He emptied his glass again and in the swirl of fumes, the numbness cushioned the pain. His mind could hardly take in what had happened. Reality just could not be so appalling. In a matter of weeks his life had somersaulted into chaos. From a highly successful company director, with income and status to match and a home and car that were the envy of his peers . . . to what? Transformed into one of the mass of unemployed, boozing himself steadily into the gutter. No job. No wife. And no mistress. Oh Sarah, why aren't you here now? With a determined effort, he swept away his longing for her with a rush of anger. First her betrayal. Now Fairchild. What the hell was going on?

He fought down a wave of panic and forced himself to his feet. He must get something to eat. That's what he needed. He would feel calmer then. He walked somewhat unsteadily into the kitchen and was about to search for ham and eggs in the fridge, when he noticed the couple of unopened bottles of whisky he had bought on his way home from the hospital. They stood where he had dumped them on the table. He stared at them silently.

Then he closed the fridge door. He crossed to the sink and ran cold water over his hands and face, but the shock of it only made him feel worse. God, if only he had someone to discuss it all with, to vent his fury and misery. Another voice to give encouragement. Reassurance.

He had not told Jenny. He had gone to the hospital in the afternoon, but she was woozy from the drugs and had drifted in and out of sleep, so he had promised to return the next day. Time enough for bad news then. After all, he had all the blasted time in the world now.

Not bothering to dry his hands, he picked up one of the bottles. This would have to be his companion tonight. Damn all women. And screw all men. He didn't need them.

He returned to the sitting-room and this time switched on the light. Might as well see his poison. He collapsed into his chair and wrenched open the cap of the bottle. The fiery smell of the liquid warmed him and he filled his glass.

What the hell did Jenny think she was doing anyway? He needed her here. Now. Not flat out in some blasted hospital bed. Why did such a stupid accident have to happen to her? Why not to bloody Lerner? Or even Fairchild? He put the bottle down and sipped the scotch. It tasted good. He leaned back with the glass in his hand and conjured up images of Don Lerner, beaten up and bleeding in the office car park. Then swathed in plaster and bandages, unconscious in a hard hospital bed. That made him smile.

He felt a little better. He tried to destroy Fairchild with the same fantasy, but found himself unable to bend that figure of authority to his will. So he gave up and drank more of the scotch.

He closed his eyes and decided to fill his mind with Sarah instead. He let his thoughts dwell on his pleasure in her warmth. Her lips and her smooth skin. The feel of her soft breasts and the touch of her fingers. Visions of her dark pubic mound and taut thighs flooded over him, until his yearning for her became unbearable.

He turned urgently to his glass for relief and was finally grateful when its golden power swept him into oblivion.

8

Jenny eased herself into a sitting position in the bed and accepted the tray from David.

'Thanks. Just what I needed.' She placed the cup of tea on her bedside table and took a bite of the toast.

David watched her in moody silence, then asked, 'Feeling any better?'

She grimaced. 'Awful, to be honest. Every blasted breath hurts.'

David stood awkwardly by the window, looking out at the drizzle, ill at ease in a sickroom.

'What time are you off?' she enquired.

'About mid-morning, I suppose.' He didn't turn round. His eyes were fixed on the dripping bird table on the lawn. A sodden ginger tom had crept cautiously through the hedge and was now silently stalking an unwary chaffinch that was picking up pieces of peanut from the ground.

'I'm meeting Graham Wells at one o'clock.'

The cat inched forward.

Jenny noted the lack of enthusiasm in his voice. The eager anticipation of his initial meetings with contacts and head-hunters had all been eroded. Too many closed doors.

She finished her toast and glanced with disappointment at the tea. David had brought her a cup of the Indian tea he always made for himself, rather than the camomile brew she enjoyed. She lay back and studied the set of his shoulders. The rigid back had crumpled and there was an uncertainty in his stance that was unfamiliar. Jenny nestled further into the pillows and relaxed.

'David, it's good of you to bring me my breakfast, but would you mind getting me another cup of tea? And making it camomile this time? I'm sorry, but I can't drink this.'

David looked round in surprise. He had almost forgotten she was in the room, so absorbed was he in the hunt taking place outside the window. The patience of the cat was impressive and each painstaking twitch of a muscle took it nearer its goal. The preoccupied bird had no idea of the fate that lay ahead.

For a moment David was about to object to Jenny's request, but instead just shrugged. 'If you like.' His attention returned to the window and suddenly he thumped the glass. 'Get out of here,' he shouted harshly.

The bird abruptly abandoned its meal and flew up towards a tree. A lightning paw shot out and tore a cluster of tail feathers from the fleeing finch, but the bird managed to escape noisily on to a branch.

David smiled to himself, as the disgruntled cat stalked off in search of other prey, then he remembered the tea. 'I'll get it for you now.' He picked up her tray and left the room.

Jenny waited patiently. Everything David did around the house took twice as long as it should. She assumed it was his way of registering protest at his unaccustomed menial servitude. Not that there was really that much for him to do. The house was kept in order by a weekly cleaning lady, so it was just a matter of putting a few meals together. Even the washing up was taken care of by the machine, and she had packed the freezer full of pre-prepared meals, so all he had to do was heat them up for himself in turn.

As a result, he had ample spare time on his hands, but he remained deaf to her pleas for a little attention to the garden. The panorama from her pillows distressed her each morning when she saw the speed at which the lawns were becoming ragged and unkempt, only outstripped by the flowerbeds. But she was damned if she was going to hire a gardener while David was just hanging around the house doing nothing. Let him take some responsibility for the care of the home in which he lived, recognise that he was reduced to physical rather than mental labour now. But the sight of the garden's neglect was a small price to pay for this unexpected turn of events. She had not foreseen this bedridden scenario in her plans.

When David finally returned to place the tray on her bedside table, Jenny smiled up at him gratefully. 'Thank you. I do hope your lunch with Graham goes well today. It's years since you've seen him, isn't it?'

'I never liked the creep. I'm only meeting him now because I'm getting desperate.'

'And he's gone up in the world, you say?'

David suppressed his annoyance, only barely. 'God knows how, but yes, he's done well for himself.'

'Let's hope he's got something for you.'

'Why the hell else do you think I'm going crawling to him, cap in hand?'

Jenny made a sympathetic face. 'It must be hard for you, I know, but don't worry. I'm sure your reputation will bring results.'

He threw her a brief, depressed smile. 'It hasn't worked so far.'

'Perhaps today's the day for a change.'

David headed for the door. 'It had damned well better be. I would hate to go grovelling to this short-arsed Graham Wells all for nothing.'

'It won't be for nothing, David,' she called after his retreating back, but received no answer.

The morning passed slowly. The rain rattled the windows and Jenny found she could not concentrate on either of her books. The hazards of Will Steger's polar expedition just made her feel cold and miserable, but she fared no better with Stephen King's latest.

She tossed them aside, deciding that the trouble was that she was bored with lying in bed, bored with the invalid role, and needed some activity. Without too much trouble, she eased herself out of bed and crossed to the bathroom. She ran a bath, keeping it shallow, so as not to wet the bandages round her ribs. When at last she was soaking in the hot water, she closed her eyes and planned what to have for lunch. After a couple of weeks of a steady diet of soup or ham and salad, David's idea of what was easy and befitted an invalid, she was in the mood for something more than the sandwiches David had left for her.

After she had dried and dressed, she flexed her back a few times and tried a few stretches. Despite the stabs of pain, she was definitely well on the mend and now that the stitches were out of her head and she could brush her hair over the scar, she felt almost normal again. Ready to spread her wings a little. She had to admit she had not been quite truthful in her response to David's hopeful enquiry after her health. Exaggerating the amount of pain she was suffering served her purpose. Kept David isolated, rattling around the house on his own.

With reluctance, she walked carefully along the corridor to the guest room. Her stomach churned at the remembrance of that nightmare, but she knew she had to go in. She opened the door and looked around the room. The only sign of all that pain was the stain on the carpet. A dirty brown smear. Taking care not to jolt her ribs, she dropped on to her hands and knees and, grunting with the effort, lay flat on the floor. There it was. Still hidden.

She considered the feasibility of carrying the hammer down to the garage while David was out of the house, but decided it was too early yet. She was still not up to that kind of exertion. Another few days and she should be able to manage it. So she left the hammer lying in the dark shadows and pulled herself upright again, but the effort made her catch her breath and she bent over gasping for a moment. When she straightened up once more, the metal foot-rail caught her eye and made her smile. David had swallowed her story of landing on its protruding spokes hook, line and sinker. So preoccupied was he with his own distress that it did not even occur to him to doubt her word. Thank God for brass bedsteads.

She left the room with a sense of relief and carefully made her way downstairs. In the kitchen, she quickly decided on a chicken Kiev from the freezer and a baked potato with cheese. She had just slipped them into the oven and was treating herself to a glass of wine, when she was startled by the telephone. The tone sounded loud in the silent house. She let it ring some time before picking up the receiver.

'Hello, darling,' Susannah Benson's voice cooed. 'Have I dragged you from your sickbed?'

'No, no such luck.'

'You mean David's not waiting on you hand and foot? What a remiss fellow he is.'

'He's gone up to London today.'

'Oh, Jenny, that's awful. You shouldn't be left to stagger around the house all on your own.'

Jenny could not help laughing. 'I'm not exactly staggering, I assure you. In fact,' she added, 'I'm just about to have a glass of wine. Then I might be staggering.'

'I tell you what, I'll come and join you. We can drink the bottle together. I know I was rotten not coming to see you in hospital, but I loathe those places. So I'll make it up to you by coming over to keep you company now. It'll be fun. I'll bring another bottle with me and you can tell me all your problems.'

Jenny was touched by Susannah's offer of a shoulder to cry on. 'That's all right, Susannah, there's no need to—'

The voice on the line was determined. 'Don't be silly. It's the least I can do. I won't have you writhing in pain without someone to hold your hand. Keep the Chablis cold. I'll be with you in half an hour. Bye.'

The phone went dead.

After so many monotonous afternoons in bed with only herself for company and David moping around moodily downstairs, she looked forward to Susannah's lively presence. Her cheerful smile and ready laugh were always a tonic for an attack of the blues.

Jenny transferred her lunch into the microwave and put the bottle of wine back in the fridge.

'But didn't Thea object?'

'No, darling, she was too far gone by then.'

Jenny was stretched out on the sofa, enjoying the latest gossip, despite her throbbing back. 'Susannah, you promised you'd go easy on the brandy in the punch.'

'I did, honestly.' Susannah held up two fingers in a boy scout's salute of wide-eyed innocence. 'But I did also happen to mix up a few rather lethal jugs of buck's fizz for the binge and I saw Thea Hatfield knocking it back like straight orange juice.'

'So while she was flat on her back asleep in the sun, you all decided to cut her hair?' Jenny laughed, causing a sharp stab of pain.

'Well, you know how scraggy it always looked. She would insist on wearing it long, even though it was as thin as rats' tails.' Susannah shook her own mane, as if in comparison. 'So off it came. When we woke her up to pour her into a taxi home, she didn't even notice.'

'But Caroline told me Thea was furious the next day.'

Susannah was unconcerned. 'Yes, she gave me an earful on the telephone, but she didn't have the nerve to come and face me until she had been to have it properly styled. Now even she admits that it looks much better.'

'It sounds like I missed a humdinger of a party.'

'You certainly did. We all drank a toast to your sickbed.'

'Do thank everybody for the flowers. They were lovely,' Jenny laughed, more carefully this time. 'I think a jug of your buck's fizz in my drip would probably have worked wonders rather than all those pain-killers they were pumping into me.'

Susannah eyed Jenny more seriously. 'So what's all this nonsense about falling on to a metal railing?'

'It's not nonsense. It's the truth. And it was a brass bedstead.'

'A bit hard to swallow.'

'I know it was stupid. But that's what happened.'

'Really?'

Jenny forced herself to keep eye contact. 'Really.' Even to herself, it didn't sound convincing and it was with relief that she heard the telephone ring.

Susannah jumped up. 'You lie still. I'll get it.'

She disappeared into the hall, leaving Jenny to quieten both her breathing and her conscience. When Susannah breezed back in a couple of minutes later, she waved her hand for the invalid to remain seated.

'It was only Caroline. Just calling to see how you're feeling. I told her I was administering Chablis to the wounds.'

She picked up her glass and raised it to Jenny. 'She said to drink your good health. And when she heard David wasn't in residence today, she told me to tell you she'd have come over herself, but she's up to her eyes in court orders this afternoon.'

'Poor Caroline, she's feeling a bit awkward about the row she had with David at the hospital.'

Susannah shifted uncomfortably in her chair. 'Yes, she told me about that.'

'She has studiously avoided bumping into him. So I haven't seen much of her since I've been out of hospital.'

'You know she's still furious with him?'

Jenny nodded. 'So I gather. The feeling is mutual, I'm afraid. David thinks she's out to cause trouble.'

Susannah gave her a long steady look. 'And is there trouble, Jenny? Trouble with David? We're not just sticking our noses in for the sake of it. We're worried about you. About the bruises and then the "accident".'

'There's no need to be.'

'So there's no truth in what Caroline says?'

'No '

Susannah made one more attempt. 'We know David must be under even more stress now, without a job. It must be very difficult for you. Both.'

'We're surviving.'

'You know what men are like. It's damned hard for them to function without their work to define their social pecking order. He must be feeling dreadful, poor love.'

'He is.'

Susannah took a deep breath, then said quickly, 'So if he took it out on you sometimes, I wouldn't be surprised.'

'He may be moody and difficult, but if you mean does he take it out on me physically, the answer is no, Susannah. He has never laid a finger on me in anger.'

Susannah stared into the guarded dark eyes and was almost tempted to believe her words, but the scar on the side of Jenny's face reminded her only too forcibly of the unsatisfactory explanations for the broken ribs and the bruising.

She shook her head in exasperation and murmured, 'Whatever the truth may be, these rumours flying round won't do David's reputation any good. It's going to be tough for the poor man to find an employer who will overlook tales of violence. I tell you, Robert is appalled. You know what a soft spot he has for you.'

'Robert knows about the rumours?'

Susannah looked at her in surprise. 'Of course. Everyone does. It was the main topic for tongues at my binge.'

Jenny could not suppress a smile and turned it quickly into a joke. 'It was the only excuse I could come up with to avoid your party,' she grinned. 'Hospital or your pool. No contest.'

Susannah laughed. 'Well, I promise I'll just accept a plain "No thank you" in future.'

'That's a relief. A dark shadow lifted.'

'Talking of shadows,' Susannah glanced round the room, 'where is he today?'

Jenny froze.

'He's usually all over me with his purrs and black hairs. What have you done with the old reprobate? Not shut him out on my account, I hope.'

Jenny's chest was tight. The effort to breathe made her wince. 'No, I haven't shut him out.' She paused. 'He's in the woods.'

'Cats are so ruthless. I pity the little mice round here, they don't stand a chance.'

Slowly Jenny smiled. 'That's true, but I don't think he'll be satisfied with such small offerings. He has larger prey in mind.'

As the train lurched to yet another inexplicable standstill, David looked around the carriage. The irritated murmuring that accompanied such delays during the rush hour was totally absent. A brief glance out of the window and then noses returned placidly to their papers and paperbacks. There was none of the frantic urgency at this hour of mid-morning.

David observed the immaculate pinstripe opposite him. Wings of white hair swept back over a tanned, well-weathered face. A neat military moustache. Off to a reunion of colonial has-beens, perhaps? He glanced around the carriage again. A few older women, with spectacles on their noses and sensible shoes on their feet were scattered about. A couple of teenagers with earphones clamped to their heads nodded and swayed in their own private worlds.

There was only a handful of men around his age. David speculated as to how many of them were also doing the rounds of the job agencies, desperately trudging round every blasted business acquaintance they knew, seeking a suggestion here, a possibility there. Humiliating themselves before jerks who had no intention of extending a helping hand. All for nothing. Absolutely bloody nothing.

But why, for Christ's sake? Why was this happening to him? Everyone knew he was good. Damned good. So why the blank wall?

David shifted the briefcase on his knees and returned his attention to the world outside. The houses slipped past hypnotically. Rows of tawdry back gardens with rusting bikes and broken tables, left to rot in heaps.

Like people left to rot. You either fought for your survival, or you rotted. Well, he damned well was not going to be one of those dismembered tables. No matter how much the bastards tried to grind him down, he would survive. Survive to trample on their graves. After all, he knew the system. He was one who had thrived on the system. Eat or be eaten. God knew, he had chewed enough chunks of executive flesh to realise how addictive was the taste.

The train started to slow again, but this time David recognised the approach to Charing Cross. The gathering of coats and errant bags bustled through the carriage. Today he was pinning his hopes on Graham Wells. Years before, at the beginning of their careers, they had both been minions together at Grantley Advertising. Wells had chosen to remain in the advertising business and was now managing director and chairman of his own small agency, just off Hanover Square. It wasn't huge, but it was healthy and still growing.

Christ, how it rankled that Wells, who had no more talent in his whole body than David had in his little toe, controlled his own business lock, stock and barrel – the magical fifty-one per cent. The thought of crawling to the likes of Wells galled David bitterly, but he would stop at nothing to get back on that roller coaster. The highs, the lows. The bumps and screams. They weren't just everything in life; they were the only thing.

As the train edged up to the platform, he let the crush of bodies surge past his seat. No need to push and elbow now. The ex-colonial opposite also waited, while the queue blocked the aisle. His snowy eyebrows raised in resignation, as he complained to David, 'Everyone is in such a damned hurry these days. It seems only old duffers like me have any time to spare.' He coughed self-consciously. 'All in a mad rush. Same for you, I expect, eh?' he added, nodding towards the briefcase.

David smiled politely and stood up. He forced a gap in the line and started to inch towards the door. His hand clutched the briefcase tightly.

The wine bar off Grosvenor Square was full. The clamour of raised voices and the clatter of empty plates kept conversation to brief snatches.

'David, it's tough at the moment for all of us.' Graham Wells settled his bulk at the small table and jabbed his fork experimentally into the veal pie on his plate.

'You don't look exactly hard done by.'

A satisfied smile spread over Wells' soft features and he leaned forward confidentially. 'Can't say I am, old boy. Can't say I am.'

Wells' education was gleaned entirely from an inner city comprehensive and the rigours of agency politics, but he liked to adopt what he assumed to be the phrases of public school.

'A juicy plum has just fallen into yours truly's lap.'

David liked the sound of that. 'What account is it?'

'Under wraps right now. Wait until it's all on the dotted line.'

David picked up his glass. 'Well, here's to success.'

'Can't knock it, that's for sure.' Wells tasted the wine and grimaced. 'Not up to scratch, but it'll fuel the engine.' He emptied the glass with a flourish, then settled down to attacking the mound on his plate.

David watched his companion as he devoured the meal with relish. Overhead spotlights shone down at discreet angles and managed to highlight the thin strands of hair dragged across his shining pate. David finished his own lunch and when he judged the moment was right, with Wells suitably replete, he asked, 'Come on, Graham, what about it? Any chance of a slot in your company?'

Wells stopped eating and his eyes narrowed. ''Fraid not, old boy. I can't help you just now. It's a bugger's world out there.' He resumed picking through the salad for nuggets of avocado.

David persisted. 'How about a bit of freelance then? You must need fresh input, especially with a new account on the go. And you know damned well I'm the best there is.'

'Sorry, old chap. No can do. I—'

He was interrupted, as two women in short skirts squeezed past their table. As the second one edged round, she stared at David admiringly and ran a hand over his shoulder. 'Hi, gorgeous, can I buy you a drink?'

David glanced up in annoyance and shook his head dismissively. She laughed and followed her friend across the room. When David returned his attention to his own table, he found Wells staring at him resentfully.

'You always could pull the birds, couldn't you? You lucky bastard. It's that corn thatch of yours that gets them every time.' Wells ran a podgy hand regretfully over his own bare pate. 'It's not what's on it, but what's in it that counts. That's what I always say.'

David refrained from comment. He had not realised Wells' dislike ran so deep.

The wine bar grew quieter, as the demands of shop and office reasserted themselves. The groups drifted reluctantly out into the rain and the place acquired a welcome calm. Wells lowered his voice and leaned forward again on the table.

'You've always been a lucky bastard. Every bleeding thing you touched turned to gold. Well, not this time, matey. Not this time. You've really fucked it up.'

'And what exactly do you mean by that?'

Wells relaxed back in his chair and smiled. He poured himself another glass of wine and offered the bottle across the table.

David brushed it aside. 'I'm waiting for an answer.'

His companion slowly sipped his wine, eyes fixed on David. 'This is a small world, my friend. A very small world.'

'I can do without the homilies.'

'But what you can't do without, as we both know, is a job. And you've put paid to that. Marketing is an incestuous business. We all know who's doing what and where—'

'Exactly,' David interrupted. 'And my reputation is one of the best.'

'A reputation is one thing. But rumours are another.'

The silence hung between them.

David fought to control his mounting anger. 'What filthy rumours? What muck is that shit Lerner spreading about? It's all a pack of lies, whatever it is he's saying.'

'No, old boy, it's not just from Lerner, I can assure you. They are coming from other directions too. Including your friend, Fairchild.'

'That's Lerner's poison getting to him. The bastard, I'll—'

'Calm down.' Wells did not bother to hide his enjoyment. Heads turned at nearby tables. 'Have another drink, for God's sake.'

David refilled his glass but did not touch it.

'As I was saying,' Wells continued, 'this is a tight business. You can't expect favours with all those rumours flying around. Even if they're not true, people don't want to take the risk.'

With a great effort David kept his voice calm, as he asked, 'What are the rumours?'

Wells sat back and laughed awkwardly. 'I'm sure it's all a load of rubbish, David. It'll blow over.'

David kept his hands on his lap to stop himself throttling his overweight companion. 'What do they say, Graham?'

'Oh, it's just a lot of hot air. I don't believe a word of it myself. Otherwise I wouldn't be sitting here, would I?'

'What do the rumours say?'

Wells regretted mentioning them now, but it was too late. 'Oh, the usual sort of thing put out after an office carve up. Incompetence and unreliability. That kind of comment.' He was too embarrassed to tell it all.

David shook his head. 'No one believes that rubbish. Everyone knows that's just sour grapes.'

'Sure. Like after a divorce, they both claim the other was useless in bed.'

'Exactly. So what else do they say, Graham?'

Wells looked at the handsome face, the angry blue eyes and the easy elegance. His own perpetual battle against flab and baldness fired his resentment and opened his mouth.

'To be honest with you, there are some really heavy things being whispered around.'

David waited, expressionless.

Wells hesitated, then continued, 'One of them is that you're . . . not well. Not well at all. And that you're drinking too much and knocking your wife about. Put her in hospital, they say.'

David stared at Wells, aghast. 'I did no such thing. She had an accident, that's all. Who the hell is . . .?' He stopped, as he remembered Caroline in the hospital corridor. Her husband was the solicitor for quite a number of London clients, including a PR company. Word travels fast.

'Look, David, whether it's true or not, it doesn't really matter a damn. It'll all be forgotten soon. You'll be yesterday's news and the bastards will be tearing some other unlucky sod to bits. So just sit it out and—'

'It matters to me,' David said in a low voice. 'What else is there? What other lies?'

'Oh hell, David, forget it. What good will it do? You can't fight gossip. You can't stop them now.'

David stared at his glass. No, he couldn't stop them now. What could he prove? Who could he prove it to? It was too late. God only knew what was being said. It explained so much. The evasive replies, the reluctance to meet, the averted eyes. He knew now that it wasn't just their embarrassment that he was out of a job that made them put down the phone. No. Any one of the agencies should have snapped him up. Someone had done a hatchet job. So thorough that he could not fix the pieces back together again. That someone just had to be Lerner. But what could he prove against the bastard? Nothing.

Anger at his own impotence seethed within him, but he held

himself together. 'Graham,' he kept his voice steady, 'if, as you say, you don't believe these vicious rumours, then for God's sake give me some freelance work. It needn't be much, just enough to keep my hand in.' He loathed himself for begging.

'Sorry, old chap,' Wells replied quickly. 'Not possible. What would my clients say? They'd drop like flies if they discovered I was using you.' He shrugged. 'Just can't be done.'

'Then why the bloody hell did you agree to see me today? Just to satisfy your twisted sense of morbid curiosity?'

Wells stared back at David, then smiled. 'You've hit the nail right on the head, my friend.'

David stood up abruptly. 'Goodbye, Graham.'

Wells watched the tall figure walk disdainfully out of the wine bar. Smug satisfaction could not quite drive away the envy.

The laughter surprised him. He had not expected Jenny to be out of bed.

David dumped his briefcase in the hall and opened the sitting-room door. The two women were sitting on the floor with a large calendar of the Chippendale male performers spread out on the carpet in front of them. They were giggling, as they leaned over the big glossy pictures of the well-muscled male bodies, near naked and glistening on a Caribbean beach. Susannah Benson was running a finger tenderly over the bulging loin cloth of a dark-haired handsome, posed provocatively with a giant turtle.

'You can come and chip in my dale any time you like, you gorgeous hunk of flesh,' she breathed with exaggerated passion.

Both women burst out laughing, totally absorbed in their entertainment. David closed the door noisily and Jenny looked up in surprise.

'Oh, hello. I didn't expect you back so soon—' she began, but David interrupted.

'You seem to have made a rapid recovery since this morning.'

Susannah stood up and moved towards him. 'Hello, David.' She gave him her wide smile. 'That's my influence. I popped round to cheer her up and it's for my sake the poor girl is putting on such a brave face.' She turned to Jenny, still sitting on the floor. 'Aren't you, darling?'

'Absolutely,' Jenny grinned and held out a hand to be helped up.

David pulled her to her feet, just a little too quickly, and Jenny winced. She lowered herself gingerly on to a chair and struggled to keep her breathing shallow until the pain eased.

'You should be in bed,' he scowled.

'Don't be silly, David,' Susannah laughed. 'We were just having fun. I brought over my favourite male pin-ups to keep her entertained in her sickbed.' She bent down and scooped up the calendar, dangling the double spread of oiled muscles before him. 'Look, aren't they scrummy? Makes my mouth water.' She turned her big green eyes on him and added softly, 'Not to mention other parts of my anatomy.'

David ignored the provocation and went over to sit on the sofa. Jenny looked across at him. It was obvious the day had not been a success.

'How did the meeting go?'

David did not want to discuss it. 'So-so. It's early days yet.' He caught Susannah and Jenny's exchange of glances and it only irritated him further. 'The man's a complete turd anyway. He always was and always will be.'

Susannah came and sat beside him on the sofa. 'David,' she said quietly, 'I'm so very sorry about the job. That fool Fairchild doesn't know what he is losing.' She put her hand on his knee. 'But I'm certain you'll be snapped up in no time.'

Her sympathy was like raw acid to him. 'Sure. It'll be fine.' He stood up. 'I'll go and get changed. No point hanging around in a suit any longer.'

As he walked to the door, he pulled the tie roughly from his neck and screwed it into a tight ball. 'I won't be needing this. They let you dig ditches and sweep roads without one.'

He threw it at the sofa, but it unfurled in mid-air and floated down to the carpet. He shrugged wearily and left the room.

Jenny's back hurt as she stretched out in bed. She had clearly overdone it today, but she had to admit, she had enjoyed the afternoon. Susannah had made her laugh. She was always amusing company and her ribald stories had briefly taken Jenny's mind off her own concerns. The merest whiff of testosterone and her friend was transformed into a blonde praying mantis. Jenny smiled to herself as she recalled that a female mantis devours its mate after the sexual act is completed.

Susannah had been reluctant to leave. She had prolonged the conversation with local gossip and tales of rumoured uncouplings, until David had reappeared. Then she had set to work with a skill that Jenny was forced to admire. Her easy flattery, her apparently artless sincerity had soothed his ragged nerves and boosted his battered ego. When Jenny had left the room to bring in a tray of cheese and pâté with hunks of French bread, she had been astonished on her return to find David laughing helplessly at one of Susannah's juicier anecdotes.

'Darling,' Susannah had cooed belatedly, 'you shouldn't be doing that.' She had jumped up and taken the tray from Jenny's hands. Then, summoning wine from David, she had amused them with a story of her latest triumph on the golf course over one of Robert's most important clients.

'So Robert has gone off in a huff to some foreign clime in the Far East without forgiving me for humiliating the silly old fool he was trying to impress,' she laughed. Leaning towards David on the sofa, she whispered confidentially, 'I'll have to make it up to him when he gets home, won't I?'

David had smiled at her indulgently. 'Lucky Robert.'

His gaze had slid very deliberately from her laughing green eyes to her breasts. However fond Jenny was of her friend and grateful for her mellowing influence over David, that was when she decided to bring the visit to an end.

Soon after, with a brief brushing of cheeks and promises to ring, Susannah had driven off in her gleaming white Celica turbo. The room had felt cold and silent without her. During the rest of the evening David had become increasingly gloomy. Eventually he had given Jenny a brief resumé of his meeting with Graham Wells, but she needed to know more.

She eased herself further down on the pillows. He had mentioned that there were rumours, but had not been specific. How much did he know? Or suspect? She had to find out. Her head was throbbing, but she did not want to take one of the sleeping tablets she had been prescribed. She was saving them.

It was late when David finally came to bed. As he slid under the duvet, rattling her ribs, she could smell the drink on him. He rolled over on his side and pulled the cover high over his shoulder. For a long time he lay like that, unmoving in the blackness, but his rigid body betrayed his wakefulness.

Jenny reached out a hand and softly touched his bare back. 'David,' she whispered.

A low grunt was the only response.

'David.' She gently ran her fingers down his tense muscles. 'I know things look bad now, but don't give up hope. We can fight our way through this mess, I know we can.' Her fingers continued to stroke his spine.

There was silence for a while, then at last David turned towards her. 'Let's face it, I don't stand a chance in hell of finding another job in marketing. Not a bloody chance. There's no point either of us pretending.' The misery in his voice filled the dark room.

Jenny gently put her arms around him, pulling him closer to her. With a deep moan, he buried his face in the comfort of her naked breasts and clung to her warmth. She slowly stroked his hair again and again, murmuring softly, 'It'll be all right. I'm here.' His fierce grip was crushing her ribs, but she kept up a steady flow of soothing reassurance.

After some time, she felt his body start to relax and his hold on her loosened. With gentle probing, she coaxed from him the contents of the rumours he knew about and his suspicions of those he didn't. Responsibility he placed firmly at Lerner's door, though Caroline came in for heated abuse for being the source of lies about his private life. Jenny continued to hold him close, as he poured out his pain and despair.

She smiled to herself in the darkness as she thought of Sarah. Her abrupt disappearance indicated that she too had been fired and the fact that she had not been in touch with David at all suggested that she had probably been informed of the contents of the two anonymous letters. Had fled in fear. Fairchild getting rid of David's mistress was a bonus Jenny had not anticipated. Perhaps even now she was cowering in her bed, too scared to

approach a hospital for tests. Jenny restrained the urge to gloat
and concentrated on gentling David to a calmer state.

At last, she raised his head and kissed him lovingly on the lips –
then more urgently to awaken his desire for her. He was slow to
respond at first, but eventually his need to assert his virility was
overwhelming.

She allowed him to make love to her very cautiously, as each
thrust jarred her newly knit bones. He was gentle, careful to please
her, as well as himself. When at last he was spent, he kept his arm
wrapped round her and settled his head on her shoulder. She lay
there silently and let him fall asleep in that position, but it was a
long time before her own eyes closed.

Her mind was racing. Beside her, David's breathing was slow and
even, though once or twice he moaned softly and gripped her arm.
What black scenes crowded his dreams? she wondered. He needed
her now. She was all he had.

9

The muted trombone of Glenn Miller drifted from the open window of the Mercedes, as Jenny approached the garage from the house. There was the first hint of autumn chill in the air, but the garden was still ablaze with colour. She glanced critically at the pot of geraniums and trailing lobelia that bordered the drive, noting a few dead heads that needed attention. The lawns cried out to be cut as well. She would have to get David on to that while she was out.

One of the up-and-over doors of the double garage stood open and David, in jeans and tee shirt, was squeezing out a sponge into a bucket of water. He looked up as she stood in the doorway.

'Thought I might as well give the Merc a once-over.'

Jenny looked at the dark blue saloon with its gleaming paintwork. It didn't need cleaning.

'But you only did it a couple of days ago,' she protested, 'and it hasn't rained since.'

David moved to the back of the garage, bent over and started sponging the car's front wing. 'I know, but it's very dusty.'

He rubbed vigorously along the curve of the wheel-arch until he was satisfied, then tossed the sponge into the bucket. It landed with a soft splat that washed a wave of water on to the concrete floor.

'Christ knows, there's fuck all else for me to do with my time.' He snatched the cleaning leather from where it was resting on the bonnet of the car and ran it quickly over the damp wing.

After a moment's uncomfortable silence, Jenny commented, 'There's plenty for you to do in the garden.'

David looked up sharply. 'No thanks.'

'The lawns need mowing.'

As he bent over the car, she heard him mutter something under his breath. He had always loathed gardening and usually left it all to her, just helping out with an occasional spade or saw when the work was particularly hard. But now things were different.

'David, I can't manage to handle the mower yet. It's too heavy. Please have a go at them. They're looking awful.'

'I'll see.' That meant 'no'.

He rinsed out the leather and replaced it on the bonnet while he squeezed the sponge in the bucket. As he did so, he noticed the car keys in her hand.

'Going out?'

'Yes, I've got a few things to get at the shops.'

David stood up and stared at her. 'But you're not well enough to drive. It's not safe. You can't even turn and look over your shoulder properly. You'd be a danger on the roads. Forget it. If you can't mow, you certainly can't drive.'

'Handling the mower and handling the car are completely different, David. The steering is power assisted and takes no effort.'

'I still say you're not driving. Not yet.' He hated her to go out, leaving him alone. Already his own company was anathema.

'That's absurd. Anyway, I'm meeting someone for coffee afterwards.'

He straightened up to his full height and picked the chamois leather off the bonnet. 'I said you should stay at home. No driving today. It's too soon.'

Jenny kept her voice calm. 'I assure you, I would not attempt to drive if I did not think it was perfectly safe. I've already arranged it.'

'Then un-arrange it.'

'No, I'm fine for driving.'

David bent down to the bucket, tossing the leather back on to the bonnet as he did so. He did not see the damp cloth roll too far and slide down the far curve to land on the dusty concrete floor. Jenny looked at it lying at her feet, then picked it up.

David was still engrossed in squeezing out the sponge and starting on the door panels. His voice was sneering. 'And which of your gossiping friends is supposed to be in for this treat today?'

'Caroline.'

'Caroline Palmer? That settles it. You're not going to town and that's final.'

Jenny inspected the collection of fine grit on the leather and replaced it carefully on the bonnet. 'Don't be so—'

David stood up and glared at her across the car. 'I'm not having you get together with that bitch. Not after what she's done to me.' The subject was closed. He walked round to the far side of the car and started sponging the other wing.

Jenny's fingers tightened on the keys. She stepped nearer the Mercedes. 'That's stupid. You have no proof at all that it was Caroline who spread those rumours. I'm sure she didn't. We've been good friends for years and I don't intend to lose her now over nothing.'

'Nothing? You call muddying my reputation nothing?'

'In this case, yes. Because the rumour is far more likely to have come from your office while I was in hospital than from Caroline. There's no such thing as friends in business.' She walked across the garage to the door in front of her Honda and swung it open.

'Jenny,' David called. 'I'm telling you not to meet that trouble-maker. For God's sake, how can you possibly want to even talk to her now? There's something called loyalty, you know. Or have you forgotten?'

Jenny stood for a second, keys in hand and answered quietly, 'No, I haven't forgotten. Loyalty. To husbands. And to wives.' She unlocked the car door. 'I'll see you around lunchtime.'

David turned angrily back to his own car and seized the chamois leather from the bonnet. As Jenny drove out of the garage, in her rear-view mirror she could see him fiercely rubbing the paintwork of the Mercedes with it.

Caroline Palmer was surprised to find the little restaurant quite full. On a Wednesday morning there was usually only a handful

of locals who gathered to sip the superb coffee and indulge in the
latest gossip over a croissant or two. A coach party of Germans en
route to Windsor had chosen to break their journey at Hambury
and had invaded the local coffee shops.

Just before eleven, Jenny walked in and Caroline watched
the teutonic heads turn. There was very little sign now of her
injuries. A faint shadow around the eyes and a slight stiffness in
her movements were the only indications of her recent trauma.
Her dark hair was brushed over the scar on her head and her
slim figure was as elegant as ever in a long navy blazer over a
silky cream blouse and tight cream cords.

Caroline smiled a greeting. 'Welcome to the Bavarian beer
festival.'

Jenny looked around and laughed. 'I'd better order a piece of
Black Forest gâteau with my coffee then.' She lowered herself
gingerly on to the chair.

'So how are you feeling now? You sounded a bit down on the
telephone. But you look just great to me today.'

Jenny smiled gratefully. 'Thanks.'

The waitress hovered just long enough to take their order
for coffee and croissants. Then she whisked away to the next
table, where she struggled valiantly with requests for 'Kuchen'
and 'Sahne'.

'I still get very tired, but this extra activity today seems to
be doing me good. It's got the old adrenaline flowing again.
Though I did have awful trouble parking the car.' She winced
at the memory of trying to peer behind her.

'I could have come and picked you up to save you driving.'

'No, thanks anyway. It's best this way. Anyway, I wanted to
get out of the house.' Seeing Caroline's frown, she quickly added,
'Now don't take that the wrong way. I mean I just needed a
change of scene to take me out of myself. That's all.'

Caroline looked at her speculatively. 'And how is David
reacting to domesticity? He must be missing his daily fix of
office ego-boosting. Suffering withdrawal symptoms?'

'A bit,' Jenny admitted. 'But that's inevitable. He's certainly
very touchy.' She pulled a face. 'Black moods of paranoia. He is
convinced he's being prevented from finding a new job because

of some master-minded plot.' She smiled ruefully. 'It's very hard for him.'

'I don't suppose it's exactly a piece of cake for you, either, having his gloomy face around all day. But you mustn't let it get you down. He'll find something soon.' She paused and eyed Jenny closely. 'He's not drinking, is he?'

Jenny looked away and her eyes fell on a blonde young woman who was talking loudly in German at the next table, trying to fathom the mysteries of 'Welsh Rarebit' on the morning menu.

'Oh hell,' Caroline moaned, 'now they'll report us to the blasted EC Commission for misrepresentation of food. It's not Welsh and it's not a rabbit.'

Jenny laughed and made a start on her croissant. But Caroline did not let her escape so easily.

'Well? Tell me. Has he hit the bottle? Sought refuge in the weak man's hard-on? Because if he has and starts in on you again, I'll—'

'No, Caroline, no,' Jenny insisted. 'He's had no more than the occasional glass. Honestly. And I promise you he's never touched me in anger.' She looked down at the flaky fragment in her hand. 'I told you. It was an accident.' This was the worst bit. Their friendship deserved better, but she needed Caroline to be convinced of David's guilt. To spread the rumours that would close the doors. Isolate him. She took no comfort from the fact that her words were truthful, knowing that her intention to mislead was not.

Caroline snorted her incredulity, but refrained from challenging her friend outright. 'So what's he doing with himself?'

'It's awful. He's tried everybody he knows. Every head-hunter, all his contacts, but he's come up with zilch. Freelance work seems to have dried up completely. Everywhere he hits a blank wall. No one wants to know.'

Caroline looked hard at Jenny. 'Perhaps there's a good reason for it.'

'Don't say that.'

Caroline sighed and patted Jenny's arm. 'Okay, my dreamer,

stay up in your clouds, but don't let them transform into black thunderheads with you trapped inside.'

'Don't worry, I won't. In fact, I'm being extremely practical at the moment, both feet firmly on the ground.'

'Oh yes? And what does that mean?'

Jenny grinned. 'I'm applying for a job.'

'What?' Caroline almost choked on her coffee.

Jenny laughed. 'It's not much of a job, but it's a start and I feel one of us should be working, just for the sake of morale.'

Caroline looked at Jenny with concern. 'You're not in a financial mess, surely? The company must have given David a generous golden handshake to be able to get rid of him so quickly.'

'Yes, it did, thank goodness, so we're fine financially with a reassuringly comfortable nest egg earning a healthy interest in the bank, but it won't last forever and who knows when David will manage to find something? This country is only too full of talented forty-year-olds dumped on the scrap heap. I'm preparing for the future.'

'So, spill the beans. What's the job?'

'A new NOW shop is opening in the High Street and they want someone to help organise and run it. I saw their advert in the local paper.'

'What in heaven's name is a NOW shop?'

'Surely you've heard of them. It stands for "Nature is Our World". Like the National Trust shops, they're big into raising funds for conservation throughout the world. Endangered species and all that kind of thing.'

'Well, good luck to you. If you get the job, you'll be raising money for David and, as we all know, the likes of him are fast becoming an endangered species,' Caroline chuckled.

Jenny smiled at her over the top of her steaming cup. 'Yes, I think you're right. Endangered is exactly how I would describe his situation.'

The envelope finally dropped through the letter box. Jenny had been waiting impatiently for two weeks. She recognised the green logo and scooped it up into her dressing-gown pocket.

The rest of the post she carried through to the kitchen, where David was sitting slumped with a mug in his hand in front of breakfast television.

He rifled through the letters and then pushed them aside in disgust. 'Just bloody bills and junk mail.' He turned back to the attractive blonde reading the news and lapsed once more into silence.

'I'm going to take a shower,' Jenny said to the back of his head and hurried out of the room.

She could hardly contain her eagerness to read the contents of the pocketed letter. Anyway, she hated morning television and loathed David's recent habit of letting it wash over him with its vivid sensationalism. It was just too garish at that time of the day.

She shut the bathroom door and leaned against it to regain her breath. She still had trouble with her ribs occasionally, especially after climbing stairs, but each day she noticed a further improvement and was already putting herself through a routine of exercises that was not too strenuous.

She pulled out the cream envelope and looked at the NOW initials printed in bright green in the corner. She shut her eyes for a moment and willed the contents to be the offer of the job. Holding her breath, she tore open the flap and lifted out the sheet of paper. Her eyes scanned swiftly down the page and she exhaled with relief. The job was hers.

She tucked the letter back in her pocket and started to run the shower. As the hot water flowed down her back, its warmth eased the ache in her ribs. Leisurely she washed her hair and when she saw the shampoo bubbles sliding down on to her breasts, it reminded her of that afternoon in the London hotel with her husband, when he had stepped into the shower beside her. Granted her a few fleeting moments of his precious time. Well, now he had all the time in the world. Hours and hours and hours of it. Alone all day while she was out working, earning the money and the status.

She smiled as she pictured the hunched figure in the kitchen in front of the colourful screen.

*   *   *

'We look forward to your starting on Monday then, Mrs Cranshaw.'

The new manager was in his mid-thirties, with a moustache and dark wavy hair. He clearly relished the prospect of an attractive female assistant to brighten his days and it was obvious even to Jenny that it was her looks that had won her the position, rather than any skills. He escorted her to the door, leaving his arm around her shoulders just a little longer than politeness required.

In the doorway, she turned round and her dark eyes smiled warmly up at him. 'I know I'll enjoy working for you, Mr Thompson.'

'I'm sure we'll get on well, but do call me Steve. We'll make a good team.' His grin revealed a chipped tooth that marred his dark good looks.

Jenny shook his hand firmly and waved a cheery goodbye. Christ, not another male ego that had to be massaged and stimulated until it stood erect. Out of the frying pan . . .

Nevertheless, as she walked back to her car, she decided she was actually looking forward to the job. Now that David was around all day, the house felt claustrophobic. She was spending more and more time down by the river. David didn't even bother to question where she went any more, so preoccupied was he with his constant typing of letters and scouring of the newspapers' appointments pages. Or even with the latest antics of the daytime soaps. Conversations tended to be brief.

Until now, she had shied away from revealing her prospective employment to him, but the time had come when she would have to confront the task. She couldn't put it off any longer. Today he was trying the London head-hunters once more, so at least she did not have to face him until the evening.

As she started the engine, she made the decision to drive into Tonbridge for a quick bite to eat and then go shopping. A couple of new outfits were just what she needed, a treat to boost her morale on her first week at work.

'Spare a few pence, guv?' A dirty mittened hand was thrust in front of his face, but David brushed it aside. That was the trouble with Oxford Street: if it wasn't hordes of tourists, it was bloody beggars.

He strode on past the John Lewis department store, using his briefcase as a buffer against the crush of pedestrians. Long years of habit kept his back straight and his step firm in public, but yet another morning of rejection and closed doors had hollowed his stomach with despair. The last agency had delivered the ultimate blow. The young manager, with a permanent smile pasted across his face, had shaken his head and murmured, 'It's your age, you see. Forty is just too high these days.'

David had clenched his fists at his side and enquired politely, 'Surely there must be something in the marketing line? Executives are always moving around from agency to agency. There are constantly vacancies created by mobility.'

The smile widened. 'I'm doing all I can for you, Mr Cranshaw. I've put your name about as much as possible, but there aren't any takers at present, I'm afraid.' He smoothed his slicked-back hair. 'As I say, it must be your age.' An apologetic slant tilted the smile.

'That's damned ridiculous. I'm not in my dotage yet, for Christ's sake.'

'I'm sure something will come up soon. We've got all our feelers out on your behalf and I'll let you know the minute we get a response. Don't you worry. We'll keep plugging away at it.' The reassurance flowed with professional ease.

David had left the office with the strong feeling that the world was now run for and by twenty-year-olds. Twenty-five was the top limit. His visit to the previous 'executive placing' agency had been just as depressing. The only response that his applications achieved was, at best, a numbingly polite letter of rejection. He had a bloody drawer full of them.

As he took a right off Oxford Street, heading without any real hope for the next agency, he asked himself for the thousandth time what the hell Lerner could have spread around about him. Incompetence? Alcoholism? Given the viciousness of business bust-ups, a potential employer should at least grant an interview to judge for himself. Wife-beating? Definitely worse, could involve police. But surely not even that would have swept with such wild fire through the marketing world. But sure as hell, something had. And whatever it was, it . . .

A swing of long dark hair jerked him out of the thoughts merrygoing round his head. A flash of green and she was gone.

David's heart was pounding as he turned and raced across the road, dodging a blaring taxi and the squealing wheels of a delivery van. He ignored the protests, as he pushed his way through groups of shoppers clogging the pavements. He had to find her. Just that brief glimpse, but he was sure it was her.

He took to the roadway and ran up to the crossroads. Desperately he searched in every direction, his eyes sweeping the mass of bobbing figures for the dark, sleek head. Where the hell had she gone? She couldn't just have disappeared. He took a guess and veered left, running on the road alongside the pavement, oblivious to the on-coming traffic. Frantically he sought that flash again and for a moment, his hopes were raised by a glimpse of green on the other side of the road. He dashed across through a gap in the traffic, but as he came closer, he saw the blonde curls and realised his mistake.

He stopped. She couldn't have got this far. He swung round and raced back the way he had come, across the intersection and down the opposite street. The crush of pedestrians was thinner here and quickly he covered the whole of the block. Nothing, no sign of her swinging walk and that dense curtain of hair.

He was breathing hard from the unaccustomed exercise, but he refused to give up yet. As he hurried down the next turning that brought him back to Oxford Street, his hopes were fading fast. He had lost her. Again. But still he continued to search. She could have gone into any one of the myriad shops on each side of the wide thoroughfare.

He pushed past a group of gawpers outside Selfridges and as he stood on the edge of the pavement, scanning the opposite side of the road through the steady stream of taxis and buses that flowed past him, he saw a flash of movement out of the corner of his eye. Off to his right, a figure with long dark hair and a green jacket was making a dash across the top of Park Lane to reach Hyde Park. There was an underpass designed for pedestrians to avoid the heavy traffic, but nevertheless, this girl darted across the road, with a group of teenage boys close behind her.

David struggled to see her clearly, but the boys blocked his view. Desperate to reach her, David ran along the road but was forced to wait for a lull in the traffic. The nearest pedestrian crossing was too far away and finally, losing patience, he plunged between two buses. An angry shout from the driver of one followed him across the street, but he did not look back.

Clutching his briefcase, he set off for the park, dodging and weaving through the meandering pedestrians, until at last he reached the underpass. He took a chance on losing sight of the girl but gaining time by avoiding the traffic. He raced down the steps and through the echoing tunnel. When he emerged at the other end into the open grassland of Hyde Park itself, he could just see the girl in the distance. She was walking briskly along one of the paths, with the group of teenagers still closely bunched around her. David could not decide whether they were accompanying her or pestering her. By now his face was flushed and he was panting hard. He took a deep breath and forced his legs to make one more effort. He ran along the path and gained strength from seeing the gap narrowing, making out part of her dark head among the taller figures around her.

One of the boys had his arm across her shoulders. That stopped him in his tracks. Perhaps she wouldn't want to see him. Could this be the father of the unborn child? Anger drove him on. Damn her. And damn the unwanted bastard.

When he was only a hundred yards from them, the path wound behind a tall group of bushes and they disappeared from view. Spurred on by the sound of their laughter, David forced a way through the undergrowth and suddenly emerged right behind them.

There were five boys. All about eighteen or so, dressed in the ubiquitous jeans and black tee shirts, with heavy Doc Martens on their feet. The tallest was obviously the leader of the pack and was the one with his arm round the girl's slender shoulders. The others were crowding round, calling encouragement in raucous jeers.

'Go on, Greg, give it to her.'

'Don't be shy. She's begging for it.'

The leader had his back to David, his arm tightly pulling her to him and his body masking hers from David's view. The sudden shrill cry of alarm from the girl was unmistakably one of fear and panic.

He stepped up behind the teenager and grabbed his arm, yanking it away from the green jacket. 'Let her go, you filthy scum.'

The moment he pulled the boy's arm, he knew he was mistaken. It wasn't her. The hair was too wavy and she was a fraction too tall. Before she even turned, disappointment thudded through him.

The band of teenagers abandoned the girl and turned on him like snarling wolves. Hardly aware of their threats and taunts or of the girl's tearful gratitude, he grabbed her wrist and dragged her back into the open area of the park, where others were walking their dogs and eating their lunchtime sandwiches.

'Fancy her yerself, do you, old lecher?' the frustrated leader called after him.

'Fucking cradle snatcher.'

'Bet you can't even get it up, grandad.'

The girl was embarrassed, but thanked her rescuer profusely. David kept a wary eye on the departing youths, as they sauntered off in search of fresh entertainment, then turned to look at the girl. Yes, there was a strong general resemblance, but her features were not as fine, nor her figure so trim.

He waved aside her thanks and walked abruptly away. He resented her for not being the one he sought. For tricking his senses. Blamed her for re-awakening all his longing and raising his carefully suppressed hopes.

A wooden bench stood empty beside the path and suddenly his legs gave way. His heart hammered and his chest hurt. He threw himself down on to the seat and dropped his head in his hands.

'Sarah,' he moaned. 'Sarah.'

Jenny was pleased with her purchases. She had managed to find a very stylish suit in a soft blue crepe that showed off her figure to perfection. The other was a heavier dog-tooth check jacket in black and white with a short black skirt, that made her feel very businesslike. She had added a white silk blouse for good measure and now felt ready for the fray next week. Mr Thompson had better watch his step.

Swinging her carrier bags loosely, she walked back down the High Street.

'You look bright and chirpy.'

The voice at her shoulder made Jenny look round in surprise. She smiled warmly. 'Hello, Caroline. What are you doing here?'

'Been seeing a client. God, he's a dreary one, too. A nine-stone weakling who is aiming to get everything he can from his Amazonian wife in the divorce court. Poor sod hasn't a hope.' She slipped her arm confidentially through Jenny's. 'But tell me, tell me, how did the job interview go?'

Jenny grinned smugly.

'You got it. Good for you.' She hugged Jenny enthusiastically, but quickly released her as she felt the slight body wince with pain. 'Hell, I'm sorry, I forgot. Are you all right?'

'I'll live,' Jenny laughed and breathed carefully a few times.

Caroline Palmer watched her with concern, but could not understand how, despite her recent injury, Jenny could appear so full of health and vitality. Her dark hair gleamed in the afternoon sunshine and there was a spring in her step. It was a pleasure to see and gave Caroline reassurance that whatever had been wrong at home before, it was definitely on the mend. Probably the prospect of earning an income of her own contributed as well.

'And how's David?'

The smile slid from Jenny's face. 'Not too good. He's up in London again today, but he didn't hold out much hope. Each week that passes seems to eat away at him. At his belief in himself.'

Caroline nodded. 'It's a tough time for him. But I can't believe he'll be out of work very long. Not with all his skills and contacts.'

Jenny appreciated the transparent attempt to infuse optimism.

'Of course,' she agreed and changed the subject. 'Look, have you finished here? As David is in London until this evening and I feel like celebrating my new job, how about coming back home with me for a wildly exciting cup of tea. We might even indulge in something stronger.'

She saw Caroline hesitate.

'I've baked a cake.'

'You've talked me into it,' Caroline laughed. 'How can I resist an offer like that?' She patted her expanding waistline. 'No willpower, that's my trouble.' She looked enviously at Jenny's slight figure. 'Come on then, Miss Skinny, lead me to it.'

Jenny was glad to turn off the congested main road and drive along the quieter suburban streets. She glanced in her rear-view mirror to make certain that Caroline was still following her. Though only just after four thirty, the rush hour traffic was beginning to build up and they had been forced to crawl bumper to bumper between traffic lights.

At the end of the leafy avenue, she swung into her own drive-way. Deciding not to bother putting away the car, she pulled up in front of the house and with skidding gravel, Caroline parked behind her. They entered the house with Jenny's packages in their arms and made straight for the kitchen.

'Let's see what you've bought,' Caroline said, as she started opening the bags.

Jenny busied herself making the tea and laying it out on a tray, while Caroline admired the new outfits. She held the blue suit up against her own bulky figure and sighed. 'It's gorgeous. All your customers will be so busy looking at you, they won't even notice how much money they're spending.'

Jenny laughed and Caroline picked up the tray. She followed Jenny across the hall to the sitting-room, but as she opened the door, Jenny stopped dead. Caroline collided with her rigid body, slopping milk on to the tray.

'David!' Jenny exclaimed in surprise. And then in dismay, 'Oh no, David.'

He was stretched out on the sofa, snoring loudly. An empty glass lay on its side on the floor where it had fallen. Beside it stood a half-empty whisky bottle. At the sound of his wife's voice, David's head jerked up and his eyes fought to focus clearly. 'Where the hell have you been?' he mumbled. The words came out slurred.

Caroline placed the tray on a low table and turned away from David. Jenny's voice was tense. 'I've been shopping. I didn't expect you back until this evening.'

'Obviously.' He eyed Caroline belligerently. 'And what is this bitch doing here?' He swung his legs to the floor, knocking over the bottle. 'I don't want her in my house. I thought I'd made that abundantly clear.'

Jenny coloured with embarrassment. 'David, for heaven's sake—'

'It's all right, Jenny, don't worry,' Caroline interrupted. She looked at David coldly. 'If I'd known you were here, I would not have put a foot over the threshold, but now that I know you're drunk, it's probably just as well I did. God knows what you would—'

David stood up, furious. The effort made his head spin and he swayed unsteadily. 'I'm not drunk, damn you.' Not drunk enough to forget the girl in the park.

Jenny tried to soothe the situation. 'We're just going to have some tea.' She turned to the tray. 'Would you like some, David?'

'Not that cat's piss you drink.' But he sat down again.

'As we're celebrating Jenny's job, you could at least drink a toast to it. Or is that what you've been doing on your own all afternoon?'

'What the hell are you talking about? What job?'

'Oh damn, I'm sorry, Jenny. I didn't know you hadn't told him yet.'

'Told me what? What bloody job?'

Jenny shrugged. 'Never mind, Caroline. I was going to tell him this evening anyway.'

'Tell me what, for Christ's sake?'

Jenny sat down in an armchair opposite David and took a deep breath to still her nerves. 'I've got a job in Hambury. Working in the new shop that's just setting up in the High Street. I thought it would help if at least one of us was working.' She paused as she saw disbelief in David's face swept aside by anger.

'I start on Monday,' she added.

'Like hell you will.'

'It's all settled. It'll help us—'

'Help you, you mean. Not me.'

'Us, David. I'm doing this for us.'

'So it's not enough for you that I'm out of work. You've got to rub my nose in it too.'

'David, that's not fair. I'm trying to help. We can't—'

Caroline cut in, 'For God's sake, David, count your lucky stars you've got a wife who is willing to stand by you. You don't deserve her loyalty, after what you've done. So just be grateful she's—'

David lunged to his feet. 'Get out of here, you bitch. Don't interf . . .' He stumbled over the word and tried again. 'Don't interfere where you're not welcome. We don't want you.'

'I bet you don't,' Caroline snapped. 'But I don't intend to let you—'

'Caroline, don't,' Jenny pleaded. 'Please don't.'

Caroline glanced across at Jenny's miserable expression and stopped. 'Okay, if that's what you want, I'll keep my big mouth shut.'

'Thank God for small mercies,' David sniped. He threw himself back on to the sofa, reached down for the bottle and poured himself a fresh drink.

Jenny came and stood beside him. 'Please, David.'

He looked up at her and laughed unpleasantly as he raised his glass to her. 'Here's to your success, my wonderful wife. My humble congratu . . . gratul . . .' He abandoned the attempt and drank the whisky.

Jenny turned and picked up the tray. 'We'll have our tea in the kitchen, Caroline,' she said quickly and hurried from the room.

Caroline stood in the doorway and looked back at David's crumpled form. 'You're a damned disgrace, David Cranshaw. You've no backbone.'

David just scowled at her and refilled his glass.

'Take a good hard look at yourself, David. Then get up off your arse and for God's sake, climb out of the mire of your self-pity. Start putting a new life together before you drown in that stuff.'

He did not even bother to turn his head, but muttered into his glass, 'Just fuck off.'

Caroline left the room, slamming the door behind her.

In the kitchen Jenny was sitting at the table with her cup untouched in front of her. Caroline took the seat opposite and for a while they just sat there in silence, both absorbing the shock of their encounter with David.

When Caroline trusted herself to speak calmly, she said, 'If he continues like this, Jenny, you can't stay with—'

'Caroline,' Jenny interrupted, looking up from the table, 'he's my husband. You don't understand.' Her breath came in short gasps. It was all going so fast.

'You told me he wasn't drinking, but what I saw in there was certainly more than the "occasional glass".'

Jenny hung her head. 'I know.' Her voice was little more than a whisper.

'You've been lying to me, haven't you?'

Jenny nodded miserably.

'So how can I know what to believe and what not to believe?'

'You don't understand. It's more complicated than you realise.'

'I just don't want to see you hurt, Jenny.'

'I won't be, I promise. I can handle him.'

'That's not what it looked like in there, with him reeking of booze and aggression.' Her disgust was palpable. 'I don't trust him.'

For a fleeting second, Jenny was tempted to open up to Caroline, to tell her the truth. It would be such a relief to shed the pretence and share the stress. But the moment passed. It would be disastrous, would put an end to all her plans. Caroline, the solicitor, would advocate the obvious solution. Just leave him, she would urge. How could she understand? That would be too simple. Too easy for David.

Jenny shook her head. 'He's not normally like this. I don't know what has upset him today. Probably more job rejections from the London agencies. It hurts to be told you're a failure.'

'Okay, okay, I get the message. But remember, I'm always at the end of a telephone. Any time of day or night.'

Jenny smiled gratefully. 'Thanks, Caroline. You're a good friend.'

'Well, let this good friend have a chunk of that gorgeous cake.'

'Of course.' Jenny started to cut a slice.

'I had better make the most of it while I can. Now you've joined the ranks of the overworked, you won't have time for home baking any more.' She took a bite from the generous portion Jenny had placed on her plate. 'Mmmm, delicious,' she mumbled with her mouth full. 'But aren't you going to have any?'

'No, I don't feel like eating.'

Caroline took another bite. 'David will certainly miss these from now on.'

Jenny looked down and stared into her tea. 'I know. There's a lot he'll find different now that I'll be working.' She raised her eyes to Caroline. 'That's why he thinks I'm just rubbing his nose in it.'

'Don't be silly. Take no notice of that. That was the drink talking. When he's sober, he'll realise how necessary it is.'

'I hope you're right.'

'Don't worry. Anyway, you'd both go mad closeted together all day. Eventually you'd end up just taking out your worries on each other. Disastrous. I've seen it a thousand times en route to the divorce courts.'

Caroline stretched out a hand and patted Jenny's arm. 'I assure you you're doing the right thing by getting a job.' She paused, then added, 'But most of all, it's important for David to realise that this is a whole new life. It's no good his hankering for what's past. He's got to start again. And your job will help to reinforce that. It's a new life for both of you.'

Jenny did not comment, but sipped her tea.

'I know it'll be hard for him,' Caroline continued. 'A person's job is their identity and unemployment means the loss of their self-image. But don't worry,' she smiled encouragingly, 'I'm sure he'll soon find a position somewhere. Just as long as it's not under the table.'

Jenny glanced up in alarm.

'Just joking.'

'He doesn't normally act like this,' Jenny said firmly. 'I've never seen him so drunk.'

'I'll believe you, if you say so. But to be honest, from the evidence, thousands wouldn't.'

'It's true,' Jenny insisted.

Caroline let it ride and steered the conversation to other topics. She related the gory details of a splendid row at the aerobics class the previous week, when one member insisted on chewing gum during the exercises. It came down to a ferocious battle of wills between Amy and the girl and eventually Amy threw her out of the class.

'It certainly added spice to the grind. We all got a great adrenaline kick out of it. Amy was amazed how well we performed afterwards.' She chuckled at the memory, as she popped the last piece of her second slice of cake into her mouth and finished her tea. 'Knowing you, I expect you'll be back at the torture class in no time. But don't rush into it too early. Take care of yourself. Get David to do more for you.'

'He does help. Honestly.'

'Yes, I can just imagine him with a pinny round his waist and a hoover in his hand.' She rose and smiled down at Jenny. 'You're too loyal, that's your trouble. What would he do without you?'

Jenny's brown eyes darkened. 'He needs me now more than ever.'

'Of course he does. The question is, Jenny, do you need him?'

A faint smile crept over Jenny's lips, surprising Caroline. 'I guess I do. Or I wouldn't be here, would I?'

'It's just that I'm worried about you.'

Jenny squeezed Caroline's hand. 'I know and I do appreciate it. But really, I'm fine.'

Kate Sharam

'Well, good luck on Monday. Go out there and give 'em hell.'

Jenny laughed and escorted her to the door. After promising to let her know how it went and to take good care of her ribs, she waved Caroline's car out of the drive. Then she returned to the kitchen and cut herself a large slice of cake.

The bottle of milk slipped from her grasp and crashed to the ground. A white lake spread its fingers across the floor and ran in pale rivulets between the dark tiles.

'Damn,' Jenny cursed, and bent to retrieve the shattered remains of the bottle. The trouble was she wasn't concentrating on what she was doing. Her mind was flitting back and forth between her fears for her first day at work at nine o'clock on Monday morning and the image of David flat on his back on the bed upstairs. She dumped the shards of glass in the bin, grabbed the floorcloth from under the sink and started mopping up the mess, careful to avoid any tiny splinters.

She had left him to sleep it off on the sofa the previous evening. Just before going to bed, she had looked in on him but he was still dead to the world and as she quietly shut the door, she had noticed that the bottle was now empty. Some time in the early hours, she had heard him noisily negotiating the stairs and he had stumbled into bed after a brief stop in the bathroom. He stank of stale whisky, so she had rolled out of bed and opened the window wider, letting in the night air that was chill but smelled sweet. She had inhaled its peaceful calm to ease her tension and in the morning she had left the curtains closed, abandoning him to his alcoholic haze.

She ran a bucket of hot water and proceeded to wash the kitchen floor until, when all trace of milk and grease was removed, she settled down to a mid-morning coffee with the newspaper spread out on the table. She was engrossed in an article on yet more proposed changes to the education system, when David opened the door.

He looked awful. His eyes were bloodshot, his skin had a grey pallor, he was unshaven and still in his dressing-gown.

'Hello,' Jenny greeted him brightly. 'How are you feeling?'

152

He walked unsteadily to the table and collapsed on to a chair. 'Horrific,' he muttered, sinking his head into his hands.

He did not see the satisfaction that spread across her face, before it was transformed into a smile of sympathy. 'Feel like coffee?'

She took the answering grunt as an affirmative. When she placed the cup in front of him, he painfully raised his head and looked at her.

'Jenny, I'm sorry.'

She waited for more.

'I don't remember much about last night, but I do recall yelling at you and that bitch, Caroline.'

Jenny kept her smile in place. 'It's all right, David. I do understand what you're going through.'

He dropped his head back into his hands. 'Hell – that's what I'm going through. Sheer bloody hell.'

She reached out and stroked the rumpled blond hair. 'It can't last forever,' she soothed. 'Just hang on in there and it'll all work out. I'm sure it will.'

David lifted his head again and her hand slid gently down his cheek. He grasped it in his own and rested his aching forehead against her palm. For a moment he stayed like that and she could almost feel the pain pulsing through him. Then he released it and picked up his coffee.

'You mentioned a job yesterday,' he said too casually.

'Yes, at the new charity shop,' she answered quietly. 'I start next Monday.'

David shrugged slightly, but the movement obviously shot a bolt through his head. He ran a hand over his eyes and murmured, 'I admit I don't like it. But just because my life has come to a full stop, I suppose there's no reason why yours should.'

The words lacked conviction and she could see they had cost him dear. They were the price for her forgiveness of his behaviour the previous evening. Forgiveness that he could no longer afford to dismiss, now that she was the only ally he possessed.

'David, I'm doing it for both of us.' She stood up and put an arm around his shoulder. 'Come on, finish your coffee and let's get you back to bed. I'll bring you some aspirin and a glass of fresh orange juice.' She smiled down at him. 'Don't worry too much. This won't go on forever.'

10

The fat woman picked up the model of the panda for the tenth time. 'I just can't decide between this cute creature or that elephant over there.' She held it out at arm's length and shook her bottle-ginger curls in indecision. 'What do you suggest, dear?'

Jenny held up the china model of the African elephant for comparison. 'They're both lovely.' She stroked the smooth curve of the animal's trunk. 'I'm sure your granddaughter would be delighted with either of them.'

'I know that. But which one of them should I choose?'

'Shall I tell you what I really think?'

'Yes, that's why I'm asking you.'

Jenny produced a brilliant smile. 'I think they would make a beautiful pair. Two of the most enchanting animals on earth.' She held the elephant right next to the black and white bear. 'Just look at them together. Your granddaughter would adore them.'

The woman pursed her orange lips, obviously tempted, but still undecided.

'They would sit on her shelf and she would think of you each time she looked at them. It's a lovely idea.' Jenny put on what she hoped was a warm and caring expression.

'You're right. I'll take them both.'

After carefully packaging the fragile objects, Jenny placed the cheque in the till and wished the departing customer a nice day.

'You've got the silver tongue and the golden charm of a siren.' Steve Thompson's deep laugh startled her.

Jenny turned and grinned smugly at him. 'Not bad for a newcomer to the game?'

'You've got the magic touch, that's certain. Each week our sales exceed our targets and I don't kid myself it's all my sexy moustache that's doing it.'

She laughed. 'I'm enjoying the work. Every person who walks in here is a challenge. Different techniques for each customer. We're lucky because at the moment we're still a novelty in the town.'

Thompson rearranged the ornaments on the display shelf to fill the gap where the elephant had been.

'I know. The poor unsuspecting innocents come in expecting to have a quiet browse and find themselves leaving with bulging bags and empty wallets. They don't know what hit them.' He walked over to her at the counter. 'But seriously, you're doing a great job.'

'Thank you. But I owe much of it to you. You've taught me a lot.'

'Much as I'd like to take the credit, I have to admit you're a natural at this selling business.' He moved towards the door at the back of the shop. 'I'll go and make us some tea. You guard the treasures.'

The relationship between the manager and herself had worked out much better than Jenny had expected. Her initial impression that he was on the prowl was soon reinforced by a succession of unsubtle passes at her during the first week. But his saving grace was his sense of humour. So after she had firmly impressed on him that she was not on offer along with the rest of the wares in the shop, he had cheerfully abandoned any further attempts at seduction. Instead, he had become an amusing and helpful companion. He had led her through the intricacies of stock control and till management and had quickly discovered her flair for window-dressing. But Jenny's true forte was in handling the customers and he left more and more of that to her.

'You're a chameleon,' he had once accused her, after he had watched her transform from the role of sympathetic daughter, when helping an elderly man choose a present for his wife, to sensitive big sister, when advising a young teenager on a gift for her mother. 'Or,' he had added, 'a bloody good actress.'

As she bent to pick up a duster, she caught a glimpse of her reflection in a wall mirror. In the check jacket and black skirt she certainly looked the part – every inch an accomplished and confident saleswoman.

The dark clouds only gathered when she arrived home in the evening. By the time she had driven through Hambury's rush hour, she was tired and her feet ached from standing all day. All she wanted to do was flop into a comfortable chair and put her feet up, but no drink arrived at her elbow, nor meal on the table.

David just sat in black gloom in front of the television, often unshaven and always moody. Once she had come home early and found him watching *Blue Peter*, his attention riveted on the details of how to build a fort out of matchboxes and loo roll tubes. She had teased him about the children's programme, but the barb had hit too close for laughter. Abruptly he had snapped off the television and stomped off upstairs.

She had little idea what he did all day and certainly the lawns remained untouched, but she had refrained from probing too much, as it only goaded him further. She still provided his meals and in return, he did the weekly shopping. Otherwise, their communication was fleeting. His sexual drive seemed to have evaporated completely and they lay without touching in bed. Rarely did he make forays up to London any more, though occasionally the odd letter would arrive for him with yet another rejection. From these she knew he was still applying for jobs, but always with no success.

A head popped round the door. 'Tea's ready,' Steve Thompson called. 'I've made us fennel today for a change.'

Jenny thanked him and accepted the cup of hot liquid with a smile. 'You spoil me.'

'It's called management skills,' he responded and they both laughed.

As she parked the car in the garage, Jenny was surprised to see David's Mercedes was missing. She let herself into the house and called out his name, but was greeted with silence.

She wandered through the rooms in case he was asleep or even drunk upstairs, but the house was empty. She found herself irritated by his absence, by not knowing what he was up to. She had got used to his always being there when she walked in, with his grunts and moody silences. As she was coming downstairs, she was startled by the front door flying open. In strode David, a confident spring in his step and a cheerful smile on his face. Clean shaven and hair trimmed, he looked smart in sports jacket and flannels with an open-necked shirt.

'Hello,' he called up to her. 'Don't look so shocked.' He tossed his jacket on the newel post and walked across the hall. 'Come and have a drink. I'm celebrating.'

Jenny stared at her transformed husband. It had to be a job. It could be nothing else. Oh God, don't let it be that. Not yet. She hadn't finished yet. Her heart thumped as she followed him and with an unsteady hand, accepted the wine he held out to her.

'Here's to success,' he grinned, as he sat down in his chair.

She raised her glass. 'Success,' she echoed.

'You said it wouldn't be forever and it looks as if you were right. A letter came this morning just after you had left for work. From Okiwa Electronics. They're a Japanese company that has just set up over here and they're looking for a marketing man who knows the ropes. And it looks like I could be that man.'

The relief in his voice was tangible. He could hardly control his excitement.

'It's not definite yet, of course. I've only had the letter from them so far, but they sound very keen.' He held up crossed fingers. 'As the company is foreign, Lerner's filthy rumours have passed them by. Their big cheese has to fly to Tokyo for a conference, so the interview isn't for a few weeks.'

'That's wonderful, David,' Jenny managed to enthuse convincingly. 'You must be thrilled. I'm sure you'll get the job.' She sipped her wine. 'But how did that make you late home?'

'Well, I just had to tell someone. To celebrate with someone. And you were at that blasted shop, so I rang Susannah.'

Jenny's eyes fixed on David's face.

'She was great. She dropped everything and treated me to a slap-up meal.'

Jenny hoped the 'everything' that she dropped did not include any items of clothing. It was not that she doubted Susannah's genuine desire to help, but when confronted by an efficient seduction scene, Jenny feared her loyalty might prove decidedly rocky.

'We had lunch at the Black Swan at Stonefield and it went on all afternoon. You know how Susannah likes to talk. And then I couldn't resist a final drink at her place, when I picked up my car.'

Jenny clasped the glass stiffly in front of her and forced herself to smile with as much sincerity as she could muster. 'How kind of Susannah.'

'Yes, we had a great afternoon. She's like a breath of fresh air. She's convinced me I've been hanging round the house too much. Vegetating to a pulp. So we've made a date for next Friday – lunch again at the Black Swan.'

Jenny's smile dropped. She had worked too hard to fail now. Damn the Japanese and damn dear Susannah. She wanted to empty the contents of her glass over David's grinning face, but instead she said calmly, 'That'll be fun. It will take you out of yourself more.'

Her mind was already racing, as he continued to tell her more details about Okiwa Electronics.

David remained in irrepressibly buoyant mood all week. The prospect of employment and a lunchdate on the horizon with an attractive female transformed him. Jenny watched the isolated figure of depression and self-doubt grow, almost physically, as each day passed, bringing with it returning arrogance and self-confidence. How could it happen so fast? The sense of failure was not yet deep enough.

At first it took time to adjust. She was not accustomed to this flurry of activity. Each evening that week, when she returned from her work, she was faced with a catalogue of fresh achievements. The hedge was trimmed, the window catch mended and even the washing machine churned gently away in its corner. Jenny listened dutifully to his accounts of his day's work, but when she found herself praising his successes and sympathising with any minor setbacks, she almost burst out laughing.

The difference was, this time round, she could afford to laugh. It was the same all over again. But totally different. He may be anticipating a playful romp with Susannah on Friday, but it was not going to be as easy as that. Her plans preoccupied her mind and she found it harder to concentrate properly on her customers. Even Steve commented that she seemed somewhat distracted these days. It was on Thursday, when Jenny returned to work after a lunchtime trip to the hardware shop, her purchase weighing down the bottom of her bag, that she found the boy sitting at the cash desk, fiddling with a couple of bongo drums.

'Hello, can I help you?' he asked, his dark eyes looking at her hopefully.

'Sorry to disappoint you,' she laughed, 'but I work here.'

'You must be Jenny Cranshaw then. I'm Jamie.'

'And what are you doing here, Jamie?'

'Looking after the shop for Dad. He's just gone out to the bank for a minute.'

So this was Steve Thompson's son. She should have guessed. He had the same mop of dark wavy hair and cheerful good looks. Steve had occasionally mentioned his twelve-year-old boy, who lived with his ex-wife in Cookham, but had not said anything about his coming into the shop today.

'So you're in charge?' she smiled.

He grinned. 'That's right.'

'Earning some money in the holidays? Make sure the manager pays you a fair wage. He's an old skinflint.'

Jamie laughed. 'No such luck. Mum suddenly had to go to Birmingham for a few days, so she dumped me here on Dad.'

'If I were you, I'd make the most of the situation. You could tidy up the stockroom for a start and there's a delivery of carvings from Nigeria to be cleaned up. They're covered in sawdust. That should be worth a few pounds anyway.'

'Great.'

At that moment a customer came into the shop and after a

cursory browse round the shelves, he selected a large, polished wooden platter with beautiful graining.

'For my sister-in-law,' he explained as he paid. 'I never know what to buy her.'

Jenny instructed Jamie in the intricacies of the electric till and bent over him as he rang up the sale. The brief touch of his warm hair against her cheek brought back such a rush of memories that for a moment she could not see clearly. She pushed them away, but still they kept coming. Mark climbing the apple tree, Mark in his first cricket flannels, Mark racing towards her on his new bike . . .

She thrust them aside, her chest tight, and concentrated on wrapping up the customer's purchase. 'I'm sure your sister-in-law will like it,' she managed to smile, just as Steve Thompson hurried into the shop.

As soon as the customer was gone, Jamie demanded, 'Dad, can I do some work round here this afternoon? As a proper job? Jenny says there's the stockroom to tidy and—'

'Okay, okay,' Steve laughed. 'If Jenny says it's all right, then that's fine with me.'

'Great. And she's already taught me how to use the till.'

'Well then, it sounds as if you could make yourself useful. As long as you pull your weight. No slacking.'

'Jamie will work hard, won't you?'

'You bet.'

'Then perhaps you can come in again tomorrow as well if you like, to earn some more,' Jenny suggested with a wink at Steve.

'Let's see how it goes today,' her boss laughed.

'Come on, Jamie, I'll show you where the stockroom is and get you started.' She let her hand rest lightly on his shoulder, as she steered him towards the back of the shop.

'Jenny,' Steve called after her.

She looked back at him. 'Yes?'

'Thanks.'

She smiled and opened the door into the stockroom.

Friday arrived. It dawned dull and overcast, but that did not seem to dampen David's spirits. Jenny's nerves grated, as she heard his whistling in the bathroom and saw him selecting his shirt with care.

If Susannah Benson only knew what she was doing. She probably really believed she was helping Jenny by inviting him out to lunch and was already preening herself on what a clever idea it was to improve her friend's home-life by coaxing David out of his shell of miserable isolation. Didn't she realise what David was like? To him an invitation to lunch came with strings attached. Strings that led straight to the bedroom. Although Susannah might mean it innocently enough, David would have other ideas.

So while David sat in the kitchen, enjoying his morning dose of toast and television, Jenny set to work. The telephones came first – both upstairs and down. Very carefully she eased the wall connectors slightly out of their sockets, so that although they still looked as if they were in place, no contact was in fact being made. She lifted each receiver to check the dead tone.

Next, taking a pair of pliers from the hall cupboard, she reached up above the front door and snipped the wire that ran to the doorbell. Her finger tested the button from outside and she was satisfied by the resulting silence. Then she walked back into the kitchen, picked up her handbag and wished David a good lunch.

'Give my love to Susannah.'

'Right, David responded without looking round.

In the garage, Jenny approached the shelf that ran the length of one side. She reached up behind a paint pot and her hand emerged clutching a small brown paper bag. The result of her trip to the hardware shop, it was bulky and obviously heavy. Inside lay a jumble of gleaming nails. They would do the job very nicely. She took out a two-inch nail and tested its point on the tip of her finger. It was sharp.

She squatted down on the ground beside the front wheel of David's Mercedes and tried the nail. It stood easily on its flat round head behind the tyre, its long point sticking up in the air. Gently she slid it forward until the metal tip just touched the rubber, then pushed harder so that it was jammed firmly against the tyre. A second nail soon accompanied the first, then she repeated the process behind the other front wheel.

When she was finished, she stood back and admired her handiwork. You would never notice them unless you were searching. When David reversed out of the garage to set off for his rendezvous, the nails would plunge like miniature stilettos into the rubber. He surely couldn't drive more than a few hundred yards before he lost all his air. That should keep him well and truly stuck at home.

The image of Susannah with her voluptuous figure and her manicured finger running lovingly over the Chippendale's crotch came into Jenny's mind. Oh God, Susannah, why have you got in the way like this? I know you're not serious, but David is oh so willing, I can't let him keep the appointment at Stonefield. No lingering lunch for him. Instead, two flat tyres, stranded by the roadside. Jenny glanced at the darkening sky. It might even rain.

And how could he ring a garage with the telephones out of order? Or even leave a message at the Black Swan. The nearest phone box was miles away. As she turned out of the driveway, she reckoned she had all options covered.

Jenny enjoyed the morning, despite the fact that she kept checking her watch, counting the minutes to when David would be turning the key in the ignition. Steve Thompson was out on a buying session, but she had Jamie for company. Together they cleaned all the shelves and she let him rearrange some of the displays. Business was quiet because, just after eleven, the skies had opened and the rain lashed down, driving all but the hardiest from the streets. By midday Steve returned and whisked Jamie away for the weekend, leaving Jenny to hold the fort alone.

The afternoon dragged slowly. The downpour continued on and off and would-be shoppers kept to their dry hearths or just made a brief dash between car and supermarket. Not one foot crossed the threshold of the NOW shop after lunch and the monotony of staring out from an empty shop at the steady rain finally wore her down. Her need to know the result of her mantrap of nails got the better of her and she guiltily shut up shop half an hour early.

As always in the rain, the traffic crept at snail's pace up the High Street and even the dual carriageway was clogged with cautious crawlers. Jenny hooted impatiently, as she tried to persuade an old Volvo doing thirty-five in the fast lane that it would be a lot better off in the slow lane. But the Volvo hung on doggedly and only at the next roundabout did she manage to squeeze past it. As she neared the turning into the avenue, the windscreen wipers cleared a misty arc of vision and her eyes eagerly swept each parked car.

The Mercedes was there. Sitting forlornly abandoned in the pouring rain only half a mile from home. Jenny thumped the steering wheel in triumph and turned, delighted, into the drive. The white Celica turbo parked across the garage door wiped the smile from her face.

What the hell was Susannah doing here? What had gone wrong with her plan?

She left the car in the drive and made a dash through the rain to the front door. The moment she stepped into the hall, she heard Susannah's throaty laughter in the sitting-room. She threw open the door and two startled faces looked up from the floor. Two figures frozen in a contorted position with shoulders on the carpet and hips high in the air.

'Squeeze tight . . .' the voice of Jane Fonda commanded from the television.

David was the first to react. He stood up, clearly embarrassed. 'Hello, back already?' His face was flushed from exertion and he flexed his legs to ease the muscles.

Jenny looked down at Susannah and was met with amused green eyes and a curving smile. 'Darling, come and join us. We're just on the buttocks exercise. Squeezing them tight, weren't we, David?'

Jenny's answering smile was almost natural. 'I thought you were meeting at the Black Swan.'

'Don't even mention it.' Susannah rolled her eyes to the ceiling. 'It's been a disaster. Poor David's had a dreadful time.' She sat up and her lavender blouse clung tightly to her sweating figure, outlining her breasts.

'Bloody vandals,' David informed Jenny, but his eyes were on

Susannah's body. 'Some maniac must have scattered nails about. I got two damned punctures. You must have seen my car near the roundabout.'

'Yes, I did notice it. Its front tyres are flat.'

'Damned right they are. To cap it all, our phone is out of order. It's always the same. Just when you need the blasted thing, it goes on the blink. So I couldn't even phone a garage or let Susannah know.'

Susannah flicked a stray strand of blonde hair back from her face and turned to Jenny. 'He can't get rid of me that easily. When I found myself stood up at the Black Swan and no response on the telephone, I drove over to give your husband a piece of my mind. I even had to bang on the window to get his attention, as the bell doesn't seem to work. What's the matter with things round here? If I didn't know better, I might suspect the man was trying to avoid me.'

David stretched out a hand and pulled her to her feet. 'What rot! Luckily Susannah's got a car phone, so she contacted the garage for me, but they can't pick up the Merc until after five. So I won't have it back until the morning.'

He watched Susannah try to tame her luxurious hair with her fingers and bend forward to brush the fluff from her trousers, giving him a moment's full frontal before she straightened up again.

'It was too late for a pub lunch by then, so we raided the fridge and Susannah decided we should work off our energy on your Jane Fonda exercise tape.'

Susannah winked at Jenny. 'Safer than on each other.'

Jenny smiled, feeling faintly reassured.

'A swim in her pool was what I suggested,' David grinned. 'It would have made an interesting change in the pouring rain, but Susannah didn't fancy it. Unfortunately.'

'We can make up for it next week,' Susannah suggested. 'We'll pick a fine day, have a swim first and then a lazy lunch at the Black Swan. How's that sound?'

'Great to me.'

'What about you, Jenny? Can't you sneak a couple of hours away from the grindstone? Join us for a swim?'

Jenny thought with a wrench of the freedom she had so willingly thrown away. 'No, it's not possible with just the two of us in the shop. But thanks for the thought anyway.'

David slipped an arm round Susannah's shoulders. 'Jenny and Robert have to be out earning our crusts for us, I'm afraid. So it's just lazy layabouts like you and me who can indulge in a midday swim.' He gave her a playful squeeze and she looked up at him, her green eyes full of laughter.

'Then before you get chained to an office again, we'd better take advantage of it while we can.'

Jenny walked to the door. 'I'm tired. I need a hot soak in the bath.'

Susannah abandoned David and followed Jenny out of the room. 'Poor old you, you're probably not really fit yet after your . . . accident. And you're working so hard, you make me feel quite guilty.'

'Good.'

Susannah lowered her voice. 'But I'm doing all I can to help, Jenny. Don't you think David seems much better? Altogether perkier?'

'He certainly is, as you aptly put it, "altogether perkier".'

Susannah gave a self-satisfied smile. 'There you are then. It must be making life easier for you.' She dropped her voice to a whisper. 'No more black moods or violent—'

Just then David came into the hall. 'What on earth are you two whispering about?'

'You, of course,' Jenny responded. 'Who else?'

'Hatching some devilish plot?'

'No,' Susannah laughed. 'Just planning for the future.'

'Well, my future lies with Japanese electronics, I assure you. That's where the biggest expansion is going to be and I'll be right in there with it.'

Jenny slowly nodded. 'That's what I call a positive attitude.' She glanced at Susannah. 'Altogether perkier.'

'I don't intend to give up the fight,' David declared firmly. 'I'm not finished yet.'

Jenny smiled softly. 'No, not yet.'

'So I intend to make the most of my last days of freedom

before getting stuck in behind a desk once more. A swim one day next week will be perfect, Susannah. Get me fitter again.'

'Right. Get your phone mended. I'll give you a call.'

Jenny walked her to her car. 'You've done your good deed for this week, so you can enjoy the weekend with a clear conscience.'

Susannah laughed. 'That's just as well, because I'm playing golf on Sunday morning against Thea, so I need all the help I can get. But don't worry, I won't forget to ring David on Monday. I'll keep him up to scratch for you.'

'I know you will. He'll end up sharper than ever.'

Susannah pecked a farewell cheek. 'Don't work too hard, darling.' She inspected Jenny's face. 'But I must say, you do seem to be looking well. Positively thriving on it.'

'I am.'

As the Toyota's rear lights disappeared out of the drive, Jenny turned back to the house. To herself she repeated, 'I am.'

'That looks good.' David dipped a finger into the bowl of warm glossy chocolate. 'Mmm, tastes good.'

Jenny tapped his finger smartly with the wooden spoon. 'Wait until it's finished.'

'We haven't had chocolate mousse ever since you started that blasted job of yours. I thought you were too busy these days for such domestic chores.' He sneaked another fingerful. Just like Mark used to.

She made herself concentrate on separating the egg whites into a bowl. 'Don't say you're not still being spoiled. Sunday, my day off and I'm slaving over a hot beater.' She switched on the electric whisk and raised her voice over its rattling whirr. 'As soon as I've finished this, I'm driving over to see Susannah.'

'What for? She was here only the day before yesterday. Can't you stay out of each other's pockets for more than a few minutes?'

Jenny kept her eyes on the whirling blades as they sliced through the foaming air bubbles. 'I promised to drop over the brochure of the new health and fitness club that's opened in town.'

'Not yet another con artist operating on you gullible women.'

'I miss my exercise class. Susannah is interested in this one, so we thought we'd have a look at it.'

'If she wants to see the brochure, why can't she get one herself?'

'I said I'd take mine over.'

'Well, do it tomorrow on your way to work.'

'No, I promised it this morning.' David opened his mouth to object further, but Jenny continued quickly, 'Don't worry, the lunch is in the oven and I won't be long. Go and read the paper or you'll leave no chocolate left for the mousse.'

He took a final dip and then sulked out of the kitchen. Ten minutes later, Jenny was in her car.

It was Robert Benson who opened the door to her. 'Hello, Jenny, what a lovely surprise. Come on in.'

She followed him into the elegant drawing-room. 'Susannah's not here, I'm afraid. She's off playing golf this morning. With Thea, I think it is.'

Jenny looked disappointed. 'Oh, what a nuisance. I wanted a word with her.'

'Anything I can do?'

'No, thanks anyway.'

'No message I can give her when she gets back?'

'No. It's a bit sensitive, you see.'

'Sensitive? What do you mean?' He gestured for her to take a seat. 'Is there a problem?'

'Oh Robert, I don't want to get you involved.'

His face was instantly full of concern. 'Jenny, my dear, what has happened?' He sat down beside her on the chesterfield. 'How can I help you?'

She smiled ruefully at him. 'You won't want to when you know what it's about.'

'Don't be silly. I—' He broke off and said stiffly, 'It's about David, isn't it?'

'Yes.'

'After what he did to me and my business, as well as to you, he doesn't deserve any help.'

Jenny looked away out the window, her face tense.

Robert Benson misinterpreted her silence. 'Don't tell me he's becoming violent again. Hasn't he done enough already? I won't let him—'

'No, Robert, no,' Jenny said softly. 'It's not that.'

'What then?'

Jenny shook her head slightly. 'It's nothing, Robert. Forget about it.' She moved as if to rise, but Robert put a restraining hand on hers.

'Come on, my dear, out with it. Don't bottle it all up. What's the blighter been up to now?'

Jenny lowered her eyes and studied his freckled hand lying on top of her own. 'It's just something I wanted to warn Susannah about,' she said finally, barely above a whisper.

'Warn Susannah? About what?'

'Now that I'm working, David is alone most of the day. He gets very depressed.'

'Serves him right.'

'I don't blame you for thinking that.'

Robert patted her hand. 'I'm sorry. I should keep my mouth shut. Carry on with what you were saying.'

'So when Susannah kindly offered to try to cheer him up by taking him out to lunch, I don't think she fully realises the effect it will have on him. She is so attractive and I'm afraid, in his depressed state of mind, he will read more into the invitation than—'

'Susannah is seeing David?' Robert withdrew his hand and sat bolt upright.

'Yes. Didn't you know?'

'No, I did not.'

'She's only trying to help me.'

Robert said nothing, but his breathing was heavy.

'She just wants to jolly David into a better mood so that it will be easier for me at home.' Jenny turned grateful eyes on Robert. 'You know how thoughtful she is. She's always been a good friend to me.'

A faint smile softened his mouth. 'Yes, her heart is in the right place, I know.'

'It's just that I can't trust David,' Jenny blurted out suddenly and put a distraught hand over her face.

There was an awkward silence and Robert shifted uncomfortably beside her. She feared she might have gone too far, so after a moment she raised her head and took a deep breath. 'I'm sorry, Robert, it's just that I don't think Susannah knows what she is getting herself into.'

Robert stood up and went over to the fireplace. From the marble mantelshelf he picked up a silver frame that held Susannah's laughing smile. He gazed at it in silence, then turned to face Jenny. His voice was calm and controlled. 'She won't be seeing David again. You need not worry about that.'

'Thank you, Robert.'

'However good her intentions may be, she should steer clear of a man like David.' He paused. 'And so should you.'

Jenny rose and walked over to him. 'Not yet, Robert. Not yet.'

'You're too loyal, that's the trouble.'

'I hope Susannah won't think me disloyal to her. It's not her I mistrust.'

'I know that.'

'And I'm sure the only reason she didn't tell you what she was doing was that she knew how you feel about David, but at the same time wanted to help me. It was difficult for her.'

Robert nodded. 'She's too soft-hearted for her own good.'

'I'm glad you think that. I wouldn't want to hurt her.'

'No, don't worry. I'll just tell her you dropped by and happened to mention her lunch with David. Then I'll come the heavy and insist she refrains from any more.'

More like win her ready agreement through a subdued display of hurt feelings, Jenny suspected. Susannah was always sensitive to when Robert was really serious.

'Thank you, Robert. I am really grateful.' She kissed him lightly on the cheek, then pulled a pamphlet from her jacket pocket. 'Here's a brochure on the new fitness centre. I thought Susannah might like to see it. You can say that was the reason I called round this morning.'

Robert walked her to the door. 'Jenny, I know you'll think

it's none of my business, but don't let David be too much dead weight on you.' He scrutinised her face. 'You're too young, too intelligent and,' he smiled, 'far too pretty.'

'I'll take care, I promise.'

'Goodbye, my dear. Good luck.'

It's not luck I need, Jenny thought to herself as she walked down the front steps, just some careful planning.

On her way down the High Street, the model in the window caught her eye. A sleek silver car with cooling slats along the bonnet.

It was a beautifully constructed replica of the pre-war Mercedes racing car. She even knew the date, 1937, of its clean sweep of most of the Grand Prix races in Europe because, the previous Christmas at David's request, she had bought him a book on Mercedes racing cars. He had admired the car's smooth lines and its huge 5.6-litre engine and had bombarded her with a string of facts and figures to demonstrate its superiority over competitors.

Jenny stepped nearer the toy shop window. On closer inspection, she realised the model was a plastic kit that you had to construct and paint yourself. Even better. She was certain David would like it. It would give him something to do, something to occupy the empty hours till she came home each day. She wondered whether her chat with Robert Benson yesterday had brought results yet. Was Susannah on the phone to David even now, easing herself out of the promised lunch date?

Jenny looked again at the model in the window and decided to buy it. It would make an appropriate gift, today of all days, considering the present she had just bought herself. She smiled and saw the reflection grin back at her. Then she pushed open the shop door.

David looked miserable. For a brief moment, he raised his eyes from the television screen as she came in. 'You're back late.'

He had not shaved and was sitting slumped in his chair, watching the news.

'Yes, I know. I had something to pick up.'

'Evening rush hour traffic is always a nightmare,' he muttered, his eyes fixed on scenes of starvation in Africa.

'It wasn't too bad, thank goodness. What's the matter? You don't look too good.'

He shrugged dispiritedly and glanced up at his wife. 'Whereas you are looking extremely pleased with yourself.'

'What's the matter? Did anything happen?'

'No, not unless you call two more job rejections, a splitting headache and a high-speed reverse from Susannah anything.'

So it had worked. 'Sounds miserable. But what do you mean about Susannah?'

'She always was an airhead and always will be.'

'But I thought you were delighted to be enjoying her company. A breath of fresh air, you called her.'

David laughed without humour. 'I should have known better. She did some fast back-pedalling today. The lunch is off, this week or any other week.'

'Why would she do that?'

'Robert, of course. He's up on his high-horse and has forbidden her to associate with me. He's got a bloody nerve, him and his cheap plastic watches. What the hell does he think will happen? That I'll corrupt her morally or something? Can't he see we're just good friends?'

Jenny bit off the retort that sprang to her lips. Good friends like you were with Robert. Like you were with Sarah. All gone now. Instead she said, 'Look, I've bought you a present to perk you up.' She held out the kit in its bag.

He looked up at her in surprise. 'To what do I owe this pleasure?'

'To my unbounded generosity,' she laughed and plonked the parcel on his lap.

He opened the bag and took out the kit. For a few seconds he stared at the box with its picture of the silver Mercedes racing to victory, then slowly turned to his wife's smiling face. 'Jenny, this is marvellous. It's my favourite car.' His voice was quite choked.

'I know. That's why I bought it.'

'I haven't done a kit since I was a teenager. I'll enjoy having a go at it. God knows, I've certainly got the time for it now. It'll be jigsaws and painting by numbers next.'

'Don't be so negative. Just you cheer up, so that you're fighting fit for the great day next week.'

'Don't worry, I won't let anything stop my being on top form for the Okiwa interview.'

'I'll do everything I can to help make it come out right.' Her face was composed, but there was a fierce determination burning in her eyes.

David was touched by what he saw as her loyalty and smiled gratefully up at her. 'You're good for me, you know. You still believe in me and I need that now more than ever.' He leaned forward and took her hand in his. 'You're all I have left.' With a laugh, he gave her fingers a squeeze. 'I'm feeling better already and you've only been home five minutes. Thanks for the car model, I really love it.'

'Good,' Jenny said briskly. 'Then you can come and see the present I've bought myself.'

'Another present? You're lashing out a bit, aren't you?'

'With all that golden handshake capital from Fairchild sitting in the bank and Okiwa just around the corner, why not? I only used a bit of it anyway. Besides, now that I'm earning a crust slaving away all day, I'm entitled to the occasional treat.'

'Of course you are. I didn't mean to—'

'But I do warn you,' she cut in, 'it's quite a treat.'

'That sounds ominous.' He put the kit to one side and rose from his chair. 'So what have you bought yourself? Jewellery? Clothes? Not yet another pair of shoes, I hope.'

'No, nothing like that. Come and see for yourself.' She took his hand and led him out of the room.

With an accompanying flourish and mock fanfare, she threw open the front door and sparkling on the gravel drive stood a brand new, bright red Toyota sportscar.

It had taken days for him to stop sulking.

He had complained bitterly about the extravagant expenditure of part of his settlement money and even about her choice of a car that was only a two-seater. But Jenny knew the real cause of his disapproval lay elsewhere. He resented her sudden independence.

Now, nearly a week later, she had persuaded him to come for a drink at The Riverside Inn, but she insisted on driving her new toy herself. The gleaming flash of red and its sleek curves turned heads and provoked admiring glances. When she climbed out of the driver's seat in the pub car park, a young man gazed in open admiration, first at the car and then at herself. David slipped an arm around Jenny's waist and led her indoors.

At a quiet table in the bar, she entertained him with a tale about an attempted shop-lifting she'd had to deal with that morning at the shop. She embellished a few touches for dramatic effect and David was suitably amused. He mellowed sufficiently to start describing his progress on the Grand Prix car kit, but once started, his enthusiasm was unstoppable. She listened attentively to every problem encountered with the chassis and every detail of the bodywork. He had suffered a brief disaster with the polystyrene cement and the aeroscreen but had managed to overcome it, so that now the car was almost finished.

When they returned home, Jenny had not been allowed to serve up the prepared supper of curry and rice until she had inspected his handiwork. Dutifully she admired the ten-inch model with a convincing degree of enthusiasm and praised his precision and expertise. The racing car still needed to be painted before it could be displayed in its full glory.

After they had eaten, while Jenny cleared the dishes, David took the fragile model car away for safety into the sitting-room. She was delighted that both presents had proved such a success, keeping David's mind occupied during the last few days. Tomorrow was D-Day. David had not said much, but she was aware that he was extremely tense about the prospect of the interview, seemingly confident of the outcome, but nonetheless apprehensive. As Jenny slotted the plates into the dishwasher, she flexed her taut neck muscles. It would be a relief when it was all over. It had dragged on too long.

While David became once more engrossed in his new passion for model-making, Jenny prepared for the next morning. She took a couple of croissants out of the freezer for breakfast and packed an apple and crispbreads into a bag for her lunch. She'd buy some of that gorgeous Brie to go with it from the delicatessen at the bottom of the High Street.

For David's lunch, she emptied the portion of rice that she had reserved from their supper on to a plate and spread it into a neat circle. There was still sufficient curry left in the bottom of the pan and she tipped it into the centre of the fluffy rice. Then, making sure the kitchen door was firmly closed, from a drawer she took the small container of sleeping pills that she had been given when she had left hospital. The bottle was almost full. Carefully she ground a number of the tiny orange tablets into a fine powder, then hastily scattered it over the curried chicken and stirred it in thoroughly. When she was quite satisfied, she covered the plate with a dish and placed it on the bottom shelf of the fridge.

In the sitting-room, David was starting to stir a small pot of silver enamel paint.

'I've put some curry and rice on a plate in the fridge for you for tomorrow, David. Just pop it in the microwave for a few minutes. It will save you having to bother about lunch.'

'Thanks,' David responded without looking up. He was pre-occupied with his present task.

Just then the telephone rang. Jenny disappeared into the hall and nervously picked up the receiver. It was all going so well, please let it not be someone wanting to disrupt anything. Surely at this time of the evening it was too late to be anyone about the interview tomorrow.

'Hello?'

'Hi, it's Caroline.'

Jenny breathed more easily.

'How's the job at NOW going? Still happy with it?'

'Yes, I'm really enjoying it. I've learned an awful lot about shop and stock management and I'm getting better and better at doing the windows. Steve's being a great help with everything.'

'That's great. And how is that other man in your life? Adjusted to your absence and unaccustomed freedom, has he?'

Jenny hesitated and lowered her voice. 'He has been very

down, very depressed, but at the moment he's much more positive because he's got the Okiwa interview tomorrow. He's very keyed up for it.'

'Of course, I forgot. I suppose I wish him luck, even if it's just for your sake. But you know what will happen if he lands this job, don't you?'

'Yes, I know,' Jenny answered softly. 'He'll revert to his old self. Old habits die hard.'

'Exactly. Take his fears and frustrations out on you and then insist you give up your job because he needs you at home to buff up his ego.'

Again a pause. 'Probably.' She stretched out another pause. 'But it won't happen again like that.'

'Why? What makes you think—'

'Because I won't let it. Not this time.'

Caroline laughed. 'Good for you, my girl. There's hope for you yet.'

'You underestimate me, Caroline. Nothing and nobody stays the same. People adapt. Life changes them.'

'Talking of changing, have you changed your car?'

'Yes, I have.'

'That's why I'm ringing. I saw you zip past me up the High Street today in a very flash hunk of machinery.'

'Do you like it?'

'Absolutely gorgeous. Your own choice, I presume?'

'Yes, my choice.'

'I thought so. It's not quite David's self-image at the moment, is it?'

'No. Miniature plastic car kits are more his style right now.'

'I insist you take me out for a run in it. I'm dying to see what it's like.'

'You'll love it. How about one day next week?'

'Great, I look forward to it. Make sure you drive carefully. You don't want to mark it.'

Jenny's smile travelled down the line. 'I assure you, Caroline, I steer a very careful path. Very careful indeed.'

Perfection. David put his brush down on the newspaper and

stepped back. Slowly he walked round the table, critically assessing the results of his morning's work.

When he stood once more in front of the miniature Mercedes, he nodded his head. 'Not bad, though I say it myself.' He rinsed his brush in a pot of thinner and wiped it on a rag.

He was pleased with the model. It looked good, and the hours of work on it had reminded him of the qualities he valued: patience, painstaking hard work and determination to see the job through to the end. He admitted to himself that this kit was his first real achievement since leaving Dern & Fairchild. What else had he done? Nothing. Nothing, that is, but drink, degenerate and drink again.

Disgusted with himself, he tidied the paint and brushes into their box and scrumpled up the newspaper. Caroline had been right, damn her. In one respect, anyway. How could he have become so spineless? It was a pathetic display of the kind of weakness he despised. But now, everything would be different. The kit had been a turning point. His watershed. After the interview this afternoon, he would truly be starting out on a new life, with a new office. And a new secretary.

With unexpected vividness, the image of warm brown eyes and long dark hair suddenly rose before him. But he forced himself to dismiss it instantly. Why should he tear himself apart for her? She did not want him and had made that abundantly clear by her disappearance and resolute silence. His new life must be without her.

He yanked his mind back to the more immediate future. The important thing now was to concentrate all his energies on the interview this afternoon. The very prospect of it raised his spirits and in his mind he ran over the path he anticipated the discussions might take. The excitement and heady rush of adrenaline fired his enthusiasm to be back behind a desk, once more a participant in the boardroom decisions.

Carefully avoiding the wet paint, he picked up the Mercedes W125 by its wire wheels and placed it on the windowsill where, with the sun glinting on its paintwork, it looked magnificent. It had taken him by surprise that Jenny should think of buying it for him – even if it was just to salve her own conscience. He still could not quite believe what she had done. How could she walk into a showroom and buy herself an expensive new car without even consulting him? And with his own money, for Christ's sake, even if it was nominally in a joint account. He would have to shift the rest of it to an account in his name only, just to be on the safe side. It was so unexpected. So totally out of character with the Jenny he knew.

She claimed it had been an act of impulse, but he found that hard to credit. Whether her action had been preplanned or not, unwise or not, he had to admit it was a lovely car and she had certainly wangled an excellent deal with the garage for her old Honda. Nevertheless he shook his head in annoyance.

Walking into the kitchen to wash his hands, he glanced at his watch. Plenty of time before he had to leave for the station, but he'd have an early lunch anyway, just to be on the safe side. He took the plate of rice and curry out of the fridge and placed it on the glass shelf of the microwave. Then setting the timer, he pressed the start button.

11

Why wouldn't they hurry up and leave?

Jenny kept a discreet eye on the middle-aged couple inspecting the intricately carved figures from Namibia, but let them browse in peace. It was obvious they had no intention of buying anything, but were just passing some spare time at the boring end of a Friday afternoon. Normally she would have viewed them as a challenge. Used her persuasive skills to convince them that they genuinely needed a set of hand-woven place mats or that the purchase of a tea-towel covered in tigers and Indian lions would be a valuable contribution towards the preservation of those species.

But this time she was eager for them to leave. She wanted to shut the shop, tear home in her MR2 and discover the results of the sedated curry. What if David had decided at the last minute to take the early train up to town and eat at one of his old haunts instead? She needed to get home right now and could feel her patience wearing dangerously thin. Steve was busy in the tiny office at the back, totalling the day's takings, so all she had to do was put on her coat and go. It was already after five thirty, but the unwanted customers made no move towards the door.

Exasperated by the delay, Jenny had just taken a few steps towards them, when the door jangled open. She turned round and started to say she was sorry but the shop was closed, but she broke off abruptly when she saw the figure of Susannah breezing casually up to the counter.

'Surprise, surprise, darling. I've come to view you in your busy sweat-shop. Or is it sweet shop?' She gazed around her with amusement. 'How quaint. You mean people actually buy these . . . objects?' She did not bother to lower her voice.

The middle-aged couple glanced uncomfortably from Susannah to Jenny and quickly took their leave.

'Thanks, Susannah. Remind me to invite you again next time I have customers in the shop.'

'Oh,' Susannah was instantly contrite. 'I'm terribly sorry. Did I put them off? I tell you what,' she picked up a bamboo desk-top pen-holder from one of the shelves, 'I'll buy this myself to make up for it. Robert will be thrilled to have it for his office.'

Jenny laughed, walked over to the door and turned the notice to 'Closed' before any more customers were tempted inside. 'I'll wrap it for you,' she said, unwilling to let Susannah off the hook, despite her own eagerness to leave.

'And how's David?' Susannah enquired casually.

'He's fine.' Jenny enveloped the delicate bamboo in a sheet of tissue paper.

'How did he take my phone call abandoning him to his lonely fate the other day?'

'Not too bad. He'll survive.'

Susannah eyed her sheepishly. 'It was grumpy old Robert. He felt David had been disloyal to him and that I was being just as bad by "consorting", as he put it, with him. So I had no choice, I'm afraid.'

Jenny smiled. 'Thanks for the kind intentions anyway. I do appreciate you were trying to help. Presumably there's no restriction put on your consorting with me?'

Susannah relaxed now that the explanations were over. 'No, of course not. That's why I'm here. I felt so guilty about it that I thought I'd come over and take your weary bones out for a drink after you've locked up here. How about it?'

'Any other evening, I'd love to. But not tonight. I've got to rush home.' She dropped Susannah's money into the till and closed it for the night.

Susannah looked faintly put out. 'Can't David wait an extra half-hour for your home-coming?'

'It's not that. He had his interview in London today and I want to know how it went.'

'Oh God, of course. Stupid of me to forget. I'll keep my fingers crossed for him, but don't worry, those Japanese tycoons won't be able to resist a blond, blue-eyed Adonis like him.'

Jenny laughed at the idea. 'Susannah, I don't think it's his looks they're interested in.'

'I know the feeling,' Susannah grinned. 'It's what's inside the wrapping that counts.'

'Appearances can sometimes be deceptive. You don't always find what you expected inside,' Jenny commented, handing the parcel to Susannah, just as Steve Thompson emerged from the office.

'Did I hear the till again? It's getting late for . . .' His words trailed away as he caught sight of Susannah leaning against the counter. Her stylish linen suit and the cut of her vivid orange blouse accentuated the fullness of her figure and highlighted the gold of her hair.

She studied the good-looking manager with interest. 'Aren't you going to introduce us?' she enquired of Jenny without taking her gaze from Steve.

Jenny hastily made the introductions and went to fetch her coat. She had seen too many male victims fall prey to the skill of Susannah's stalking to bother to hang around for the outcome. Already Susannah had draped herself over his arm and was being given a guided tour of the ethnic range of goods from India.

'What superb workmanship,' Jenny heard her breathe in admiration, as she held an enamelled jewellery box in her hands. 'I simply must have it.'

Jenny called goodbye and slipped away.

An accident on the dual carriageway delayed her even further. The queues built up and stretched back for nearly a mile, as homeward-bound cars took it in turns to edge slowly round the mangled steel. When at last she was free of the congestion, Jenny put her foot down and used the full power of the sports car.

The Mercedes was sitting in the garage. She felt its bonnet. It was cold.

She hurried into the house and standing in the hallway, listened for any sound. Only silence. She glanced in the kitchen.

No David. When she checked the fridge, the cold curry was gone.

Had he eaten it? Or maybe thrown it out? Perhaps the sleeping tablets had given it an unpleasant flavour. She was about to shut the fridge door, when she noticed a newly opened bottle of wine sitting in the rack. She picked it up, saw that only a small amount of the wine was missing, half a glass at most, and held it thoughtfully in her hand. Then decisively she shut the fridge, walked over to the sink and tipped the bottle, watching the pale liquid slide noisily down the drain. When it was empty, she placed the bottle on the table.

His car was in the garage, so he must be in the house somewhere. Her heart was beating fast as she went quickly back across the hall and opened the sitting-room door.

A sigh of relief escaped her.

He was stretched out in his chair, head lolling to one side and legs extended straight. His breathing was slow and regular – the soft, shallow rhythm of deep slumber. He was dressed in his best suit, all ready to make a good impression, but instead of a punctual arrival at the Okiwa offices, he had obviously come to sit down for a moment after lunch. Feeling drowsy probably. Then a gentle drifting into dark oblivion. Or was it a sudden collapse, overwhelmed without warning by devastating tiredness?

Jenny walked over to him and gently shook his arm. No response. She looked at his still face, softened in sleep and suddenly fear took hold. He could be unconscious. In a coma. Too many tablets. The wine. In a panic, she shook him harder and this time broke the steady rhythm of his breathing. He mumbled something incoherent, though his eyes remained firmly closed. Relief flooded through her and she took a deep breath to steady herself. She had to keep calm.

She looked at her watch. Six thirty. Even a Japanese company must have closed its office at this hour. It would be safe to rouse him completely now. He wouldn't be able to get through to Okiwa Electronics even if he tried. A blond strand of hair had fallen over his eyes and she brushed it aside, calling his name.

Again no response.

She bent over him and said softly, 'You're going to have to wake up.' She placed her hands firmly on his shoulders and shook him violently. 'David, David.'

This time his head jerked up and she felt his body tremble beneath her hands. A brief moan of protest escaped from his lips, but once more he subsided into the depths of sleep.

'David, wake up.' Again she shook him roughly. 'Come on, open your eyes.' She felt the prickle of fear once more. How could she rouse him?

She lifted her hand from his shoulder and lightly tapped his face. The only result was that his head lolled further over and she could feel herself starting to get desperate. Determinedly she swung her hand back and slapped him hard on the cheek.

It worked. His eyes shot open and a moment's panic filled them as he fought to recognise where he was and who his attacker could be.

'David, what's happened? Why aren't you in London?' Jenny demanded, her face close to his.

She saw the blue eyes struggle for comprehension. His mouth opened, but no sound emerged. The effort was too great and the tide of sleep swept over him again. His lids started to close and his jaw went slack.

'Oh no you don't, my sleeping beauty.' She struck him across the face again.

At the second blow, David reacted. Abruptly he sat up and pushed her away from him. 'Stop it,' he shouted thickly, his eyes still confused.

Jenny stood back, genuinely relieved that he was at last fully conscious. 'I'm sorry, David, but I just had to wake you. I couldn't get you to answer. Why are you sitting here fast asleep? Shouldn't you be up in London?'

David stared up at her with glazed expression, then sank his head into his hands. He rubbed his face roughly, as if trying to clear away the mists in his mind. When he lifted his head, there was dawning awareness in his eyes.

'What time is it?' The words were slow.

'Gone six thirty.'

'It can't be. I only sat down for a moment.' He shook his head, as he attempted to drag the memory of the afternoon to the surface. 'What the hell happened?'

'Do you mean . . .' she paused, '. . . you've missed the Okiwa interview? You just slept through it?'

He nodded in dumb disbelief.

Jenny dropped into a chair, as if stunned. 'David, how could you?'

He stared back at her, horrified. 'It's not possible,' he murmured. 'It's just not possible. I couldn't have fallen asleep.' His eyes were still heavy, drooping lower and belying his words. 'I was all ready to go.'

Jenny looked at him in silence and then asked quietly, 'Did you have anything to drink, David?'

His eyes flew fully open and he glared at her. 'I did not get drunk. I'm not a fool.'

But the thick fog in his head and the dull ache behind his eyes caused him to question his own words. It certainly felt like a hangover.

'You haven't answered my question. Did you have anything to drink?'

David hesitated. He forced his mind to recall his actions at lunch. 'Yes, but only one glass of wine. Nothing more.'

He took her silence as a sign of incredulity.

'Go and have a look. I opened a bottle of Chablis. The rest is in the fridge. Look, I'll show you.' He stood up and for a moment the room swayed round him. 'I did not get drunk,' he repeated adamantly.

He walked unsteadily out of the room, determined to prove his point, but the uncertainty of his step added to his confusion. In the kitchen, he flung open the fridge door. There was no wine to be seen.

David looked quickly back at Jenny, standing in the doorway. 'I know . . .' He broke off abruptly as his eye caught the bottle standing empty on the table. He walked slowly over to it and examined its label. Yes, it was the one he had opened at lunchtime. It didn't make sense. He was sure he'd only had a small glass and then placed it in the fridge.

Yet his head ached and he had slept all afternoon.

He looked up and saw Jenny staring at him, waiting. He shook his head. It only made it hurt more. 'I was sure I didn't drink it all. But . . .' He looked again at the empty bottle in his hand, bewildered. '. . . I admit it appears as if I did, but even if it's true, you know I can handle my drink better than that. One bottle of wine wouldn't make me fall asleep. A bit more relaxed, perhaps. But not asleep.'

Jenny came forward, took the bottle from his hands and dropped it in the bin. 'Perhaps you've reached a point where that is no longer true. You've been drinking too much for weeks now. Maybe you are in a worse state than you realise and have reached the stage where you're so brimful of alcohol that even a bottle of wine will knock you out, blank out your memory.'

'That's crazy,' David exploded. 'Don't make up some stupid theory just because I fell asleep.' But he was shaken and confused.

'All right. Whatever you say, but let's think of Okiwa now. Is it too late to ring them? To explain?'

David glanced at the clock. 'They'll have gone home to their kareokes by now. And what the hell can I say to them anyway? "Sorry, I fell asleep"?'

'No, of course not. You must say you were ill.'

David rubbed his hand across his face. 'They'll never buy that. And even if they did, the fact that I didn't bother to inform them would wipe out my chances. They don't want anyone unreliable.' He sank down on a chair. 'It's no good. Let's face it, I've messed it up completely. My one and only chance.' He crashed his fist down on to the table. 'I'm a total disaster. Even when I get a chance, I balls it up. What in God's name is happening to me?'

Jenny came and stood beside him. Her fingers stroked his hair and ran over his broad shoulders. 'Don't despair, David. You're not finished yet.'

The weekend was bad. David's mood never altered from one of black misery and nothing Jenny said could lift even a corner of it. Self-recrimination seethed within him and the pain of it could only be deadened by bouts of furious activity followed by the oblivion of the bottle.

He spent hours splitting logs, far more than they needed for the autumn fires, until the sweat ran freely from him and the muscles in his bare back hardened in the faint warmth from the watery sun. Even when the clouds darkened and heavy showers interspersed the brighter intervals, he did not pause. Again and again he raised the axe above his head and slammed the blade down to bite deep into the raw wood. Even during the worst downpours he seemed oblivious to the rain pounding on his naked skin. The fury within possessed him and drove him on. When his arms could no longer hoist the axe one more time, he showered and collapsed, exhausted, with a full bottle of Scotch beside him. He refused to eat but sat with silent determination, drinking himself into oblivion. Jenny did not attempt to interrupt his frenzy but left him to get on with his own form of self-destruction.

The nights were long and the waiting endless, but finally Monday morning dawned chill and overcast. At nine o'clock Jenny rang Steve at the shop to say she would be in late that day, apologising and only explaining that she had a slight problem at home, but left it at that. David had not surfaced yet and was unlikely to for some time, judging by the state he had been in the previous night, but she had to stay until he contacted Okiwa Electronics. Could not leave until she knew for certain how the Japanese company was going to react. Would they offer him another interview? Surely it was too late.

To her surprise, David staggered downstairs in jeans and sweatshirt at nine thirty. He did not even look at her but snatched up the telephone. She watched silently as he spoke first to the personnel department at Okiwa Electronics and then to the managing director's secretary. He got no further. Jenny could tell as he quietly explained the circumstances which had caused his absence that the situation was hopeless. He reasoned and argued forcibly, but to no avail. He was told very politely that the position had already been given to another interviewee, one who had succeeded in turning up on Friday. He would, of course, be officially informed in writing. Many regrets that he had so unfortunately been taken ill.

David slowly replaced the receiver and stood staring at it

for a while, as if time had stopped for him. Jenny noticed his hands were shaking and there were beads of sweat on his face. He looked suddenly older. Was this really the man she had kowtowed to for so many years? A part of her melted at the sight of his haggard face and the self-doubt in his eyes. For a fleeting moment her determination wavered.

His voice was husky. 'The job's gone.'

'David, I'm sorry, but . . .'

'Forget it,' he snapped and ran a hand over his weekend stubble. 'I need a drink.'

'It's not even ten o'clock yet, David. That's not the answer. You can't . . .'

'Don't tell me what I can or can't do. You're not my keeper. Never have been and never will be. If I feel like a drink, I'll damned well have one. So keep your nose out of my business. I don't want your good intentions.'

Her moment of weakness was crushed.

David strode over to the cocktail cabinet, only to find he had exhausted its supply of whisky the previous evening. 'Why the bloody hell haven't you bought enough scotch? What is this place, a Mormon dry state? Goddammit, I have to do everything myself in this house.'

He grabbed his car keys from the drawer and stormed out of the house, slamming the door behind him.

Jenny waited for a sense of calm to return to the house. She breathed deeply a few times, suppressing the earlier shreds of sympathy. She could not go on much longer.

David had plummeted into the abyss. Everything he touched had crumbled to ashes in his hand. But she knew she must not underestimate the strength and determination of his character, for he could hack footholds for himself up the sheer sides of despair by willpower alone. No, she must prevent that. She wanted him to know what it was like to lose all belief in yourself, all self-respect. The drinks cupboard would have to be kept well-stocked while she was at work.

Before leaving for Hambury, she went upstairs to tidy the bedroom and found the bed an untidy tangle of duvet and pillows. David's suit of Friday still lay in a crumpled heap on the floor as Jenny had kept a low profile this weekend and had avoided clearing up behind him. But now that he was out of the house she efficiently changed the bed linen and then picked up the jacket and trousers, but the stale smell of whisky wafted up to her from the wrinkled material.

She bundled the suit into a ball for the cleaners and carried it with distaste downstairs, where she dug out a plastic bag to dump it in, but before doing so, she automatically checked its pockets. In one she found a soiled handkerchief which she tossed into the laundry basket and in another, a few coins. The side pockets of the jacket were empty as usual, because David did not like to spoil the lie of his suits, but in the inside breast pocket she found his Sheaffer fountain pen. She pulled it out and as she did so, her fingers brushed against a hard piece of paper deep inside the pocket.

She reached in further and drew it out. It was a small colour photograph, one of those cut from a strip of four taken in a photobooth. Wide brown eyes laughed happily out at her and a warm smile revealed perfect teeth. The long dark hair hung loosely, framing her face, and a man's hand was resting on her shoulder. Jenny instantly recognised the ring on the man's pinky finger. Anger tore through her and she flung the photograph from her as if it burned her fingers. Her breath came in gasps and her heart hammered furiously.

The suit dropped from her hand to the floor and she turned angrily on the dark material, stamping on it as if its owner were still inside.

'You bastard, all the time you were hiding her away.'

Is that what he drew his strength from? His secret hopes of reuniting with this dark-eyed beauty? Is that what kept him going? She had not expected this.

In control once more, she bent down and picked up the photograph lying on its face on the tiles. There was a smudge of dirt across the smiling mouth.

'So you're still his lifeline, are you, Sarah Archer?'

Very deliberately, she tore the photograph in half, and then into quarters. From a kitchen drawer she took out a lighter and holding the pieces of glossy paper over the sink, she flicked the flame into life. But just as the fire was about to engulf the fragments, she abruptly withdrew it.

'No, that's too clean and simple for you.'

She put down the lighter. 'I know just the place for a piece of dirt like you.' She walked swiftly to the door, the crumpled pieces of disjointed face in her hand.

At that hour of the morning Hambury was quiet. David came out of the off-licence carefully clutching the two carrier bags and retraced his steps towards the car park.

His head throbbed and a sharp pain stabbed continually behind his eyes. But he did not resent the hangover, even though it made the light too fiercely bright and the cars too deafening. Anything to distract him from the numbing agony he carried inside. He struggled to keep his mind on the effort of putting one foot in front of another. His body did not seem capable of functioning on its own any more and he had to concentrate very hard to make it keep moving. His coordination seemed to have gone and he had fumbled the change when paying for the whisky. The coins had slipped through his fingers and fallen noisily to the shop floor. Instantly a youth standing next to him had ducked down and retrieved them for him. As if he were an old man.

The car park was at the rear of a row of terraced houses with only half a dozen vehicles spread out over the flat expanse of tarmac. A run-down pub backed on to it and its yard was piled high with metal barrels and plastic crates awaiting collection. The tall figure of a young man leaned casually against the yard wall, as if waiting for someone.

As he passed him, David did not even raise his aching eyes, but concentrated on heading for the sanctuary of his car. Only another shot of scotch was going to make any inroads on the fireball of pain that was burning inside him.

He did not see it coming. The blow knocked the breath out of him and sent him crashing face first into the wall. The carrier bags in his arms exploded in a shrapnel of shattered glass and golden liquid. Before he could even start to realise what was happening, hands seized him from behind and swung him round. For a brief moment, he was face to face with dark eyes seething with hatred, then an iron fist hammered into his jaw and another smashed into his mouth.

David felt his lip split open. As he staggered backwards, his brain was reeling, desperately trying to focus on his attacker. The young man came at him again. He was fast. David tried frantically to fend him off, but his reactions were too sluggish. The fists slammed into his stomach, doubling him over in agony, as vomit shot from his mouth. Another vicious blow landed on the back of his defenceless neck and sent him crashing to the ground. David rolled on to his side, his whole body shrieking with pain.

Just in time he saw the foot swinging at him. He jerked his head backwards a split second before the boot shot past his eye. A snarl of frustration escaped from his assailant, as he fought to keep his balance. In that moment's delay, David seized the chance to struggle to his feet and back off a few steps. He could feel blood flowing down his forehead, where it had cracked against the pavement and he brushed it quickly from his eye. He needed every scrap of vision he could get.

The young man had not finished yet. He stepped towards David again, his fists ready to strike.

'For God's sake, what's this about?' David's voice was hoarse. 'If it's money you want, I'll . . .'

The young man's foot shot out and caught David behind the knee. His leg buckled and he would have fallen again, had he not grabbed hold of his attacker's shoulder. For a second they were face to face again and this time David did not hesitate. He head-butted the other's nose.

It exploded in a spray of blood and pulp. The youth screamed and pulled free, clutching his face. David followed him, thudding a string of punches against any part of his body that came within striking distance. The retreating figure kept his head averted to avoid further damage to his nose, but David managed to slam another blow into his face. With a howl the youth darted back, opening up a gap between them, but then he turned to face David again. Blood was pouring down his shirt from his shattered nose and he was breathing heavily through his mouth.

'Now get out of here,' David snarled at him. 'Get out before I . . .'

David was not expecting it. He thought his opponent was finished.

Two quick steps and a boot swung hard up into his crotch.

David collapsed on to the pavement, as agony flared from his groin. He was not even aware of the foot swinging again. This time into his face. His head shattered into piercing shards of blinding light and he did not hear the raised voices and running footsteps.

'I'll go and ring the police.'

'They'll have a telephone in the pub. You had better ask for an ambulance as well.'

'Yes, he looks pretty bad.' A pause. 'Smells drunk.'

The voices sounded far away, but he knew they were talking about him. Handkerchiefs wiped blood from his face and gentle hands eased him on to his back. He tried to speak but only a moan escaped his lips.

'Hang on, Henry. I think he's coming round.'

David managed to open his eyes a crack and saw a large face, full of worry, floating only inches from his own.

'How are you feeling?' the woman asked. 'You don't look good.'

David lay very still, trying to ignore the screaming pain in his head and to concentrate on speaking clearly.

'I'm not drunk,' he said, but even to his own ears the words sounded slurred. He attempted to sit up, but he would have fallen again, had not strong arms caught him and eased him into an upright position.

'Take your time. Don't rush it.' Watery blue eyes looked with kindly concern into his, as the man holding him steadied his weight.

David tried to smile gratefully back at him, but his swollen lips would not work properly. He closed his eyes for a moment to wait while the ground settled in one place, then looked again at his benefactor. He was probably in his mid-sixties, with a ruddy complexion and fine broken veins across his nose and cheeks. His wife kneeled on the hard pavement beside him, clutching a blood-stained handkerchief in her fingers.

'What happened?' she enquired. 'The other man ran off when we shouted, but we've got his description. We can tell the police that he was tall and had—'

'Emma, not now. The poor fellow's hardly conscious.'

David attempted to speak again, but with no more success than before. He flexed his limbs and found that, except for the sickening pain in his groin, his body still seemed to function normally, if disjointedly. It ached all over and his knuckles were split where they had crashed into hard bone, but otherwise there was no permanent damage.

The trouble was his head. The pain rattled round it like a violent thunderstorm and his thoughts did not seem to communicate properly with his body. What he needed was a drink.

'Could you help me to my feet, please?' he managed to mumble.

'Oh, I don't think you should stand up yet. You must sit here,' the woman urged, 'until we call an ambulance.'

'I don't need an ambulance.' He started to struggle to his feet and two pairs of arms immediately wrapped around him to raise him up. They held on to him while he steadied himself and then released him reluctantly. The woman held out the soiled handkerchief.

'Take this to stop it dripping,' she offered.

David became aware now that he was fully upright, that the blood was streaming from his forehead and lip again. One eye would not open properly and he touched it gingerly with the tip of his finger. The flesh around it was swollen and tender.

'I think that's where he kicked you, just as we were coming,' the woman observed. 'He was vicious. We must telephone the police right away.'

David accepted the handkerchief and staunched the flow of blood. 'I'll ring the police later. All I want now is to get home and have a . . .' He stopped and turned his head, very slowly, to look at his bags of shopping. The four bottles were in pieces, shattered by the wall.

The elderly man followed his gaze and nodded sympathetically. 'Would you like me to pop in the pub there and buy you some more?'

'Henry, I really don't think he should, you know.'

'Nonsense, dear, it's exactly what he needs.'

David handed over several notes and urged his rescuer to buy a bottle for himself as well out of it. The man's eyes sparkled and he disappeared into the yard. By the time he returned, clutching two bottles of scotch for David and one of gin for himself, David was able to move more easily. Under great protest, they helped him to his car, wrote down their names and address for him and then watched anxiously, as he put the car in gear and drove cautiously out of the car park.

'What's the matter with you today? You're so jumpy.'

Jenny looked at Caroline Palmer in surprise. 'What makes you say that?'

'Because you've been as nervous as a kitten ever since we got here. When I knocked over that pile of flowerpots you nearly jumped out of your skin.'

'Don't exaggerate. I admit I'm a bit tense, but that's all.' She gently replaced the azalea she was holding in the rack of plants and made an effort to keep her mind on why they had come to the garden nursery. 'I think a couple of these would be perfect for the spring. And don't forget that crimson camellia.'

'You're right, I'll take them.' Caroline selected the healthiest of the azaleas and added them to the collection in her trolley. 'So why are you so tense, Jenny? I thought you were enjoying the charity shop.'

'I am. Really. It's given me all sorts of ideas.'

'Ideas for what?'

'For the future.'

'Come on, spill the beans.'

'It's too early yet. Give me a bit more time.' She bent over to inspect a tray of alpine plants. 'How about a small rockery? Do you think Andrew would oblige with some stone hoisting?'

'I don't want to get too ambitious. Let's keep it simple to start with.'

Caroline had persuaded Jenny to accompany her to the local garden centre during her lunch hour to help her choose a variety of plants for a new flowerbed and shrubbery that she had decided to create in her colourful, though undisciplined, garden. Every autumn it was the same: she was seized by a sudden urge to redesign the layout of her garden and in a surge of enthusiasm, over-laden borders would arise where lawns had previously stretched and Jenny was always roped in to temper the excesses with her more expert knowledge.

'So if it's not the shop, what is it? David?'

Jenny nodded and moved away further down the aisle between the displays of red-hot pokers and winter irises. Caroline trundled after her with the trolley.

'What's he up to now?'

'He didn't get the job.'

'The one with the Japanese firm?'

'Yes. He heard this morning.'

'Oh hell, that must be a terrible blow.'

Jenny recalled his black scowl and bitter words of the morning. 'He was devastated.'

'I just hope he doesn't take it out on you. If you want to come and stay with us for a few days until—'

'No, Caroline. I appreciate the offer, but no. I have to be with him now. It's important.' She had not forgotten the smiling photograph in his jacket. 'I can't leave him completely alone at a time like this.'

'He doesn't deserve you.'

'Oh yes, I think he does.'

'How can you say that after he put you in hosp—'

'I told you, he didn't touch me.' Jenny looked her friend straight in the eyes. She wanted her to be convinced. 'You don't understand the situation, Caroline. But trust me, I know what I'm doing.'

'I hope you're right.'

Jenny headed for a pile of bags of compost. She selected a couple of peat-based ones and hoisted them on to Caroline's trolley. 'These will improve the soil. You still need an ericaceous compost for the azaleas though.'

They pushed the trolley round the corner, adding the occasional plant and bag of fertiliser. Jenny tried to relax and enjoy the outing, but her mind kept swinging back to speculating on the situation at home. What was David up to now after today's disappointment? Telephoning the job agencies again? Writing yet more applications? Was he finding solace in the bottle or, worst of all, was he seeking consolation with Sarah?

He had not returned by mid-morning when she had left for work. She had kept an eye out for his Mercedes as she drove into Hambury, but there was no sign of it. The tense knot in her stomach refused to release its grip and now she was feeling weary. The weekend had been a succession of disturbed nights with little sleep, so she was not surprised at the odd look Caroline had given her when they had met at the nursery gate. She knew she was not looking her best, but the bright smile she turned on went some way towards disguising the strain. She had to hang on. It was nearly over now.

At the cash desk, Jenny waited while Caroline paid and then helped her unload the purchases into the Escort's boot and on to its rear seat. As she slammed the boot lid shut, Caroline smiled and said, 'You won't recognise the garden when that little lot is in. Thanks for your help.' She eyed Jenny more closely. 'Are you sure there's no help I can give you?'

Jenny put an arm round Caroline's shoulder and kissed her cheek affectionately. 'Don't worry about me, Caroline. I do appreciate it, but honestly, there's no need to be concerned.'

Caroline gave Jenny a hug and opened her mouth to reiterate her doubts, but something in her friend's face stopped the words in her throat. Something new. A firmness of purpose in the eyes that convinced her that maybe Jenny was right. There was no need to be concerned.

She smiled fondly at her. 'Okay, I'll leave your life in your own hands and keep my nose out. But don't forget, I'm here if you need me.'

'Thanks, I won't.'

'I'm the one who should be thanking you, for all this horti-cultural advice.'

'All part of the service.'

'Talking of service, how is the shop doing? Emptied Africa of its carvings, have you?'

Jenny laughed, 'Yes, they're all weighing down mantelpieces throughout Hambury. I'm working on the hand-woven rugs next. So beware!'

'I'll come in and have a look at them,' Caroline promised. 'By the way, did I see someone else working in there with you, when I drove past the other day?'

'Yes, that was Jamie, Steve's son. He is just filling in occasion-ally during his school holidays.' Jenny smiled. 'It's been good having someone young around all day. I'll miss him when he's back at school.'

Caroline studied Jenny speculatively. 'You get on well with Steve, don't you?'

'Yes, I do. He's fun to work with.'

'How much fun is "fun"?'

Jenny eyed her friend impatiently. 'Don't go charging up blind alleys, Caroline. There's absolutely nothing between us and I don't intend to let anything start.'

'So he's interested then?'

'You're incorrigible,' Jenny laughed. 'The point is I'm not interested in anyone but David.'

Caroline pulled a long face. 'More fool you. Steve's very attractive, even with the teeth.'

'Then you have him. He's fancy-free.'

'Thanks, but Andrew might have something to say about that.'

'So might David.'

'Point taken. One of these days I really will learn to keep my mouth shut.'

Jenny laughed, 'That'll be the day! Well, I'd better be get-ting back.'

'Okay, I'll let you go. Thanks again for the help – and I really am sorry about David.'

Jenny paused as she was climbing into her car and said softly,

'Yes, I'm sorry about him as well.' She started the engine and disappeared out of the nursery in a flurry of gravel.

Not again.

Jenny stood at the end of the bed and looked down at her husband with distaste. After her nervous impatience all day, she had returned home from work to find the house silent. There was only the telltale sign of the car in the garage.

She relived David's black despair of the morning and the angry venom that had driven him from the house. Surely not to do anything stupid. The thought of the Mercedes in the garage reassured her and she went upstairs to the bedroom. The smell had hit her first. Their room stank like a distillery. David was stretched out on the bed, flat on his back, his arms out sideways and his mouth hanging open. He was snoring loudly.

And he was drunk. Unconscious drunk. An almost empty bottle of scotch stood on the bedside table, no glass in sight. So he'd reached the stage where he drank straight from the bottle. Jenny moved round the bed until she was standing beside him and stared intently at the signs of battle on his face and the blood all over his clothes. He had obviously got drunk somewhere, picked a fight and come home to bathe his wounds in more whisky. His face looked terrible. Dried blood was smeared down his cheek and over his chin. His lips were cracked and swollen and a huge bruise covered one side of his jaw. But worst by far was the eye. It looked like he'd gone ten rounds with Rocky and the make-up girl had done a particularly good job in transforming it to a narrow slit with multi-colour paintwork on the swelling pad. At some stage his stomach had obviously rebelled against the amount of alcohol and had vomited its contents over his shirt and bedcover. He looked and smelled disgusting.

Jenny stood gazing down at his unconscious form for a long time.

'This is it, David,' she breathed at last. 'You've reached it now. You've hit rock bottom, haven't you? The bottom of the pit.' She leaned down and whispered softly in his ear, 'And you have no idea how you got there, have you?

No idea who pushed you over the edge and pulled the ladder away.'

She straightened up, the strength of her emotions taking her by surprise.

'How could you be so bloody stupid? So all-consumingly blind to anybody but yourself. Besotted with your absurd ego to the exclusion of all else.' The image of her arrogant husband strutting his tyranny over her life suddenly overflowed her mind, swamped her sense and filled her with fury. 'You didn't mind who you hurt, did you? Who you trampled over in your rush to indulge your own desires and ambitions. But now, David, it's over. Now you're finished.'

She breathed deeply to still her pounding heart, but it was impossible to contain the rage that surged through her veins. The words tumbled out, louder and louder.

'I am a person too, but you never bothered about that. You never cared that once I loved you. Or that once I loved our son.' Tears pricked her eyes and his face dissolved into a watery blur. 'And then there was Shadow. You destroyed him too. So casually.'

She brushed aside the tears and bent over her silent husband once more. Her hands reached out and clasped his battered face, her eyes inches from his. Her voice was calmer, lower, the words coldly deliberate.

'You destroyed me as surely and intentionally as I have now destroyed you. You systematically pulled and twisted me apart until there was nothing left of me. Of my own identity. Nothing to hold together. Just a battered shell of gaping holes.'

She held his face tightly between her hands, as if trying to force her words into his skull. 'It's you down in that black abyss now, David. Not me. I'm sticking that tattered shell back together, filling in the empty holes with new life to make myself whole again. You didn't think I could do it, did you?'

She released her hold on him and stood up straight, looking down on his unconscious form. Her lips curved into a slow smile. 'But I have, David, I have done it. You are the one who is now full of fear and foreboding, alone and isolated down there.'

She stepped away from the bed. 'What happened to all those

friends you had? You don't understand where they went, do you? All those business "friends" of yours disappeared into the woodwork at the first whiff of HIV. And my bruises did for the rest. Even your little playmate Sarah deserted you, however long you carry her picture round with you.'

She turned her back on him and moved over to the window to open it wide. The fresh air that flooded in eased the lingering stench of vomit. For some time she stood staring out at the garden and the fields beyond. She would be sorry to lose them. The sweet-smelling breeze brought scents of the trees and fields, and she breathed of them deeply before turning back into the fetid room.

She smiled down at him, stretched so broken on the bed, a calm confident smile. 'This is the end, David. I've finished with you and I've finished with us.'

She walked over to the dressing-table and from the drawer took out a pair of scissors. Without hesitation she returned to the bed and lifted a lock of David's blond hair in one hand. Very deliberately the blades sliced through the fine threads.

'There, David, the bond is broken. You are free. To do what you want, with whoever you want. And I am free of you.' She studied the small bundle of fair hairs in her hand and murmured once more to herself, 'Free.'

She replaced the scissors in the drawer and went into the bathroom where she dropped the lock of hair down the loo and flushed it away. She watched the swirl of water wash away all trace, then rinsed her hands in the basin.

'A little more time,' she said softly. 'That's all I need from you now. A little more time.' She looked in the mirror and the face she saw framed in the glass smiled back at her and was at last content.

The police could not help. With only the description of the dark young man to go on, they had no hope of finding David's attacker. The elderly couple were eager to offer assistance, adding details of clothing and appearance, but nothing that would lead to his identification or present whereabouts. The question as to whether the attack had been an attempted mugging or just a brutal instance of mindless violence was left unanswered.

David himself displayed no interest in discovering the identity of his assailant. At first Jenny assumed it was the combination of shock and hangover that kept him slumped silently in his chair each day. But as the weeks passed and there was no change in his morose behaviour, Jenny knew the apathy and despair had taken deep root.

Slowly his face healed. The swelling subsided and the cuts mended, the bruises paled to a sickly yellow and then disappeared altogether. Each morning, Jenny drove off leaving him still in bed and returned each evening to find him entrenched in front of the television, the inevitable bottle at his side. He hardly spoke and he barely ate. Jenny left him to his own desires. Meals were placed on the table, but if he chose not to come or only ate a few mouthfuls, she did not comment. The discarded food was dumped in the bin or on the bird table.

She watched him grow thin and he looked even taller. He stopped shaving altogether and a bristly blond beard sprouted on his chin. The fair hair that he had always kept so clean and silky grew lank and greasy, but his eyes were unchanging in their dull misery.

The days gradually fell into a pattern. Jenny enjoyed her work and the daily company of Steve Thompson. He made her laugh and they took to stopping for a quick drink together at the Sea Trout pub before going home in the evening. The quick drink inevitably stretched to a longer chat over a second round, but it seemed to make no difference to David what time she came home, so she did not bother to curtail her enjoyment over a lengthy hour or more. And all the time she was making plans.

One evening each week she attended an exercise class, now that she could no longer go to Amy Stafford's daytime session. She even persuaded Susannah to join her and they made a habit of stopping off for a Chinese meal on their way home.

The weekends were the worst. The house sat silent around them. She tried to fill it with the sound of her favourite Chopin, but the soft strains of music failed to lift the black mood that hung in the air. Jenny handled the bills, the shopping and the garden on her own and without complaint. The activity kept her occupied at home and away from the sight of the whisky bottle slowly emptying.

Every evening she went to bed alone, knowing that the stumbling footsteps would wake her in the early hours of the morning. David was always deep in drunken slumber within seconds of his head touching the pillow and every morning she was up long before he woke, so that as the weeks went by, her only sexual fulfilment lay in the fantasies she took to bed with her each night. But each morning brought the prospect of an end to the charade ever nearer.

The branch would not snap. Jenny jerked the blades together harder and swore loudly. The action almost tipped her off her perch on top of the step-ladder and she clung for safety to the bough above her head.

The first few drops of rain, that had been threatening all afternoon, began to fall, stimulating Jenny to greater effort with the shears. She had allotted this Sunday to a real blitz on the garden and in the morning had succeeded in getting all the lawns cut, the edges trimmed and the flowerbeds thoroughly weed-free. After a brief hiatus for lunch and the radio news, she was quickly hard at it again, hacking back the shrubs to a manageable size once more. The extent of their summer growth never ceased to amaze her, with the weigela and lavatera entwining together in profligate abundance. And now she was on the last lap, pruning the apple trees.

'Don't you dare chuck it down yet,' she shouted at the darkening clouds above.

Her arms ached from working above her head and she still had one more tree to do. She climbed down the ladder and picked up the long-handled shears from the grass. They were better for the high branches, but she found their five-foot handles difficult and unwieldy to use. Nevertheless she struggled on with them in a determined hurry to finish quickly.

A jagged bolt of lightning streaking across the sky startled her and a moment later a rumble of thunder assured her of the storm that was on its way. The rain fell with an abrupt increase in force, soaking her hair and clothes in seconds, but undeterred, Jenny dragged the steps over to the last tree and rapidly yanked the shears open and shut, snipping the outstretched limbs back to the required length. Her upturned face was drenched and she squinted her eyes against the curtain of rain. She was damned well not going to give up now, when she was almost finished. She cursed as one of the falling branches hit the top of her head in its descent.

She turned to position the step-ladder further round the tree and as she did so, the sight of a figure standing at the French windows caught her eye. It was David. Staring at her through the rain-washed glass. Warm and dry in the protection of the house.

'You bastard,' she yelled, knowing he could not hear. 'I'm out here playing lumberjack in the monsoon and all you can do is watch. Get out here and help, you lazy layabout.'

He just stood there watching her, but the house was too far away for her to be able to make out his expression. Ignoring him, she returned to her task. She attacked the tree with renewed vigour, slicing off the green wood and circling the tree with the ladder as swiftly as she could. But in her hurry to escape the downpour, she lost patience and over-reached when stretching for one particularly rampant branch.

As she felt the ladder slipping sideways beneath her and her feet slithering into thin air, she grabbed frantically at the bough beside her and her fingers hooked thankfully round the rough bark, though her legs were kicking wildly, seeking a foothold. But the whole garden was soaked and the sodden bark beneath her fingers offered no safety. She heard herself scream as her grip slid off the slippery surface and she crashed to the ground.

She had not fallen far – maybe five or six feet – and the ground was soft, but she landed awkwardly on her back and had the breath knocked out of her. She lay still for a moment, recovering from the shock, then stood up shakily. Her ribs ached and her elbow was grazed.

She attempted to brush the mud off her jeans and sweatshirt, but they were so drenched by now that all she did was spread it further. She glanced self-consciously up at the house and was infuriated to see David was still standing at the window, watching her ludicrous antics on the ladder. With clenched teeth she turned away, ignoring him and grabbed a length of fallen wood off the wet grass, tossed it into the wheelbarrow and then scurried round the base of the tree picking up all the twigs and severed branches. She gave a despairing glare at the tall thick stem that had caused her downfall, waving mockingly at her in the wind, but everything was so slippery now, including the ladder, that she did not dare risk another accident.

Ducking her head against the driving rain, she emptied the barrow on to a heap at the bottom of the garden and replaced her tools and ladder in the shed. By now she was so wet that she was starting to shiver and her teeth chattered uncontrollably as she hurried to the back door. With relief she burst into the kitchen out of the rain and kicked off her muddy shoes on the mat.

'Here, this is what you need.' Before her stood David, his arms holding out a big bath towel. 'Get out of that wet stuff before you catch pneumonia.'

Jenny dragged the clinging sweatshirt over her head and then the tee shirt underneath, soaked quite literally to the skin. But when her shaking fingers tussled in vain with the button and zip of her trousers, David came to help and pulled the jeans off her chilled legs. At that moment, standing with dripping denims dangling from his hand, he stopped and looked at her.

Jenny suddenly became aware of the ludicrousness of the situation. Standing virtually naked in the kitchen with her hair plastered to her head like a dark skull cap, rain still running down her face and wearing only a pair of wet socks that left damp footprints wherever she stepped, she suddenly felt vulnerable. Her panties had disappeared somewhere inside the wet jeans, leaving her dark triangular mound glistening wet.

She saw David's eyes travel up from her groin to her cold-hardened nipples and then he came close to her, wrapping the warm towel round her shivering form. He rubbed her back vigorously and Jenny felt the blood flowing back into her icy skin. Her taut muscles relaxed and the ache in her shoulders eased, but abruptly she moved away from him. Yanking the towel tightly round her still damp figure, she stepped round to the other side of the table.

'Thanks,' she murmured without looking at him and headed for the door.

'Wait, Jenny.'

She glanced back at him.

'I've made you some tea, to warm you up.' He picked up a steaming mug from the table and handed it to her.

Grateful for its warmth, she sipped the camomile brew and wrapped her hands round the mug. 'Thanks,' she said again, this time more sincerely.

He stood watching her silently until she started to find his gaze disturbing. Swiftly she finished the hot drink and turned once more towards the door.

'Jenny.'

She was impatient to be gone. 'Yes?' This time she was expecting some snide comment about the foolhardiness of tree climbing in the rain.

'Did you hurt yourself?'

'No, not much.'

'Is that how you fell on the brass bedstead before?'

Jenny froze. What was he implying? Did he suspect? 'Something like that, yes.'

'This time your ribs survived?'

'Yes.'

'Good.'

She looked at his tall angular frame and his ragged beard that failed to disguise the hollowness of his cheeks, and suddenly it dawned on her that he wasn't being suspicious or prying. He was just trying to make conversation. They were so unused to communicating any more that his attempts came out clumsy and stilted.

'I'm fine,' she assured him and hurried from the room.

As she showered and dried herself, she ran over the scene in the kitchen and tried to find an explanation for it. The very fact that he was trying to engage her in conversation was a significant change in behaviour. What did he want? What was he up to? She pulled on a clean pair of jeans and thought about the possibilities. Surely he couldn't be suffering from a belated attack of conscience. No, far more probable was the likelihood that he had at last felt the need for human companionship. He'd found despair was a lonely hellhole and realised he needed a helping hand to pull him out.

Well, nobody had pulled her out when she'd needed it. She'd had to climb the slippery slope all on her own. Suddenly remembering Caroline and Susannah's frequent words of sympathy and offers of help, Jenny knew she was not being strictly honest with herself. Okay, so she'd had the good fortune of loyal friends, but David did not have any only because he had not earned any. Did not deserve that kind of loyalty and support.

She ran a comb through her wet hair and pictured him hunched in his chair downstairs. Miserable and alone. That's what she wanted, wasn't it? That's what she had worked for. But somehow the image brought her no pleasure. Where was the satisfaction she had anticipated? She stood up and pulled a warm dry sweater over her head. Her plan had been a success. This was the end she had aimed for, but now she was realising she had been mistaken. This wasn't the end. Not for her.

When she returned downstairs, she was relieved to find David slumped silently in front of a rugby match on television. Perhaps the momentary kindness in the kitchen had been an aberration.

But that evening she did notice that for once he ate most of his meal and came upstairs not long after she had gone to bed herself.

The manure slid off the shovel and David forked it in round the base of the shrub. He didn't know one bush from another, but he was sure they all benefited from a good dose of well-rotted horse muck. After yesterday's rain, the stuff was damned heavy to cart around and squelched unpleasantly, as he filled each barrow load. And the smell only seemed to make his headache worse.

As soon as he had heard Jenny's car drive off that morning, David had got up and showered himself awake. The two glasses of whisky of the night before had not been nearly enough to guarantee unbroken dreams and he had tossed and turned all night. A couple of hours' sleep just as it was getting light had been his ration. He was tempted to repair the lack with the balm of the bottle, but he had forced himself to reject the idea. He would not give in so soon. Surely his word was stronger than that. He had promised himself he would stay off it for one day. Only one day, for God's sake. Not much to ask.

When he had watched his wife battling through the rain in the garden the previous afternoon, he knew he could no longer go on like this. Something had stirred in him as he witnessed her display of spirit and he remembered a time, not so long ago, when he had possessed that same will to win. Where was it now?

He trundled the barrow back to the manure heap at the side of the hedge. Each summer Jenny bought numerous sacks of it and left it to rot all season, before spreading its pungent nutrients around the beds in the autumn. He sank his shovel deep into the cloying pile and tipped it on to the brown mess at the bottom of the barrow. As he did so, a gleam of white in the dark clump caught his attention. Probably a bit of bird's eggshell that had blown into the mound, but it was very white. He peered at it more closely. No, it was a piece of paper. Well, that didn't matter, it would rot down over the winter with the rest of it. He again dug deep and emptied another shovel load on top of the first and this time, another small scrap of paper stuck out clearly from the side of the growing heap.

He was wearing gardening gloves, but even so, it was with distaste that he lifted out the fragment of white. He turned it over clumsily in the thick fingers and stared in disbelief at the other side. It was half a laughing mouth and a smooth sweep of flawless cheek. He'd know it anywhere.

'How the hell . . .?'

He dropped the shovel unheeded to the ground and, mindless of the stink and stickiness of the manure, he scrabbled in the barrow for the glimpse of white he had seen in the first load. Within a moment it was safely in his hand. He brushed the stains and flecks of straw off it and examined it closely. One eye smiled back at him and he felt a surge of longing for her. He held the two pieces of photograph together and she came alive in his hands.

He remembered the moment. The day they had decided they should have a picture of each other and had bundled into a photograph booth together. It had been a squash and she had sat on his lap. The passionate kiss, the laughing embrace, his playful peck on her nose, they had all been recorded in the miniature squares. But she had insisted on keeping all the pictures with him in for herself and had only allowed him to have the single one of her with just his hand on her shoulder.

The other half of her face. Where was it? The thought of the amount of manure he had already spread and dug into the garden appalled him. It could be anywhere. Please God let the second half still be in the main mound. Frantically he started to search, indifferent now to what, only a moment ago, had been repulsive to him. All he could think of was finding the rest of that face.

It did not take long. They were not far from where the first two had been. With relief he wiped all four pieces of photograph thoroughly with his glove, trying to rub away the brown stains that streaked across them. But even those marks and the creases in the paper could not conceal her fragile beauty from him. He held the completed face flat on his palm and only just restrained himself from kissing the soiled paper. Instead he threw his filthy gloves to the ground and rushed into the house with his prize.

The disinfectant removed the smell and some of the marks,

but could not quite rid all the stains from the hairline creases. Unfortunately it also blurred the picture in places but not enough to dull the sharp edge of his pleasure. He carefully taped the pieces together so that the photograph was whole once more, then he sat down at the kitchen table and gazed at the face.

'Sarah,' he murmured, as he ran a finger softly over the thick dark hair. 'Where are you? Why did you go?'

He remained there for a long time.

At the end of it, he stood up and fetched the two bottles of scotch from the cupboard. He unscrewed the caps and smelled the strong fumes that escaped. Instantly his stomach hungered for it, but before he could change his mind, he lifted them above the sink and tipped them upside down. Several times his hands shook with the effort of fighting the urge to stem the amber flow, but his grip remained firm until the last drop had gone.

There was only one way the photograph could have got into the manure heap. In pieces.

Jenny.

She must have found it in one of his suits, torn it up in anger and buried it in the pile of dung. Taken what was not hers to take. He'd not had the slightest idea that she knew about Sarah. How long ago had she realised? He shrugged and stared at the empty bottles. It didn't make any difference now. It was all irrelevant because Sarah had gone. Deserted him. Jenny was the one he was left with. The one who had stood by him as his world had crumbled. She was the one he needed now and that was why he was doing the garden today. He would damned well show her. As well as show himself.

He picked up the photograph from the table and with a huge effort of will, he scrunched it into a ball. He crushed it tightly, as if trying to squeeze out the pain, threw it deep into the bin then quickly left the kitchen.

In the bathroom, he looked in the mirror. The face that stared back was a stranger's. Totally unfamiliar. The beard was thick now and hid the bottom half of his face, but he saw that his mouth had settled into a thin bitter line. His eyes were sunken and bloodshot, his cheeks hollow. He picked up his electric razor. He could start again, make this the first step. But did he want to? That was the real question. Was it worth the massive effort? Wasn't it so much easier just to drown in the numbing waves of alcohol?

He looked into the hard blue eyes and sought an answer, but the only expression that gazed back at him was one of weariness. He wasn't young any more and he felt he had aged a century in the last six months. His brain raced haphazardly over a series of splintered scenes, their jagged shards slicing through his mind, and relentlessly he lived again the recent destruction of his life. Of himself. He recalled the drunken stupor that had cost him the Japanese job, Jenny's patience as she poured him into bed, her acceptance of the silent evenings and barren nights. Always Jenny. Always there.

She was the one person who had stuck by him against all odds and he knew that if he could just make the first effort, she would be there to help him. The strength she had shown surprised him. He could rely on her. After all, she was his wife, wasn't she? She owed him loyalty. He switched on the razor and the soft noise of its motor was like the sound of his own engine whirring into life.

Jenny came down the steps of the bank with a smile on her face and the forms clutched in her hand. The meeting had gone well, even better than she had dared hope. Now it was time to go and see Caroline Palmer.

The High Street was busy with the crush of early afternoon shoppers, all jostled by the keen autumn wind that chased any scrap of litter along the pavement. Halfway down the hill Jenny turned into the doorway marked with the brass plaque that announced Palmer, Paige and Irving, Solicitors. The receptionist was pleasantly efficient and waved Jenny through to Caroline's office.

'Thanks for seeing me this morning, when I know you're probably flat out.'

'That's all right. What are friends for, if not to abuse?' Caroline laughed. 'Sit down and tell all.'

Jenny chose the more comfortable-looking of the hard leather chairs arrayed in front of the desk and looked about her. This was her first visit to Caroline's office and she was interested to see how much of it reflected her friend's warm but forthright personality. The decor was discreet and the furniture of good quality, but the pictures on the walls were bright and colourful and the shelves brimmed over with a haphazard jumble of books. A bunch of anemones gave a cheerful splash of colour to the desk.

'I need a bit of advice.'

'Advice on what? Divorce? It's my speciality.'

Jenny frowned in mock annoyance. 'Won't you ever give up? No, Caroline, it's not about divorce.'

'More's the pity.'

'Just concentrate on what I'm here for.'

'And what's that?'

'I want you to look over a contract for me.'

Caroline leaned forward with interest. 'A contract? Certainly, I can help you there.'

Jenny drew a pile of papers from her bag and placed them on the desk. 'I've got to get back to the shop now, as I have already been longer than I said I would. So I'll leave this with you and collect it at five thirty, if I may. Tell me then what you make of it.'

Caroline gathered the documents into her hands and raised an eyebrow. 'Better make it four o'clock, if you can, as I'm out later.'

'Fine. Steve will have to cope alone again.' She stood up and at the door turned to say, 'Thanks, Caroline, I'll be back later.' But a vague grunt was the only reply and Jenny smiled as she saw her legal friend already engrossed in the small print.

Jenny knew the moment she turned into the drive that something was different.

She was back later than usual. Susannah Benson had breezed into the shop just before closing time to pick Jenny's brains on what kind of multi-gym equipment was best to buy for her new-found keep-fit enthusiasm. She had invited herself along for Jenny and Steve's customary drink at the Sea Trout and they had all spent a pleasant hour poring over the various sports catalogues Susannah had brought with her. It had been with real reluctance that Jenny had eventually left the two of them in the warmth and laughter of the bar. To return home to what? Darkness, coldness and silence. She had shivered at the thought of the evening ahead. She could not let it go on much longer.

But to her surprise, when she drove through the gates, the house was shining brightly with a welcoming glow. The instant she stepped through the door, she could feel the change. Sounds of activity issued from the kitchen and the lively rhythm of *Rhapsody in Blue* drifted into the hall. As she opened the kitchen door, she was greeted with an unexpected smile and a glass of wine, and it was with faint bewilderment that she gazed round the room. The table was carefully laid, with even a single rose from the garden in its centre and inviting aromas hovered round the oven. And then there was David himself.

He had changed. The beard was no more and his hair was combed and clean. But the real difference was in the eyes. The dead weight of hopelessness was gone and in its place was an energy that she had not seen for a long time.

'Welcome home. You must need this.'

She accepted the proffered glass and sipped the cool wine, giving herself time to adjust. 'This is a pleasant change.'

'The first of many, I promise you.'

She heard the eagerness in his voice. 'Do I take it then that this is a permanent transformation?' she enquired cautiously. 'Or shall I come home tomorrow and find, just when I've got my expectations up, that you have reverted to living in the bottle again? That today was just a flash in the pan.' She saw him flinch.

He stepped closer to her, took the glass from her hand and placed it on the table. Then he put his arms around her tense figure and looked down into the wary dark eyes. 'You have every right to be angry. How you've put up with my self-destructive behaviour, I don't know.'

Jenny continued to stare at him but made no comment.

'I've put us both through hell, I admit it, but my only excuse is that I was totally in shock. It was that damned Lerner's fault.

My world came crashing down and buried me under the debris.'
His eyes dropped under the strength of her gaze. A mumbled
'I'm sorry' was just audible. Then with an effort he smiled, the
hollow-cheeked ghost of the old Cranshaw charm. 'The drinking
is over.' He squeezed her arm as if to prompt a response, but
in the face of her continued silence and unswerving stare, he
laughed anxiously, 'Apology accepted?'

The silence hung between them for an uncomfortable time,
then Jenny said solemnly, 'Yes, David, I accept your apology.'
Did he really think that's all it needed?

He bent and kissed her, running his hands possessively over
her shoulders. Then he pulled her tight to his chest and whispered, 'I promise it'll be different this time.'

She could feel the rapid beat of his heart and his desire
hardening against her. She pulled away and picked up her wine
from the table. She had not expected this. Not so soon.

'So what has prompted this sudden urge to turn over a
new leaf?'

David waved a hand vaguely, as if brushing aside the past. 'I
guess I just came to my senses. Now I've got to get back on my
feet and start functioning again. My life's not over yet.'

She nodded slowly. 'Yes, who knows what the future will
bring?'

'Absolutely right. So it's time I got back in shape.' He ran a
hand over his clean-shaven chin. 'I've made a start and intend
to keep on the straight and narrow from now on.' He waved
a hand at the table. Beside his place mat stood a bottle of
Perrier water.

Jenny glanced at it in surprise. 'So I see.'

He gestured towards the oven. 'And the meal is nearly
ready.'

David had never cooked her a meal in his life and she could
not believe he was about to alter that track record now, new
leaf or not.

'What is it?'

'Pizza.'

That was more like it. Straight from freezer to oven to table.
But it was better than nothing.

'Good. I'll just go and put my feet up.' She headed for the door. 'Call me when it's ready. And don't forget the salad.'

'Now you're home, I thought you would do that.'

'No, David,' she shook her head firmly. 'It's important to finish what you've started. You do it.' She picked up her glass and left the room.

The small present was to cheer himself up. David felt the need of something to lift his black mood. During the last three weeks he had been trekking round the jobs agencies again and with monotonous regularity had come up with nothing. The bastards were still fighting shy. He just had to hang on in there.

It seemed a hopeless task and at times his need for a drink was desperate, especially today when he had read in the *Financial Times* that Dern & Fairchild were expanding. They had bought a small advertising agency and, on the principle of new brooms, he knew they would be looking for fresh talent. Somewhere some lucky bastard with half his own experience and expertise was going to walk into a highly paid marketing position.

'Don't be so bloody stupid,' he reminded himself. 'You wouldn't want to work for that malicious crowd again, even if they asked you.' But he knew they would never ask.

So he had driven into Hambury to give himself something to do and keep his mind off the empty drinks cupboard, as he had no more job agencies to chase and had noticed the kit in a shop window. He opened the bag he was carrying and peered inside. He was going to enjoy this one. It would be a beautiful model of Nigel Mansell's Williams championship car when it was completed. He recalled the sense of achievement he had got from making the Mercedes kit and felt the need for another injection of pride in himself. Anyway, the kit would keep him busy. Keep his thoughts off the bottle.

He was finding that hard. The temptation to wipe out all the pain with a few quick shots of scotch and to hell with the consequences was at times overwhelming. He knew he could lick it eventually, so what did the odd relapse matter? Half a dozen times it had happened and after each occasion it had been that much harder to climb back on the wagon. Strangely, Jenny had not seemed unduly distressed by his occasional fall from grace. When she had returned home and found him out for the count in his chair or, once, flat out on the kitchen floor, she had calmly made him comfortable with a blanket and left him to sleep it off. The next morning she had not even mentioned it.

A light drizzle started to fall, prompting David to pull up his raincoat collar and duck under a shop awning. His eyes rested casually on the window and his interest was instantly caught by the array of enticing red and black lingerie on display. The day he had bought Sarah a set of filmy red underwear edged with black lace rose vividly before him. The female assistant had been extremely helpful, holding up each minute, but costly, garment for him to admire and encouraging him to run his fingers over the gossamer material. Sarah had paraded in them for him in the privacy of her room that evening, so that when he ran his fingers over them again, the warmth of her flesh made them infinitely more desirable.

'Hello, David. How's it going?'

David jerked himself back to the High Street and turned to see Steve Thompson standing at his elbow.

'Thinking of buying a present for Jenny?'

David realised he was still staring blindly at the window display. He stepped away, embarrassed and quickly shook his head. 'Not really. I was just . . .'

'. . . Keeping abreast of the fashion scene?' Steve laughed at his own joke and David felt obliged to smile politely.

They had only met on a couple of previous occasions, when David had come into the shop to see Jenny, but David found her boss's easy manner irritating and faintly resented his overfamiliar relationship with his wife.

'Any luck with the job hunting yet?'

'No,' David replied shortly. Then softened it with, 'I'm still hammering away at it.' How much had Jenny confided in him?

'It's a miserable business. Touch wood,' Steve tapped the top of his head, 'I've been lucky so far. NOW is a great company to work for and they're opening more branches all the time.'

David was not in the mood for a commercial for the charity

business. 'Good,' he said dismissively and turned to leave, but Steve's hand caught his arm.

'Don't dash off yet. I'm glad I bumped into you. I've been wanting to have a word.'

David braced himself for what was coming. It was bound to be some kind of recrimination. So Jenny had sobbed on his shoulder after all, damn the woman.

'It's about NOW's future.'

David relaxed.

'We're expanding fast in the south-east, as I was saying. Our area manager feels we need more professional marketing advice to guide us along the right lines, but, to be honest, we don't want to fritter away too much hard-earned cash on it. So we're putting out feelers for freelance consultants. I wondered if you might be interested.'

David managed to keep his voice calmly under control, as he replied, 'Certainly, I could help you out there, I'm sure.'

'That's great.'

'I'll let you have my CV. It will give your boss an idea of my areas of expertise.'

'Sounds impressive.'

'I'm sure you'll find I'm more than sufficiently qualified for the job.'

'Well, I hope you won't find the job too small because—'

'No, I assure you. No fear of that.'

'Good, let me have your details then and I'll pass them on to my area manager.'

'Thanks, Steve, I appreciate it.'

'Think nothing of it. Anything to help you and your lovely wife. Good luck.' Steve waved and hurried off up the hill.

David was irritated by the remark about his wife, but not even that could cloud his pleasure at the prospect of work coming in at last. The advantage was that it was out here in the sticks, away from the mainstream gossip and rumour. Lerner's poisonous lies would not have stretched this far. He tucked the kit under his arm and strode eagerly back to the car park, his mind racing with the possibilities opening up. If only he could land this client, then he could progress by word of mouth to a growing clutch of local companies needing freelance London-standard advice and analyses. It might not be big time, but it was a start.

As he passed the off-licence, he was tempted. Just a small drink to celebrate. Only one. It took all his willpower to keep on walking past without stopping. Anyway, there was nothing to celebrate yet. He had been premature in his expectations of the Okiwa Electronics job and look how that had ended. This time he was determined to be more circumspect. Instead he promised himself a glass of wine to drink a toast if he eventually did land the work. See how he handled that and then go from there. One step at a time.

As he approached the car park, he automatically scanned the area for the tall dark figure that had so inexplicably attacked him before, but there was no danger lurking and only preoccupied shoppers climbed in and out of their cars – no lone young men threatening to waylay unwary pedestrians. Nevertheless, David gave the pub yard a wide berth and skirted round the opposite side of the tarmac.

He slipped the Mercedes into gear and drove easily out of the town. Despite his determination not to be too optimistic, he could not prevent his mind racing ahead. As he pulled off the dual carriageway on to one of the narrower roads that formed a network around Hambury, his head was full of plans and preparations. He could feel the adrenaline flowing freely, as his system kicked into a higher gear. He just could not resist the urge to hope and plan, the need for action. Even if nothing came of this charity shop work, it was worth following up the idea of pursuing the local companies. They may be small fry but it would be a beginning, a first step towards—

The loud blare of a horn shattered his thoughts and startled him out of his reverie. His eyes searched instantly for the cause of the disturbance and looming in his rear-view mirror he saw a car right on his back bumper. It hooted angrily again and again.

'What the hell . . .?'

The crazy driver was obviously impatient to overtake, but the road was so twisting here that the idea of passing was ludicrous. David put his foot down harder and for a moment the Mercedes pulled away, but the following car quickly caught up and attached itself to within an inch of his bumper once more. The hooting started again.

'You bloody menace,' David shouted. He could see a dark-haired man at the wheel. 'Get off my tail,' but it had no effect. As the road started to drop steeply downhill, he decided this lunacy had gone on long enough. With a curse, he started to brake.

The crunch from behind snapped his head back and catapulted the Mercedes forward with a jump. 'You damned maniac, what the hell do you think you're doing?'

Again he attempted to brake, but once more the small car behind slammed into his rear. He caught a brief glimpse in the mirror of a mangled bonnet, then put his foot down and accelerated away out of reach. But he had underestimated his pursuer, who was not to be shaken off so easily.

They were both racing towards the bottom of the hill, when David glanced in his mirror and saw the car veer out into the opposite lane. It was unbelievable. The maniac was going to try to overtake him just when they were hurtling towards a bend. He slammed on the brakes. It only needed a car to come round in the opposite direction and they would be in a huge pile-up.

As the small car came abreast of him, David looked sideways at the lunatic driver. To have such a death wish he had to be high on drugs. Fierce eyes glared back at him and a wide grin stretched the face into a contorted mask. But before David could recover from his astonishment, the car swerved and slammed into his side at high speed, buckling his door and jerking the steering wheel through his sweating palms, forcing the Mercedes out of control.

Its heavy body crashed through the flimsy hedge lining the road just where the earth fell away in a steep green slope. The engine raced as the wheels left the ground while it spun in a cumbersome arc and landed with a sickening crunch of steel and shattering glass on its side. The driver's side. It skidded a few feet further down the slippery bank, finally coming to rest with the upper wheels spinning wildly.

David could not believe he was not dead. The seat belt had held him firmly in place but he was covered in glass. A trickle of blood seeped down one side of his face and his whole body was battered and shaken. But he was still alive. As he tried to move, pain shot up his right leg, stunning him into immobility. The twisted steel had sliced into the flesh and crushed the bone below the knee. Blood soaked warmly into his trousers.

'Please God, make someone come and help me.'

He did not move a muscle, but lay absolutely still trying to control the pain. When at last he heard the sound of the ambulance siren and voices calling, his mind was still full of the dark face staring back at him from the other car, as it rammed him off the road. It was the same young man who had attacked him in the car park at Hambury.

But even more bewildering, he was certain the car had been the gold Fiesta owned by Sarah Archer.

'So you can't tell us any more than that, sir?'

The policeman looked unconvinced and his ambitious grey eyes stared hard at David.

'For heaven's sake, I'm not hiding anything, if that's what you're implying,' David snapped. 'I was forced off the road by a crazy joy rider and was lucky to escape with only a broken leg. Shouldn't you be out there looking for the maniac before he succeeds in killing someone?'

He sat forward aggressively, his face flushed with annoyance. What the hell was this blue uniform up to? He just kept going over and over the same points, as though the pieces of information would miraculously produce a new picture if he kept moving them around.

'I assure you, we are endeavouring to do so,' the young ginger-haired constable responded pompously and the clichéd phrases only irritated David further.

'Then why keep grilling me as if I were the culprit? Let me remind you, I am the injured party.'

David's leg was stretched out in front of him encased in a white shell of plaster and he tapped it lightly as if to emphasise his point. Constable Grant's eyes did not relent as he stared at the damaged limb.

Jenny sat watching the exchange and wondered what was going on. It was quite obvious the policeman thought David was holding something back, and she had to admit it did seem like that. But why on earth would he be protecting the person who had run him off the road?

The Mercedes was a complete write-off and David had spent the night in hospital, but other than the broken leg, had suffered only minor cuts and bruises. That morning Jenny had brought him home from the hospital and had been surprised at his morose silence. A vituperative outburst summoning retribution down on the head of his attacker was more what she had expected.

Constable Grant was trying to pacify David's display of anger. 'I am well aware that you have been through a very shocking experience. It's just that you do not seem to have a very clear picture of the car or of its driver. I'm just trying to jog your memory.'

'I've already told you all I know. I was in fear of my life, for God's sake. You don't go gazing at the cars and people around you when you're fighting to stay on the road.'

'So you're certain you can't recall the exact colour of the car, sir?'

'Just that it was pale,' David reiterated. 'Maybe cream or beige, I can't remember.'

'And a smallish car, you say. Maybe a Fiesta.' The constable jotted a note on to his pad.

'Yes, or a Metro. It was just a blur in my mirror.'

'I do understand that, sir. It must have been extremely frightening for you.' He glanced across at the wife and found her gazing speculatively at her husband. So she didn't believe him either.

'It's just that it's a bit of a coincidence.'

David looked up quickly. 'Coincidence? What do you mean?'

'Well, sir, you reported an assault on you in Hambury car park not long ago. You were beaten up by . . .' He paused and consulted his pad, but only for effect. '. . . by a tall dark, young man, I believe it was.'

Jenny intervened, 'Are you suggesting there could be a connection between the two incidents?'

'It is possible, yes. These two incidents were both vicious attacks. And your husband says he thinks that yesterday the car we're looking for was driven by a man, probably youngish, which puts him in the same category as the attacker in the car park.' His voice could not hide his scorn at the inadequacy of the description. 'He is unfortunately not able to recall whether the man in the car was fair or dark.'

David stared with irritation at the constable, but said nothing.

'So you do think they are connected,' Jenny commented thoughtfully. She looked at David, but he did not meet her eye.

Constable Grant turned back to David. 'What is your opinion of that possibility, sir? Do you think it might have been the same person in both attacks?'

David studied the plaster on his leg, as if turning the idea over in his mind. Eventually he looked up at the policeman. 'I honestly don't know. You could be right or you may be barking up the wrong tree completely. I admit it does look like a bit of a coincidence and I'm sure in both attacks it was a man. But my vague impression was that the one in the car was slightly older and not so dark.'

'But you admit you did not see him clearly.'

'Yes.'

'Then it is possible you could be mistaken and it was in fact the same man?' Grant persisted.

A pause. 'Yes.'

Constable Grant smiled smugly at achieving the answer he had been pressing for. 'Then I have to—'

David interrupted, 'But my feeling is that they were not in fact the same man.'

'What makes you say that?'

'I don't know. I can't explain why.'

Irritation showed on Grant's face, as he reminded David, 'But you said it was only a vague impression. Nothing positive.'

'That is right.'

'Then, as I was saying, I have to ask you if there is anyone you know who might wish to see you harmed? If the two attacks were isolated incidents of the kind of mindless violence that is all too common today, then that is one matter. It is hard to find these people, but we try.'

Grant paused to study the effect of his remarks on David. Jenny watched him intently. 'But if, on the other hand, we can trace a thread of motive behind these actions, then we have a much greater chance of success.'

David continued to regard the constable without expression.

'So, sir, is there anyone who might have a grudge against you? Someone who might want revenge for something?'

'Of course not. Nothing like that. In business you always make enemies, but not bad enough to do anything serious.'

'Anyway,' Jenny added, 'my husband has been out of the rat race for the last few months.'

Grant pounced on that. 'May I ask why you left, sir?'

'Because I chose to, damn it. That's got nothing whatever to do with this business.'

Jenny could not understand it. Why was David reacting so belligerently? Even for him, this was over the top, when all the young policeman was trying to do was establish the facts. And perhaps he was right. Perhaps there was a connection.

'Constable, haven't you managed to find any other drivers who saw my husband's accident happen?'

'It wasn't an accident,' David growled.

'Incident then,' she corrected.

'No, Mrs Cranshaw, we have appealed for witnesses, but unfortunately none has come forward yet.'

'But surely someone must have seen the two cars together somewhere along the road.'

'That's quite possible, but we haven't heard from anyone so far. We're still pursuing enquiries.'

Jenny turned to David. 'You don't remember seeing that same car in the car park when you were attacked in Hambury, do you?'

'Of course not. For heaven's sake, I'm not even sure what make or colour it was, so how could I possibly say if it was in the car park?'

Jenny studied his scowling face and was suddenly certain the constable was right. The connection was there. But what on earth could be the reason? What was David hiding?

'So there's no reason you know of,' the policeman pressed on, 'why anyone would want to see you injured?'

'No, I've already told you there is nobody I know who could

possibly want to cause me any damage and I don't believe the incidents are connected. It's obvious this disaster was caused by a crazy drug-head, high as a bloody kite, who gets his kicks scaring us poor bastards shitless.'

Jenny stood up, hoping to encourage the policeman to leave. 'I agree with my husband. He's just been extremely unlucky.'

'I'm afraid I can't help you more,' David commented. 'I've told you all I know.'

Constable Grant looked at the hostile eyes and knew he would get no further. If that was how Mr Cranshaw wanted to play it, that was fine by him. He would just put out a few more appeals for witnesses and the forensic boys would identify the make and colour of the other car from the paint smears. But that would be that. There was no hope of finding the dangerous offender without co-operation from the victim.

'Very well.' Grant rose and made for the door. 'I'll keep you posted if we uncover any further information.' He turned and looked again at David's plastered limb. 'I hope your leg is better soon, sir.'

'Thank you.'

Jenny escorted the policeman into the hall and he took a lingering look at her legs as she walked ahead of him. But when he climbed into his car and turned to wave goodbye, she had already shut the door on him.

'David, my poor darling.' Susannah leaned down and flung her arms round his neck. 'You must be in agony. Let me kiss you better.'

She placed her soft lips to his and he could smell the fresh odour of sweat on her body, her cheeks glowing with vitality from recent exercise. It was the evening of their weekly aerobics session and she had descended on him in a flurry of concern.

'That's enough, Susannah, you're supposed to be kissing him better, not suffocating him,' Jenny commented as she left the room to fetch cold drinks.

Laughingly Susannah withdrew her embrace and stood looking down at David in his chair. She patted the white plaster supported on the stool. 'Can I sign my name on it? I'll write something wicked to amuse you when you're bored.'

'Thanks for the offer, but no thanks. How did the class go?'

'Exhausting.' Susannah collapsed into a chair. 'But I just had to come home with Jenny when I heard you'd been so brutally mangled.'

'I appreciate your concern, Susannah. As always, the epitome of Florence Nightingale.'

Susannah grinned. 'Do you think a nurse's uniform would suit me? Playing "doctors and nurses" was always my favourite game at school. Best of all I liked to be matron, as that meant I could examine all the boys.'

'I bet you did. You've missed your vocation.'

Jenny entered at that moment, carrying a tray of glasses and orange juice. 'What vocation is that?'

'David thinks I'd make a good nurse.'

Jenny laughed out loud at the idea. 'The poor male patients would come out of hospital more exhausted than when they went in.'

Susannah giggled delightedly, but remembering David's injury, she brought the conversation back to him. 'Does it hurt dreadfully, David?'

'I'll survive.'

'I'll come and massage it for you when the plaster's off. I can work wonders for limp limbs.'

'You're incorrigible,' Jenny laughed.

'Darling, I'm only teasing.' Susannah's eyes widened in mock innocence, as she shook her luxurious mane around her shoulders and assured David, 'I'd not harm a fly.'

'No,' Jenny commented, 'you'd just unzip it as fast as you could.'

Both women burst out laughing, but David only smiled politely. Jenny noticed the dark shadows in his eyes, went over to his chair and carefully lifted his injured leg off the stool on to the floor.

'Come on, time for bed. Susannah, you can have the pleasure of helping me get him up the stairs.'

'Delighted to have the honour.' She finished her drink with a flourish. 'I needed that. I don't think I've got a drop of moisture left in me after all that leaping about.'

'I'm sure you'd manage to find some if the need arose,' Jenny teased. 'Now come and help me get David on his feet.'

Together they pulled him upright and then, with their arms wrapped around his waist and his weight on their shoulders, they helped him hobble up the stairs. When he finally collapsed on the bed with a groan, Jenny commented, 'Say goodnight now, Susannah. Time to go.'

'Don't I get to help him off with his trousers?'

'Definitely not.'

'Well, I'd better go and help Robert off with his instead then. Bye, my darling, take care.' She bent over David on the bed, so that her breasts brushed his chest and kissed him warmly on the mouth once more. As she straightened up, she suggested, 'What you two need is a proper holiday. You've both been in the wars recently and should take a break. Get away from it all.'

David grunted without interest and concentrated on easing himself into a more comfortable position.

'Really, David, I mean it. Just that trip up to London for the day bucked Jenny and me up no end last week. A change of scenery does you good, so imagine what a couple of weeks in the sun would do for—' She broke off, realising that David was staring at her.

'What trip to London?'

Jenny stepped in quickly. 'Susannah and I treated ourselves to a day in town last week.'

'Weren't you supposed to be working?'

'I took the day off. Steve didn't mind.'

'But you didn't think it worth informing me?'

'No, I didn't.' For a moment they stared at each other, then Jenny turned to Susannah. 'Come on, I'll see you to your car.'

Susannah blew David a final kiss and accompanied Jenny downstairs. In the hall she queried David's mood. 'He seems very down in the mouth. None of my teasing would cheer him up.'

'I know. He's been very quiet since the accident. Not exactly depressed, just quiet and unresponsive.'

'He'll snap out of it soon, I expect. It must have been a helluva scare for him and being stuck indoors now with that blasted plaster on his leg can't exactly improve his temper.'

'No, it doesn't. He hates being alone all day, especially now he can't drive anywhere.'

'Poor lamb. No job, no company and no mobility. What a mess he's in.'

'By the way, thanks for letting slip about the London jaunt. I told you not to mention it as it's part of the surprise.'

'Oh hell, I'm sorry, Jenny. It just came out without thinking.'

'Never mind. It's done now.'

Susannah leaned close and whispered conspiratorially, 'How's it going? All fixed up yet?'

Jenny smiled. 'It's almost there. Not long now.'

'Any news on work for David? Not that he'll be doing much with that snowy straitjacket on his leg.'

'There is one possibility with the NOW charity in the pipeline.'

'Well, that should raise his spirits.'

'It's not definite yet, but he's keeping his fingers crossed.'

Susannah's wide mouth drooped in an expression of exaggerated sympathy. 'It must be rotten for you both. I wish I could persuade Robert to offer him something, but the old sourpuss has really dug his heels in. He won't even consider it. He claims it's because David has proved he's unstable, what with the drinking and . . .' she hesitated '. . . you ending up in hospital.'

'I told you, he didn't—'

'I know, I know.' She pulled on her fleecy jacket and fluffed up her hair. 'Anyway, I'm convinced the real reason Robert is being so stubborn is that he's sulking over David deserting him for a rival company. You know what spiteful little boys these men are at heart.'

'But business has always been cutthroat,' Jenny reminded her. 'Sentiment has never stood in the way of ambition. It's the same everywhere.'

'I know that, but there's no point arguing with him. He just won't listen to me. The old grouch is determined to stay with Fairchild and is having lunch with him next week.'

Jenny kissed her on the cheek. 'Don't worry about it,

Susannah. David will survive. He is the one responsible for causing this mess and he's the one who will have to dig himself out.'

'But you're in it as well.'

'Yes, that's true,' Jenny said thoughtfully. 'But it was my own choice.'

Susannah looked at her oddly. 'None of us chooses our disasters.'

'Don't we?' Jenny smiled. 'I think perhaps we do.'

'That's absurd. But it'll certainly be a disaster for me if I don't get home soon. Robert doesn't even know I'm here. Sorry I can't be more hopeful about some work from him, but you never know, he may come round in the end.'

She ducked out into the cold wind and as Jenny closed the door behind her, the sound of David's voice drifted down the stairs. He wanted help to undress. As she headed back upstairs, she told herself, 'Be patient, just a little longer.' This broken leg was a disaster she could have happily done without, but no way would she let it make her deviate from her chosen path.

The telephone call came as a complete surprise. The week had been a busy one and Jenny had arrived home tired from work, so it was with reluctance that she abandoned her chair to answer the insistent ring. As she hurried into the hall, she flexed her shoulders in an attempt to ease the knot of tension at the base of her neck.

'Hello?'

'Hello, Jenny, it's Phoebe.' Phoebe O'Brian was her new fitness instructor, whom Susannah had dubbed 'Dobbin' because of her long nose and horsy laugh.

After a brief exchange of pleasantries, Jenny asked, 'Is there a problem about tomorrow?' The instructor had never rung her at home before and as the next class was scheduled for the following day, Jenny could only assume it was about to be postponed for some reason.

She listened in silence to the long-winded response and eventually hung up without further comment. She stood staring at the receiver, trying to figure out the cause of the telephone call. It didn't make sense. She walked slowly back into the sitting-room and resumed her seat. David, engrossed in his Mansell racing car model, did not even look up. Jenny held her book in front of her eyes once more, but in reality all she saw was Phoebe's plastic smile.

'Who was it on the phone?' David suddenly asked.

'My exercise class instructor.' She noticed he seemed relieved by her answer.

'What on earth does she want?' but his attention was already returning to the miniature wheel in his hand.

'She says the class is too full and she wants to cut back the numbers. So I'm out on my ear.'

David looked up in surprise. 'I thought you said the class was already very small.'

'It is.'

'So why is she turning away clients?'

'That's what I want to know.'

David shrugged and lost interest, but after a few more moments' thought, Jenny put aside her book and went to ring Susannah. Phoebe had not mentioned her, but if there was no room for herself, then in theory, Susannah should also be given the heave-ho, as they had joined at the same time. She let it ring for a long time, but there was no answer. Frustrated, she replaced the receiver, with suspicions already stirring and filling her with unease.

'Never mind,' she reassured herself, 'you will easily find another class to attend and you didn't much like Phoebe anyway.'

But when she resumed her seat, she found it very hard to concentrate on her book.

'Great news!' David waved the letter in front of her face, his eyes alive with enthusiasm. 'The NOW area manager wants to see me in Tonbridge next week. To discuss the possibility of a consultancy, he says.'

The permanently worried expression of recent days was wiped away by the few typed lines. 'Thank God you took that job with them, because it looks as if this might be the start of my new career. David Cranshaw, freelance marketing consultant. I won't get my hopes up high, though, until after the meeting.' But his voice betrayed that it was already too late for such restraint.

He was waiting for her response.

'I would think you stand a good chance of getting the position, given your past experience.'

'Damned right I do.' He rifled through the rest of the morning's post, dumped the junk mail in the bin and poured himself another coffee, though he felt like something stronger. 'If only I didn't have this blasted ton weight on my leg. You'll have to drive me to Tonbridge when the time comes.'

'I'll be working.'

He looked up sharply. 'Then take the afternoon off. This is important.'

She studied him as he reread the letter. 'Important to you, yes,' she said softly, but he paid no attention. He was already impatient for the intervening days to pass. It was a sharp contrast to his recent preoccupied moodiness. She had not been able to fathom why he had become so withdrawn and silent, even taking to the bottle again occasionally, and in the end had put it down to the pain in his leg and the shock of the accident.

'This is just the shot in the arm I need. This morning I'll start getting stuck into those facts I've dug up on charity businesses. Might as well impress them from the outset.' He hobbled out of the kitchen.

Jenny pulled on her raincoat and glanced out the window. The dismal weather had not let up for days now and though the forecasters had promised only showers today, it looked as if another Friday morning was going to be a wash-out. As she backed her MR2 out of the garage, she got the now familiar kick at driving the sleek car and she resented the mess the rain and mud would make of its gleaming paintwork. She would have to try to make time at the weekend for a thorough hose-down, though at the moment David was making use of her car as a taxi and herself as a chauffeur. She pressed down on the accelerator. Not for much longer, he wouldn't. He could take a cab to the interview if necessary.

She switched the wipers on to fast speed to sweep a path

through the drenching spray. It was ironic that it should be the NOW charity chain that was about to offer David a consultancy. Ironic that she should be the cause of the job falling in his lap, after all she had done to achieve the very reverse. But this time it was different. This time her view of the way ahead was from a completely altered angle that widened at each step forward. Well, David could have the NOW charity, if that's what he wanted, for her thoughts were already racing in a different direction.

The heavy rain blanketed the dual carriageway and the traffic bunched into a solid wall. Jenny glanced at the clock. She was going to be late. As she sat peering out impatiently between each sweep of the wipers, she recalled once more the phone call from Phoebe last night. Again her stomach lurched uncomfortably. Her nerves were on edge and she was relieved when the traffic started to flow more freely, with the prospect of the day ahead to take her mind off her fears.

But when she saw Caroline Palmer standing waiting outside the shop door, huddled under a dripping umbrella, she instantly jumped to the conclusion something had gone wrong. Not now, please not now. Not when she was so near.

'You're late,' Caroline greeted her.

'It's a monsoon out there. The traffic was hopeless. But to what do I owe this early-bird visit? No emergency, I hope.'

'No, no, nothing like that.'

Jenny felt relief wash over her and turned to unlock the door to shield her face from view. 'So what's the trouble?' she asked over her shoulder.

'Let me into the dry before I drown out here and I'll tell you.'

Once inside, Jenny set about opening shop, attending to lights, alarm and till. Caroline looked around and ran her fingers through a display of silk scarves from India.

'Gorgeous colours. You ought to—'

'Never mind those, Caroline. Why were you lying in wait for me? Has something gone wrong with the documents?'

'Of course not. Not with me handling it,' she smiled. 'Don't be so paranoid.'

Jenny laughed and relaxed. 'Okay, I admit I'm a bit jumpy. Just tell me what you're here for.'

'I'm on my way to the office and just stopped by to ask you to drop in this morning to sign the papers. I'll be out the rest of the day, so it has to be before lunch, that's all.'

'Yet more papers?'

'These are the final ones, I promise. After today, it's all set.'

A surge of excitement robbed Jenny of words, but she hugged her friend tight.

'There's just one problem.'

Jenny quickly released her. 'What? What's the matter?'

'It's David.'

'Oh. Oh, that.'

'Yes, that. You've got to get his signature.'

'I know.'

'It's no good, you can't put it off any longer, Jenny. You can't go ahead without it.'

'I know.'

'It's all set for the first of the month. That gives you one more week.'

Jenny sat down on the stool. 'I'll get it by then.'

'What if he doesn't want to co-operate? Refuses to sign?'

'He'll sign.'

'I hope you're right. It would be awful if he—'

'I promise you, he'll sign. Believe me, Caroline.'

Caroline nodded. 'Okay, I believe you, but I wish you luck.'

At that moment, the door jangled open and Steve Thompson walked in. 'The traffic out there is a nightmare.' He shook off his drenched raincoat. 'Hi, Caroline, how's business?'

'Hectic, so I must make a dash for the office now or Andrew will think I've been washed away down a drain.' She headed for the door.

Jenny stood up. 'I'll come over about eleven in my coffee break, if that suits you.'

'Fine. See you then.'

'Caroline.'

Caroline turned and looked at Jenny, so poised and confident in her present role. Only the dark shadows in the eyes betrayed the tension. 'Yes?'

'Thank you.'

Caroline chuckled and held up two crossed fingers. 'It's not over till the fat lady sings. But I put my money on you.' With a brief wave and a shake of her umbrella, she ducked out into the rain.

Steve stared at Jenny. 'What was that all about?'

'Nothing much. Just something she's arranging for me.'

'Right, let's concentrate on the window today. It's time for a thorough revamp.'

Jenny smiled as they started to remove the native drums and rugs from the window. Steve was capable of stripping it, but he relied heavily on her to create the new display. How would he manage when she was gone? She felt a twinge of guilt. She would have to tell him next week.

During a break in the rain, an unexpected rush of customers kept them both busy and Jenny was grateful to have her mind distracted from her worries about David and his signature by the demands of a querulous old man, who was looking for a specific ebony carving from Thailand of a native fisherman that his daughter had seen in the window the previous week. It had unfortunately sold the day before, but Jenny managed to induce him to buy a different carving from the same Thai village, this one of a dancing maiden. With assurances that he could have a refund if his daughter was not pleased with it, he left satisfied.

By lunchtime, Jenny was feeling positively buoyant. The trip to Caroline's office had been brief but gave her a rush of adrenaline that had her surpassing even her usual skills in designing an eye-catching window display. When she came back into the shop after a final inspection of her handiwork from outside, Steve congratulated her.

'It looks great. I expected no less.'

Jenny nodded her thanks. It was all good practice. 'By the way, Steve, David heard from your manager this morning. He's set up a meeting for next week.'

'That sounds promising. I know he was very interested when I sent him David's details. I wish him luck.'

'Thanks for putting his name forward in the first place. He's very grateful.' The lie came out easily.

'With his experience and reputation, I'm amazed he hasn't been snapped up before now. We're lucky to get him.'

'Luck has nothing to do with it.'

'What do you mean?'

'I mean you make your own luck.'

Steve laughed, 'That's certainly true. It was, though I say it myself, my excellent judgement that made me offer you the job here in the summer and it's as a result of that, we are now acquiring David's skills for the whole area.'

Jenny's mouth widened in an amused smile. 'Yes, each a connecting link in a chain.'

'And talking of chains, how about trying that new wine bar at the top of the High Street for lunch? I hear it's got chains hanging on the walls. Very kinky.'

'I think it's intended to be medieval, Steve,' Jenny laughed. 'But yes, that sounds good to me.'

Just as they were about to leave at one o'clock, the telephone rang. Steve hurried back to his office, promising to keep it short, while Jenny waited patiently in the shop, but after five minutes she wandered over to enquire whether she should go on ahead. To her surprise, he was standing with his back pointedly turned to the door and was speaking in low tones into the receiver.

Jenny stood there uncertainly for a few seconds, trying not to look as if she was eavesdropping, but all she heard was a muttered, 'I can't believe it. Are you sure he got his facts straight?'

There was silence, while he listened to the reply and Jenny felt it was time to interrupt.

'Steve,' she said quietly.

He jumped as if shot. He whirled round to face her and his expression astonished her. It was one of guilt. And fear.

Quickly he recovered and apologised awkwardly, 'Sorry, Jenny, I got caught up discussing something.'

'That's all right. Don't let me stop you. I'll go on ahead.'

'No, no, it's for you actually. It's Susannah Benson.' He said a brief 'Bye' into the phone and handed it over to her. 'I'm afraid I won't be able to make that drink for lunch after all,' he said quickly. 'Something's come up. It'll probably keep me out all afternoon, but I'll be back to cash up at five thirty.' He hurried past her, grabbed his jacket and dashed out of the shop.

'Good heavens, Susannah,' Jenny said into the receiver, 'what on earth did you say to put such a fire in his tail? He's rushed off like a scalded cat.'

There was a long pause, then Susannah's voice replied too casually, 'Nothing, nothing at all. God knows what's got into him. I just rang to . . . to say I'm sorry you won't be in the fitness group any more.'

Jenny listened to the taut and subdued voice and hardly recognised it. 'So you haven't been asked to leave?'

'No.'

'Doesn't that strike you as odd? As we joined together.'

'Phoebe felt she had to drop just one person and I'm afraid it was you. Sorry, but you can always exercise at home with your video tapes.'

There was an uncomfortable silence.

'Susannah, what is going—'

'Got to dash now. Bye.' The line went dead.

Jenny stared, bewildered, at the receiver and then replaced it on its cradle. What was all that about, for heaven's sake? And what was the meaning of that long secretive conversation between Steve and Susannah? Had she actually got her hooks into him and was in the middle of a passionate affair? It would certainly explain Steve's embarrassment at perhaps being caught arranging an assignation. If that was the case, it was obvious why he had deserted her for the afternoon: the lure of a cheap hotel room.

But Jenny could not bring herself to believe it of Susannah, because although she was an outrageous flirt, Jenny was certain Susannah cared too much for Robert to hurt him like that. It all just didn't make sense.

Her mind still reeling, she locked up the shop and spent her lunch hour in the packed supermarket, dutifully stocking up for the weekend.

The clock struck two. David stretched his back muscles to ease the ache caused by a morning spent in his study, hunched over the keyboard and screen that he kept for his own exclusive use. Jenny may be acquiring new skills at her job, but he still did not trust her to meddle with this expensive hardware. He reached forward and switched off the VDU, but he could not turn off his mind so easily. Facts and figures about the target markets of the charity business still whirled in his mind.

He stood up abruptly to break the chain of thought and his leg instantly protested. Questions about the extent of diversification required were replaced by the one question that had burned itself into his brain ever since his Mercedes was forced off the road. Why had Sarah turned on him? Why had she sent someone to lie in wait for him and try to mangle him to a pulp? Not once, but twice.

It was obvious the young constable had suspected there was more to the attacks than David was admitting, but what more could he add without handing Sarah over to the police? He had to find her first. For Christ's sake, he could have been killed in that car. But how on earth could he get hold of her? When he had telephoned her ex-flatmates, they had assured him that she had not been in touch since she left and her mail was just gathering dust in a pile. He had even tried Dern & Fairchild personnel office, claiming to be a relative who had lost touch. But it was another dead end. They had informed him that Miss Archer had collected her back pay and documents in person, so they had no forwarding address.

He had been over and over it in his mind. Round and round in circles. Every second of that last lunchtime together he had replayed a thousand times. But it got him nowhere. He just couldn't come up with anything that made sense. Even if she was pregnant, why should she hate him? Surely, he was the one who had been wronged.

His head ached with the effort and he decided to take a break by making himself some coffee. God, he was sick of being on the wagon, as well as sick of this plaster on his leg. How was he going to put up with the damned thing for six long weeks? The pain in his leg made him hurry with the cafetiere and it was with a sigh of relief that he eventually sank down into his chair in the sitting-room and sipped the strong dark brew.

Using the remote control, he turned on the television, letting himself wind down with the afternoon film. Black and white it may be, but Katharine Hepburn and Cary Grant together were irresistible. Their ludicrous antics amused him and his laughter eased the disquiet of his mind. It was just when Hepburn was swinging wildly on top of a twenty-foot ladder that the doorbell sounded. Damn, he did not want to get up. His leg was comfortably settled and he was not in the mood for Jehovah's Witnesses or itinerant tradesmen. He was tempted to ignore the unwanted visitor in the hope they would go away, but a second more demanding ring of the bell persuaded him to make the effort.

He stumbled to his feet and resented the painful process of hobbling to the hall, so it was with a frown that he swung open the front door.

She stood before him as lovely as ever.

He gasped in disbelief and blinked twice to make certain it was not another of his dreams. Her tentative smile convinced him she was real. Only she could promise so much by such a slight movement of her lips.

'Sarah.'

'Hello, David.'

They both stood there, not speaking, their eyes locked on each other. David drank in every detail of her fragile face, her abundant dark hair and her slight figure. No sign of any swelling.

At last he stepped back and held the door wide. 'Come in.'

Sarah walked into the hall and he shut the door behind her before she could change her mind and escape. He was not going to let her go this time, not without explanation.

She stood quietly, but her eyes were tense and her body looked poised for flight. She wore a thick camel coat, the collar pulled up against the cold, a coat he remembered wrapping round their naked bodies, when they had made love one chilly evening in the woods during a business trip out of town. He limped towards her, but she exclaimed, 'No!' and backed off two paces, though her gaze remained fixed on his.

'David, I've missed you so much.' Her eyes filled with tears, but he did not dare approach her again in case he frightened her away.

'Sarah, why did you disappear? Where did you go?'

She struggled for control, but when she spoke she ignored his questions. 'I had to come to see you, David. I have sat in my car so many times further down this road, just on the off-chance you might come out and I'd get a glimpse of you. I've seen your wife going off to her job in Hambury.'

David's expression changed to one of surprise.

Sarah laughed nervously, 'You'd be amazed how much I know about your comings and goings. I've watched—'

'Sarah, I—'

She did not let him finish. 'No, David, please listen. Let me say what I've come to say.'

He wanted to take her in his arms, to hold her tight and never let her go, but he made himself keep his hands at his sides and say quietly, 'I'm listening.'

'David, I'm sorry. Whatever you did to me, I would never want to hurt you. You must believe that.' She struggled once more against tears and her voice was low. 'As soon as I found out what my brother had done, I knew I had to come and see you. To know you were all right. To say I'm sorry.'

She glanced down at the white plaster and he edged a step nearer.

'So it was your brother? In the Fiesta? And in the car park as well?'

'Yes, but I swear I didn't know what he was doing. Not until I saw my car all pushed in and he confessed everything. Told me what he had done to you.'

'But why would he want to kill me? What have I ever done to him?'

Her eyes were shocked, but she kept her voice calm. 'It was what you did to me, David. That was his reason. He was just repaying the injury. I am the one who could have been killed.'

David stared at her, confused by her words. 'What on earth do you mean by that?'

'You know only too well.' She turned away to hide the emotion in her face and he took the opportunity to come closer.

'Sarah, I don't know what the hell you're talking about.'

She looked round in surprise at hearing him so near and the sight of him just an arm's length away broke down her defences. 'Oh, David,' she sobbed, 'David, you look so well. Not ill at all. I've been so worried about you.'

He stepped forward and wrapped her in his arms, hugging her tight to convince himself it was really her at last, not another phantom of his dreams.

She buried her face in his chest and he smelled the fragrance of her hair, felt the trembling of her body. He did not care that he had no idea what she meant, nor that she was the cause of his beating and his broken leg. All he knew was that she was here, in his arms.

'Sorry I'm late.' Steve Thompson's dark hair glistened from the rain, as he pushed open the door. 'I didn't mean to keep you waiting.'

'It doesn't matter.' Jenny looked up from the till. 'I've started cashing up for you.'

It was gone five thirty and she had turned the shop sign to 'Closed' after a quiet afternoon on her own. She picked up her raincoat, wished him goodnight and was about to leave, but Steve stopped her.

'Come into the office for a few minutes, please, Jenny.' His voice was distant and formal.

What on earth was this about? She followed him into the cluttered little office and stood waiting, while he sat in the chair behind the desk and placed a long brown envelope in front of him. He stared at it silently for a moment, then cleared his throat, obviously nervous and ill at ease. Jenny came over and stood before the desk, smiling down at him.

'What's the matter, Steve? Didn't your afternoon go well?'

He did not look at her. 'No, my afternoon was awful, to tell the truth. I had to make a decision that was very unpleasant.'

Jenny was surprised by the seriousness of his tone.

'And that decision is this,' Steve continued, his eyes flitting up to Jenny's very briefly before settling once more on the envelope. 'I'm sorry, Jenny, but I've got to terminate your employment with this company. I shall not require you in this shop after today.'

It was like a blow in the pit of her stomach. She couldn't have heard right. He must be teasing her.

He pushed the envelope across the desk. 'Here is your pay to the end of the month and I've included one month's notice.' Still he did not look at her.

Jenny sank into the chair in front of his desk, disbelief battling with reason. She attempted to speak, but only a faint croak emerged. She swallowed and tried again. 'Steve, what is this about? What's happened? We were getting along so well and the business is doing fine, so why . . .?'

The words died in her throat, as Steve raised his eyes and looked straight at her. There was that fear again, entwined with embarrassment. But definitely fear.

'Why, Steve, why?'

There was silence. Her boss sat very stiffly in his chair and then, with an obvious effort, said, 'I could spin you some tale about not needing a full-time assistant any more or that head office is sending over someone from another branch. But I don't want to do that. We've been friends and you deserve the truth.'

Jenny gripped the edge of her chair and felt a wave of nausea sweep through her.

'I have to say I think you've been less than honest with me, Jenny, to say the least. But nevertheless I will be straight with you.'

Her mind registered the hurt and anger in his voice, but she could feel nothing. She was numb with shock.

Steve took a deep breath and then the words came out in a rush. 'I have been informed that your husband was sacked from his London job because he has AIDS. Obviously that means you could also be infected. I don't know whether you've been tested or not, but I can't risk employing someone who might be a carrier.'

He paused for her response, but when there was none, he hurried on, 'I am sorry, Jenny. Sorry for you and sorry for David. But I am not willing to put myself, my customers or my employers in danger for you. Or my son.' He shuddered visibly. 'Most of all not my son. So you have to leave and I—'

'Steve,' she managed to whisper, 'it's not true.'

He stared at her, then said uncomfortably, 'You are bound to say that, aren't you?'

'No, no, it's all a mistake.' She remembered only too well typing the letters to Fairchild on her old typewriter and her satisfaction as she slid them into the open mouth of the postbox. In her wildest imaginings, she had not expected them to rebound like this. 'None of it is true. David is perfectly healthy, I promise you. He hasn't got AIDS and isn't even a carrier. It's just a malicious rumour.'

Still she saw incredulity on his face.

'I'll have a test and that will prove I'm telling the truth. I swear I'm not HIV positive.'

His gaze wavered uncertainly. 'And will David have a test too? He can't possibly be employed by this company as a consultant if I'm not convinced he's clear.'

She hesitated. How could she ask David to be tested for AIDS? What possible explanation could she give?

Steve took her hesitation as confirmation of guilt. 'So you're not so certain, after all.' He rose, picked up the envelope and held it out to her. 'I'm sorry, Jenny.'

She accepted it dumbly and rose to walk out, but stumbled as her knees buckled beneath her. Steve reached out and steadied her, but quickly withdrew his hand. She stared at him in amazement and he instantly looked away.

'I'm not a leper, you know,' she said quietly. 'I'm still the same person I was this morning. Nothing has changed.'

'Oh yes it has. The difference is that this morning I was in ignorance. And now I'm not.'

'You condemn me with no trial? No proof? Just irrational fear for your own skin.'

'And for my child. When I think of him in here with you . . .' Steve turned his back on her and walked out of the office.

She followed him, suddenly seething at the injustice. 'Even if I were HIV positive,' she shouted at him, 'I wouldn't be instantly poisonous. Half the things we sell here are probably made by people suffering from the disease, but that doesn't worry you. It's no reason to sack me. You're a bloody coward, Steve Thompson. You listen to unfounded rumours and believe them rather than me.'

He faced her and she flinched at the sight of the bitterness in his expression. 'You are the one who is the coward, Jenny. You could not bring yourself to tell me the truth, but chose to trick me and this company into trusting you. And your husband.'

Jenny wanted to scream at him that it was all lies, lies, but forced her voice to remain calm. 'This is ridiculous, Steve. We have been good friends over the last few months. I wouldn't risk you or your son, you know that.'

'Do I?' His words were as chill as the rain outside. 'I can no longer believe or trust you. You would lie just to keep this job.'

Again the irony. Next week she would have handed in her notice. She watched him walk to the door and hold it open.

'I am only willing to believe you, Jenny, if you show me a clean bill of health from the hospital.'

'I told you, I will get one.'

'For both of you. That means David as well.'

She glared at him furiously. 'I could sue you for this. Wrongful dismissal.'

'I would deny this conversation ever took place. Your word against mine.'

'You are being unjust, Steve. I am telling you honestly that it is a pack of lies. David and I are both healthy. Please believe me.'

He stared at her, then said firmly, 'I am not willing to take the risk without a medical clearance.'

'You are an absolute bastard,' she exploded. 'Even if I did have AIDS, it wouldn't make me untouchable. You wouldn't risk soiling your lily-white soul by working with me.'

He did not reply, but continued to hold the door open for her.

'And who passed on this totally false information to you?' she demanded, coming closer.

His eyes gave nothing away. He was just waiting for her to go.

Suddenly Jenny remembered the telephone call at lunchtime. 'It was Susannah, wasn't it?'

She knew she was right by the flush that rose to his cheeks. Of course, it was obvious now. Susannah had mentioned that Robert was having lunch with Fairchild this week, so Jenny should have anticipated that this might happen. But how far would the poison spread? Any amount of blood tests would not stem the flood of whispered gossip and hinted innuendoes. Without doubt, that explained Phoebe. The exercise class had been the first casualty, now this. Where would it end?

Without another glance at the manager, she walked out of the shop and hurried down the hill. She had to see Susannah.

'I'm sorry, she's not in.'

Jenny was certain Robert Benson was lying. Before she had even finished parking her car in the gravel drive, the oak door of the house had opened and Robert had stood grimly on the top step. Barring her entrance. Instead of the usual warm smile of welcome, she was greeted with a curt nod of the head and a brusque 'Good evening'. The eyes that looked at her out of his rubicund face were the same as Steve's. Full of fear. But this time, instead of anger, there was pity.

'I'd like a word with Susannah, please, Robert.'

That was when his eyes had flitted uncomfortably away and he had started lying to her. He was so patently bad at it that, in other circumstances, she would have laughed.

'Robert, I must speak with her.'

'I've told you, she's out at the moment. I'll get her to ring you when she comes back.' He retreated into the house and started to close the door.

'No, Robert.' Jenny pushed against the heavy door with a release of pent-up anger, sending Robert staggering backwards. Ignoring his stricken expression and startled cry, she strode past him, through the panelled hall and into the drawing-room.

Susannah was standing nervously by the fireplace. 'Hello, Jenny.' Her voice was shaky.

'What the hell have you been spreading around about David and myself?'

'Jenny, I . . .'

At that point Robert hurried into the room and instantly took up a protective stance beside his wife. 'I was the one who learned the truth. Fairchild told me everything about David's dismissal.'

'None of it is true.'

'Then why didn't David fight Dern & Fairchild in the courts for wrongful dismissal? God knows, it's easy enough to prove you're not HIV positive.'

'Because Fairchild hid behind other excuses and claimed it was because of financial cutbacks.' She recalled Steve and his declared intention of denying the truth about her own loss of job. 'Like many others do. Employers are too frightened to cite AIDS as the cause because they know it's not a valid reason for dismissal.'

Robert stared at Jenny's impassioned face and his natural kindness struggled to the fore. 'Jenny, my dear, let's sit down and talk about this more calmly.' He gestured for her to take a seat, but he and Susannah chose the sofa a fair distance away. 'I think you are being naïve. There's no smoke without fire, you know, and we all know David was not the most . . . I have to say it . . . loyal of husbands.'

Susannah swerved the conversation off that topic. 'Has David been tested then, given the all-clear? Is that what you're saying? Tell us, Jenny, and we will believe you, I promise.' Her green eyes were guilty.

Jenny shook her head impatiently. 'No, of course he hasn't. He doesn't even know that he's accused of having AIDS.'

Robert and Susannah exchanged glances of disbelief. 'Then how is it that you know about it?' Robert demanded.

Jenny's cheeks flushed with colour and she cursed her lack of forethought. Quickly she sought an explanation. 'Steve told me. After you rang him, Susannah.'

'Then how do you know it's not true?' Robert persisted.

'Because I do. There's nothing wrong with David's health.'

'It would explain the drinking,' Susannah suggested softly.

'So would losing his job,' Jenny insisted.

'He has got very thin recently.'

'That's because he wasn't eating.'

'And the attacks,' Robert commented thoughtfully. 'It would explain the two attacks on him.'

Jenny stared at him aghast. 'What do you mean?'

'Well, AIDS is a very emotive subject. It causes a lot of enmity. Perhaps someone was wreaking revenge.'

With heart racing too fast, Jenny tried to explain yet again. 'But you don't understand, he's not infected. He's as healthy as you are.'

They both remained silent on the sofa, wanting to believe her, but quite clearly already convinced otherwise.

Jenny said quietly, 'Susannah, it was not right to tell others these false, malicious rumours until you had spoken with me about them.'

'I know and I'm sorry. I honestly didn't mean to. It was you I was ringing at the shop, not Steve. It just all came out.'

Robert interrupted, 'He had a right to know, as your employer.'

'Not if it's untrue.'

Their eyes locked together and eventually Robert lowered his gaze without further comment.

'And Phoebe? You must have told her as well.'

Susannah nodded miserably. 'I was so frightened, Jenny. It wasn't fair on the rest of us to keep it secret.' Her eyes suddenly grew wide with horror. 'Oh my God, I kissed him last time I was at your house.' A shudder shook her body.

Robert immediately put an arm round her and drew her to him. 'We'll get you to a doctor first thing in the morning.'

'You are being ridiculous, the pair of you. I swear there's no danger of AIDS. I've already lost my job because of you, and probably most of my friends. All for no reason.' Jenny stood up. 'Even if I were HIV positive, it would be no reason to treat me like a pariah.' She looked at the embarrassed faces, both carefully avoiding eye contact and gave a faint shrug. 'At least I'll know who my true friends are this way.' She started for the door.

Susannah leaped from her seat and rushed over to Jenny, barring her exit. 'No, Jenny, don't leave like this. I'm sorry for what I've done. I didn't mean to hurt you.' Tears filled her eyes, so that Jenny suddenly felt sorry for her groundless fear and she smiled ruefully.

'I was going to chuck in the job anyway.'

Susannah was grateful for the hint of an olive branch. She put her arms round Jenny and hugged her tight. 'Forgive me?' she murmured against the flushed cheek.

Jenny gave her a reassuring squeeze. 'Of course.' She stepped back and looked hard into the moist green eyes. 'I'm telling the truth, I swear to you.'

Susannah managed a watery smile. 'I do believe you.'

Robert intervened, 'But we'll have you checked, just in case.'

Jenny opened her mouth to protest, but then saw the relief on Susannah's face at the suggestion. All right, let them find out the truth for themselves, if that's what they wanted. What did it matter? Without another word, she left the house.

As she drove home in the dark, Jenny fought to gain a shaky control over her spiralling emotions. Humiliation kept her cheeks burning, but anger at the injustice combined with pain at the betrayal to hollow a sense of sickening loss inside her. First Steve, then Susannah and Robert. All terrified at the first whiff of rumour, scared their own skins were in danger. This was what she had forced David to endure.

Feeling unsteady, she kept her speed down, so that the cars streamed past her, their yellow beams snatching and distorting the images around her. The same way the glaring lies had twisted the reality of her life. She took a deep shuddering breath and her pulse settled to a steadier beat. The time had come to end it. End the lies and the pretence.

Only David's signature stood in her way. She stared grimly out into the blackness ahead, her lights piercing a path through the cloying night. For a long time her thought focused on her husband and then abruptly she pressed down hard on the accelerator. When she finally pulled into the drive, she was surprised to find the house in darkness. No light in any window. It looked cold and deserted. With a faint feeling of unease, she walked in and turned on the lights. Silence blanketed everything. She opened the sitting-room door, but the room was black, the only sound the rain rattling against the windows. She flicked the switch and brightness filled the room.

Sitting silently in his chair was David.

Jenny stared at him in surprise. 'What are you doing in here in the dark?'

He gazed up at her so intently that she felt uncomfortable for a moment, but then he murmured, 'I must have fallen asleep.' He studied her more closely. 'What's the matter? You look a bit shaken.'

Her colour was still high, but she brushed it aside with a casual 'Nothing much. I had a dust-up with Steve at work.'

Again his eyes bored into hers. 'Tell me about it.'

'There's not much to tell. We had a disagreement. He accused me unjustly of something and as a result, I'm not working there any longer.'

It was David's turn to look surprised. 'It must have been some dust-up. What did he accuse you of?'

She almost told him. Almost came out with the whole truth, but then she remembered the signature. With a shrug she turned away to block his probing gaze. 'It's not worth going over again, I'd rather just forget it. Anyway, I've got a boot load of shopping to bring in.'

David did not ask again the reason why she had been fired.

It was later, while she was preparing the meal that the knife slipped and sliced into her finger. Jenny cursed and took another swig from the glass of wine that stood beside the chopping board. It was no good. Her hands were still shaky and it was impossible to concentrate properly. She glanced round and found David standing right behind her.

'Look what you've done to yourself,' he said, wrapping his arms around her, so that he could look down over her shoulder at what she was doing. Slowly he raised the bleeding finger in his hand and lifted it to his lips. 'You're your own worst enemy,' he whispered in her ear.

Very deliberately he kissed the cut and then with her body

still enclosed between his arms, he took up the small knife. They both stared down at the sharp blade. Suddenly Jenny felt nervous and started to panic, but she gasped in horror when he swiftly drew the blade along the fleshy ball of his left thumb. The blood welled from the deep cut and dripped on to the chopping board, but he took no notice and holding her hand firmly in his, pressed his own wound hard against the scarlet gash on her finger. He rubbed them against each other, keeping them bonded tightly together.

'There,' he said solemnly, 'blood brothers. That's what we are now. So don't worry about a job. I'll look after you.'

His voice sounded odd and she pulled away to look round at him. For a second, his eyes stared intently down at her and she could not penetrate their expression, but a caring smile quickly drove away the unnerving stare and he released her finger.

'I'll get us both a plaster,' he said and fetched the packet of pink strips from a cupboard. He peeled the backing off one of them and rested it lightly on his own thumb, so that its small square of lint started to turn red. Before she could object, he quickly took it off again and placed it over the cut on her finger, pressing it down and wrapping the sticky ends round firmly.

'Blood brothers,' he repeated and held out his own still dripping thumb for her to kiss.

Jenny did not appreciate this strange charade and was about to protest, but he pushed the injured thumb closer to her lips, forcing her to brush a reluctant kiss on top of the wound and feel the oozing blood enter her mouth. It tasted salty and warm. Immediately she swallowed to get rid of the taste.

He smiled at her and covered the cut rapidly with another plaster.

'What did you do that for?' Jenny demanded. 'Why cut your thumb like that?'

'I told you. To make us blood brothers. That means we are responsible for each other's lives.'

She shook her head in distaste. 'You're crazy.' She wasn't in the mood for humouring his antics.

'Who is to say what is crazy and what is sane?'

'David, I'm not interested in playing games.' She went back to chopping onions. 'The meal won't be long.'

At the kitchen door David turned and watched her speedy movements with the knife. 'Do be careful, Jenny. You might hurt yourself.'

She did not glance round, but was relieved when she heard the door close.

'Go away together for the weekend?'

'Yes, just the two of us.'

'No, David, I don't think that's a good idea.' Jenny did not want to go away with him.

'Why not? It would do us both good.'

'No, I don't feel like driving for miles. I'm tired after working all week and I want to rest.'

'That's why you need the break. To give you a chance to relax and forget about Steve Thompson and his shop. Get right away from here and be pampered for a couple of days.'

'I don't know. It's not what I—'

'Come on, Jenny, the weather forecast for the weekend is good and I want to take advantage of it. A bit of sea air in our lungs will buck us both up.'

His face was eager and his tongue persuasive. Maybe it would not be such a bad idea after all, if it put him in such a cheerful mood. Perhaps it would present the ideal opportunity for finding the right moment to request his signature on the form. Reluctantly, she smiled at him and nodded. 'Perhaps you're right. It might do us good.'

'I'm sure it's just what you need.'

'All right.'

'So you'll come?'

'Yes.'

'Good.' He pulled out a tourist guide book. 'Look, I've already chosen the perfect place.'

She didn't really care where they went. 'So you've been planning this?'

'Only today. The idea came to me out of the blue. I thought

we haven't been away for a long time and are stuck in a rut. This will be a new start.'

'A new start,' Jenny echoed. 'So where is this place we're heading for?'

He waved the guide book at her. 'In Devon. It's a thatched country pub not far from Totnes, complete with roaring fires and ye olde Englishe landlord, as well as being within easy reach of Torquay in one direction and the windy expanses of Dartmoor in the other, or so the book says.'

'Sounds ideal. It's just a question of getting there.'

'I've got it all planned. If we set off bright and early in the morning, we will be there for lunch. It's motorway nearly all the journey, so it won't take us long.'

Jenny studied the map he handed her, plotting the route she would choose the next day, and as she glanced up, she caught David watching her intently.

'Looking forward to it?' he asked.

'Yes.' She said it mechanically, her mind elsewhere as she turned back to the map, away from his stare and concentrated on jotting down the road numbers. 'Sure your leg is up to it?'

'I'm sure. Don't worry, it'll be no trouble, even with the plaster.'

'You'll have to take it easy. Gentle strolls along the beach.'

'No, I fancy a few bracing cliff-top walks myself. My plaster can manage that, especially if I bring the crutch along with me.'

'Good idea.' She didn't want him getting overtired and crotchety. The intention was that he should be relaxed and in a good mood. Handing the map and book back to him, she stood up. 'I'll go and pack a few things into a bag for tomorrow, if we're making an early start. Why don't you ring that pub and book a room?'

'I'll do that right now.'

Jenny handed him the mobile phone and left him to it. This would be the end of it all. The final act in the drama. She was so preoccupied with her own thoughts that she failed to notice David's long purposeful stare, as he watched her leave the room.

*   *   *

As they came over the brow of the hill, their first sight of the island took her breath away. It sat in emerald splendour in a blaze of sunshine, as the waves washed round its jagged shore. The day was bright and the pale blue sky warmed the slate grey of the sea, while the wintry wind whipped up white horses to a frenzy.

'It's glorious.' David had been right. This break was exactly what she needed. Spread before her, the green hills on either side of the narrow road rolled down to the wide curve of the bay, and a quarter of a mile out to sea lay Burgh Island, a small grassy outcrop boasting only an incongruous Art-Deco hotel, an ancient pub and a tiny handful of buildings. The tide was out, revealing a wide expanse of golden beach and a broad causeway of firm sand that stretched across to the hotel. At high tide the island would be completely cut off, only accessible by boat or by the extraordinary ancient tractor that crouched on the causeway ready to run trips through the waves.

Jenny drove expectantly down into the village of Bigbury and parked close to the beach. The cold wind had swept the sand smooth and driven any tourists back to the warmth of their cars. At this time of year there were very few visitors anyway, so Jenny and David had the beach to themselves, except for a couple of dogs bounding away excitedly, as their owners released them from their leads.

'I like it here,' David commented, as he carefully manoeuvred his metal crutch down the slope to the sand. 'When I came here as a boy, I climbed up to the look-out post on the very top of the island.'

'It's beautiful. And so cut off, away from everything.'

'Yes, it's very isolated,' David said softly, as he stared out over the waves.

He had been quiet on the drive down, but that had suited her own mood. The traffic heading to the West Country had been light and they had made good time. The hotel had lived up to the description, full of dark beams, oak furniture and willow pattern plates. Horse brasses and copper kettles were kept to a discreet minimum and the lunch they had been served on arrival was of the freshly home-made variety, accompanied by a genuine log fire, rather than a gas imitation. The dining-room had been empty except for one other elderly couple and whether it was the sense of privacy or just the wine at work, David had become more relaxed and his tongue looser.

Jenny feared that he would query the connection between her own loss of job and his meeting with the area manager the next week, but he made no mention of it. He seemed determined to blank out all reference to work and stress, and instead just kept the conversation light, for which Jenny was thankful. It made the whole exercise that much easier. Anyway, she had to admit, now that she was here, she found the environs extremely calming.

'There's somewhere I want to take you,' David had said, as they finished their coffee.

'Oh? Where?'

'It's a tiny island off the coast about half an hour from here. I went there as a child once.'

'What is it called?'

'Burgh Island. It was famous in the thirties as the haunt of Noel Coward, Agatha Christie and even the Windsors. It got very run down later, but a few years ago I read in the paper that it had been completely renovated in all its Art-Deco splendour.'

'Sounds intriguing.'

'We'll go there this afternoon.'

'If you like.'

On the trip over, the sun had obligingly made an appearance, so that now both sea and island had a sparkling clarity that drove all but the pleasure of the moment from Jenny's mind. She readily accommodated David when he hobbled over and placed an arm across her shoulders, resting part of his weight on her.

'I'll need a helping hand here.' He smiled down into her face and pulled her closer. 'This is going to be interesting.' He laughed as he tested the crutch on the sand. It promptly sank several inches into the loose dry grit at the top of the beach, but once they were on the firmer sand, only its tip disappeared and it bore his weight well, with Jenny's support.

She tucked her scarf more securely round her neck against the tugging of the wind and they set off on the causeway. Halfway across, Jenny turned and looked at the tracks they had made in the damp sand.

'It looks as if we're being pursued by an invisible monster,' she laughed, pointing out the trail of footprints, round holes and scraped ruts made by the plaster.

'It may think it's invisible, but it can't hide its tracks,' David murmured so quietly that Jenny almost missed it. 'Come on,' he added, 'let's race it to the island.'

Clinging on to the crutch and to Jenny, he hobbled onward at a faster pace and when they reached the slipway at the far end, abandoning his hold, he turned to face the imaginary monster. With a swashbuckling flourish, he waved the crutch in the air, thrusting and jabbing at his unseen enemy. 'Your days are numbered,' he called out to the wind.

Jenny watched her husband, faintly bemused by his odd antics, but when his plastered leg suddenly slipped out from under him after a particularly violent lunge, sending him toppling to the ground, she hurried to his side.

'David, are you all right?'

'Not quite St George's standard yet, it seems.'

'Are you hurt?'

'No,' but he rubbed his elbow ruefully.

She expected more evidence of sorely grazed pride, but he shrugged off the accident indifferently, as if his mind were elsewhere. Just then a sand-spattered spaniel came bounding off the beach and shook itself vigorously, spraying grit all over them. The dog's owner hurriedly apologised and helped Jenny get David on to his feet again.

'Thanks very much,' Jenny smiled and returned the crutch to its rightful place once more.

'You should take care,' the dog owner commented. 'This wind could blow you into the sea, if you're not careful.'

'We'll be careful,' Jenny assured him.

With David's weight once more across her shoulders, they

made their way up the slope past the old Pilchard Inn and on to the grassy path that ran round the island. The centre of the island was a steep hill topped by an ancient look-out post that had once been for spotting the shoals of pilchards that years ago had abounded in local waters. The path skirted the rocky cliffs before veering inland.

Carefully Jenny and David followed the track and the higher they climbed, the more strongly the wind blew, buffeting their backs and tearing at their clothes. When the path narrowed, they were forced to walk in single file until a flat grassy expanse opened up and David sank with relief on to a rock.

'Hell, that's better,' he said breathing heavily, as he rested the leg stiffly out in front of him. 'Things aren't always as easy as you expect.'

'It's a steep haul up to the top. Take a few minutes' rest.' Jenny turned away and looked out at the view from the cliff top. In the distance the mainland was washed by weak sunlight and the fierce wind swept across the green hills. Her eyes were drawn to the surging waters around them that never ceased their perpetual motion and she stepped nearer the cliff edge to scan the rocks below, pounded into jagged teeth by the force of the sea. A black cormorant suddenly swooped down from a cranny in the cliff face and dived into the water. Jenny watched fascinated as it emerged triumphantly with a fish in its beak and flew to a safe perch on a rock to enjoy its meal, but within seconds, a screeching mob of seagulls descended from nowhere. Jenny yelled at them in vain, but they drove the cormorant to retreat further along the shore. She stood nearer the edge, peering over as she tried to follow the beleaguered bird's progress.

'It's the survival of the fittest.'

She was startled by David's voice right behind her, but did not take her eyes from the black bird. 'They're vicious.'

As a particularly strong gust of wind blasted across the island, she felt David's hand rest on her shoulder. She watched the cormorant fly off in retreat and the white gulls claim the fish and the rocks for their own. As Jenny scanned the cliff for a glimpse of any other cormorants, she felt the pressure on her shoulder increase and sensed David's body move closer to hers. A sudden rush of vertigo smothered her mind, making her turn abruptly and cling to David's arm to steady herself. The movement took him completely by surprise and he stepped quickly back from the cliff edge. Jenny's pulse was racing uncomfortably, but as she looked round at his face, she was astonished at the sight of his laboured breathing and the tense expression on his face.

'David, you've overdone it. You shouldn't have come up here.' She needed to keep him good-tempered.

Slowly his eyes relaxed and he nodded in agreement. 'I think you're right. I've had enough.' He looked out across the icy waves. 'Enough for today. Time for scones and clotted cream in true Devonshire style at that Art-Deco hotel. With luck, the tide will be in by the time we've finished and I can ride back in that extraordinary sea tractor.'

Jenny picked up his crutch and handed it to him. 'After that you had better lie down for a while. Give your leg a rest.'

'We've only got today and tomorrow. I don't want to waste them.'

'Yes.' She slipped her shoulder under his arm and felt his weight descend on her. 'That's all we've got.'

'Would you care for some coffee?' enquired the pretty blonde waitress, as she stood beside the couple's table.

Jenny shook her head. 'No, thank you.'

The waitress turned her most charming smile on the tall attractive man, hoping to catch his eye. 'What about you, sir?'

He looked up and noticed her properly for the first time.

'Coffee, sir?' She felt the colour creep up her cheeks as he stared at her.

'Yes. Thank you, that would be very nice,' and added with a smile, 'The meal was excellent.'

She hurried away, eager to please.

David dismissed the brief temptation from his mind and returned his attention to what Jenny was saying.

'David, I'm certain that freelance is the right way for you to go.' He had just commented that one never knew what the future had in store and she was quick to reassure him. 'There must be a whole string of smaller companies eager for your expertise on a retainer basis, even if you don't get the NOW consultancy.'

She was relieved when he smiled. 'I'm sure you are right.' He put his hand out and wrapped it round hers on the table before she realised what he was planning. The two pink plasters rested together. 'But don't let's talk business tonight. This is our escape from it all.'

'From reality?'

'Why not?'

She wanted to tell him why not – that her reality had become too inviting to abandon so readily – but instead she smiled at him and freed her trapped hand to raise her glass to him. 'To escape.'

He laughed, touched his glass to hers and echoed her words. 'To escape. And to you, for all that you've done for me.'

Something in his voice made her study his face more closely, but his smile remained warm and admiring.

'You've been a tower of strength and I know how much I owe you. That's why I wanted us to have this break together.' He reached out and again took her hand in his. 'You deserve it. I want it to be special.'

Just then the coffee arrived, relieving Jenny of the need to respond. The waitress hovered longer than necessary, hoping for another of the smiles, but he was engrossed in his wife and eventually she moved on to the next table.

'You're looking very pleased with life ...' he paused, 'despite just losing your job. I admire your sanguine frame of mind.'

Jenny's heart thumped. 'It wasn't something that I really cared for. Anyway, Steve proved to be so unreasonable that I'm glad to be gone from there.'

Still he did not ask what the disagreement had been about.

She did not want to think about it, let alone discuss it, as her rage at the injustice had not yet totally abated.

'As you said,' she added, 'let's not talk of realities. I'm more interested at the moment in making today and tomorrow a success.'

He smiled. 'Yes, I want them to be a success. Did you enjoy this afternoon at Burgh Island?'

'It was beautiful. I hope it didn't put too much of a strain on your leg.'

'No, it wasn't too bad, but I'm sorry it didn't end up quite as I planned.'

'What do you mean?'

At first he did not reply, just stared at her blankly, then seemed to pull himself together. 'Well, we didn't get up to the look-out post, like I did when I was a child. I wanted to do that again.'

'Never mind, some other time, perhaps.'

'Perhaps. But it's you I want now.' Very deliberately, David lifted his gaze to Jenny's face and the hunger in his eyes was unmistakable. He pushed aside the coffee in front of him untouched. 'Let's go upstairs,' he said quietly and stood up.

Her heart sank as she realised what he had in mind. It was, of course, inevitable on a weekend away that his thoughts would turn in that direction, but nevertheless, she had hoped his injured leg would act as a deterrent. His hand fastened firmly round her wrist and he led her out of the restaurant, up the narrow stairs to their room. The dark timbers and low ceiling gave it a warm intimacy and the bed was covered in a heavy rose damask. But David did not wait to pull the cover aside.

The moment the door closed, he drew her to him and kissed her long and hard. His hands ran down the curve of her spine, pressing her close to his body and his breathing became heavy and uncontrolled. For a second Jenny almost pulled free from his grasp, but knew what the consequences of such an action would be. Black temper and a fit of grumbling sulks would not win her the signature tomorrow. This was the very last thing she wanted from him. In exchange, what did it matter if she offered the simple act she had performed so many times before?

His fingers sought the zip at her back, slid it smoothly down and slipped her dress from her body. His lips savoured the skin of her neck and shoulder, while his hands released her breasts from the flimsy material of her bra. As he lowered his head to her nipple, she asked herself again, what did it matter? At the back of her mind, a nagging doubt beat an erratic tattoo. Was she selling herself cheaply yet again, like she had all their married life? Wasn't her body worth more than a measly signature on a piece of paper?

David swept her back on to the bed and flicked off her panties, so that she was lying naked beside him. Very slowly and deliberately he ran his fingers over her skin, stroking, teasing, tantalising, until her body took on a will of its own. It responded to his expert touch with tingling nerve ends, flushed cheeks and swollen nipples until the pulsing need of her body betrayed her. She brushed aside the questions, forgot everything except her physical desires of the moment.

She stripped his clothes from him, rolled him on to his back and swung herself on top. Her mouth found his and her tongue probed deep, as she rubbed her breasts back and forth against his chest. She wanted satisfaction too fiercely to be patient, arching her back as she sank down on him, her breath coming in rapid gasps as his rhythm matched hers. He moaned briefly beneath her, but she did not hear as, with a stifled cry, her body shuddered out of control and she collapsed beside him.

They lay like that in silence on the damask cover until the chill in the air finally made them stir. Swiftly Jenny slipped into bed and David followed, stretching out on his back and staring up at the ceiling, a slight smile curving his lips. In the darkness Jenny turned her back to him and somehow, in a way she did not quite understand, she had the old familiar feeling that he was playing some kind of game and in a vague sense, she was aware that she had just lost. She had let herself down.

But it was the last time. After tomorrow there would be no more games, no more lies. Tomorrow would see an end to it all.

The pebble arced high in the air, then plummeted down into the water, causing rippling circles to spread across the waves. The wind of the previous day had dropped to just a steady breeze, but the sea was still choppy and dark under the canopy of grey cloud. Jenny launched another stone into the air, but this time missed her aim. It bounced off the side of the old wooden jetty and spun off at a crazy angle, startling a seagull from its somnolent perch on one of the posts.

They had found the deserted cove quite by chance. Having decided to explore further along the coast, they had followed a narrow road that curved round the side of a wood and suddenly dropped down to the edge of this small shingle bay. The tide had turned and Jenny watched tensely as more of the dark wooden structure of the jetty was slowly revealed by the retreating waves.

Beside her, David was sitting sprawled on the shingle, the white plaster of his leg now smeared with dirt. The only sound was the rhythmic roll of the waves and the deep rumble of the stones, as they were ground against each other in the fierce grip of the sea. Jenny emptied her handful of stones with a final fling that sent them scattering noisily over the water and decided the time had come.

'David.'

'Mmm?' He continued to gaze out to sea.

'There's something I have to tell you.'

'What about?'

'About me. About us.'

This time he turned and looked at her. 'What about us?' His

relaxed, cheerful mood had suddenly evaporated, leaving a cold hard stare.

She took a deep breath. 'I have decided to open a business of my own. I'm going to—'

A harsh scornful laugh burst from David. 'What the hell do you know about business? Absolutely nothing.'

Jenny clung to her determination to remain calm. 'I'm going to open an up-market dress shop in Tonbridge. If it does well, I hope to expand to other towns.' Her enthusiasm swept her onward. 'I've taken out a lease on a unit in the perfect spot. It's in the main street between—'

'And when did you arrange all this?'

'I've been planning it for months. It has taken me some time to find the right place, but this one is ideal. I'm convinced it will be a success.'

David was staring at her with an expression of angry disbelief. 'You obviously did not think it worth mentioning these plans to me.'

'David, try to understand. It was something I wanted to do on my own, to prove to myself I could do it. If I had told you, you would either have squashed the whole idea flat or have taken over yourself.'

'Damned right I would. You don't know the first thing about—'

She didn't need to listen to his insults. 'But I've learned, David. I know enough now to have completed all the contracts, designed the shop interior and arranged for shop-fitters to start. I have been over numerous fashion warehouses in London, including French and German ones, so that I have a good selection of excellent names lined up for stock.'

'And when did you manage to fit in all this activity? While you were supposed to be at the shop in Hambury I presume?'

'Yes. I cut back my working hours.'

'Very convenient.'

'I learned a lot from Steve. However badly the relationship ended, I do owe him that.'

'So you think you know enough to succeed on your own?' His voice was sceptical.

'Yes.'

'Been over all the legal contracts with a toothcomb?'

'Yes. Caroline Palmer helped.'

He picked up a pebble and hurled it at the retreating waves. 'I might have known she'd be in there somewhere, stirring her cauldron.'

Jenny bit down on her sharp response, reminding herself what she needed from him next. She took several deep breaths. 'The bank has agreed to finance the venture against the security of my fifty per cent ownership of our house.'

David's eyes narrowed. 'Has it, indeed?'

'Yes.' From her jacket pocket she drew a folded sheet of paper. 'This is the form that requires your agreement. Will you sign it, please?' It was out at last. She held her breath.

Without a word, David took the form and his eyes skimmed over it. 'So they won't lend you the money without my agreement, as I own the other half of the house.' He looked up at her and smiled. 'Is that right?'

'Yes.'

With a sharp laugh, he tossed the paper towards her and the breeze carried it a few feet away, but Jenny did not take her eyes from David.

'Well, dear wife, you can forget your little scheme because I'm not signing.' His eyes took on a cruel pleasure, as he added with emphasis, 'Not now. Not ever.'

It was final. There was no point reasoning with him and she would not stoop to plead. She knew he would not change his mind. Jenny stood up and retrieved the sheet of paper, then looked down on his triumphant smiling face. Stepping closer to him, she said in a low voice, 'David, there's one more thing I have to tell you. I am leaving you. Our marriage is over.'

A furious scowl darkened his face, but before he could speak, she continued, 'As soon as we are back in Kent, I will start divorce proceedings and I will expect fifty per cent of the house in the settlement. If you think you can put an end to my plans, you are mistaken. You can't stop me, only delay the date of the opening.' She leaned down, her face only inches from his. 'You have no power over me, David.' Deliberately she let the paper drop on to his lap.

For a moment she thought he was going to lose control, so violent was the rage that swept through him, but unexpectedly he suddenly smiled in a rictus imitation of a grin. 'That's what you think,' he laughed maliciously and let himself fall back flat on the pebbles, his laugh growing louder and louder as he stared up at her.

She could stand it no more. Could not bear to be near him. Without a word, she turned and strode away down the beach, her heart hammering in her chest and her breath coming in shallow gasps. He had put an end to all her hopes. Everything she had planned. Oh yes, of course she could pursue the whole idea when the house was eventually sold, but that would be months, even years, away, and by then she would have lost the lease on the shop in Tonbridge. With an effort, she calmed her racing mind and tried to accept the postponement of her plans.

'You'll have to be patient that's all. On Monday go to the bank and discuss the new situation with them.'

But the anger and frustration would not be so easily soothed and the rasping turmoil drove her to lengthen her stride, until she found herself standing by the jetty that stretched out its blackened struts into the sea like the stumps of rotten fangs. The old timbers were worn smooth by the wind and waves, and in places had rotted into jagged holes, as if a monstrous fish had taken great bites out of them. She climbed up on to the surface planking and as it seemed solid enough, ventured further along its length, peering down through the cracks between the shrunken slats at the mesmerising motion of the waves.

All around her the sea surged in a rolling swell to the distant horizon and its calming influence helped clear her mind. Her thoughts focused on the future, already sifting ideas and planning the next steps. She was not beaten yet. Glancing back at the beach, her eyes registered that David had not moved, still lay stretched out on the stones, but her mind shut him out. She gazed at the shifting colours of the sea and the rush of the foam, as the waves crashed against the wooden struts of the jetty. The salt spray tasted like memories of childhood on her lips and she held out a hand to catch some in her open palm.

From somewhere behind her, the gull swooped down, obviously convinced she was offering food. All summer the birds had been fed snippets of sandwiches and crisps by tourists, so it was with a raucous cry of expectation that the gull descended to her outstretched hand. The sudden flapping of huge wings round her head and savage beak plucking at her fingers startled Jenny. She leaped backwards with a cry of alarm, flailing her arms to drive off the demanding bird.

As she jerked away, she twisted awkwardly, catching her foot in the uneven planking and toppling headlong over the edge of the jetty. Suddenly the dark waves were rushing towards her and in desperation she clawed towards one of the wooden uprights. Her fingers hooked round its edge, stemming her fall and she gasped with relief as, for one brief moment, she hung suspended by her hand just inches above the foaming water. She struggled wildly to grasp the post with the other hand as well, but just as she touched it, the top of the strut crumbled beneath her weight and a chunk of rotten wood came away in her hand.

She plunged down into the sea.

Her scream of terror was cut off as the icy water closed over her head. She sank deep below the surface, her mouth and nostrils filled with water, driving her into mindless panic. Frantically she struggled to reach the surface, but her heavy clothes dragged her deeper until her lungs were burning and she could not stop herself gasping for air. The rush of salt water that flooded into her mouth sent her into a frenzy of fear and gave greater strength to her legs. Fierce kicks drove her to the surface until her head burst above the waves and her lungs shuddered for air, as she drew a choking, agonised breath.

Before she could take another, she felt herself going under again. Only determined kicking forced her back to the surface. She tried to think, but could not quell her panic. As she went down for the third time, she knew she would drown if she could not calm down, for the icy water was already slowing her movements and the weight of her water-logged clothes was too much for her.

With a supreme effort she kicked herself once more to the surface and succeeded in dragging several gasps of precious oxygen into her lungs. She managed to keep herself afloat this time while, with numbing fingers, she struggled with the buttons of her jacket and when at last she shook herself free of it, it was a great weight lifted from her.

Her body bobbed higher in the water and with her head raised further above the waves, she forced herself to think. The jetty, she had to reach the jetty. Its wooden struts were her only lifeline. Thank God it was only a matter of a few feet away. With renewed hope she struggled towards it and even when an icy wave smashed into her face, blinding her, she did not stop, but struck out strongly for the safety of those wooden posts.

Gradually it dawned on her. With horror she realised she was getting no closer. Fleetingly she stopped swimming and was instantly carried another few feet away from her goal. The ebb tide and the currents – they would sweep her out to sea. Fear gave her savage strength and she gained a yard of lost ground, but still the jetty remained beyond her grasp. Another wave smashed over her face and she spat out a mouthful of salt water. Her arms and legs were beginning to feel like lead and each movement demanded more effort.

She wasn't going to make it. The realisation instantly paralysed her and she sank once more down into the dark waters. The instinct to breathe drove her to fight the numbing cold and her chilled limbs battled against the weight above her, forcing her head once more above the waves. She was shivering uncontrollably. She knew she couldn't make it without help.

David. Where was David?

The question filled her with hope and she turned her face eagerly towards the beach. It was deserted. There was nobody to be seen. Her heart thudded with sick despair and the tide managed to carry her further out. It was then that she looked up and saw him. His dark figure, leaning on the crutch, was standing at the end of the jetty looking down at her.

Relief flooded her mind. 'David,' she screamed. 'David, help me.'

He did not move. Nor utter a word. Just stared silently down at her helplessly bobbing head.

'Dav—' but a wave filled her open mouth and she convulsed in a spasm of choking. When she could breathe again, she looked up and was thankful that David was still there. Ignoring the risk of drifting further out, she stopped swimming to tread water, so that she could raise herself higher in the icy sea and shouted at the top of her lungs, 'Hold out the crutch to me, David.'

He did not move. Perhaps he had not heard.

With desperate strength she fought a few strokes closer and spitting salt from her mouth, tried again. 'The crutch, David. Stretch it out for me to reach.' Her mind, as well as her body, was feeling numb and the words were an effort of will.

At last David was reacting. He raised the crutch, and her hopes with it, waved it at her – and then turned and hobbled off with it towards the beach.

She could not believe what her eyes told her. He would not leave her here. To drown like an unwanted kitten. Her throat tightened in fear and shock froze her limbs, so that yet again she sank below the waves. This time she thought she would never come up, but the will to survive made her fight her way to the precious air once more. As her limbs struggled against the ebb tide, her eyes sought her husband and she spotted his retreating back half way along the jetty.

'David!' she screamed again, but this time without hope. He did not even glance round.

Rage flooded over her, sending adrenaline surging through her body. She kicked and swam and struggled, resisting the power of the waves with every scrap of her determination to live. Slowly, very slowly, the jetty was coming closer, until it was only inches from her fingers. Just as she was reaching out to grasp it, the dead weight of a huge wave broke over her, dragging her backwards once more by the force of its undertow.

Screaming her fury, Jenny struck out again for the black stake, but her arms were too heavy now and would not obey her commands. Hope was running out of her with every wave that washed over her, her kicks grew slower and she sank lower in the cold water. She just wanted to close her eyes and give up the fight.

With a jolt she realised she had done just that. She opened her eyes to discover she had drifted another precious metre away from safety. The cold was numbing her brain. From deep within her, she drew on her final reserves of strength and kicked herself into action for what she knew would be her last effort. There was no more left. No, she would not let it end like this. The future was too bright to let it drown in this murky sea.

Keeping her breathing steady and her eyes focused on the wooden strut, she drove herself on, as inch by inch she broke free of the current's hold, until at last her fingers groped against the slimy post and she flung an arm around its solid strength.

For long minutes she clung there, holding on to life. Her limbs felt numb and her lungs burning, but she was alive and she had a future. Determinedly she started to climb the wooden structure, ignoring the protests of her body but it was painfully slow. When finally she collapsed on the sodden boards and lay there shuddering, her whole body was wracked with tremors. She started to retch helplessly, as her stomach voided the salt water from her system and then the shock hit her. Uncontrollable sobs tore through her, as she clung tightly to the planking beneath.

Eventually, when the worst had passed, she sat up and looked towards the beach. David was there, stretched out on the shingle, calmly observing her. Slowly she dragged herself to her feet and unsteadily made her way along the jetty, halting every few yards at first because her knees kept buckling under her. Gradually the blood flowed back into her frozen limbs and she threw off her sodden sweater before it chilled her even further. But all the time she did not take her eyes off David for a second. When she reached the end of the jetty, she stumbled over the uneven pebbles until at last she stood before her husband.

'You left me there to die.' Spoken aloud, the words sounded even more terrible than in her head.

He looked up at her, his gaze hard and unrepentant. 'Yes.'

The shock of that single word was greater even than the waves closing over her head. She sat down abruptly. 'Why, David? Why would you want me to drown?'

He stared at her for a long time. 'An eye for an eye. A life for a life.'

'What do you mean?' Her teeth were shivering and she fought back a wave of nausea. 'I haven't taken your life.'

'Oh yes you have. Very cleverly and very deliberately, you stole my life from me.'

Jenny's throat went dry. He knew. Knew what she had done. For a fleeting second fear twisted inside her, then unexpectedly came relief. Relief that it was all over, even more completely than she had intended.

'I stole nothing from you. You were the cause of your own downfall.'

From an inside pocket David pulled out a long brown envelope and held it out to her wordlessly. There was nothing written on the outside.

'What's this?'

'Take it.'

With fingers that were not yet steady, she accepted the envelope, opened it and drew out two sheets of paper. The wind snatched at them, so that she was tempted to release them to its careless grip, but instead she made herself flatten them out. They were two typed letters.

It came as a shock that jolted right through her. Whatever else she had been expecting, it was not this. Her heart raced painfully and it took a huge effort to keep her voice calm. 'Where did you get these?'

'They are two letters that were sent to Fairchild, while I was working for him. As you can see, they are both anonymous and both claim that I have AIDS. That I have been tested and found HIV positive.' He paused to let the words sink in. 'Don't bother with lies and acting innocent. I matched it with our typewriter. The same partly blocked "o" and the tip of the "y" missing. I know you sent them, so don't deny it.'

She could feel her cheeks flush guiltily, but looked him steadily in the eye. 'I don't deny it.'

'You thought I would never see them, didn't you?'

'Yes.'

'And I never would have, never discovered the real reason

for being treated like a leper. For losing my job, my income and almost my sanity. Never found out that you were behind it all. No, I would never have known why . . .' he paused and smiled triumphantly '. . . if it hadn't been for Sarah.'

But the name no longer had the power to hurt Jenny.

'Sarah Archer? Is she back again?'

'Yes, Sarah is back again, waiting for me to return from this fiasco here. It was she who opened my eyes. You certainly had me fooled. God, how could I have been so fucking blind?' His voice had risen until he was shouting at her.

She had heard enough. Her soaking clothes clung to her body like an icy glove and she could not stop the trembling that shook her limbs. She had to get to the rug in the car.

'David, think what you like, do what you like. It's over between us.' She decided to make one last attempt. 'It would make it easier if you would sign the bank guarantee giving agreement to use of the house as collateral. We will be selling it anyway, so—'

'Why should I make it any easier for you?' Struggling for control, he turned his head away towards a seagull that landed a few yards away clutching a razor-shell in its beak. With a raucous cry it proceeded to tear it apart.

'David,' Jenny said quietly, 'we are all responsible for our own actions. Answerable to ourselves. Nothing I did warranted letting me drown.'

His eyes jerked back to her and his voice was harsh, as he snapped, 'But you didn't, did you?'

'No, I survived. By my own efforts.'

'And it was your efforts that almost destroyed me.'

'No, David, you did that yourself.'

'It was you. You. It's so obvious when I look back on it. Your sudden interest and attention. Your visit to the office.' His hands clenched in tight fists of fury and he leaned threateningly towards her, so that she could feel his hatred like a dry heat radiating from him. 'It never even occurred to me that it was you who had intentionally hidden that message from Fairchild on my desk. Dragged me off for some sleazy sex to prevent me returning to the office.'

'I didn't have to do any dragging. You were panting at the leash. It was your own decision.'

The contempt in her face goaded David beyond bearing. His hand shot out and slammed into her cheek, rocking back her head viciously.

'Well, you got your revenge, my treacherous wife, but don't think you can walk away from me without paying for what you did, because you can't.' A satisfied smile spread over his face. 'You will have to pay the price.'

Jenny rubbed her cheek, stared at him without comment, then rose to her feet. There was nothing more to be said. She forced her frozen limbs into action and set off up the shingle slope of the beach.

'Jenny,' he called after her, 'don't you want to hear what that price is?' His voice was louder, deeper, more threatening.

She hesitated, then turned to face him. 'The price is already over and done with. I spent too many years paying it. The debt is cleared. The only thing I don't understand is, if you knew about the letters and have your cosy little companion tucked up somewhere waiting for you, why did you suggest this holiday? You don't invite someone you loathe away for a romantic break.'

'At the sea shore there's always the risk of a freak accident.' His smile did not waver. 'Anyway, you do if you've got AIDS and you're trying to pass it on to them.'

She stared at him dumbly, her mind refusing to accept the words.

'Sit down, Jenny,' he said almost pleasantly, 'let me tell you about it.'

As Jenny sank down on to the stones, all colour had drained from her cheeks, even her lips were white as she tried to speak. 'What do . . .?' The words wouldn't come.

'Sarah came to see me on Friday. She told me about the letters that said I was HIV positive. Don Lerner had relished showing them to her when he kicked her out. As soon as we put our facts together, it was obvious you were the culprit. She immediately obtained copies of the letters from Fairchild and that only confirmed it.' He was explaining patiently, as if to a child. 'But there was something else she told me.'

His eyes watched her every expression. 'Sarah has AIDS.' He laughed and its harsh sound startled the nearby gull. 'How's that for irony? Her previous boyfriend was into drugs, so she must have caught it from him and has undoubtedly passed it on to me.'

Jenny stared at him in horror. Her mind was a whirling tumult of images. Steve Thompson's rejection of their friendship, Robert and Susannah's eyes so full of fear. And that was only the beginning. She stood up, eager to be free of him.

'You may be wrong,' she said and was amazed at how collected her voice sounded. 'It is not always passed so easily.'

David struggled to his feet with the help of the crutch and hopped clumsily over to her, thrusting his face aggressively into hers. She stood her ground and stared defiantly into his triumphant eyes.

'This weekend,' he gloated, 'I made sure we shared everything. And I do mean everything.' He reached out, seized her left wrist and lifted up her cold hand. His thumb ran along the raw scab on her finger. 'Blood brothers, remember?'

She recalled the taste of his warm blood in her mouth and then the feel of him deep inside her last night in the hotel bed. She knew there was slight hope she could have escaped the virus. A wave of fear swept over her and she snatched her hand from his, fighting down the images of wasted bodies that crowded her mind. The blood was pounding too fast in her ears. She dragged her eyes away from the sight of his twisted pleasure and forced herself to think. A long deep breath slowed her pulse and she headed again for where the car was parked.

But his voice would not let her escape. 'You don't like it now that you're the one in trouble, do you? See how you feel when your so-called friends drop off like flies, when no one wants to know you.'

She lengthened her stride, did not look back. She had made her decision. Whatever life she did or did not have left, she was not going to let him soil it. Behind her she heard his limping footsteps and the sound drove her to hurry. Her limbs were not functioning coherently, her mind and feet seeming disconnected, but finally she reached the sanctuary of the car.

However strong the urge to drive off immediately, she knew she had to strip off her icy clothes first. Keeping on only her bra, pants and sodden trainers, she hurled the rest into the boot and grabbed the rug to wrap round her shoulders. Its warmth gave her strength. David was coming closer and her shaking fingers fumbled the key in the lock at first, but in desperation she used both hands and managed to slot the key into its hole. She swung the door open, leapt into the driving seat and again struggled to still her trembling as she inserted the key in the ignition.

She threw the car into reverse and rapidly backed off the grass verge where it had been parked. Just as she slammed it into first gear, the passenger door was yanked open and David collapsed on to the seat beside her. She glanced at him, then put her foot to the floor.

'What the hell do you think you're doing?' he yelled, but she did not slow down. The car shot on to the road, the passenger door still flapping wildly and the off-side wheel crunched over the metal crutch that David had abandoned in his hurry to get into the car.

'Slow down, you fool, you'll kill us both,' he shouted at her and grabbed for the wheel. She jerked it away from him, sending them veering across on to the wrong side of the road.

'Look out, for God's sake, you'll . . .' The words died in his throat as a car came round the bend heading straight for them. In the nick of time, Jenny swerved back on to the left side of the road, but kept her foot flat down on the accelerator.

'Jenny, stop it.' He leant out to grab the open door and pulled it safely shut. 'What are you trying to do?'

'What does it matter what I do? If we're both going to die anyway, now that your girlfriend has signed our death warrants, why should you care how it happens? One death is as good as another.'

'No, Jenny, no, don't,' he shrieked in panic, as she only just held the car on the road round a fast bend. 'It's not true. I lied to you.'

For a terrifying second Jenny took her eyes off the road and stared at him. 'Lied about what?' Her voice was calm, despite the fact they were hurtling straight for a bank of trees.

'Watch the road,' David yelled, his eyes wide with terror.

She yanked the wheel over sharply and with a screech of metal, the off-side wing just scraped along the trunk of a fir, leaving its red paint smeared on the bark. 'Lied about what?' she repeated.

'About Sarah having AIDS. Please stop, Jenny. Stop now.'

The speed didn't slacken, but a length of straight road allowed him to breathe more easily. He snapped on the seat belt. 'I was just paying you back for what you did to me. None of us is infected. I made it up because I wanted to frighten you.'

A faint smile touched Jenny's eyes. 'And you succeeded. Just like I am frightening you now.'

'Yes, you're damned well succeeding all right. I admit it, I'm bloody terrified. Now stop this before you kill us.'

A bend loomed ahead and David braced himself in his seat. 'We're not going to make this one,' he yelled, but the Toyota screeched round on two wheels, just as an old Capri approached in the opposite direction. An angry blare of horns registered its fear.

As Jenny regained control of the speeding car, she said softly, only just audible above the roaring engine, 'You don't like not being in command, do you? You still want me to continue to do as you say, jump to order and obey instructions.'

'For God's sake, stop this lunacy.'

'But you've got Sarah to do your bidding now. You don't need me. So do as I ask.'

'What the hell do you . . .?' His voice froze as he saw the van in front of them. They were racing headlong towards its rear doors, just as a motor bike roared towards them on the right. There would not be room to overtake.

'Jenny,' David screamed, sweat breaking out on his face. He braced his good leg against the car door.

For a split second Jenny touched the brake, just enough to allow the bike past before they shot past the van, as if it was standing still.

'Thank God,' David breathed again. He did not dare touch the steering wheel or handbrake at this crazy speed. Thank God the country road was not busier. 'If you want to kill yourself, that's up to you, but let me out first.'

Jenny nodded, her eyes riveted to the road ahead. 'Now we're getting somewhere. It's called give and take, instead of just take.'

He clutched at the straw. 'What is it you want from me?'

'Sign the document.'

Frantically David rummaged in his pocket for the crumpled form and a pen. 'I'm signing,' he yelled, as he scribbled his name on the line. Despite the quaking motion of the car. 'There you are, you've got what you want.' He tossed it on to the rug on her lap. 'So for Christ's sake, stop.'

To his relief, the car slowed, if only a fraction, but it was enough to get them round the next bend safely and past another startled car.

'What now?'

'There's one more thing.'

'This is extortion. I'm not giving in to any more of your demands. Just damned well stop this car or I'll—'

'Or you'll what? Cry? Beg? Plead?'

'Don't be—'

'Is that what Mark did?'

'Oh my God, is that what this is about? Don't be so bloody stupid. That was—'

'Years ago?' Her foot thumped down on the accelerator and the car leaped forward.

'No, no . . .'

'Yes, David, it's frightening, isn't it?'

A curve in the road was followed by a small junction where a blue sports car was just crossing in front of them. At the speed they were doing, they would hit it slam in the middle. David threw his hands over his face and prepared for the impact, but Jenny hurled the wheel over to the right, just missing the sports car's bumper by a fraction of an inch, but at the last minute catching her rear wing on a fence post that sent the Toyota into a spin.

David cowered in his seat, convinced they would be hit by an oncoming vehicle as they pirouetted across the road, but the car finally came to a total standstill, untouched and facing the right direction. David was shaking too much to get out of the car.

'Is that what it was like for Mark?' Jenny demanded. 'Did he scream and beg you to go slower? Did you ignore his pleas until it was too late? That skinful of alcohol made you feel indestructible, did it? Well, you were right, you were indestructible. Only a few cuts and bruises were the price you paid. But what about our child beside you? What about his price? His life. Didn't you care? Wouldn't you listen to his cries?'

David lifted his hands away from his face. 'I didn't mean to, Jenny. It was an accident.'

'Like Shadow was an accident. Like leeching the life out of me was an accident.'

'I may have played around a bit, but I never hurt you intentionally. I didn't mess up your life.'

For a long moment Jenny looked into her husband's frightened eyes and then she reached down and released his seat belt. 'No, you didn't mess up my life.' She sat back in her seat, her eyes intensely bright. 'No, I did that myself. I made the choices that kept me with you. Kept me on self-destruct.'

She took a deep shuddering breath. 'But not any more. I have a life to live.'

David wiped his face with his hand and made as if to reinsert the seat belt catch.

'No, David. Get out of my car.'

He frowned in annoyance. 'You can't expect me to—'

'Just get out.'

'And if I refuse?'

'We'll have another joyride until you're feeling more amenable.' She revved the engine warningly.

'Okay, okay, but how the hell will I get home?'

'That's your problem.'

'Please, Jenny, be reasona—'

'No.'

'We can—'

'Get out. Now. This is the last time I say it.' Her eyes told him she was not making idle threats.

He opened the car door and eased his plastered leg on to the ground. The moment he slammed the door behind him, the Toyota headed off up the road at a sedate speed.

As the car climbed the long straight hill, Jenny glanced down at the paper on her lap. It was signed. Somewhat shakily perhaps, but undoubtedly his signature. She had what she had come for. And more. No longer did she hold him responsible for what had been her own fault, her own paralysis of will. He had his Sarah to go to, to repeat the pattern of the past, but for her this new life would be different. She would not make the same mistake again. All decisions would be her own and all consequences would be hers to face.

In the rear-view mirror she saw the abandoned form of David standing with a hopeful thumb extended to passing traffic. Rapidly the figure grew smaller and smaller, until it was only a tiny speck in the mirror. At the top of the hill, Jenny rounded a curve and he was gone. It had been a long haul. Smiling, she pointed the car towards her future.